The Dust of Texas

by

Wil Michael Peck

Published by Advanced Concept Design Books
Lago Vista, Texas

This is a work of Historical Fiction. Historical individuals and places and events are mentioned. Villages are actual name places.

Copyright © 2011 by Wilfred Michael Peck
Published by arrangement with
Advanced Concept Design Books, an imprint of
CID, Inc. Tx
6706 Bar K Ranch Rd.
Lago Vista, Tx. 78645

Library of Congress Control Number
to be assigned
International Standard Book Number
ISBN 13: 978-0-9826162-2-2
ISBN 10: 0-9826162-2-8

For information, address
rseibert@advancedconceptdesign.com

First paperback printing July 2012
Printed in the United States of America
derek@kustomkwikprint.com

1st Edition Copy July 2012 10 9 8 7 6 5 4 3 2 1

LaPoint Series II
The Dust of Texas

Dedicated to the horses and scouts that opened the southwest to exploration and settlement.
==================================

Much appreciation goes to those who inspired and encouraged this yarn, beginning with my Grandma Alice from Plum Creek, who told me my first frontier Texas tales as a young boy, and continuing through many teachers, to those who helped edit the Dust of Texas.

Muchas gracias to Hank Young of Cortijo Jerez, Durango, Colorado, for introducing me to the Andalusian horse, and for the cover photo of his stallion
"Escobar"

==================================

What follows is a work of historical fiction, based on actual events that occurred following the war of secession, when scouts and wranglers developed the ranching culture, and pushed it through the dust of Texas.

By Wil Michael Peck

LaPoint Series
Book II

The Dust of Texas

Table of Contents

Chapter One: Occupied New Orleans

On another drizzling overcast morning in late February of 1865, a handsome young man called Joshua Alexandre, of the trading house Robinoix of New Orleans & St. Louis, left the Union army headquarters at the St. Charles Hotel after making further supply contracts. He was riding his dappled gray Andalusian stallion on the brick pavements of the French Quarters, heading for the Robinoix Traders' offices after a short breakfast at Café Du Monde, away from another tedious meeting with Union officers over delivery of supplies to the city. The strong chicory coffee and beignets were one of the small pleasures left to the city living under occupation for years. The glorious war of secession had been a short one. The glory had faded with the illusion of possible victory as the Yankee gunboats blasted their way to New Orleans in the spring of '62 and took over the main port on the biggest river. From that point the city was under the union heel, and the people treated like rebels under subjugation instead of an occupied Confederacy.

During the previous fall, Sheridan had led his troops on a burning and pillaging raid in the Shenandoah Valley, leaving a wasteland. Soon thereafter Hood's battalion was mowed down at battles of Franklin and Nashville, and Sherman occupied Savannah after leaving a wake of devastation, looting, burning, rape, and murder in his wake of total war on the South. The newspapers bore a constant and grim litany of bad news, and everyone prepared for worse to come in the second term of an administration that had suspended the bill of rights and much of the constitution even in the North. Since secession and Lincoln's invasion of the Confederacy, New Orleans had slipped from bad to worse, and struggled through subjugation. The fear of slave revolt was pervasive throughout the south where the Confederacy was still in control, thanks to Lincoln's clever Emancipation Proclamation, which freed only the slaves under secessionist control, and left the ones in federally occupied New Orleans still bound. General Grant was angling to catch General Lee with a superior force, and the war's end seemed only a matter of time to realistic men like Josh, who was only twenty-five, but well educated and experienced for his age. He knew the dream of a new Confederation of States bound by a common belief in "government by consent" was lost.

The white mist had turned to a cold drizzle as the stallion cantered along Decatur street, heading upstream along the great Mississippi. Two colored boys were coming up from the river bank with poles and a catfish about two feet long.

"Hey Mr. Joshua, Ah know whah ya got dat hoss!" yelled the taller of the two.

"Where's that?" said Josh as he moved Scorpio into changing his front lead every two steps, with his right hand still on his thigh, smiling at the boys.

"Under yo rump,"

"That's right."

"I know how you be guidin' him too."

"How's that?"

"With your rump." The stallion stopped pacing forward and stood erect, his front hooves slowly raising high and pawing the ground.

"Right again, did you boys have to stay up all night to catch that catfish."

"Yassah, gonna sell it at tha market."

"Take it to the old blacksmith at Robinoix Traders, he'll buy it. You know where that is, don't you?"

"Yea, sho we do. Blacksmith McBride himself. We take it up deah."

"Alright, tell him I sent you."

"Yeasuh Mistah Joshua."

A slight nudge got the stallion cantering again as the rain increased. It was the forth rainy day in a row, and the dreary wet weather had Josh wearing an oilskin duster covering a gray Chihuahua bitch in a tiny black sweater and snuggling under his coat. With the reins looped on the wide Spanish saddle horn, the rider cradled the little dog close to his vest and guided the horse with subtle pressure of his legs over the shiny wet cobblestones. Despite the dark misty weather and grim mood of the occupied city, long under the boot of the Federal occupation, Joshua could not help but be consoled by the brimming spirits of the horse beneath him and the tiny dog at his vest. He began to put the stallion through changes in his lead on every second pace, and had him prancing down the cobblestones, signaling with just the seat in the saddle on the lead changes. It was something that pulled his mind from the troubles, and he knew the horse loved to go through his paces.

New Orleans, the crescent city, once the jewel of the South, the major port on the Mississippi that shipped the goods from the interior of the growing country, had been occupied by federal troops for several years, and the young but capable, Joshua, had been left in charge of the Robinoix trading office in New Orleans, which aided in keeping the citizens alive and the Union officers content with its many mercantile connections. So he had endured many meetings with Union officials, and dreaded each of them, though the Banks regime was far better than the reign of General Butler, the one they called "the beast."

This contract-dickering session had been particularly galling, and Josh had held his tongue and his anger and made the agreement, controlled and diplomatic as usual. Supplying the city and Union officers with trade goods was one way Josh ensured continued protection for the Robinoix plantation on the Bayou Teche in St. Martin Parish, over 100 miles west of the City, as well as continuing business for the old family trading firm that was first established during the fur trading era soon after Lewis and Clark got back from the far reaches of Louisiana.

The war over secession was grinding to an end on all fronts. It was an end that was long ago predicted by Alexandre Robinoix, who had left his illegitimate son, Joshua, in charge of the company while the city suffered under its third grim year of Union occupation, a sullen depression gaining a greater hold every day in the South as the realization set in that a way of life was ending in economic and social ruin, and a new one had to be created from the wreckage. With the federals clamping a stranglehold on the main shipping port of the Mississippi, it was obvious the South was headed for ruin, and they were a subjugated people, no longer living under government of consent.

Everyone was doing what they could to survive and hold on to what they had built, while living under the heel of a federal occupation that had been brutal at times. The early days of occupation under "Beast Butler" had shocked the city into sullen submission with a ruthless hanging for disrespecting the federal flag. The Robinoix protested but carried on, and at that time the Robinoix holdings, both the trading company and the rural farm land holdings along the Bayou Teche, had survived, battered and stripped, but intact, through a careful balancing act on Joshua's part, involving endless talking and compromise, and the skillful management of the plantation by his mother, Corina.

Constant foraging raids had left the plantation nearly bare, but at least it was still intact, as was the trading business. All of the horses at La Point plantation but Scorpio and a line-backed dun Andalusian stallion called Buck had been confiscated by one bunch or another, but the federals allowed the company two mules for transport of vital goods.

The Robinoix family, with their history of intimate involvement in the opening of the West since the Louisiana Purchase, with their long ago secret contract negotiations in France, and their later involvement in the opening of Texas, had been pro union and pro compromise all along, but to no avail. Alex foresaw that the Republicans would try to bring in a heavy tariff, a national bank, and a northern cross-country railroad, but he still argued against secession, on pragmatic grounds. The futility of fighting an industrial state with great manpower reserves was apparent from the beginning to the Robinoix family, but they had to watch demagogues make glorious speeches that eventually led to secession and to war.

As representative from the Teche district, Mister Alexandre Robinoix, the owner of plantations and the trading company, argued that secession was constitutional but impractical with the radical Republicans in power, and voted against secession. Although at first he drove cattle for the Confederacy from Texas, he would not serve in the Confederate army, and spent much of his time out around Taos during the war, leaving Joshua with more responsibility at the crescent city offices. It was through his sustained and diplomatic efforts that the trading business survived.

Although on paper Joshua was a mustefino, one-sixteenth negro, and born a slave, he had been raised at an orphan's boarding school from the precocious age of four, educated and trained to help run the horse-farms and the business, among other things. After over a dozen years of eduction and training at the orphans' boarding school, Joshua had been sent to France and England for schooling, then given his freedom papers when he began to run the New Orleans office, supplying the city with necessary goods.

New Orleans was kept alive by supplies arranged by Joshua, but it was a city festering with resentment at the heavy-handed Federal occupation, and women had been abused as prostitutes for not being polite to soldiers, under Federal Order #28, issued by the erratic and vindictive General Butler.

When General Butler required an oath of allegiance to the Union from all involved in the company business, Joshua had complied, though Alexandre Robinoix had disappeared soon after to run herds from Texas to Arkansas to supply the Confederate army. Soon after that Alex dropped out of sight.

No one had heard from him since, as the long dreary years passed in New Orleans, once the shimmering jewel of the south, now under the Union boot-heel. But the buffalo robes from Comancheria and Taos, shipped down through Bent's fort, the old adobe trading post on the Arkansas river where it slips through the plains in sight of the big mountains, keep coming in, as beautifully finished as ever. McBride the blacksmith surmised that Mr. Alex was in the mountains around Taos, and the clerks at the warehouse agreed, since the bales were packed in his precise way with tags in his handwriting.

On that misty morning in February '65 Joshua was glad the aggravating and tedious bargaining meeting over supply contracts was over, and he enjoyed the springy movements of the fine animal beneath him, one of the few treasures so far spared by the war and occupation. The pure blooded Spanish horse, the finest result of a line involving horses imported from Spain in his grandfather's time, and a continuous selective breeding program on the La Point plantation, was neither large, with big rump and belly, nor tall, like the Union mounts, being only fifteen and ½ hands high. But the stallion was extremely muscled, quick, and surefooted, with a thick arched neck holding the proud head high. A high perceptive intelligence and willingness to learn marked the stallion with nobility and grace of movement. Without extra bulk, the dappled gray was light on his feet, with rapid accelerations, and controlled spinning turns in either direction, exercising lead changes with subtle commands from the rider. They moved as one across the cobblestones or the short-track at Metairie. The Andalusian could also thrive on grasslands and outperform the big grain-fed Union mounts in the field, as they were expert at rapid turns and kicks in both directions.

People stood and watched when they paced along Decatur, past the coffee company owned by the Robinoix

Traders, with the trained prancing movements of the stallion responding to the slightest pressure of the rider's rump, leg, or foot to execute gait and lead changes every two steps. Riding his horse was the treasure for Josh that the war had not taken away.

As the high-stepping stallion and rider approached Jackson square, the sounds of music emanated from a small cafe, where a band of black and white musicians were holding a jam session, with banjos, horns, and drums topped by accordion and mouth harp. It was a new sound they were developing, full of syncopation and improvisation. Joshua stopped the horse in front of the small dive and listened, glad that the disaster had not completely damped the musical spirit of New Orleans. Scorpio pawed the cobblestone with his front hoof while the music rolled from the open doorway.

"Lookee heah now, dat's de hoss from Congo square, dat keeps time with his feet," said a man with a mouth harp, leaning in the doorway. When he saw Scorpio dancing in place, he stopped playing and broke into a grin, then stood up and started a slow shuffle to the music.

"Good morning, Uncle Willie," said Josh as he guided Scorpio into a lead change every two steps, and had him skipping to the music, his steel shoes clacking on the bricks.

"See out theah, dat be Massa Joshua, maybe he come ta play conga drum."

"Naw, fool, he work all day every day. He coming from the army headquarter, I believes."

"There he be now, dat dancin' hoss. Come on now, Massa Joshua, make 'im prance. Heah now," said another old musician as he stepped out the door and begin to blow low trumpet riffs at the horse and rider. Joshua smiled and nudged the horse, who began to pace in place, stepping high in time to the music, changing his lead as his smooth lips rolled back to reveal white teeth that matched the smiles of the early morning revelers watching him. The music picked up in spirit as the players heard the horse stepping high on the cobblestones, catching the beat of the song.

"Now ya got de beat, Massah Joshua," sang the white haired old darkie, "Now ya got de beat ta travel on."

Josh smiled and tipped his hat to the morning music makers as the horse slowly pranced away. The Spanish stallion clattered his hoofs on the worn bricks of St. Peter's street alongside Jackson square, and then towards the Pirates' Alley beside the Cathedral. On a subtle command the horse stopped the lead changes and began to walk smoothly along the wet streets.

In the square stood a statue of General Jackson, erected about a decade before, a man that Joshua's Robinoix ancestors had fought with against the British at Chalmette battleground, supplying cotton bales upon which to build the cannon emplacements in the swampy bottom-land. They also had supplied an Andalusian stallion for the bony General to ride, one resembling the bronze charger Andy sat astride in the square. Later some family members had worked with Jackson on the acquisition of Texas, and backed him as he fought the national bank. The pigeons were huddled on Andy's upraised hat, hunched against the drizzle, leaving their droppings.

Josh was heading to the Robinoix offices on Burgandy Street, past the ancient Cabildo building where his ancestors had witnessed the Louisiana Purchase transfer in 1803, to a back apartment behind the blacksmith shop where he stayed while in the city. He hoped to pack there for a month on the bayou to settle his inner turmoil over the southern situation, and his own position of limited options, which had always been his lot in life, a life that had been planned and controlled by Alex Robinoix. He had lately been wishing he could light out for new territory, the shining mountains of the west or to Texas. A small herd-gathering ranch was there, on the San Antonio River near the Indianola and Chihuahua cart trail, close to the small Tejano river- crossing called Alamita, under family ownership. His old friend Gabe had been urging him to head out west for over a year, since both were fed up with living in an occupied city. But the St. Louis office had drug their feet about sending a new manager until then.

The special horse-shoes fashioned by old Gabe, the company blacksmith, gave the horse better footing on the cobbles. The narrow alley was in dark shadows from the tall buildings lining it, the abundant southern gulf moisture dripping from the eaves, and the stallion quickened his pace towards the corner of Pirates Alley and Royal Street, his hoofs ringing on the pavement. The big dark ears on the stallion pricked to the left as they walked down Pirate's alley, putting Josh on alert.

While passing in front of the Cabildo alley, a stifled scream pierced the heavy mist of the morning, and the stallion gave a startled side-step motion as horse and rider came upon a group of Union soldiers intent on assaulting a mulatto girl. Josh was enraged and reacted quickly, stuffing the chihuahua into his saddlebag, where she barked and snarled under the loose flap.

"Stop it, damn you," said Josh, in a loud voice.

"Get away, ya bastard! She's justa yalla gal," yelled the soldier in front of the girl. "Mind yore own business, and get back afore ya get cut up!"

"This is my business, and you get away, or I'll be the bastard that makes you regret it."

"Hey, get away with that beast," yelled the soldier as Josh nudged his stallion forward. Scorpio rose on command to his hind feet and walked towards the startled group in the narrow alleyway, flailing at the nearest ones with his front hooves while snorting and flinging saliva at them with his tossing head. The two soldiers holding the girl fell in terror, and a couple more pulled knives and circled, then the fight was on, with the chihuahua snarling in the saddlebag.

After driving the men in front of him back, Scorpio quickly settled onto his front legs, then with a rapid turn the stallion kicked his powerful rear legs and caught the closest knife-wielding assailant with full force, hurling him into Pirate's alley in a twisted pile. Then the horse reared up and struck the one on the other side with his front right hoof, knocking him back into a wall, his knife clattering down the bricks of the alley. The men that the horse struck did not get back up, and the others cowered in terror, slipping on the wet bricks trying to get away from the crippling blows of the stallion's hooves.

With two down the horse and rider soon dominated the others with a few rearing and smashing stamps of his steel-clad hooves, freeing the girl to escape down the Cabildo Alley. They were in a panic to get away from the war horse and its enraged master. The commotion caught the attention of a federal patrol marching down Royal street by the park behind the cathedral, and they began a quickstep towards Pirate's Alley, but the event unfolded before they got to the corner.

Within a few seconds of whirling action, Scorpio and Josh had broken up the assault and shattered more than a few bones, leaving trampled federal soldiers behind them as they clattered down the alley to pick up the running octoroon girl and carry her away. The soldier who had taken the full kick of Scorpio's rear legs was badly broken, with a twisted and dislocated shoulder and broken ribs, and was gasping, laying on the wet bricks, coughing blood. The rest of the attackers were on the ground in serious pain, or hunkered under a bench by the little park behind the cathedral.

The federal foot-patrol finally reached the scene after Josh and Scorpio had clattered down the Cabildo alley and out of sight up St. Peter's street. The sergeant recognized the horse and rider, from seeing them at headquarters many times, and filed his report to a certain adjutant he knew was friendly with the trader. He had also jailed the injured assailants, though two had to go to the hospital, with one barely clinging to life.

Chapter Two: The War at Home

When Josh came pacing up on his shiny wet horse to the blacksmith shop beside the Robinoix Trader's office, he sighted a grizzled, gray-bearded, thick-bodied old man with a balding head marked by a huge knife scar along the top of his forehead. The blacksmith was nailing a shoe onto the left rear hoof of a big dark long-eared jack mule. His hand movements were a little unusual because his left hand was somewhat mangled into a stiffened claw, requiring help from the other hand at times, though he could still grip with it. The smell of coal smoke hung heavy in the shed, and the warmth from the forge felt good to Joshua after his ride in the cold rain. A rough sign was nailed to a cypress wood support post, NO CREDIT. STAY BACK. HOT SPARKS. Another post held the sign, PRICE DOUBLES IF YOU HELP.

With the last nail in his jagged yellow teeth and the mule's huge hind leg between his knees, the stout blacksmith drove another nail in, his arms still powered by huge triceps, biceps, thick forearms and wrists, and bulging shoulder deltoids, despite his gray fringe of hair and worn and weathered face, crisscrossed with lines like an old map. The mule farted with a long hissing sound as the stout old man drove in the last nail.

"Leon, you son of a gun, ya could'a waited on that til I was done back here," said the blacksmith as he wrinkled his nose from the pungent mule gas. "Damn that mash you been giving 'em shore makes some powerful gas when they ain't workin'."

"They're going to be working soon, Gabe. We have to leave now."

"Couldn't hear ya. Speak up, dammit."

The mule flashed a big-toothed grin and seemed to laugh, his big lips curled and quivering. Then he swung his long dark head around and looked back at the jenny in the stall, pointing his ears at her and hee-hawing to elicit a like reply. Gabe went to greasing the lid of a Dutch-oven sitting with other gear on the table.

The sweating blacksmith wore a leather apron over his bare and powerful chest, grizzled with gray hair and a line of scars across his belly, and there were lots of scars on his arms and back. He put his tools away in boxes affixed to the wall of the smoky shed and put his hands near the forge to warm them.

"You got things about ready to go, Gabe?" asked Josh as he brought his horse under the shed roof out of the rain.

"What?" With the rain drumming on the roof and the old man's ears weak from all the gunshots that had gone off right beside them, and the constant ringing of steel hammers, his hearing wasn't all that good. The mules' ears were pointed towards Josh and Scorpio, who shook water from his mane.

"I said, are we ready to go?"

"Speak up, dammit, Josh. You know my ears ain't that good." He turned his left ear towards Josh to hear better.

"Are we ready to go?"

"Right now?"

"Yeah, or sooner."

"Waugh! Well yeah, I reckon I could be, as you can see 'round here, been busy as hell, got most of the possibles lined up, sawbucks repaired, panniers ready, Parcheesi greased, mules shod, galena, powder, molds, sourdough starter, compasses, fire starter glass and flint, knives, cooking gear, medicine pipe, kinnickinnick, whiskey jug, greasing the biscuit pans,   ...yeah, just about ready for a jornada."

"And how about you, are you up to a long ride?"

"Waugh, I'ma feelin' up ta snuff, but I thought we whar leaving early in the morning, maybe the rain might blow outa here..how cum we gotta make beaver now?"

"Change of plans" said Josh as he took grain in his cupped hands and fed his mount. "Scorpio kicked in a soldier's ribs when I broke up a rape down by the St. Louis cathedral. Soon as I file the order forms in the office and get my bags I'll be ready to go. The clerk can handle everything until the new manager gets here. Pack up both mules soon as you can. I'll be ready in a half hour or less."

"Waugh. That fast,huh?" The old man picked up a small block of green sandstone and began to sharpen the foot-long knife of layered steel from the belt scabbard hanging on a post. His face acquired a serious and thoughtful expression, with a small crease on his brow between his eyes, his good ear turned slightly towards Josh to hear better.

"More than that. There's a good chance we're in for a scrape. Put a couple of pistol rigs in the pack, the new colts, and the Sharps carbine and 1851 Model long-gun, also that ten gauge, and both Spencer repeaters, and plenty of ammo. I'm getting my Whitworth long-gun from out of the case, to carry with me on Scorpio. Actually, you should pack all the ammo and weapons we can carry. It all might just get confiscated here. I don't know how this latest mess will play out. Scorpio mangled one of them pretty good."

"Bashed in a yaller-leg bug-tit, did-ya? Yore pal the lieutenant came by 'bout an hour ago, said you got in a scrape with some rowdy soldiers over a mulatto gal…that right?"

"Yeah, it was Camille, and they pissed me off. I've gone round and round with the officers about this, and finally got general agreement on it. Then they just do it anyway."

"Wal, the Lieutenant said there could be trouble. One of 'em is connected politically, the stove-in one. He's apt ta go under from punctured lungs and stove in ribs."

"Yeah, I know. He stopped me at the door as I was storming into the headquarters at the hotel with my blood boiling, told me to lay low until he figured out the upshot of it all. That was after I had to take Camille home and settle her down."

"Yeah, I can jus' picture that, if I had tha time. Didn't seem ta settle you down any, though."

A long and low rumble of thunder rolled from a darkened cloud overhead and the rain beat harder on the roof, necessitating much louder speaking.

"Wal, I know ya been chaffering for quite a while. You gonna tell me exactly what happened to speed things up? And why we carrying all the hardware now, 'nuff for two mules? You gettin' loaded for Ole Ephraim, huh? I already had all the possibles I thought we needed."

"Later. Let's just say it was the last straw. I've had it with this place, time to head west."

"I can see you got yer blood up. You got that dark look."

"I guess that was the last straw for me. I can hardly believe it happened, but all of sudden there it was in front of us, and we reacted. I didn't even know if Scorpio would actually kick a man until he did it."

"He took it to 'em, huh? Used your Vienna riding school war kicks?"

"Yeah. Finished the whole group in a few seconds, before the patrol got there. I've already gone round and round with the colonel about this mistreatment of women in the quarter. I'll tell you the rest later, just get everything ready. Pack extra supplies, good coffee especially, chicory too, and two bottles of brandy, lots of mama's mosquito repellent and healing salve, and a few of those knives you've been making. And all the clean water we can take."

"Turned Scorpio on him, ya did! Now that's skookum! Dang. I seen it coming, seen it, seen it, like a black panther inside ya. Knew it would bust out sooner or later."

"Well, it did, I guess."

"Now you figuring they'll be coming to confiscate your horse, huh? We goin' to Plantation LaPoint, or Texas?"

"Maybe both. I've got to talk to my mother about it before I decide. She was wanting to go back to Santa Domingo with that bunch until the war mess settles down and Mister Alex shows up, if he ever does. I want her to come with us to Texas, leave this wasteland. It isn't going to come right here for a long time, under the federal heel. I've already sent word to the St. Louis office to send a manager, two weeks ago, and he'll be here soon. I've had it with living in this city, smooth-talking Federal occupation lords, and spending my life doing what's required of me instead of what I want to do."

"Let's go, then, this place gives me moss-back depression...let's go ta Texas, to the rancho. Can't be as many federals there, and Pancho is there still, I reckon, with the horses, 'less the Comanche got 'em. You won't have to chaffer with federals anymore, just work with horses. Come on now, ah know that's what you always wanted. Now's your chance."

"Maybe. I've got to talk to Mama Corina first....need to convince her to come with us."

"Not likely, she keeps that place humming. She can't be spared there."

"We'll see. Pack everything we might need if we head that way, and I'll get what I need and inform the clerks here. Make sure we have the Sharps long rifles, and both Spencer repeaters. I'll bring the Whitworth when I come back down."

"Yassah, boss, ya don't have ta tell me twice. I been ready ta leave this swamp since the Federals moved in. Warn't my damned war anyway, never owned a slave and don't intend to. I'll put in some ponche for trading to redskins in Texas. Waugh, gemme some dry ground under my feet for a change."

"Never owned one but never had trouble bossing me around when I was one, huh?"

"That was my job."

"Well, both our jobs are over now."

"Wal let's go."

"Alright, I won't be too long rounding up a couple of things," said Josh as he left the shed and walked into the brick house adjacent to it. He went into the back room where he pulled down a panel from the ceiling and hoisted himself with athletic ease into the attic. He returned with the big gun, scooped up his saddlebags and the Chihuahua, and was ready to go.

Thirty minutes later they both rode out leading dark mules with full packs, heading for the Bayou Teche country, over a hundred muddy miles to the west. The blue-roan stallion led the small train, with the big mule Napoleon in tow, then Gabe on the line-backed dun named Buck, with Josephine, a slightly smaller, dark brown jenny, pacing along behind. Soon the smell of wet leather and warm wet horses and mules pervaded the air with the moist squeaking of their saddles and wet plodding of hooves.

The rain was increasing steadily as they left the city, and the Chihuahua Suzette was riding in a canvas pack on Napoleon, the huge macho jack. The wind had grown colder and stronger, driving a wet chill into the old blacksmith's bones. Both riders wore sheepskin vests with dark oilcloth slickers covering them, with broad-brimmed, felt hats that poured rivulets from the rim.

Joshua had to show the federal pass at several checkpoints for them to continue, with quite a long wait at the river. Silver coin changed hands several times to smooth travel. By midnight they made it to La Fourche, in the swamplands, the rain splashing across the flat black water, and spent the night and most of the day at the home of friends, resting. Then they left by seldom-used trails to travel at night, with more light rain on their hats and shoulders.

It took two more nights of riding in intermittent rain, slogging through continuous gumbo mud, through forests primeval and around swamps impassable, hiding by day in thickets so tight no one would enter willingly, to finally approach the old swamp hideout at the mission school near Grand Bayou.

The isolated boarding school had been established decades before by the father of Alexandre Robinoix, to teach orphans, illegitimate children, and mulatto children who could not attend the regular schools. Mister Alex had brought in monks from southern France to teach the boys, who boarded at the old buildings on the isolated island. Josh had spent his childhood there, with only occasional visits with his mother.

The rain had finally let up some by the time they had threaded the old trails to the landing. They unsaddled and unbridled the horses and mules to rest their backs, rubbed them down and grained them. Then they carried the tack and left it on the shore in a shed hidden by luxuriant greenery. In a hidden spot behind the shed Josh uncovered a pirogue shoved back up in the cypress knees, and together they paddled it over to the dock on the dark bayou where it fed the lake. They then slept at the old school dorm, the place being abandoned since the start of the war. The dark shapes of alligators swirled through the water along the shore, and turtles flopped into the water from their resting places upon the approach of the small flat-bottomed boat. Long curly gray tendrils of Spanish moss hung from the lower branches like veils to pass through into memories of better days.

"Brings back memories, eh Josh? All the fish we caught from this boat, crabs and crawfish too. Jambalaya, crawfish pie, hot fresh bread with garlic butter. Dang we ate good here. And them renegade friars was alright fellows."

"Yeah. Those were the best days. But I think they were monks, not friars. I remember how I used to tump the boat over and dunk you in the dark water," said Josh as he gave the boat a little lurch.

"Gol-dang Josh don't start that again! You know I can't stand no more cold water!"

Josh laughed and kept paddling. In the dark shadows back from the little dock a large stuccoed house in Spanish mission style with wide porches loomed in mossy elegance. They found the key in its usual hiding place and went inside. The place was musty and full of spider-webs, but after clearing a place on tables there, they felt safe enough to fall into deep restful sleep in their ground tarps.

Joshua had spent the great part of his childhood here at the school established by the old Creole French father of

Alexandre Robinoix, who had been a friend to Andy Jackson. There the lonely boy fell in love with horses, and studied academics under imported French monks. As he grew older he learned other skills like horse care and training, black-smithing, weapons accuracy, sword and knife fighting, forging knives of Damascus steel, and pottery and brick-making for the masonry work they did to complete the school. His dozing was filled with those memories, and thoughts of his occasional visits with his mother, whom he had been separated from at an early age.

The mission school was the only place where the mixed blood children and orphans of the area could receive a good education, away from the eyes of a strict society that forbade the education of those with Negro blood. The white society looked the other way while the rich and eccentric Robinoix family did what they pleased. Joshua was just one of many mixed race illegitimate children who boarded and schooled there, hidden away.

Around the mission island was a maze of swamp and bayous full of wildlife, and Josh was taught to cut for sign, to hunt and kill with care and respect, and prepare the meat, by an Attakapas native who had somehow survived the white mans' diseases and made his living hunting and trapping the lowlands. Later a Choctaw came and taught him horse training in the most gentle manner. Then Gabe came and hectored him into repeated practice of various weapons. Josh had always spent his spare time at the stable of horses and the green wet meadows, riding them in broad circles.

Josh remembered those days with bittersweet fondness, for he knew they were all over, as was his chance for the life he wanted there on the bayou horse farm called LaPoint Plantation. The war had been a giant fool's errand, and the devastated land was the reward for foolishness, from Josh's point of view. He agreed with his father that gradual, compensated, emancipation was the best approach to the slavery issue, and stood against public financing of a transcontinental railroad, the creation of a profligate national bank, and the outrageously high tariffs that the black republicans called for. But it was all for naught as events had unfolded in the worst way, with at least a half a million men killed and the South in ruins.

Exhausted, he still felt restless, so he paced the floor and ate dried sausage and French bread. Gabe McBride, a much older man used to retiring early, was snoring while sitting up against a post, so Josh laid him down on his bench before flopping down on a table himself. Then Josh fell into a fitful sleep full of disturbing dreams, with images of his mother and an old swamp woman from nearby in them.

In the morning Gabe had coffee and a breakfast of potatoes and eggs scrambled with peppers ready by sunrise. He had found some hens nesting in the old brick kiln, and dug potatoes from the old garden.

"Damn, you're up early. And something sure smells good."

"I get up ta take a leak at three every morning. Just stayed up and stirred around with a candle lantern. Lots of old memories here. Good ones too. Remember I'd paddle out and put those melons on that raft for you to shoot, and you shot that old Sharps from the pirogue sitting sideways that time and flipped yourself into that black water, and then those gators went under on the shore? Gol-dang, never saw anyone scramble back on an upturned boat so fast, kept a hold of the gun too. Ya paddled it ta shore upside down with your hands flailing like paddle wheels and the gun under yore belly. Shore was a sight."

"Yeah, I remember you laughing about it a lot. Mostly I remember when you first arrived with that greasy poultice on your head wound and aloe juice dripping from your wrapped up hand. I was shocked, and all they would say was you had been scalped, but they didn't finish."

"Can't blame ya. I was a sight, I reckon, too weak ta talk about it, or even think about it."

"Lots of good times back here then, learning to cut sign and shooting, fishing, gator hunting, gar spearing. You taught me everything you knew about the wilds."

"Naw, taught you everything you know, not everything I know."

"Yeah, right. Well, I got a feeling we might never have those times again."

"We can start over iffen we gotta, Josh."

"Yeah, maybe it's time for that. I'm done with living in New Orleans as company factor."

"Good. It all went sour when the federals occupied the city, far as I'm concerned. We'll jus start over in Texas."

After eating, they both rode over to the LaPoint

plantation, leaving the mules in the shed with grain and fresh hay. The little dog Suzette, acquired by Mister Alex years before on the Chihuahua trail, rode in Joshua's saddlebag, in a silk top-hat to keep her hairless belly warm, her pointed snout occasionally peeking out when strange noises or smells disturbed her and set off her low snarling growl.

They could see strange colored smoke from a distance when riding the bayou road towards the plantation. Josh picked up the pace and the horses got into competing in speed with each other, with Scorpio edging ahead. When they got to the long entry drive lined with huge oak trees, they could see the big house and barns were gone, nothing but piles of smoking ruins.

"Oh no, oh no, oh no," said Josh as he spurred his stallion and rushed forward, leaving Gabe behind him cussing.

"Damn, ah's always feared it'd come to this," said Gabe as he spurred his mount to keep up with Joshua's swift running stallion. They moved quickly down the long oak-lined entry drive to the house, surveying the damage as they rode. Horror gripped Josh as he raced his horse.

Joshua quickly dismounted as his stallion slid to a stop in the wet ground beside the smoking ruins of the big house. A crumbled mass of charcoal and brick foundation steamed and emitted tendrils of smoldering smoke. The little bitch Suzette jumped out of the saddlebag, down the stirrup to the ground, and began running around sniffing the ruins. A small garden shed was still standing, and out of it emerged a dazed and frightened looking teenaged brown-skinned boy, his eyes teary in the smoke fumes. The dog ran over barking at him until she recognized him, and then jumped into his arms as he squatted down.

"Suzette! Joshua! Yal come back."

The buckskin stallion carrying Gabe came thundering up the drive. "Burnt us out. This is what I left Texas to get away from, murderous pillaging savages. That about tears it," yelled Gabe as he stopped in the mud, leaving skid lines, and dismounted.

"Chester, what happened?" asked Josh as he approached the boy. Gabe walked in a circle sniffing the air. "That's a bad smell, Josh. I know that smell, from when I was a Comanche captive and they built that mesquite fire under my hand. It's human flesh, and horse, burnt to a crisp. Ain't smelt

that since I smelt my own flesh burning. Damn em to hell!
Bunch of savages, Bug's boys." Gabe's face went pale and he
quickly turned and took a few steps towards the bushes before
he bent over and heaved his breakfast. Josh focused on
Chester.

"Chester, look at me! What happened?"

"It was one of dem federal foraging parties, like befoah,
or das what we thought, come to take the last of our feed corn.
But dis time it was a different bunch, real mean….had a captain
dat was right near crazy, yelling everyone into a frenzy like,
screaming 'bout infidels and Bible talk such-like, 'bout grinding
de balls to dust and driving de infidel from de land an all. Dey
took all deh garden stuff and loaded the corn in de wagon,
yelling at everyone to hurry up, treatin' us like trash, ya know. Ah
run to de back poach and yo mamma told me to grab de
silverware and hide it in dat cubbyhole in de pantry, long with de
brandy. But ah didn't have time for de brandy befoah dey come
in, so ah hid under de table with Janie while yo mamma tried to
order dem out. Dey started to loot de house and yo mamma
tried to stop em, and dey got yo mamma and carried her upstairs
fighting like a wildcat agains dem, and de three of dem had dey
way with her up dere over our heads. Mama Corina was cursing
dem de whole time too."

"Worse than Comanches," said Gabe, slamming his bad
hand down into his other fist. Joshua said nothing, but his face
darkened with pain and rage, his eyes burning with salty water.
Gabe walked up and took a hold of Josh's forearm.

"'Deh's nutin ah could do, dey had me and Janie locked
in de pantry downstairs while dey was upstairs. We heard a
terrible struggle for de longest time as she fought dem, and then
finally it got quiet, and we heard dem clumping along de hall
upstairs. Den we smelt smoke and heard dem running down de
stairs, and we heard dem break lamps in the parlor and kitchen
and set de whole place on fire. It took to burning awful fast and
ah knew we was done for with dese ole dry cypress boards, but
an awful panic got a hold of me and ah found dat heavy ole meat
cleaver yal kept back here. And ah just chopped and chopped
on de basement doah til ah got a hole thru, den kicked it out and
we crawled out and went out de back and on down to de bayou,
where we laid under de watah by the reeds. Ah's sho glad de
tile floah yal put in kept de kitchen floah from burning fast as de

rest. Janie ran away down to St. Martinville, ah reckon, long with de rest, what was left."

"My mother...?"

"She gone, burnt up.... Ah never seen heah agin, since yesterday afternoon...nobody left but me. Ah reckon dey done kilt heah or she burnt up in de house-fire. Leswise ah nevah seeh heah come out. Ah's awful sorry bout dat, Joshua. Mama Corina was de best lady ah evah knowed, with her garden and cooking and healing plants and such. Can't be no LaPoint Plantation without her."

Josh stood reeling, tears in his eyes, his stomach churning, the whole horizon unsteady. He could not feel up or down nor anything but Gabe gripping his forearm and waves of dizziness. In a grim flash he understood the horrible premonition he had been feeling all during the ride there, and the jumbled dreams. For over a week his nights had been filled with fleeting images of the times he had spent with his mother before he had been torn away from her at age four and placed in the orphanage, to keep from being sold by the bitter white wife of his father. The mother and horse farm he longed to return to were both gone, and he felt a deep pit form in his center.

"My mother. They killed my mother and burned the farm, with the horses in the barn." He spoke the words softly.

"Sons-o-dirty-bitches," said Gabe. "There's never any call for this. Thought we had an agreement with the federals over this. Thought Plantation LaPoint was protected, Josh."

"We did, plenty of agreements, and I gave up my pound of flesh for years to keep them in brandy and cigars while keeping the people alive with beef and flour."

"We got ta strike back fast, like with Comanches."

"Alright, we will. Somebody's got to. This can't stand. Saddle up, we're going to spot them if we can. Nothing to do here now, it's all in ashes....we're too late. Come on, Chester, bring Suzette and climb up behind me," Josh mounted and offered the boy his stirrup and his hand. Suzette leaped from Chester's arms onto the saddle in front of Josh, and he put her in the right saddlebag.

"There's a loaf of bread and some cheese in the left saddlebag. Eat."

The boy grabbed at the food and was soon stuffing it into his mouth. Gabe walked around and surveyed the ruins in disgust. "World gone loco," he finally said as he moved to mount Buck, who was shifting around nervously at the smell of burnt horse-flesh.

"Tell me Chester, could you recognize them if you saw them again?" asked Josh as he pulled the youngster up onto the rump of the horse.

"Oh yeah, ah never forget dose faces. One had a red beard and hair like a devil. He's de boss. Bright blue eyes, sorta wild and cold like. Had dem captain's bars, had some broken teeth in front, and a knife scar on his face. Other had curly long blond hair, like yoahs but more white like straw, and longer even. De other was big, real big, and dark-haired with a beard like a spade. He be even taller den you, lots heavier. Dem soldiers been heah before, getting hay and corn for hosses after dey took all our mules so we couldn't plow de gardens but wif dem ole mares, den dey come back and took all de vegetables yo ma had stored and hid away....but dat Captain's de one dat riled em up for de hell dey brought. De hosses got burnt up in de barn, lawd gawd deh was screamin. Ah didn' know what to do so ah just slept in de shed. Ain't nobody alive 'cept me and Janie, and she run off. De others from down at de cabins went down to camp by town. What we gonna do, massah Josh?"

Gabe looked at Josh with the same question in his eyes.

"It's up ta you now, Josh Robinoix, yore plantation, yore ma," he said. "Those danged republicans have turned loose the dogs of war, and it's time ta fight back. You're the last of the LaPoint plantation."

Josh fought back tears and could not speak when he thought of his mother, but when he thought of the men who did it, the restraints of his previous life fell away, and he said, "Alright then. I'll take that name now, Gabe. LaPoint. I'm all that's left of it."

"What ya gonna do, LaPoint?"

"I'm going to kill the lowdown curs who did this."

"I'm with ya."

"Let's go."

They started back down the entry road at a fast walk, under passing shadows of the huge moss-draped live oaks, trees planted by his Robinoix ancestor nearly 100 years before. "Gabe, you brought the telescope, binoculars, and all the rifles, huh? You're sure?"

"Seguro. I packed both the Whitworth and the Sharps, and both tha Spencers, plus two big colts and lots of ammo. We gotta get em now, you know. This can't stand, even for a day. Far as I's concerned, this done dug up the hatchet. You gotta do like we done to the Comanche, hit em back hard and fast, only way to stop this kind of thing. They done forfeited their right to life. I can do it with the big '53 Sharps if you don't want to, or the Whitworth. This here done got my bristles up, like back in 40 on the Blanco when the Comanches burned me out. I'm wrathy as Old Ephraim. We got to rub 'em out."

"Save your breath, I'm already set on it. I'll do it. She was my mother. But I'd just as soon see their faces up close."

"Wal, close or not, they got to die for what they done. And you got the hair of the bear in ya, I always knowed it, yore daddy's son. Still, I'd like to put em under myself, for your ma. Corina was the finest woman I ever knowed, 'ceptin my Arapaho-Cheyenne squaw, who was a healer too. Your ma saved me, by God. She got my burnt up hand so much better I can use it without much pain, even though there ain't much left of it. And she got my scalp flap to grow back together with them herb and aloe potions of hers."

"Yes, she was a wonder, alright. I spent lots of my life missing her."

"Hell, I couldn't have stood this wet place without that mosquito repellent she made. She's a real healer. I want to take down one of them, for her. I can still shoot that Sharps if I got a rest. Maybe I ain't the curly wolf I was, but I can still throw hot galena in the right spot if I need to."

"Alright," said Josh. "We'll take the best chance we get to put them under. Here, let's cut thru the back trail to avoid patrols. We can get to their post at New Iberia just as fast. They are probably out foraging now, so we will set up in some of those tall cypress by Spanish Lake with spyglasses, so Chester can point them out when they come in with their days haul. Then we'll take him to St. Benard's in Breaux Bridge. Fr. Jean will look after him while we finish this thing."

"Thought you couldn't stand those priests and all that popish mess."

"No, not all of them. Just that corrupt bunch in the city. Fr. Jean is a good man, who used to bring us books at the mission school, and I can't blame him for contradictory theology. He has a good heart, and he will take good care of Chester."

"Ah wanna go wif yal,"

"Can't do it, cousin. We are going to the killing grounds. You have to get somewhere safe for now."

"Den de Mission School!"

"It's closed down, Chester. Nobody there."

"Alright den, ah go to Father Jean's."

"Alright, let's slip on over there, the way to handle this is ta Indian up on 'em, " said Gabe.

"I'm almost ready."

"Come on, ah'll follow you," said Gabe as he took off in the lead, forcing Josh to urge Scorpio to a quick burst of speed.

"Not too good at following, are you old scout."

"Gotta strike when the iron is hot," said Gabe over his shoulder.

Riding the muddy and overgrown back lanes and trails, the shady alleys under spreading branches draped with Spanish moss dripping with dew, they arrived at the shimmering dark and misty body of water called Spanish Lake, and Josh found a tall cypress that would give him a bird's eye view of the federal camp. He stood on a big cypress knee, leaped up to grab a lower branch, using it to swing himself up.

"If that don't beat the dutch," said Gabe "ya dang painter cat."

There was a diamondback water-snake hanging on the branch he needed to step onto, so Josh eased it off into the water below by using the tip of his black riding boot. The snake fell with a splash in the dark water, then emerged swimming in serpentine motions into the brush. Josh moved up the tree, pulling the boy from branch to branch.

The Federal camp had once been a recruiting and training center for the Confederates of the area, a camp where the local Yellow Jacket Battalion trained, but had since been occupied by Federals while the Yellow Jacket boys were spread and scattered after the defeat at Opelousas.

Josh and Chester found a comfortable perch on the smooth branches and waited for about an hour, while Chester filled Josh in on what had happened while he was gone. When Josh stopped gathering information, his mind went back to his mother and the plantation and its horse barn, and that was too painful to endure, so he kept asking questions about the marauders.

When the mosquitoes found them they spread the ointment made by Mama Corina on their bare skin, inhaling the strong fragrance of citronella and eucalyptus. Then they grew quiet and just sat watching the great blue-gray herons and snow white egrets doing their afternoon fishing. The turtles, alligators, and snakes carried on their daily hunt below to care for their young. For hours they waited with clouds sliding by overhead, until the Federal foraging parties started coming in. Chester fell asleep in the crotch of the great cypress boughs. Josh could not help but remember the visits with his mother over the years, and think of how they would never happen again, so he was glad for some more activity to pull him from his sadness when he saw the Federal patrols returning on the levee road.

The first party of federals had a wagon load of corn and vegetables. Josh had by then shown Chester how to use the glasses on various water creatures around the lake, so it was easy for him to focus them on the Federal foragers. But Chester didn't spot them in the first two parties that returned.

The third party contained the men they were looking for, and Chester pointed them out to Josh, who had a picture memory that was nearly flawless. Grimly transmuting the pain of loss in the well of his stomach into his plan of action, he marked their faces, and how they rode, and how they moved when dismounting and walking. Then after waiting for the activity outside the post to quiet down, they slipped away through the thick woods and went back down towards the mission hideout, dropping the boy off with a familiar priest at St. Bernard's.

After that they headed northeast through Picouville, crossed Bayou Benoit on a small ferry, then rode slowly down the bayou road to the old mission school across the water, where they spent the night. Josh could not sleep and spent hours currying the horses and mules until he was too tired to think. Then he spent another hour writing in a leather bound journal until he could write no more and went back to currying the stock. Keeping busy with the horses eased his discomfort, and Scorpio sensed his pain and tried to soothe him with gentle nudges of his soft muzzle.

It was a long night for Josh, full of memories of the few times he was with his mother, who stayed running the plantation when he went to the boarding school. His restless dreams had him arising early with Gabe and leaving very early after another fine breakfast of potatoes and eggs, washed down with lots of black coffee mixed with chicory to a shimmering blackness like ink.

That morning the fog was thick as they paddled the pirogue across the still dark waters, and then they were trailing both mules with all their supplies, so they didn't retrace their trail as quickly. But they were able to unpack and tether the mules in the back pasture along the bayou at LaPoint Plantation, then slip into the brush outside Camp Pratt, with all their weapons, waiting at sunrise, which lit the thick fog up like a white curtain. Climbing with a brass telescope in his back pocket, Josh whipped his body up around a branch and scampered up the tree to wait and watch.

The third foraging party to leave the post was six men and the red-bearded captain. The captain seemed to be reading from a big black book to the men as they slowly plodded along. It looked like the Bible, perhaps, or a field manual. Josh used the small telescope and identified the blond-headed and black-bearded perpetrators riding beside the captain. Josh studied them and marked everything about them in his picture memory. He wished he could just shoot them there and then and be done with it, but knew it would be suicide with mounted troops camped nearby. They headed southeast down the old Spanish trail, with Joshua and Gabe following at a safe distance behind.

Trailing them down the Jeanerette road, south along the rich farmlands by the Bayou Teche, the well mounted riders finally saw the patrol turn into the front drive of a plantation there, and race up to the house. Josh and Gabe dismounted under spreading branches and Josh swung up onto an old cane-hauling wagon for a perch to use the telescope.

The federal soldiers put everyone into a panic when they came rampaging into the front yard. The few chickens that were left went squawking and flapping on the run out towards the brambles. The stocky captain with a reddish beard was shouting orders to round up everyone on the front porch, gather the valuables and hide them in a wagon load of corn and horse grain. Soldiers were hustling about while the panicked residents were crowded onto the tall porch under guard. The blond went to picking out females for the captain's pleasure, and probably his own. The house servant he grabbed began to scream and struggle.

"Oh no, they're at it again," said Josh while peering through the telescope. "They're on another rampage. Let's rush those curs and blow them to hell."

"Waugh, I can barely see them through these branches," said Gabe, who was using the binoculars and standing on a fallen tree trunk. "But it don't look good."

"So lets go get them."

"Like hell! Rush a whole squad armed with carbines? Let's don't bite off mor'n we can chew and get put under in the attempt. We got ta get a perch ta rain down some fire on em with the Whitworth or tha Sharps, stop 'em in their tracks."

"Maybe that barn loft, down in that pasture, in the bottom land there. Can't hardly see it for the mist on the ground. Might be a shot up above it."

"Yeah, that's the way my stick floats on it too. Lets go."

"What the hell does a stick floating have to do with anything, anyway?" asked Josh. Gabe said "Waugh, already told ya, shows ya where the beaver went under......" and mounted up.

Sprinting their horses down through the misty bottom land to an old weathered cypress-board barn on the property's back pasture, Josh and Gabe stabled the mounts and climbed to the loft with their rifles and ammunition pouches. The view from the front was obscured by tall magnolia branches and wide live oak trees with green foliage, and Gabe proceeded to cussing. "Gol-dang, can't see em from here, lets find another spot. I want ta plug that captain for what he done, put him under. It's time to make wolf meat of that murderous scum."

Josh carried the Whitworth long-rifle, for he preferred the spinning elongated slugs for accuracy at a distance. The hexagonal bullets and hexagonal twisting inner tube made it the most accurate rifle in existence. He had been out-shooting Gabe and his Sharps for years with it. Josh kept silent and scanned the room while jamming the long ramrod down the barrel, packing the big slug against a big load of powder. He replaced the ramrod and looked up out the hay loading window.

"We gotta get another perch," said Gabe.

"Wait," said Josh, looking up at the pulley rope hanging from the beam where hay was loaded into the loft. LaPoint set down his Whitworth, cut a length of the pulley rope and stuffed it into his pants, then crouched down and leaped up. Grabbing the beam with both hands he swung his body up and flipped over onto the roof. Quickly he put a foot loop in the rope and tied the end to a weather vane on the ridge so he could lay against the ridge with both hands free, without sliding off the mossy slick cypress shakes. He had a shooter's perch and rifle rest with a bead on the house and yard.

Gabe broke into a grin as he peered up to where Josh had scrambled. "Damn boy, that's shining work, sure nuff, you're neigh onto half cougar cat, I swear, the way you can climb. Here, take yore Whitworth. Remember it's single trigger now, not like the old Sharps."

"Yeah thanks, how could I know that after firing it six hundred times, anyway?"

"Well, yer pap tole me ta make sure ah learned ya. Can you see them varmints?"

"Not real well with all this fog, give me a minute to use the telescope,...wish we had a better telescope on this rifle itself, this 4 power isn't much," said Josh as he carefully brought up the big gun with the long heavy barrel, then put the other brass telescope to his eye, braced it and focused. It was difficult to balance on the roof ridge and hold the heavy barrel of the British-made Confederate sharpshooter's rifle. Josh tried to find a good position as Gabe spoke up from down below.

"This fog and mist will keep them from seeing the smoke from your shot, if we're lucky. Take this ammo parfleche with long bullets for the Whitworth, watch it, it's greasy and slippery." Josh reached his long arm down. Gabe handed the cartridge bag next, then the spyglasses. "Here, better hang em all on your neck to keep em from sliding down the roof."

"Yeah, I got 'em, thanks grandma, yeah, I got clean underwear on, mittens too, just keep knitting...now I can see two of them rounding up everybody on the front porch. I can't sight in on the captain with the feathered hat, he's just stepped in the doorway with a woman in his grip....looks like Mrs. Broussard. But the other two are there, plain view...blondy on the porch behind a post with the kitchen gal, damn him, now the big one with the spade beard is walking towards the barn with a kerosene lantern...I got a bead on him, in the clear."

Gabe had the binoculars and was peering through the

branches below. "Yeah, I can see them now, sorta. Drop the son of a bitch. Rub him out. Make wolf meat."

"Alright, alright, you can shut up now, or earlier, to suit me."

Twenty seconds passed slow, ticking like drops of water from the window frame.

"Wal?"

"Hell, I can't squeeze it, Gabe. I don't know if I can do this. Shooting from ambush doesn't sit right. If I gotta kill I'd rather do it face to face. Lets rush in there with the Spencers and pistols."

"Hellfire, this is real war, what part don't ya understand? We're in it now. They done made war on yore family, the worst kinda war, and your kin done been wiped out...and we're the only ones to avenge 'em."

"But ambushing don't suit me."

"They're ambushers, and we're ambushing them for what they done. They got it comin' for rubbing out our folk, yore folk. Lucky for them I ain't got one close with a blade.'

"I'd rather do it with a blade, eye to eye."

"Well we ain't got tha chance for that. They kilt your ma, Joshua Robinoix. Shoot tha sonsabitches."

"Don't call me that."

"Listen. Yore ma didn't get no chance, and neither should they. Now quit yore quibbling debate and kill em. They got it comin."

"Damn. Seemed like the right thing til it come to squeezing the trigger."

"This ain't no duel of honor, Joshua, this is war. You takes your shots when you can. They done gone beyond the pale, and got it coming."

"Yeah, I know you're right. Here, take the cartridge bag, I've got two more slugs with powder. Won't have time for more than that. It's hard to hold it up here. Let me get a better rest on this roof ridge."

"Who's stopping ya, I always told ya to take a good barrel rest, didn't I? Just go through the procedure. Sight in, deep breath,…"

"Shut up, Gabe," said Josh abruptly as he focused and sighted in. With scarcely any breeze, and a target at 600 yards through a white mist, it was something he had done hundreds of times in practice, but this was a man instead of a bucket or melon or a bulls-eye target. Josh went through the procedure in the old ritual taught him by Gabe when he was a teenager, but paused at squeezing the trigger, and breathed again, and again. The sweat begin to drip into his eyes, burning them.

He held a bead on the big man's chest as the black-bearded fellow walked towards the barn. There was no wind to affect the shot, only heavy damp air. The sweat kept beading on Josh's face despite the coolness of the day. He could feel and hear the blood pounding in his ear as he bent his head down to sight along the heavy barrel. He tried to steady his breathing, deep and slow.

A long silence, perhaps a half minute passed. Gabe finally spoke up. "Well, gol-durn, I said I'd do it. Get down, we'll get another spot where we can both shoot. With my eyes I gotta get closer anyway. Come on down. You ain't never shot at anything but watermelons and paper targets, 'cept for that duel, and ya only shot to wing him. And it's been six months since you fired the Whitworth. We don't have to take 'em now, we can find a better spot...maybe a tall tree like you climbed before."

"Alright, this isn't to my liking anyway, lets get closer...lets ride in on them with repeaters and revolvers..." said Josh as he put the brass 4X telescope on the long Whitworth back up to his eye.

"Wait, Gabe, oh no, that's a damn torch he's making, soaking it with kerosene...that big fella is fixing to set fire to the horse-barn. Stop, damn-it! He's lighting a torch and heading that way. There's horses and mules in there."

"It's up to you, Joshua. Time for palaver is done gone. You're the only one that can stop him."

"Damned if I do or don't, to hell with it, I can't let him burn those horses, or another plantation house with folks in it."

"Put him under. Throw hot galena into him, Josh. Rub him out."

With the heavy barrel resting steady on the ridge line, and his mentor urging him on from underneath him, Josh sighted his final line, took a deep breath and let it out, then methodically squeezed the trigger and saw the big flash of fire erupt from the end of the long gun.

Crack! The powerful accurate Whitworth sent its oversized load of fire and hot lead towards the barn-burner as he stood lighting his torch. An instant later he flew backward with a shocked look on his face, releasing the torch where it hung in the air for an instant as the slug tore a large hole in his chest and sprawled him six feet back from the torch as it fell sputtering on the muddy ground. A booming echo rolled down the wet valley bottom. The man didn't make another move except to quiver a bit, mouthing words while his gaping wound leaked a pool of blood into the muddy yard. LaPoint watched him in the looking glass to make sure he was dead.

"You get him?"

"Yeah, dead center, we're in it now.....now hold still while I get the other one, he's got hold of a girl on the porch.....so I have to go for the head. I have to reload, and my gut is reeling from this. I feel like throwing up, so better step back. And be still."

"That was a shinin' shot, in this fog, boy. Like I always said, you're the hair of the bear."

"Will you shut up before I puke a hairball on you?"

"Yeah, I reckon I might, or just step back from tha window a bit. I'd like to shoot the other but thar's no way I can swing up thar like a dam cougar. Go ahead and take em, like I showed ya. I told you it'd come in handy some day. Figured it'd be with Comanches, though."

"Be still." Josh clamped the reloading pouch under his knee and took aim again.

"Alright. But just remember ta.."

"Be still, quit your hectoring for a second. I'm done reloading."

"Did ya remember ta..."

"Shut up, Gabe, please, quit with the mother-hen..."

Josh, his stomach reeling and guts heaving from what he had done, took two deep breaths like when he first learned to use the old Hawkens, Sharps, and Whitworth long rifles as a teenager in '53.

A flood of memories drifted through Josh's mind as he sighted for what seemed like an eternity on the small target, waiting for his churning guts to settle down and quit the slight trembling in his hand. He tried to steady his deep breaths again, to kill another man while still reeling from killing the first.

"Come on, the fat's in the fire, Joshua!"

The darkness that had been growing in Josh through

years of contempt emerged and took over his guts and his fingers. When Josh grew still and squeezed the trigger, *Crack!*....he saw the flash and had that certain feeling acquired from hundreds of practice rounds that his shot was true to the target. He saw the soldier's head jerk back in a red mist as the boom echoed down the valley. He quickly switched to the telescope to see the effects, laying the smoking rifle down on the roof and holding it with his knee.

When he focused in the long-glass he saw a big red splotch on the wall of the porch and his target, the man's head with a red hole in the forehead, with his body sliding down the wall, leaving a red smear on the white boards. There was a fist-sized red and black hole in the wall where the bullet had gone through the cypress planks. The girl that the soldier had been holding was shrieking but unharmed, and she soon climbed the railing and took off running at a lively rate towards the brush where the hens had earlier scampered. Josh quickly began reloading, intent on finishing the job.

"You gotta make beaver now, eh, Josh?" said Gabe.

The enraged and panicked captain had bolted out the back of the house when the second shot came slamming and splintering through the parlor wall. He slipped in the mud while rounding the corner and fell cursing, but quickly rose and began scurrying again for his mount, who was tugging on his reins in nervous agitation. The other three men had stopped loading corn into their wagon and were looking around for where the shots came from. They were looking too close though, and couldn't tell much in the thick white fog.

"Snipers again! It's those Yellow Jackets, I'll wager. Secesh bastards. Probably that Thibodeaux bunch again. Where did those shots come from, you pie-eaters?" yelled the Captain as he grabbed the reins of his fractious horse and jerked them, spooking the already nervous animal into a turn that nearly threw him off as he mounted.

"Can't tell, Captain, sir. Must have been over that way, maybe from those bushes or those trees yonder."

"Well get mounted and get your rifles out, we got rebs to kill." The nervous horse kept turning in the yard by the big live oak trees, getting more fractious by the moment.

"Yes sir, captain. What about the corn wagon?"

"Damn the corn wagon, ya gol dang Philistine idiot. Get

your weapons ready. Those are big slugs to come through that wall like that. Sniper rifle. They got a bead on us too. We're getting out of here and maybe engaging some rebs. It's killing time for them Yellow Jacket bastards. Get your carbines out."

The spinning of the spooked horse put the Captain in Josh's sight at the time he reloaded and set the heavy barrel down on the ridge-line rest, so he popped off a quick shot, but wasn't quite dead on, and the big bullet nicked the captain's earlobe, taking it clean off as it whizzed by, leaving a spurting upper stump and a red streak on his cheek that splashed blood onto his shoulder.

The captain jerked back and yelled in pain, "Hellfire….I'm hit. Damn the Reb secession bastards. I saw the flash this time. It came from that barn over there, near the top…see that smoke?....a big gun sniper. Damn, bleeding like a stuck hog." He jerked his kerchief from his neck and held it to his ear as it turned red from the pulsing spurts of blood.

"They took my ear off, by gawd, and vengeance will be mine. You two dumb sonsofbitches get saddled up and attack that barn…the rest of ya take shank's mare up there with your carbines and pepper that loft with fire when you get close enough. Damned sharpshooter, is what…those Yellow Jacket snipers again…they don't know when they're whipped."

Two of the soldiers dropped the shovels they were using on the dried corn and ran for their horses which were tied to a railing by the porch. Just before they got there another big octagon slug came whistling in and knocked the rail off the posts, scattering the horses and stopping the soldiers in their tracks. They went back scurrying for cover as they finally saw where the fire was coming from.

"Go get 'em on foot, forget chasing them horses. You got your carbines, slip over there, you two give 'em covering fire. Get with it, start shooting, damn-it, aim for the hayloft of that barn yonder."

"Hell, no way we can hit it from here, Captain."

"I know that, damn-it, but maybe they don't ….get moving towards it, firing as you go."

The corporal grabbed his carbine and mounted his horse, which he had tied by the barn.

"Come with me, Sam!" yelled the captain, at which instant he whirled his horse and took off down towards the green bayou, with his head squirting blood. The red-headed captain with a copper beard put his yellow bandana up to his ear to staunch the flow as they beat a hasty retreat along the bayou. The soldiers on the ground began the racket of a covering fire towards the barn that echoed along the big cypress of the still water, sending the birds squawking off upstream.

"Captain's having a conniption, Billy. Squirting blood out his ear. Creased his cheek too, looks like. Ugly bastard gonna get uglier. Says we gotta rush that barn."

"Ah ain't rushing no barn with Yellow Jacket snipers in it with these piss-ant carbines. That ground is so boggy we can barely walk through there. We'll get picked off like Griz did. Just take cover and fire that way, Carl."

Atop the barn, amidst the sulfurous smell of gunpowder, Josh muttered a curse. "Hell, I rushed that one, just nicked him…side of his face, I think." He peered though the telescope and saw the riders coming their way, and the several soldiers advancing with carbines on foot, while the Captain beat a retreat along the bayou. Rifle fire erupted from the soldiers on foot, falling short.

"Time to go, I'm coming down, I didn't get all I need to."

"Wal, it ain't like a buffalo stand, Josh. You done good, stopped em in their tracks, ya did."

After a few more seconds of scanning with the long-glass, Josh saw that the foot soldiers were reluctant to approach, and were instead taking potshots in the direction of the barn, but landing far short. One of them hit the shed in front and made a racket, but that was the extent of the damage. Josh handed the long heavy Whitworth down to Gabe and swung his body down into the hayloft. When he did his head slammed into the jamb, and raised a knot on it immediately.

Gabe was scoffing at the lame shooting from cover by the soldiers when he heard the bang from Joshua's head knock. "Hell, watch out, you okay?....ain't no big rush, them boys don't want no part of them Whitworth overloads. No way they'll hit anything from there. You buffaloed em ." Slipping down the stairs from the loft and out the back of the barn, they quickly moved to their nervous horses. When they started to mount, Gabe noticed the knot on Josh's head. "What the hell happened to yore noggin, pard?"

"Banged it when I climbed back in. Ain't bleeding, is it?"

"Naw, but its a rising knot that's gonna give you a black-eye, that's for sure. You alright?"

"Well, no, I have been better. I'm actually not even sure I'm here anymore. I just shot two guys, felt like puking my guts up, and then saw stars when I bumped my head. Now I'm dizzy and my head is throbbing. I feel like I've been thrown from a horse on my head. I usually avoid this sort of stuff."

Gabe had to guffaw at that, and figured Josh would make it alright, though he looked strange, and his eye was swelling up and turning colors.

"Wal, ah reckon yore usual self done been left behind for shore now. Ya gotta make up another one."

"Yeah," said Josh, rubbing the knot on his head, "and I'm not too sure how that's working out, either."

"Yore gonna have a black eye for a while, ah reckon," muttered Gabe.

They took a back trail to the pasture at the ruins of the plantation where they had left the mules. Their willow draped trail was full of muddy streaks as they hurried without regard for their back-tracks. It took several hours to return to the tall trees around the plantation LaPoint.

Napoleon and Josephine were glad to see them, and let them know until Gabe shushed them with feed bags full of oats. Josh did the same for the horses, going over them with curry-comb as they ate. He was still reeling from the killings he had just committed, and feeding his horse and caring for it seemed to steady him. After a while Josh seemed somewhat centered again, and the horses more contented.

Gabe looked at him with narrowed eyes, studying.

"Ya feelin' up to beaver yet?"

"Yeah, whatever the hell that means," replied Josh. "I'm not who I was the other day."

"Waugh. Naw, ya ain't. Stomach knotted up, I reckon. You be ganted up for war now." Josh just nodded. Gathering the packs and gear and loading the mules, they moved to the woods along the bayou to plan their next move.

Gabe took his big knife and slivered some cypress to get a fire going, while Josh broke small dead twigs from standing trees where they were dryer. Josh used a candle dripping wax to get the flame going hot. Squatting around the smokeless fire they made dark coffee and laid low, stuffing French bread chunks, beef jerky, dry boudin and cheese down, and feeding the animals.

"Wal, I gotta say, for a while thar I didn't think you could do it, Josh. Sorry I doubted ya. I know it wasn't easy under those conditions."

"Neither did I, until he started to burn those horses in the barn. Then something just snapped inside me. That kind of man doesn't deserve to live as much as the horses do. But still, it's a bad feeling in the pit of my gut. Especially the second one, seeing his head exploded like that. Sort of like those watermelon, huh? Damn. Sort of sickening image, hard to forget."

"Aww no, don't get me started, I whar right next to Owen Whistler when his head exploded all over me, back on the Cimarron. Most sickening feeling I ever had til then. He was dodging arrows from above while a bullet caught him in the cabeza and blew it open. They made wolf meat of ole Owen. Never got time to bury him."

"Hell, I didn't mean to get you started, Gabe, it just don't go down easy, killing from ambush....It isn't like a duel, face to face."

"I know, it's that way the first time, til ya realize it's war, not some affair of honor. The whole point of practicing to be a sharpshooter is to take them down from a distance where they can't hit you. Don't let it get you down. They deserved it. What else could we do, take em to the sheriff or the federals? "

"Yeah, I know. Too late to worry. What's done is done. I don't regret finishing what they started. But if I'd have listened to you and left New Orleans at Christmas, we could have avoided this."

"Why hell, ya done all ya could do, made all the right moves, sometimes the world just gets overrun with wild wolf packs This is just such a time. And we're in the wolf pack killin business now, like it or not. We got to get that Captain. He's the one causing the worst of it."

"Yeah, I know. I'm set on it now, after taking down the henchmen. It just took me a while to wrap my mind around it. I was so glad I avoided the war and all the senseless slaughter. Now here I am, a killer like most everyone else, a sniper to boot. Feels like I crossed a line I can't cross back. For a moment I regretted it. But I've crossed over for better or worse now. I wish I had killed them all."

"Yeah, I know how you feel. The first time is the worst. It'll pass, 'cept for maybe at night. Let's get out of here now, go to Texas. Ain't nuthin left for us to do here. That captain's gonna lay low and lick his wounds. They'll be scouring the countryside for us by tomorrow morning."

"I doubt it. They'll think it's another skirmish with the Yellow Jackets. Most of them came home after Opelousas and have been tangling with the federals ever since, as a home guard. I got to finish this, Gabe. I don't want to leave it undone."

"Alright, what's your plan?"

"Well, we got two of three, with just one left, I'd like to meet him alone and face to face. He's the main culprit."

"You think you marked his face with your shot?"

"That was my feeling, maybe his cheekbone, maybe his ear, but....How the hell can I tell at several hundred yards. He jerked like I skimmed him, and I saw his coat turning darker as he road off. I figure if I had grazed his head hard he wouldn't have been moving so fast."

"Well, he'll damn sure lay low, now he knows a Confederate sharpshooter is after him, and done kilt the two who was with him when he done in yore ma. If yore shooting skill in New Orleans gets connected with this, they may know who to search for. They could dig that elongated Whitworth slug out of tha wall, and it's a rare gun, and the Federals know you got one. Then this scrape could get a little tighter."

"Yeah, I've been thinking along those lines too. But hell, those guys probably raped a lot of women along the Teche, and there's deserter camps, and jay-hawkers, and just plain old marauders all around here. He can't be certain it was anyone connected with LaPoint, or just more sniper fire from Yellow Jackets, or relatives of women they raped."

"But ya got him for certain?"

"I think his ear is smarting now, maybe his cheek. Sure was squirting red. Hope I hit the vein in the neck . Bleed out, you damned murderer, woman killer." Josh spat on the ground.

"Wal, he'll be easy to spot, with that red beard and hair, and ear shot off."

"Yeah, I can spot him. I'll never forget that face. I even dreamed of it. And I'm not sure about the ear, but I know I grazed him. Let's rest here tonight and figure out our next move in the morning."

"They will be out looking for us in the morning."

"Yeah, but they won't find us, because we'll be at their camp watching them. They'll never figure to search that mosquito bog down by the lake, under their noses."

"Wal, glad we brought yer Ma's repellent. She's helping us from the grave, huh?"

"More than you know. My dreams are full of her. I dreamed we were at Congo square together, like when she took me to play drums when I was a kid."

"Really? That's shinin', fer shore. You better pay heed to what she conveys in them dreams, afore she moves on."

"I am, and I have a trail opening in my mind."

"Alright Josh, you calling the shots now, yore Booshway and I'm your Segundo. All them years of training that Alex had me put you through, you gotta call up every bit of it now. And I ain't talking 'bout black-smithin' and bricklaying, neither. We may have to shoot our way out of here with every weapon we got. Wish you would have hit that captain a few inches over, and this would be finished, with nothing left hanging."

"Yeah, me too. I rushed the shot when he was turning on his horse. Don't fret, ole fella. We'll finish it soon."

"Don't call me ole fella, wolf-pup, 'til you can out grip me. Taught ya all you know, not all I...."

"Yeah, so I've heard. You saying you're not old? For years you've been saying you're getting too old for this stuff."

"I'm one of the few in my crowd that lived to be old, anyway. Lots gone under. 'Cept Mr. Alex, and he was tha best."

"Yeah, so you've told me. All he ever did was set me to work at something or another. And I screwed this work up royally, with nothing but ashes to show for it. Let's go."

They returned to their camp, hidden in heavy wet woods, and were greeted by the overjoyed Chihuahua Suzette and the lonely mules, Leon and Josie. After hand-feeding the stock with oats and corn mixed with molasses, they bedded down in the underbrush, wrapping in cowboy roll tarps and wool blankets. Suzette slept curled in Josh's belly after her meal of dry sausage, cozy and content.

Josh had strange dreams with his mother and the men he had killed in them, and awakened hours before dawn, making a small fire for black coffee, then awaking Gabe, who rolled out complaining of his rheumatism from sleeping on the ground, and went to telling about the old days of sleeping on a buffalo robe under two feet of snow up on the Llano Estacado, coming out the Cimarron canyon from Taos, dodging Comanches with a load of beaver pelts. Josh had heard it all before but this time it meant more, since the area might be in their future.

After coffee, bread, and sausage they mounted and rode in the moonlit night to Spanish Lake, brushing the overhanging black branches on the small trail. The lake was shining black and silver ripples in the moonlight, and smelled of rotting vegetation. Alligators roiled the surface with their eyes bulging above the dark waterline, searching for dinner. Big blue and white cranes did lazy slow wing flaps as they skimmed along over the placid surface. Sounds from the federal camp echoed over the lake.

Chapter Three: Shadows on the Teche

The next morning dawned foggy again as they waited near Spanish Lake watching the Federal encampment for the departure of the foraging parties. Josh climbed up with his telescope to watch the departing horseback groups of five to eight men, sometimes with a wagon, sometimes mules for hauling booty back. Several parties left, but their target wasn't among them. He noticed they carried carbines, accurate only at short range. Later a couple of ambulance wagons left towards Brashear City, but they were covered and escorted by a cavalry unit, so it was impossible to tell who was in them.

Disappointed, Josh and Gabe holed in the dense woods during the day until Gabe figured the saloon in New Iberia frequented by the federals was open. He went and began drinking and listening until he was nearly too drunk to walk straight, but had learned what he needed. Then he staggered off into the twilight and returned through back trails to the hideout near the LaPoint plantation. When he swung off his horse he nearly fell from the muddy landing, and he saw Josh come out of the bushes with his head shaved, and his facial skin darkened with a mix of coffee, charcoal, and grease, grinning with white teeth set off by his black skin. His clothes were dark as well, so that he was nearly invisible when he quit grinning.

"Gol-dang, almost didn't know ya. Ya gone from a black eye to a black man! You're missing your mane. Somebody come by and lift yore scalp for ya, boy?" asked Gabe with a chuckle.

"Something like that."

"Or you done beat em to it. I guess you done decided we going to Comanche country, huh?"

"Maybe, don't know. Just had the feeling I should change my appearance, and you always told me that a Comanche would ride an extra hundred miles for a sun-bleached scalp like mine."

Gabe busted out laughing and nearly fell down. "Oh shit, too much tangle foot to take a gander at that!" he said.

"So I see."

"Dang, you look a sight. Shore don't look like that New Orleans gentleman. No more factor dressed in foofarraw, huh? Look at that dark skinhead. Yore crowning glory done shorn away. Comanche wouldn't give a spit for that scalp, now. Mine either, now that it's half fallen out and ain't copper colored any more."

"So maybe we'll get a pass and just slip on by them on account of bad hair, huh?"

"Might be. So you ready to head west? That little herd-gathering ranch is still there on the Rio San Antonio, just waiting for us. Pancho is a mustanger deluxe and Rosita a great cook. Maybe Mister Alex knew it would come to this and bought it as a place to move to, huh? He had a knack for the long vision, ya know."

"I guess so, Gabe. Texas looks like the last option now. I can't do any more ambush killing and get a good nights sleep,... and I doubt I can catch him alone, now that he knows we're after him. You must have found out something, it's nearly midnight, and you're drunker than I seen you in years. Tell me."

"Hell, I had to buy some rounds to get them soldier boys talking. The captain we're a hunting is called J. P. McSheran, and he's gone with everyone glad of it. Even that riff-raff at the Federal camp is glad he's gone. Some sort of a crazy Bible spouting abolitionist madman, or so they say, come to smite the infidels, but mainly intent on looting and raping. They said he come in 'bout half bled out after circling around back to the camp. They said he'd been attacked by a whole passel of Rebs too, blaming it on the Yellow Jacket battalion, like you reckoned they might. Said you marked him good too, took all but a small upper part of his ear off, sliced his cheek with hot lead, and put him in bed from loss of blood. He bled so much from you taking off most of his ear that he fainted and fell off his horse when they got back to Camp Pratt, and smashed his nose in on a wagon wheel. He left in that hospital wagon, head wrapped in bandages and out cold, with the other seriously injured, for better medical facilities at Brashear City. We ain't gonna find him now."

"Well hell's bells, that about tears it. Texas is sounding better all the time. I got his name."

"Yeah, and we know he has a misplaced earlobe, scar on his cheek, and a busted nose, maybe our trails will cross later."

"Guys like that invite killing. I'll get him if someone else doesn't get him first."

"Yeah, could be, and if that warn't enough for ya to

decide to head out, there's more. They got a warrant out for your arrest over that scrape in New Orleans. Already got a notice out over the telegraph, couriers too, stating John A. Bobindough, wanted for attacking federal troopers in New Orleans, 900 reward. John A. Bobindough. Sounds like some kind of sourdough biscuit mix, maybe. I expect your pal the Lieutenant made a mistake lettering yore name."

"How the hell did you find that out?"

"By getting the telegraph guy drunk and getting him to show me the warrants list he had in his coat. Turns out that guy you and Scorpio stove in was the nephew of a congressman, and they done sic-ed the hounds on ya."

"Well, that was never really my name anyway...just something to put on paper for the federals. I don't need the Robinoix name."

"Why, Alex Robinoix is your pap, and you're the spitting image of him, and got his makings too."

"That's what you say. He hasn't ever called me son, or given me his name. I'm just a crossbreed bastard from the bayou, trained to be an overseer, you know. Just another mulatto offspring that happened to get educated to be of some use. The Robinoix title isn't stuck to me too damn hard. I'll become LaPoint."

"Wal, that wife of his that died later woulda had you kilt by her brothers or sold off if Alex hadn't stopped it and slipped ya off in tha night."

"So you say. I'm not stuck on the name, or the role that was carved out for me either. Both are useless now, time to start over."

"Wal, might as well shuck tha name then, cause somethin' like it's been put on their long list, sort of. LaPoint suits ya well enough."

"That have anything to do with them burning out the plantation after all our agreements?"

"Can't say for sure, but I doubt it. That was finished last week, just been smoldering all this time. They been looting and burning out places and raping women all up and down the bayou, 'cording to local talk. The great Texas overland expedition came through here and stripped it, mostly, and what's done been spouted up after that been stole by one side or the other, renegades, rebel deserters, jay hawks, marauders, what have ye. Then they got the Thirteen Corps that was in on the siege of Vicksburg wreaking general havoc. That captain came in about two months ago with them destructive marauders, used ta be red legs, guerrilla looters and killers, some say, and things got a lot worse after they arrived. They come down from Missouri, been burning and pillaging up there."

"It's all gone to hell on account of the damned war, just like Mister Alex said it would," replied Josh in a low grim tone. "He was right about that, anyway."

"Damn I know that's right, after several years of washing down federal crap with rainwater in New Orleans with union boots stomping round every corner, and watching you swaller yore bile and chaffer with 'em. Now they burning out everything down here too."

"The stupid cretins. It all comes from those black Republican radicals. Why, they don't have to burn things down to forage, they're cutting their own throats, demolishing farm production, and sowing hate that won't ever go away."

"Yep, hit's a damned free-for-all, might as well be on the frontier with the savages. At least on the Llano Estacado you know who your enemies are, and they don't spout tha Bible at ya."

"Yeah, pretty near everyone, according to what you've said, especially Comanches and Kiowas. Don't sound like much of a paradise on the high plains."

"Well, there's other ways to Taos, Joshua, and thar's a chance Mister Alex is there. Somebody's been sending those fur shipments in. We could go there and hunt."

"I know. It's just that, I spent the last several years trying to save what we had, like Mister Alex told me to do, and thought I had it done. Now it's all for nothing, and I lost my mother, the woman he loved, and the Robinoix home. In the end I failed. What could I tell him if I saw him? How I lost everything for him?"

"It's just the times, Boy. Right now they're gonna be looking for a sharpshooter with a Whitworth because of that octagon slug you left in the wall of that house. And you're known for a sharp eye and a Whitworth in New Orleans."

"There's lots of sharpshooters around, so they got no proof...Whitworth is the standard Confederate sniper gun. John Bobindough isn't even close to my name. Hell, I don't even have a name, really."

"Thar's damned few Whitworth rifles with those long slugs of lead around, and they knew you had one, from that time you took it to a shooting match, remember?

"Yeah, I do, dammit, showing off those slugs you made for accuracy."

"Alright then?"

"Alright then, yes, I'm done, let's leave this place, go to Texas. We'll ride at night until we get clear of this mess. Scorpio and I will go in blackout."

"What's yore whole notion, Josh?"

"They will be looking for a pale gray horse with black mane, and a rider with a blond mane, come on and look..." They walked to where the stock were tied and waiting. Scorpio was now jet black, with a shorn mane and docked tail.

"So you both goin' darkie on me? I ain't gonna put that greasy black stuff on me, gol-dang-it."

"Don't you get it, Gabe? You don't need to. I'm the one they're looking for, huh? A white, well-dressed businessman from New Orleans with long blond hair on a dappled gray horse with long mane and tail. I'm gonna pass for a shave-head darkie on a black horse with a cropped mane and tail. I can be your slave, or captive, or helper, depending on the situation."

"Alright. Alright. Might work as good as any other, if we're caught. But gol-dang, Josh. I'm too tangle footed to ride all night."

"I figured for that, got a pot of black coffee, thick enough to stand a horseshoe up in. Tonight we'll go back to the mules and move west a couple of hours til we find a good hiding spot away from the plantation, then we can take turns sleeping and standing watch. You get the first sleep."

"Alright then, let's get away from this dang Federal camp, they're too close for comfort. And I need more of that mosquito repellent of your ma's."

"Here. I keep some in my pocket. Listen good now. I spent the time scouting, and I met with old Cypress Sally, who has lived on the swamp edge for years. We went in her pirouge and marked a trail through the marsh along that long canal off the bayou, back of her houseboat. She showed me where the water is shallow and the bottom will support a horse and rider. In that little swamp to the south I met up with a party of Yellow

Jackets led by a Captain Thibodeaux, whom I used to know. He filled me in on things around here, and showed me some trails. They are keeping an active home guard, picking off marauders when they can. He's got a map of a lot of trails they use to avoid Federals. Helped me get my bearings again, after being gone for these last years. Come on. We'll walk the horses. Follow right behind me; you could get mucked down in the dark, and I learned the trail in daylight. But don't step outa my tracks or I can't account for how deep you'll sink. There's quite a few gators and snakes too."

"Aw crap, you know I hate them critters. Why not take the road?"

"So grab a stick to brush them away. I picked up some broken chunks of brick to throw at them if I have to. You know I can drive off gators."

"Ah reckon, if ya can see 'em in this light."

"Then come on, gators come with the territory around here, stamp your feet."

They got the horses to high stepping and they did the same, stamping their feet in the mud, hoping to drive the serpents from their path. The progress was slow, but they only encountered banded water-snakes and small gators, which Josh brushed away with a long cypress bough. They walked their nervous horses for a mile and then heard an unearthly deep growl that vibrated the mud at their feet. The horses spooked and tried to retreat, and Josh saw a huge alligator in the shallow water to their right. It was rearing his toothy snout up and emitting deep bass toned growls that evoked terror. The extended head was immense and powerful, slightly open with sharp teeth gleaming in the moonlight, while the long back was set in a high arch, with heavy tail curled behind in the shallows.

"Hot damn, it's a giant gator, take the horses back!" said Josh as he whirled Scorpio and handed his reins to Gabe and grabbed the sack of brick chunks slung from his saddle horn. He grabbed the first and readied it to throw just as the gator made a charge at him, hurling the heavy chunk into the eye of the beast at five yards as Gabe jerked the horses back. The gator recoiled and Josh struck his nose with another tumbling piece of brick, then another into the eye area, and the gator retreated back into deep water with even louder growls, thrashing through the mud and water lillies. It was all Gabe could do to hold the horses, which were both emitting loud shrieks and tugging their reins, anxious to retreat.

"Damn, you hammered him with every throw. Just like when ya was a kid. Nice chunkin'"

"Yeah, thanks. Wasn't sure I still had it in me, not too hard to hit when they're that close. But I only have three chunks left, and might have to shoot the next one."

"Holy crap, I hope thar ain't more as big as that one, big enough to charge men."

"Maybe not, but if I have to fire, it might bring trouble from the Federals, so let's hope for better luck."

"That fuggin' monster might come back."

"I don't think so. I hit him in the eye. That always works."

"Hit was a bunch o shinin' shots. Let's get on before he recovers. That was as big as ole Ephraim. Never seen one like that."

They were trembling on the trembling ground, and tugging on nervous stock, but followed the small levee trail until they left the marsh below the lake, then returned to their hideout near Plantation LaPoint, where the mules were glad to see them. They packed the mules, fed and watered all the stock, stowed Suzette in the left saddlebag in the top hat she used for a sleeping bag, then took off in the darkness, heading west. Wrapped in thought and silent except for the clomping and splash of hooves, they rode through the dark shadows of tall cypress trees draped with gray tendrils of curly moss hanging limp and saturated in the fog.

Several hours later they stopped at a cemetery outside Abbeville, and found an overgrown spot to hide in, so Gabe slept while Joshua sat up with Suzette in his lap, thinking over their situation and working on his plans, then later rubbing down the restless stock until the first pale light of dawn showed in the east. He went over and gently nudged the leg of Gabe as he slept, knowing not whether the old man would spring out of his bed with a knife flashing for the Comanches in his dreams.

When Gabe awoke he was startled again by the sight of Josh with skinned pate and blackout now over all of his visible skin, and started a dry chuckling. Gabe had never thought of Joshua as a Negro until seeing him in this disguise, and he couldn't help but laugh at the sight of the former New Orleans gentleman with the long blond mane as a bald darkie.

"Jeeves, you're a sight to scare old Ephraim, a fiend from the darkest pits of hell, with a cup in his hand. Morning to ya. Am I dead? Seems sorta wet for hell."

"If you are, then I am too. I think it's time for us to be reborn. Here's your coffee, Gabe. You seem to be enjoying my costume." He gave another big grin and did a low bow, "Yas masah, yaa-sah!" causing Gabe to chuckle again and spill his coffee.

"Oh hell yeah, I do. Ya seem sorta like an overgrown Chester, come to think of it, 'cept for your sharp narrow nose and blue-green eyes. Not sure yore gonna convince anyone yore a darkie."

"Well, I'll give it a try. Being too light was the reason I got taken away from my home and mother in the first place, if you remember."

"Wal, ya know Alex done that to save yore hide."

"I'm just saying, I've always been in disguise. I'm a bastard born in slavery running a business in New Orleans like a white gentleman, Gabe. Once I was on the run because I was too light to live in the slave quarters, and looked too much like the master to suit his wife. Later I passed for a white gentlemen in European universities. It's not like I ever fit in anywhere. I'll just pretend I'm a tracker and look down a lot, cutting for sign like you taught me, eh?"

"Wal ya better tell 'em yore a Seminole tracker if anybody asks, or better yet, let me do the talkin'.".

Josh laughed. "Well who could stop you talking? Just carry that shotgun across your saddle-horn and don't get into idle chatter....and maybe we won't get seen and can slip right thru to Texas."

"That'd be some shinin' luck."

"It's a dark night and I'm a dark man now, on a dark horse. We'll ride at night and hide by day, luck or no luck. And you know, Chester is Uncle Alphonse's boy. So we're cousins."

"Wal, come to think of it, yeah I thought about that once or twice. When I knew him in Taos he always had a right fine Mexican gal with him," said Gabe as he rounded up the mules by lead lines. "Dang if ya sure don't make me feel white, though." The mules started braying as he tugged them, and he shushed Leon with his hand.

"Shaddup, Napoleon, Texas is awaitin'."

As Josh approached Scorpio the horse seemed to give a long laugh in his face, his white teeth flashing in his dark head, which he shook furiously as if to complain about his missing long mane, which was cut short like Joshua's head. The dark color of his legs had been extended up his body to his head by Josh, and he looked to be a different horse. He rattled his head from side to side in complaint at Josh, and his reaction made both men burst out laughing as they set out walking for Texas.

"Ya shore done a job on him," said Gabe. "Turned him back to dark, just as he was going into a sorta dappled gray."

"Yeah, and in six months he'll be nearly white."

"Wal, it's gone ta Texas for us then, and maybe Taos too, let's ride."

"Goodbye. Going to Texas, can't be worse than this," murmured Josh LaPoint as he nudged his stallion gently with the pointed toe of his boot, then tugged on the line to Leon the jack mule, who was still making a big racket.

"Skocum. Lead on, LaPoint," said Gabe, who pulled Josephine and started her braying.

"Shuddup, ya dang mule," hissed Gabe.

They rode all the wet and dreary day and into the twilight, huddled against the chill, listening carefully for sounds of horses as they each led a mule along the overgrown trails. The pine forests lining the wetlands and bayous were dark and dreary in the rain, while the hardwoods were hard to ride around, with their low branches. They barely covered three miles in an hour of pushing through the sloppy gumbo mud, and the hours rolled by slowly when they had to hide from patrols and other groups of night riders.

Several times they were alerted by Suzette to the pounding of horse's hoofs behind them, and slipped off the trail into thick brush where they could dismount and hold the noses of their stock as the groups of riders passed. The swampy land soon gave way to higher prairies, piney woods, and better footing for the horses and mules. .

Often during the ride the little Chihuahua bitch Suzette would ride in front of Joshua, her terrific alertness and the set of her ears telling Josh where danger approached. Several times they dodged groups of horsemen, once by getting saddle deep in a swamp beside Injun bayou. Once they got a mule stuck and had to lasso him with two ropes to pull him out braying and squealing, alerting anyone around, which fortunately, nobody was.

By daylight they were still slogging through wet ground only fifteen miles from where they started, their stock exhausted as they were. They heard vague sounds of riders in the distance and wondered if they had been going in circles in the dark. They kept pushing away from the patrols on mud covered mounts, back into wetter ground.

In the swampy bayou-land that morning they were riding on a muddy levee trail that was slippery from the horse traffic that had traversed it before, when they heard a large group of riders coming. With no place to go but into the swamp, they cut off the levee and took to the shallow water and set out through the huge cypress tree butts with their pointed knees sticking out of the water like elegant wooden fins, some extending two feet high above the murky waterline.

With his years of fishing and hunting the swamps in summer as a child, Josh took the lead in finding ground solid enough to hold them. Gassy smells and bubbles rose as they trailed off through dense timber growing in two feet of water. The horses sunk to their knees in the primordial goop, the water above their chests, but they were able to keep moving, heading for another levee and bayou several miles to the south. Turtles and water snakes slid from their slimy perches as the travelers progressed through the swamp. Alligators cruised just below the surface, lurking at a close distance, looking like just another floating log except for the ever watchful eyes projecting above the water. Various cranes and ducks took off ahead of them, announcing their arrival. After two miles of this slogging they came upon a cabin of rough-cut cypress boards, the diagonal saw-marks showing lines of green algae, resting on a log raft of cypress trees, some three feet thick. The houseboat was floating at the end of a small canal, perhaps five feet deep, that drained that area of the vast swamp.

An old mulatto woman with caffe au lait colored skin and green eyes was sitting on the porch with a cane pole, her cork floating in the canal a few yards away. She was watching them while smoking a corncob pipe that hung from the corner of her mouth, with gentle puffs of white smoke coming from her occasionally. The swamp beside the canal was not as deep, and easier to traverse, so they could get close to the cabin. The old woman, dressed in overalls and long-sleeved shirt, hailed them when they stopped splashing, their horses still panting from the exertion of slogging through the mud.

"Took yal long enough. Knew yal was coming, knew it a long time. Since I seen ya earlier on, knew you'd pass by. Dreamed it up."

"Hello. Good day to you. Gabe, this is Cypress Sally."

"Yessah, that'd be me. I'm still here. What you get is what you see. Who yal running from now?"

"Federal patrols."

"Ya come de right way, de doan come heah, 'fraid o gators and snake,.....and haints." At that she cackled mischievously and looked like a little girl for a second, with crinkled green eyes and a gapped-tooth smile. She puffed on the pipe and looked at their faces in turn.

Josh had to laugh with her, but felt tears forming in his eyes afterward, stirred by old memories of visiting with Sally and his mother. Gabe tipped his hat to her and nodded.

When Joshua had been allowed to visit the LaPoint plantation after the white wife of Mister Alex Robinoix had passed from long term illness, a younger Sally had often been there visiting with his mother in the garden, planting special herbs and making healing potions on the wide back porch as Joshua worked with the horses. He treasured those rare memories of visits with his mother, and seeing old Sally brought back a flood of images. She had always lived in the swamp near Cypress Island and gathered healing plants from the verdant outpouring of nature in those wet bottom lands and marshes with lush overgrown islands along the bayous.

"Yal need potions?"

"Mostly we need to find the shortcut to the big south levee and evade a Federal patrol behind us. We've already nearly lost a mule to the muck today."

"Dey doan come in heah, dey scared o us...all us heah swamp creatures. Even de cranes. Yal got a long ride now, ain't dat right, Mastah Joshua?"

"Yes, leaving for Texas, Sally."

"Why sho, only natural. Cain be helped."

"You know about LaPoint plantation?"

"Sho, hon. Corina pass by dis way when she go, cause we ole friends. She bade me give ya a potion ta keep ya awake on a long ride, way from this wet land to da dry land, da dusty land. Dat de ole blacksmith?"

"Yes, Sally, old Gabe McBride, blacksmith and scout."

"Scout is right. He a fine lookin' man too, scout too. Ah'd let 'im scout me if yal had de time. He take yal 'zackly wheah yal needs ta go, dat's fo sho. Wait heah hon, ah'll be right back." She stepped into the house and returned in a few seconds with a burlap bag with bottles of potions. Josh moved his mount to right beside the end of her fishing porch. "Listen heah and doan get 'em mixed up. Look now at de picture on each label. I know ya don't forget nothing. Dis fo if ya needs ta stay away few a long time, on a long ride. Dis fo horses and mules, ta do de same. Dis heah fo ta see in de darek. Dis is fo bites from vipers, cut de bite and suck de poison out and spit, den make a poltis o dis on it till it starts ta heal. Den dis heah make a poltis ta heal any wound. Dis is ta keep de bugs offen yal. Dese heah roots are ginseng, for dat ole man, make him young again. And heah's a lil bag of chicory, hard ta find wheah yal goin, for yo coffee, keep yo stomach well when ya drinks too much coffee. Heah, look at de pictures I drawn on de labels."

Each bottle had an appropriate symbol which Josh could remember. He studied them for a few seconds, then replaced them in the bag and took it. "Thank you Sally, you're a good friend. Now that Mama is gone, you are the last old time healer around here. Who will know the plants and potions, when you're gone?"

"Ah knows. Ah knows. Won't be no priests nor doctors knowin' it. And ah getting a lil bit old."

"How old are you, Sally?"

"Oh, 'bout hundred, ah reckons. I's born on Santa Domingo."

At that instant they heard shooting a couple of miles back, a few scattered shots, then a barrage of fire. A bugle call sounded above the firing, which echoed through the big trees in the swamp, making the direction of the fight difficult to determine.

"Yellow Jackets done jumped de federals again. Now is yals' chance ta slip away, while dey fightin'."

"Can you point the way for us to go without getting bogged down, to catch that old levee that goes southwest?

Sally stood on the end of the porch and pointed. "Dat

way. Dey woan catch yal, but ya got's ta travel at night til ya come to da deep pine forest, and higher ground. Hide in de day and travel at night. Dey fights de war in de daytime round heah, and dey aftah yal for sho now. Ya gotta go while dey got's deh minds on sumthin else. You de one got's ta point dey way now, you de son of Corinna and Robinoix. LaPoint. Like a knife, it all follow de point."

"Thank you Sally. We'll be going now." Josh felt overwhelming sadness wash over him with the feeling that somehow he was losing the last touch with his mother when he left Sally.

"Yal gonna be missed, like yo mama be missed. Yal gotta long ride, and ya gotta beware when ya come to dat dark river wif all dem pointed sticks. Nasty pointed sticks in de mist, I seen. Goin be bad trouble deh, goin be vipers and suchlike lurking ta kill. Yal gonna do alright if yal don't get too tired like. Yal gotta kill 'em first."

"We'll use your potions, like my mama did."

"Alright now. Yal best keep movin, dem soldiers is all up and down de levee lookin for yal back deh, but Captain Thibodeaux and de las o dem Yellah Jackets fight dem when dey can. See dat blue crane flying dis way up deah? De swamp tellin me dat mo soldiers be comin. Go dat way. But ah gots ta tell ya dat yo leavin one war and goin to anothah. Be careful when you see dem walls o Jericho, Joshua, wif all dem pointed sticks. Yo gotta be awake fo sho den. A poison place it be. Danger. Danger. Danger."

"Walls of Jericho, pointed sticks, stay awake, be careful. I'll remember that Sally."

"Go on now, go finish dat war, point de way. Cain be helped. Dey takes de killing, like vipers. Cain be helped. Save yo healing fo de hosses. Cain be helped. Go on now. Go on, heah now, dis be de time for Joshua ta point west."

They rode off in the direction she pointed with her bony crooked yellow finger tipped with a long sharp nail. Josh could not help pondering whatever she was talking about, which wasn't clear at all, no matter how much it ruminated through his mind in the swamp. And he kept remembering with sadness the time he was working with his mama in the garden and Sally visited with swamp plants.

"Damn this is foul smelling mud," said Gabe, "And that

woman shore spewed out a mess of notions and potions, huh?"

"Yeah, and she was sweet on you, too."

"Yeah, I reckon that's about all I can attract now, a hundred year old mulatto swamp woman."

"She's a good cook, and catches whatever she wants in the swamp. And she knows herbs like my mother did."

"Yeah, I'll keep her in mind if Texas don't work out, and hell freezes over. Whoa-ee, yore shore churnin' up a stench in that yellow mud."

Continuing through the murky water, through miles of water-hyacinth and floating sticks, they tried to keep course by lining up huge cypress trees in the distance. The horses sank to their chests in water at times, as did the mules, protesting as they bogged down with constant braying. They were soon exhausted fighting through the mud, but they slowly moved on through the miasma emitted by their passing, and they would be impossible to track.

Within an hour they came to the levee and ascended it, finding solid ground at last, so they could make time. The horses were covered to their chests in foul smelling yellow mud, some with an oily sheen. They headed west at a fast walk and found dryer land and rolling pastures bordered by dense trees, so they used what cover they could find to stay out of sight, avoiding detection by patrols.

Finally they came to firm grassy meadows and piney woods with likely hiding places, and the mist hanging low on the ground as the sun set. On this land they finally made good time, moving at a fast pacing walk. At twilight they came to a small settlement around a store, about 50 miles west of where they started at dawn, and made a stop in the brush, where Josh fed grain to the stock and watered them. He was glad they had escaped trouble for the first day's ride.

Gabe went to the crossroads store and got some grub, fresh water, and local information, which he shared with Josh. The store-keep had told Gabe that there were many light engagements in the area between patrols and deserters, and the local home guard, and marauders of all kinds. The Federals usually patrolled until dark and returned to their encampments, was his opinion.

The travelers camped in a small cemetery nearby and slept part of the night, though Josh was again bothered by strange dreams and was ready to go when he saw the first light in the east. His mother had appeared with Cypress Sally in his dream, and they had taken turns telling him of many things to come, which were only vague images in the back of his mind as he rode through the wet and misty forested land.

They kept due west all day until they came to a lumber mill at twilight, near a cypress ringed lake by a town called Charleston, where they slept in the tool sheds behind the main operation. They had successfully dodged patrols and groups of marauders for the second day of riding, slipping through the dense pine forests, but Josh could see that Gabe was tiring from the long hours in the saddle. He wasn't the man he was back in his years of rangering in Texas, and this was his first long horseback ride in years. So they scouted out a spot in the dense pine forests under shadows of the gleaming moonlight west of the lake and took turns sleeping and standing guard while the stock grazed and rested, with Suzette and Scorpio ever on alert with their pricked up ears. The weather cleared a bit and a mild wind from the south started blowing, a sign of spring to come. The fat moon was lighting parts of the ground and leaving dark shadows to hide in.

Awaking Gabe at twilight, and giving him a ginseng root to chew on and Sally's night potions to drink, they lit out towards the Texas line, traveling in the evening now that there was less swampy land to traverse, and more solid footing for the loaded animals. Suzette and Scorpio keep hearing riders behind them, and they quickened their pace all they could in the dusk. Within a few hours they were approaching the Sabine river crossing, but Gabe was confused as to which crossing.

He hailed a teamster just sitting on his wagon smoking a pipe in the dark. "Hey there, driver, good evening to ya, is this here Millspaws crossing?"

"Used ta be called that, and Jericho too, but now they call it Niblett's Crossing."

"Wal, is there a ferry crossing still?"

"Yeah, you could call it that, bunch of snakes and lizards running it. I come across a couple hours ago just to get over before the river came up anymore. Resting my stock now. Keep going the way you be. Yonder down that road there about two miles."

"Any troops there?"

"Not no more, war's 'bout played out around here, Smiley's Confederates scattered a while back, lots of other dead with measles and buried in that graveyard yonder, along with regulators, moderators, and 'bout every other type of gunshot corpse. This place been a killing zone for years. I got waylaid on the other side of the crossing, 'bout a mile past. Took my whiskey and tobacco and two new model six shooters I had traded for, to ward off bandits. Ain't no troops around when you need 'em to keep the roads safe for commerce. I hear most of the federals staying east of here, round Charleston."

"Alright, then, thanks, safe journey to ya. Want a twist o tobacee?"

"Sure I do. Yal pass many federal patrols between here and Charleston?."

"None that we couldn't dodge."

"Them's some fine looking mules yal got, yal wouldn't want ta sell 'em, would ya?"

"Naw, much obliged for the information, though. Good night to ya."

Josh remained silent throughout the encounter. He knew that Gabe had passed this way over a dozen years before, and was content to let the older man be the guide, since he remembered every trail. Soon they approached the small town of Deweyville, and passed through it quietly.

On the outskirts of town they came upon a dark skinned man with a wagon bogged down in muddy ruts on the road. He was stuffing tree bark and sticks in front of his wheels, covered in the dark slime. He looked up at them for a brief while, the moisture on him shining under the full moon, then went back to his efforts to free himself. He had two worn out looking mules with boney asses trying to tug the wagon out from a deep slush. The travelers circled the mud bog on a narrow path found by Josh and Scorpio, then stopped and looked back.

"Let's tie the mules and give him a tug with Buck and Scorpio," said Josh. "That's the way my stick floats."

"Now don't go to mocking my palaver boy. I didn't learn to talk proper at no danged 'lightenment academy like some favored son, ya know."

"Favored in some ways. Well, we gonna pull him out or not?"

"Yep," said Gabe, as he dismounted and tied the mules to

trees near the road, watering them and putting feed bags on them. He got two lariats from the packs, pitched one to Josh, and remounted. They backtracked towards the bogged wagon, with Gabe in the lead. Gabe swung his lariat to the man and told him to hitch it to the right side of the wagon, then played out the coiled line and went forward until he was in front of the wagon in a position to pull. He put a daly around his saddle horn with the rope while Josh did the same thing on the other side. Then, with the driver urging his team, they both pulled and helped the weakened mules roll the wagon from the slush. When they got it out the man thanked them profusely, saying he would pay if he could, but had already been robbed that afternoon, and didn't have feed for his mules.

They spared him some grain for his mules and talked to him. Gabe handed him a wet towel to wipe the mud from his hands and face.

"Here, wipe that mud off with this here. Did ya get robbed?" asked Gabe as Josh fed their stock by hand with the grain molasses mixture, remaining silent.

"Back the road a piece. Thank ya again, kind gentlemen. Them's some powerful hosses for being so compact. I was a might afraid of yal when I first saw ya, and yal pulled me outta de bog."

"No problem, pard. We couldn't rightly leave ya thar when we could get ya out easy. I'm called Gabe, that their fella is my helper, Joshua."

"Samuel Ashworth is my name, a free man of color I am."

"You know this area well, been here long?"

"Yah-suh. Ah sho do. My people came over here long time ago, back in '33, and I'm getting out, had enough. Can't hold onto nothing anymore. Thought it was gonna be a place we could live in peace, build up our own holdings. No suh. No such thing. Even robbed me on tha way out."

"And whar about was that?" asked Gabe again, as he coiled the lariats and hooked them onto the saddles of their sweating mounts.

"Back cross tha river there, few miles back. Took all my goods, feed for mules and myself, suh. I thank ya for all your kindness too, for I'd probably been stripped to my teeth if I'd stayed stuck in that bog. Stuck in the bog, that's what its been round heah, suh. Ah'll be thanking de Lawd in my prayers for yore arrival."

Josh heard and felt the man was hungry, so he took bread, cheese, and sausage from his saddlebag and walked up and offered it to the man.

"Thank ya, suh," said Mr. Ashworth. "Are you a free man of color too, suh?"

Josh nodded his head.

"Well suh, this just ain't the place for such as us to make a new life any more. I lost just about everything in the fighting 'tween de Moderators and Regulators, and what I managed ta hold onto done been stripped in the interval by white thieves. I done give up on it."

"So it's all gone ta hell here too, huh?"

"Yah-sah, one time we thought we could make something for ourselves heah, free blacks and redbones, but I done shucked dat dream. Lawd, ah feels better aftah eatin' something. Was sorta dizzy when yal drove up. Them robbers took to my head with boots for their amusement, 'stead of killing me and drawing buzzards, ah reckon."

"How many was they?"

"Oh, I reckon 'bout eight or so. Came at me just in the upgrade of a little draw about a mile from de crossing, actually, suh. Is yal going dat way?"

"Yes, we are.

"Well, I hope yal are well armed.

"We are."

"Would yal consider waiting until morning and letting me travel with ya, suh. I kin shoot one of them repeaters pretty well."

"Wal", Gabe looked at Josh. Josh hesitated for a moment, then gave a slight negative shake of the head.

"No sir, we can't do that. What we done for ya is about our limit. We got ta keep on alone."

"Tonight, suh?"

"Yep."

"I wish ya all de good luck, suh. I feel like yal was a blessin' ta me, and wish a blessin' on yal. Maybe them robbers be drunk and asleep by now. But keep yore powder dry, suh, and be ready to shoot when ya see a tiny draw with a creek in it, bout a mile from de landing."

"Thanks for the blessin'," said Josh.

"Well, alright then," said Gabe. "Well be on our way, and good luck to ya, sir." Josh tipped his hat and they parted company as the free black drew his wagon and team onto a dry patch alongside the road for a rest.

They continued along the tree-lined shadowed road until they came to a hand-painted sign at the edge of the buildings that said, *Niblett's Bluff, river ferry.* The road was slippery and sloppy with the ruts of wagon traffic. There were a variety of earthen fortifications along the river, including a ditch and heaped up mud redoubt with abbatis, the sharpened branches and sticks protruding up and out at odd angles, to pierce any federals who cared to lunge that way. Suddenly Josh saw an image of Cypress Sally in his mind, talking about the walls of Jericho with pointed sticks.

"Hey, did that teamster say this place was called Jericho crossing once?'

"Yep. Quite a nasty looking mess, huh?"

"Yeah, and danger lurking, she said."

"Who said?"

"Cypress Sally."

Gabe began grousing about it as they rode closer. "Gol-dang, look at the sharpened sticks, like a fuggin' porcupine! What kinda shiftless morons would leave them thar for tha stock ta get injured on?" said Gabe.

"It's an abbatis, remember? I showed you that book on ancient fortifications with a picture of one, and they probably got catfish guts and alligator innards on the ends of the sticks to fester the wounds. Don't let our stock even get close to them."

"You don't say. So that's tha way yore stick floats, young coon?" said Gabe.

"Yeah, ole coon. And don't fall off your horse onto them sticks either."

"Wal doan shoot yore foot with yore pistol, neither. Dang yore sure fulla sass for a darkie, ain't ya?"

"Yas sah, massah. I done took a swig o Sally's stay awake juice and one nip of her eye tonic."

"Wal now's tha time ta share some. I got a creepy feelin' bout this place, smells like death."

Josh passed the bottles one by one to Gabe, and then they drank from canteens while studying the area.

"See anybody lurking?" said Gabe.

"No, but I got a bad feeling too. Something weird about this place."

"Wal, don't get too spooky on me, makes the mules nervous."

"They should be. And watch out for all those damned sharpened sticks, and snakes, with this high water. And the damned slippery footing."

"Aw shuddup and stay behind if ya ain't got nothing better than palaver 'bout sticks and snakes and muddy ground, as if I ain't dealt with neither. Come on, ya danged mule. Walk in slow, Josh LaPoint, we about ta make Texas."

"Well go on, scout."

"Well alright then."

They saw no soldiers or irregulars about the scattered fortifications, nor was there much activity amidst the ramshackle buildings, only the dim kerosine light from a bar on the outskirts. There was a musty damp smell from the river-bottom, and a fog along the shore. The fog was mixed with the smell of wood smoke and burning trash, and dead fish.

Down by the foggy river bottom there were a few old lanky shiftless-looking guys huddled around a small fire on the bank by the dock, under the edge of a makeshift shed roof, passing a jug around and trying to sing to French harp and fiddle. It was a vile noise that only approached music at brief instants, a caterwauling resembling a pack of dogs howling at times, but Gabe approached them after tying his horse and mule to the rail of a small stock pen. Josh waited with the stock, hand feeding them. The ferry was chained to a big oak tree branch and tied to sticks driven into the banks, and the river was running bank full, with lots of driftwood and litter floating down.

The horses got spooked at something and both tried to turn and bolt, tangling the mules and putting Josh into concern that they would get spiked. He urged Scorpio forward down the muddy incline and quickly straightened out the line to his mule, heading for the ferry crossing to Texas, tugging the braying mule in protest, followed by Gabe, who did the same.

Chapter Four: Ferry to Texas

"Howdy boys. Whar's the ferryman," Gabe asked as he strolled down the slippery bank to the fire, his gait stiff from the long ride. LaPoint waited up the rise, tending the stock, cleaning hoofs and hand-feeding grain.

"Ferryman?" replied the nearest lounger, raising himself up on his elbows. "Char! Ride on tha ferry now! Whar ya at? Why he's right here somewhere, belly up by tha fire, last ah seen him. Char! Whar ya at, Ben? Is old Char on the can, Nathan?" The rest of the crowd began muttering as well.

"Char on a bender."

"War is what we got 'round heah, dats fo sho."

"I seen Char on his bed in tha cabin," said the accordion player, "Clutching his bag of silver coins in one hand and the jug in the other."

"Yal work on tha ferry? Does it run at night?" asked Gabe?

"Sometimes."

"Fer silver coin."

"Yeah, sometimes is right," offered another.

"Naw, Goines, you always talking trash. Yassah, dis is de ferry, and de ferryman is here, somewheres," said another darker-skinned man with long straight black hair who sat on a little crate warming his hands.

A third man stood up and spoke, twanging a Jew's harp softly in his hand as he did. "Ferryman be our pal Silas B. Charcoal, yonder in that shack up thar. Old Char, we calls 'im. He went down bout two hours ago, got too drunk and sleepy, waiting for paying customers. We's having a few toasts 'bout them re-electing our fellow Melungeon, Abe Lincoln. He might even be kin, says ole Goines, theah." He started shuffling a little to the music as he looked up at Gabe.

"Speak fer yerself, I ain't no Melungeon," said his pal nearby with the jug.

"Dis stranger won't know what yore talkin' 'bout, Melungeon."

"Happens I do," said Gabe. "I's raised near Melungeons, in the Appalachians. Didn't know they was down here too."

"Thas right, the man knows," said Goines, hoisting

another brown clay jug for a quick snort that bobbed his protruding Adams apple a couple of times. "No payin' customers today. Nothin' but deserters today, or gimped up parolees with paper script. Now, earlier today I seen ole Char on a bender, but he done gave out."

"Char's fer sure on a tear earlier today, 'bout ole Lincoln, warn't he?" said the harmonica man. "He shoulda been a preacher."

"That shack there?" asked Gabe.

"What bout that shack there, stranger? Lookin' fer gals?"

"Iszat whar this ferry captain abides?"

"Char on a rum bender, cain be a preacher like dat, " the man closest to the fire muttered again.

"Naw, that's whar tha tavern owner got some gals for a fella need some company fer a while, and Char, he ain't no captain, he's jus plain ole Silas Charcoal, another red-bone running the ferry on account of he's got kin in the right places and a good pullin' arm and kin read and write and do figures. Iffen he didn't go with one of them gals then my guess is he be sleeping in that shed yonder, below that lil blockhouse that the Confederates left."

"That lil bitty shed thar?"

"Why Silas ain't Melugeon, he's downright educated. Jus' ax 'im."

"He's red-boned as I am."

"Tha's right mister, but he gonna be hard to wake."

"Oh yeah, ole Char on de bed or flooh, ya kin fergit it. Hits over fer yal til a new day dawns."

"You could join us here at our fire and wait til morning, you and your companion there. Or roust up a couple of those gals to bed yal down til morning and pull your cream for ya too, if ya got coin."

"You doan' wanna be goan' through that no man's land in the dark o night. All kinds o haints over thar, cross that river," said the man who was shuffling.

"Yal ain't gotta worry bout Confederate troops here, anyway. The ones that didn't die of measles is all skeedadled. Nothing much worth fighting over is left. Shipping's dried up, lumbering too. Nothing but fighting over spoils, and not much of them. Yal come set by the fire here, warm the bones..." offered the friendly man with the Jew's harp.

"No thanks, gotta keep movin' while we can. I'll wake him up. I'm a paying customer." Gabe walked stiff-legged up to where Josh was holding the stock and trying to soothe them.

"You missing yore regular New Orleans gals enough to shack up here for the night with some bar gals?"

"Very funny. We need to keep moving like the devil's on our trail. I'm ready to be in Texas. Let's cross this creepy area now, I don't like it. Neither does Scorpio."

"I know. Buck too. Smelling blood, I reckon."

Gabe turned back to the campfire circle, then walked past it towards the little shack above the bank. The boys around the fire passed the jug as they watched him go.

"Going to Texas, here's another one, party of two, travelers on a dark road,.... Going to get kilt and scalped by savages, or et by Kronks or Tonks."

"They already tried that. Ain't strange ta me," said Gabe, as he stopped and faced them, bowlegged and stiff from his long ride.

"Wal suit yerself, then. Ah ain't trying ta tell ya how to do, jus' try ta be neighborly, being as we got a fire and jug and all...and your friend kin come down to tha fire and warm himself, iffen he inclines that way. We got nothing 'gains darkies."

"He stays with the stock," said Gabe as he stood on the rise above the fire, scanning the woods across the river and the trees around the landing.

"Mistah, ole Char ain't takin' any confederate paper money anymore, so ah wouldn't even bother lessen ya got silver coin. He's funny that way now, being the war's about dead along with the South and all. Confederate paper ain't worth a mule fart. He won't take no script atal. Just silver coin."

"Wal, dats for sure, yal not gonna have no luck lesson ya mention silver coin, ah tell ya that right now. That's one of Char's sayings, 'no silver, no ferry'".

"Yasuh, that's what he say, no silver...." piped in another.

Fatigued and impatient, Gabe cut him off. "Aww shuddup, wouldya? Ya danged repeating parrot. We got silver coin and no time to waste." Gabe then turned and stalked up the little rise to the shack and proceeded to knocking on the door with his big fist. The whole door-frame shook with the power of his pounding, for he was a bit tired and cranky.

"Lookin' for the ferry man, old Char!" yelled Gabe.

Raucous laughter rolled from the fireside loungers, sort of a high cackling mixed with hacking phlegm.

"Good luck to ya, stranger."

"Oh yeah, good luck with Char, rousting him outa bed an' all!"

A phlegm-choked gargling voice emerged from the shanty. "Hey, cut that out, quit pounding, go way. Who the hell is banging on my door in tha middle of tha night?" A scraping, then a banging crashing noise ensued. "Go way, Curley...said I don't wanna go ta town."

"We're travelers that need to use the ferry, on urgent business. Come on, ferryman."

"Ferry opens when I wakes up and got a load o paying customers, lemmi lone, back ta sleep."

"I said we's on urgent business, and we got silver coin to pay, and a load, four stock, two men. "

"Go the hell away, I says."

"We can't wait til daybreak. We'll pay your usual fare and a bonus, in silver coin, for crossing right now."

"River is up, mister. Cottonmouths crawling in the dark escaping high water. I don't like ta cross in the dark when it's up. Some of my river-sticks have washed away on the other side, and tha dock's bout half gone too. I gotta get them boys out thar ta help me drive in more sticks on both sides of tha river tomorrow before it's right ta cross again."

"Aww get up, ya possum. You want this money or don't ya?" Gabe rattled his bag of silver coin.

"Silver coin, ya say? Alright. Ya gol-dang bulldog. Gemme time to put my boots on." The door opened and a double barreled shotgun came out followed by a skinny man with a hawk nose and bloodshot eyes, wearing long johns, black rubber boots, and a ratty tattered reddish brown cloak that flapped in the south breeze. There was a sour odor that nearly swamped Gabe's senses when the lanky ferryman stepped out with the shotgun.

"I've bout had it with not being able to get a decent night's sleep round here. I told ya to come back at daybreak, but naw, ya got silver coin, ya say. Well, let's see it, says I." He raised the shotgun and tried to prod Gabe in the chest with it, but Gabe turned sideways quickly and dodged the tip as he pressed forward in a hurry.

Josh cringed on his saddle when he saw that, for he knew what would come next, and unhooked the loops on his pistols. Gabe's reaction was instantaneous, and threw a shock of panic into the ferryman, who had not expected such a rapid move from a thick gray-bearded man. It was as fluid a knife move as Josh could imagine, and he was amazed at the old blacksmith. The moonlight had flashed off the long blade of Gabe's big knife as it quickly slid from its scabbard to the man's throat as McBride stepped in past the shotgun. With one powerful jerk of his blacksmith's arm he had wrenched the shotgun from the weaker man's grip while the blade lightly pressed against his throat below the chin, pinching the bobbing Adam's apple.

"Whoa! Whoa! Don't cut me! Mercy!" said old Char in a trembling tone. He wriggled like a trapped animal to try to escape the blacksmith's vice-like grasp.

"And why shouldn't I? Poked a shotgun at me! Now you gonna try ta weasel on me?"

"Hold on now, hold on, no need ta get riled and go ta slicing with an Arkansas toothpick. I'll take yal across, long as ya got the silver coins. Folks come roust me with paper silver certificates and want a ferry ride every night. Don't go to cutting on me; there's one ferry and I got the padlock key hid. You stick me and you wander the riverbank in flood tide, trampling serpents and looking for a crossing that ain't there. So jus' simmer down."

"Take us across, now. And it ain't no Arkansas toothpick."

"Wal Bowie knife or whatever, doan be astickin' me..."

"Ain't now Bowie knife. Now come on!"

"Alright, I'll take ya now, but like I said, if-fen you's smart you'd wait til daylight ta cross over into no man's land, after them boys get the river sticks drove in by the landing, on account a tha high water, ya see. The ferry gets all twisted by the current and hung up in them branches at the high water landings. 'Sides, I need a helper to pull on both lines with tha river on a rise like it's been."

"Mister Char, I'm 'bout half wore out from a long ride, and ain't got much patience left. You got one chance to avoid feeling how sharp this blade is, so get with it. We're crossing right now. I can pull the damned line." Gabe stepped back, sheathed his big knife, and leveled the oily shotgun at the man.

"Aww, hold your horses, mister. I'ma coming. Don't go having another conniption. That thar gun ain't got no shells anyway. On account a hits a ten gauge and the shells is kinda rare and I ain't got round to loading any lately, on account of powder is scarce and…"

"I reckon you'll feel it if I hit you over the head with it," replied Gabe.

The wiry old ferryman put a slouch hat on his head. "No need for that, I's just a little jumpy after drinking rum all night waiting for paying customers. Nuthin' but bummers, bad eggs, deadbeats wanting credit, and chickenshit balderdash all day. And then that cheap rot-gut green cane rum after some more salt horse meat. Dang. War is hell on business and my stomach too. My haid's bout ta split open. Ah, lemme take a hair o tha dog." He grabbed up a jug and took a long snort, the spillage running down his wiry arm. Finally lowering the jug and drawing a deep breath, he offered it to Gabe, who shook his head no.

"Suit herself, but don't begrudge a man his drink, huh? Been a hell of a day. All we had thru here is graybacks, thick as lice they are, deserters with no silver, nothing but worthless script. Beat up, half dead, starving, broke, gimped up deserters straggling back from that lil ole war they thought was gonna be a big party. Everybody that gets the news knows the war's lost. Lee's been on the short end of the stick since he lost Jackson. Yep. Nothing but deserters and parolees. Stone cold broke motherfu…"

"Alright then, I got the drift. Like I said, we got silver. We pay our way. So get moving." They began to amble towards the landing.

"Wal, alright then. Yassah! Got a bigwig with silver, ah have now. Yassahree. Man's got to cross the Sabine heading for Texas right now. Got two mules fully loaded by somebody knows how to pack mules, and two muscled-up little stallion horses. Going ta Texas, ya say? Passin by? Well dang my hide, lookee here now, there's a whole bunch of ya. Two horses, two mules, one man and one darkie. Double fare bonus in silver coin, that's what ya said, right? Oughta be more, on account of it's dark and all, and the river on tha rise, and cottonmouths."

"Don't waste your breath and our time. Let's go."

"Wal, lemme get my pulling' gloves on."

"Right now."

"Alright, I got 'em," said Char as he stomped down to the ferry in his boots and long-johns, with the ratty brown coat flapping in the breeze and trailing a sour stench. He kept flapping his mouth too, talking to nobody in particular in the dark.

"Gol-dang, they inaugurate that damned red bone gorilla one day, so I get just a lil drunk on that green sugarcane rum, and the next thang ah know some bullhead's jerking me out o bed to ferry cross in tha dark, after ah been celebrating and passed out. Can't wait til morning like anybody else. Shore in a hurry ta get ta Texas, huh? Got somebody hot on yore tails, do ya, causing ya to absquatulate in a rush?"

"Shut up and get going fore I let the air out of ya with my pig sticker," said Gabe.

"Alright, alright," said the ferryman. Then he peered squint-eyed at the fire and yelled in his scratchy voice. "Hey, come on, a few of yal come with me to help pull rope, I'm bout give out at the start."

"Aw naw, not now, we on company Q," came a voice from the fireside circle.

"Yeah, we don't go on shift til morning, too many cottonmouths. I done got struck at twice today."

"Come on, gol dang it, fore this bullhead sticks me with his blade. Yal want pay, yal get up and pull rope."

While a few of the fireside loungers started getting up and inching towards the ferry in unsteady gaits, the scrawny old ferryman went to a tree on the bank and fetched the key to the padlock from a hole in it, then unlocked the chain as Gabe gathered the mules with his dun stallion. Old Char's rum-addled buddies staggered over to the ferry and cautiously walked aboard, holding on to the ropes for balance. Then they just squatted on the wet logs with their jug, showing no inclination to do anything other than wait while Char untied the lines. A sour rank smell fouled the breeze down the river.

The log and plank ferry was tied up against a bunch of sticks and branches that had been pounded into the bank like fence-posts for a landing. The dark rush of the high water had it straining against the improvised dock. Many of the sticks had sharpened ends, as if they had been purloined from the abandoned abbatis. The riders approached with caution in the misty gloom, each with a wary nervous feeling. The horses and mules were still skittish, ears pricked and moving in all directions, nostrils swelling with the unpleasant smells.

The two big ropes across the river looked like half rotten old logging lines, several inches thick, and they were fastened to tall oaks on the higher bank, and swooped across the river in a low arch that dipped into the current in the middle. One of them went through a set of steel loops on each side of the ferry, which sat crooked with its nose up in the mud of the bank, jammed against a bunch of sticks pounded into the shoreline. The big logs upon which the plank deck was placed were waterlogged and riding low in the funky smelling water. A couple of pale-bellied snakes with big knotted heads hung dead from a fence railing, along with huge catfish heads and an alligator jawbone with lines of sharp teeth.

Josh had remained mounted and silent the whole time, and was first to move along, to dismount and lead his horse and mule onto the rickety ferry. Using oats in his hand, Josh led the other stock onto the creaky ferry, trying to ease their nervousness. He always exerted a calming control over the livestock with the use of his hands, body position, and voice.

The weight of the loaded horses and mules set the ferry down lower in the water, and it was all the skinny ferryman could do to get everything ready, in his rum-addled state. They had to push off with poles as the rear stuck in the dense black mud. He paused to catch his breath when he had all the lines done, scanning his clients with narrowed slits for eyes. His helpers slipped around and got in the way, eliciting a stream of cussing from old Char. Then he started studying the stock as Josh secured them on the deck by tying slipknots of their reins to the railing.

"Them's sho some mighty fine horses and mules yal got, now. Ain't seen many good mounts round here lately, 'cept under soldiers. Mules either. That is some powerful looking jack. Good looking jenny too, with packs done up right. Whar yal say you're from?"

"We didn't. And keep back from them mules, they bite."

"Ye didn't did ya? Sorta on French leave, ah reckon? Wal, don't matter much ta me, long as ya ain't moderators."

"Wal, we ain't that, we got business in Texas, just passing thru here. But if I was staying I'd pull these gol-dang sharpened sticks up around here, whole place looks like a booby-trap."

"Aww, that's the leavings of them soldier boys, and ya might never tell when some're comin' back, so we jus leave their stuff alone, 'cept to borry a few sticks when ah need em, like when the river rises and washes things out, and some danged ole bear wants ta cross in tha dark."

"Yeah, wal, it don't make for a pleasant atmosphere, sorta gives a hostile feelin'."

"Just sticks, is all. River sticks, poles the soldier boys left. All kinds of driftwood comes down here. We use 'em up when we need 'em, for pilings and corrals and such. I use 'em fer firewood too."

"Well, goldang, ya oughta have more respect for the livestock than leave them piercing points for 'em to get wounded and fester on. Come on now, let's get this barge moving. You can have yore river, sticks, and ferry job too, just get us across and out o' here." They started a slow pulling on the lines and the ferry sank deeper as it left the shore. It was hard to get the waterlogged mass moving against the strong current.

"Your darkie got a mean look, doan talk much, huh?"

"Nope. Only when I want him to."

"Is he red bone or Cherokee mix?, or just plain darkie?"

"I reckon he's a Seminole tracker, my guess," said the other guy, who was up pulling on the line behind Char.

"Ain't my business what blood he is, long as he does his job, which is tracking and killing. Like yore job is moving this ferry, right now. So pull harder."

"Wal, don't pitch another conniption, hoss, here we go, hang on, she may proceed ta driftin' and pitchin' when we get out in tha real current. That's how cum I gots ta have you and yore darkie on the other line a hauling even with me to keep her headed straight...can't hardly see my sticks over there, some of em's under water or gone, ah reckon, and ah don't know how hard we gotta pull, with this load on, them mules loaded heavy and all, may need yore man to do some real hard pulling too, 'cordin ta how strong that current's gotten to in the interval...now ya watch out for water moccasins, had a man get bit last week,...oh yeah, nearly forgot."

The ferryman grabbed a hollowed-out cow horn hanging by a leather sling and blew a faltering bleat from it, started coughing, spit, then blew it again. Then he slung it over his shoulder and began slowly hauling on the thick rope by leaning his wiry body weight against it, nudging the ferry forward into the murky water with the help of his pals and Gabe. Everyone pitched in and leaned on the ropes to haul it over.

Out in the current the tall lanky ferryman began to let up on his tugging and slow the raft, so Gabe began to pull harder on the thick knotted old logging rope, and with his immense arm strength they moved steadily to the darkened shore of no man's land. Josh helped heave with the crew on the other side as they moved out into the current. With Gabe's powerful arms pulling and his lungs starting to pant, the ferryman began to talk as he sidled close to where Gabe had set the shotgun down, drooling brown juice from the plug in his lip.

"Yore darkie got a peculiar sharp look about him, and he's a-usin' it on me mighty freely when he gives me a sideways glance now and again, ah reckon." He spit a stream of brown juice into the dark water, and slowly wiped his chin of the spittle while Gabe hauled on the thick wet rope.

"You keep him pulled up short, heah now? I don't want him near me, thankee, while I'm tugging on this line here. Makes me nervous, looking at me like a damned panther at a rabbit, by gawd. Hellfire it's slippery, ain't it, and I'm still too drunk to be adoin' this...Curly, pull like you mean it back there..." he said as the livestock shifted for better footing with the current tugging on the raft, causing the whole affair to tilt and pitch.

"So what's the latest news with the war?" asked Gabe as he hauled harder on the thick rope, "Lee win any battles?"

Old Char took the question as a chance to lay off even pretending to pull on the line, spit another brown stream of tobacco, then begin a discourse in his drunken drawl. "The Galveston newspaper said that the Confederate congress finally approved the official design for the flag. Mighty nice of them to do that, now that the war is 'bout lost. Least wise, it gave me sumthin' else to raise tha jug to."

"How old was this newspaper?"

"Why it was fresh off tha boat. March 10, it was."

"March 10, ya don't say. What is today's date, do ya know?"

"Why hell yes, I got record books to keep. I ain't ignorant of lettering and figuring. It's March 13, an unlucky day for some, maybe so."

"What else the newspaper say?" asked Gabe as he hauled on the rope."

"I tole ya, Lincoln was inaugurated for the second time, as if onct wasn't bad enough. I figured onct them bankers got their railroad bill through congress without the Southern senators blocking it, they'd have got rid of ole crazy Abe. They'll get rid of him soon, done wore him out. One look at his picture in the paper and you know he's gone crazy as Sherman."

"Aw go on now," said his buddy. "He's always been one of them Henry Clay inner circle types, and a railroad lawyer. They ain't gonna push him out. He'd jail anyone who tried. They'll come by in the night."

"Sho fine lookin' hosses and saddles," said another, "mules too."

"Mules too. Got some long rifles on 'em."

"Lincoln brought this war on, ya axe me. We always had tha right ta secession."

That gave Char his opening, and he took it. "That's right. This whole mess wouldn't started if the railroads had not pushed them radical republicans in there with that railroad lawyer running the show. Used our own money from the tariff again us for years, sucking us dry, and then passed the Morrill tariff, worst of all. The railroads and bankers bought the danged election, used the newspapers and them German revolutionaries ta do it, don't ya know?'

"Aww, I know all that, but let's get this ferry movin' ta Texas."

"Then they done thrown up an even bigger tariff on everything we buy while they pass a bill for transcontinental railroads that bypasses the South and gives away the country to tha railroads. Next they'll be packing that place with immigrants fresh off the boat in New York City, so them railroads can have somebody ta overcharge til they bankrupt, then buy up all the land for big plantations and ranches."

"We shouldn't a got him started," said one of old Char's buddies.

"Yep, ole Char on a bender or on a tear, ah know that's right."

"Let's everybody pull the danged rope now, instead of stoppin' ta talk," said Gabe.

"Them mules is sho packed good, mighty stout too," said

another rope puller, panting, as the others muttered back.

"Good packer, tracker too. I think that's a Seminole tracker, from the eye on him."

"Got mighty big saddle horns, could be vaquero."

"Never seen a black vaquero, Quint."

"Could be darkie-mex breed."

"Somebody done whacked him in de eye, says me."

"You fellas could pull harder if ya quit jawin' 'bout my tracker," said Gabe as he tugged on the line.

"Seminole. Ain't friendly neither. Sorta piercing gaze. Well, let's heave, boys, sooner we get done, it's back ta tha fire."

"Come on boys, pull the danged thang," said Gabe, panting.

The ferryman went on with his mumbling Lincoln rant while everyone else started pulling harder to move the heavy log ferry across. A pungent breeze floated down the center of the river, smelling like a flood that had scoured the land and sent manure down the creeks. Progress was slow against a stiff current.

The sound of frogs singing was layered over with the drone of the ferryman Char on his log stump. "Yep, inauguration ball they calls it. Hits plumb crazy what they're doing,...everybody knows that them Lincolns are crazy, him and his wife both. She's just looking for a railroad mansion and so is he, with a spare bedroom for his secretary. They done riled up all them crazy churchwomen abolitionists over that lying book, *Uncle Tom's Cabin*, got 'em screaming 'bout taking our slaves away, our property. I spent my hard earned money on two slaves to pull on these damned ropes, help me build up my place an all, and they done up and run off when Lincoln told em they was free. Is that any way to treat a man's property rights? They up and run off on account ah his danged emasculation proclamation. Where's mah compensation?"

Another voice in the dark took over as old Char took a dip of snuff. "Hell, Lincoln only freed the ones in the South on account of he was losing the war and wanted to start a slave revolt down here. And now the war's being won by ole drunken butcher Grant and his railroad buddies. And Sherman done burnt Charleston down to ashes, and 'bout got Fayettville surrounded and stove in. He's burning a scar right through the South, total war on his own countrymen."

The next shabby lounger spoke up from his wet perch as he pretended to tug on the line. "Ah yeah, hits total war now, pillage and burn, ole Attila ain't got nothin' on Sherman and his bummers. Hit's a losing fight, I tell ya boys. They's pouring starving Irishmen off the boats of New York into the federal army and using 'em like cannon fodder. Ole Grant doan care how many bodies he stacks up long as he prevails and gets enough liquor and ceegars."

The other fella added his two cents worth. "They're piling the carcasses like so many rotten Irish potatoes, or sawing their legs off and setting off down here ta try to beg free ferry rides. Why, after the siege of Vicksburg we had nothin' but walking corpses come thru for days."

"Don't ah know it," said the other guy. "We gonna be the first part of their empire. They'll get rid of ole crazy Abe and make Grant king, then keep him drunk all the time while they rob the place blind. He can sic Sherman on anyone who resists. Gov'ment by consent done been replaced with rule by bayonet."

Old Char took another long brown spit and wiped his chin. "I tell ya, I ain't no Bible thumper like some round here, but that Sherman's a beast from hell, just plumb insane."

"Wal I am a Bible thumper, by God," said another, "and I tell ya Lincoln, Sheridan, Grant, and Sherman are the four horsemen on the apocalypse, that's for certain. If he comes down here I'm jumping a boat for Mexico."

"Why hell, they threw Sherman out of tha army for being crazy, then Grant snatched him up and sent him ta killing everybody. I think he got the syphilis up thar at them West Point taverns and it's rotted his brain. Lots of those soldier boys catch it up at Bennie's Tavern, that's why we got these crazy generals piling up bodies."

"Me too," added the other. "I may go anyway. How we gonna live with a forty-nine percent tariff on everything we buy? Why hell, it's ole Henry Clay speaking through that lying lawyer, Lincoln. Railroads, national bank, and high tariff, that's what it's all about. Bleed the south ta death with taxes to siphon off in corruption. Ta hell with state's rights and consent of the governed, it's rule by the gun now, boys. Lincoln's the new Caesar, and his legions are on their way."

"That's danged right," replied Char, warming to the rant. "We's part of the Republican Caesar's empire now, and they're just getting started. Gonna take Mexico next, if Grant gets his way, take over from the Frenchies...won't be no place ta run then, them Carlota colonies for Confederates will be overrun and massacred, so's he can wipe out the last resistance..."

"Lincoln's a ceegar?" asked the drunkest man squatting alongside the rope. "I thought you said he's a railroaded lawyer and drove his wife crazy."

"Lincoln's plumb shore Melungeon, I reckon, and yonder fella is a Seminole lookin' fer prey. Dark skin, high nose, light eyes, hunter look." replied his pal.

"He'd better pray, where he's going."

"Lincoln ain't no ceegar, Grant likes tha ceegars, with his whiskey."

"Caesar, ya dang fool. He's a Caesar for the railroads and national bank. Like that thar ole time Roman, caused a civil war ta take over the government, 'till they assassinated him. Stuck him with knives on the senate floor, I heerd."

"It warn't no civil war, we didn't try to take over them! They done come and made war on us. All we wanted was to govern ourselves!"

"Did yal leave yer units?" asked the most sober helper. "Lots o boys is goin' on home, or down ta Mexico, Carlota colonies for secessionists.   I'd throw in with ya if yal was heading down thar."

"Oh yeah, be fine til Grant invades down thar," offered another voice in the dark.

"Oh yeah, he'll kill all the secessionists and deserters first, then the French, take over the whole damn place like they took over Texas and the Spanish west."

"Who is that Seminole scout after, anyhow?"

"Lincoln is a railroad lawyer ? Is that why we never heerd of him till that election that drove everything apart in '60?"

"Shuudup with that, Quint. Can't hear the stranger."

"Naw, we ain't deserters. We're bounty hunters, serving warrants, catching escaped thieving slaves. I'm too old to be marching around in no fool war over darkies I never owned, and he's ...well, lets just not talk bout him...don't want to get him riled. I use him for tracking and catchin'. He memorizes the warrants for me and looks folks over to see if they match the pictures."

"He's part Cherokee, and part Seminole, ain't he? I can

tell. He's got that look of a hunter after something, or somebody....his eyes."

With constant tugging on the ropes, the ferry made slow progress against the midstream current. It seemed suspended in the dark flow of the fetid night, with the gurgling sounds of the small eddies behind it, the song of frogs and crickets in the velvet black shoreline. The more Gabe and Josh pulled, the more the others let off and pretended to pull, letting the current bog their progress in the dark.

"That scout looking fellow is a darkie with a big knife and pistol, and a mighty fine stallion."

"Seminole. Got a sharps fifty on the mule, I wager."

"Seminole can be mighty black if they double dipped."

"Naw, that tracker be sorta green eyed. Too dark for Melungeon, ah say," drawled another drunken voice. "He ain't got a wide nose, but he sho is dark. Dark as lampblack."

"Any fool can tell he's a Seminole, one them scouts the federals use. Got that hunter look in his eyes."

"Looks like tha angel of death, you ax me."

"Lincoln look like tha angel o death, ya ax me."

"Seminole, I tell ya."

"Wal," muttered the man with a low tone, "Ah prophesy that they ain't gonna live long onct they cross the river. They be goin ta death's country, if Char wakes dem toll-road boys up."

"Looks to me like Char on the prowl, too."

"So's that Seminole. He ain't gonna be easy ta tangle with."

"Wal, don't sic 'im on me, huh? Dey say dem slave-catcher darkies is de meanest of all. There's plenty o free colored round here, ya know, place was settled early by Red bones and free colored, even before tha Austin bunch. Some of em got rich here too. But not fer too long. You still gonna pay in silver, ain't ya?"

"Like I said." With a final heave Gabe pulled the ferry into shore while the hung-over ferryman again pretended to pull on the greasy rope. Then he staggered over and tied the lines to sticks pounded into the dirt, with a lead line to a big oak tree on the shore. After unloading they paid the ferryman in silver coin with a bonus, just as they said they would, then Gabe handed the shifty-eyed Char a few more coin for the shotgun and the cow horn.

"I'll be takin' these off yore hands too."

"Buying my shotgun and horn, are ya?" said the ferryman as he bit on the coin, then spit another reeking stream of brown juice. "You'll play hell finding shells for a ten gauge, jus' like me, mister. But go on ahead, I'll use the coin to get something I can make more use of. I jus' ain't got the eyesight to load shells properly anymore, ta tell that truth."

"In an earlier day I'd bent both barrels over your head when you pulled it on me. As is, just consider yourself lucky to be still sucking up all that air. And I expect to see some varmints up the trail that you signaled with yore horn."

Gabe and Josh saw their suspicions were right from the look on the ferryman's face as he handed the cow-horn over.

"Why, the hell you say, this here's just for folks ta signal me from either side to come get em, is all. They musta slept through it, or left off, being the river's high and all. They stay in that shed yonder."

"So you blow it in the dead of night with high water when you figure they ain't thar?"

"Why no, not-at-all, jus' a creature of habit, ah guess....ya done rousted me out o bed and all, not myself rightly when ah's half asleep and half drunk...ain't that right, boys?"

"Sure Charcoal," replied the taller of the two buddies who had accompanied Char to help pull it back. "Creature o habit, we is."

"Well, ah got some habits myself. Like coming back ta kill those that tried ta have me killed. Best thing for you to do is forget ya ever seen us, and be thankful ya lived through it. Maybe I'll see ya later, Char. Don't forget we paid in silver for the crossing."

"Yassir, Ah am, ah do, ah will fo sho, and good night to ya. Yal be careful now, ya heah. You in no man's land now, yal betta clear out the river bottom a few miles so as to avoid any more rise in de river ..." With a wicked little broken-toothed smirk, old Char turned away and mumbled as he began to untie the lines.

While the travelers walked their mounts and mules away, the ferryman muttered to his pals, "Course, lotsa good an empty shotgun do 'em when Simon and the boys swoop down with hot lead. Then we'll see who's top dog with a knife to tha throat. I'll own that knife after the dealings done, ya old snapping turtle sonofabitch. I'll be listening for the shots that kill that old bulldog."

After walking their stock a ways, Josh motioned to Gabe and they got together for a talk as the ferryman muttered to himself and the ferry thumped against a makeshift dock. Gabe found the ten gauge shells from the packs and then checked and loaded both shotguns. As they stood to confer beside one of the branches driven like fence-posts into the shore, a cotton-mouth viper which had wrapped around it, lifted his head and opened his mouth wide, the big fangs and white mouth shining in the moonlight.

In a move swifter than thought, Josh reached out and grabbed Gabe's left shoulder and pulled him back from the rearing snake head. At the same time Gabe's good right hand was pulling his big knife, and with a roundhouse whack he chopped the snake's head off.

"Damn, old fella...pretty swift move..."

"What'd ya yank me fer, nearly messed up my aim?" said Gabe.

"I didn't know if you saw it. It was fixing to strike."

"I saw the sum bitch soon as he moved his head. Thought it was part of that branch til then."

"Well, nice swing with that blade. Remind me not to wake you up too soon when you're carrying it."

"Cypress Sally warned us, pointed sticks, danger."

"Let's seek higher ground."

"Well alright then, this place makes me jumpy. And my neck hairs is bristling. I think we're nearly in a real scrape."

They both mounted, leery of more snakes in the dark. "Why'd he blow that horn, I wonder?" said Josh in a low voice, leaning towards Gabe from the saddle.

"Ah's pondering on tha same thing, I reckon he gives a signal to some scoundrels over there for ta waylay us in tha dark. Is that what yer thinking?"

"Yes. To wake them up and get them ready to jump us, like they did that other fella."

Walking the stock a ways while the ferryman mumbled and fumbled with his lines, Gabe and Josh then stopped and made ready for battle, tightening girths, pulling out pistols, making ready more shotgun shells.

"I feel a scrape coming," said Josh, placing bullets in the

one empty chamber in both of his pistols. "I've been feeling it since the landing, Suzette too. We should have grabbed that horn before he used it, but I was tugging like hell to get us across against that current."

"I got it in my saddlebags now."

"Well great, but the mule's out of the barn now."

"Waugh. Good horn though. Like the one I used in my ranger days."

After checking the packs and feeding the mules some handfuls of oats, Gabe handed Josh the other ten gauge shotgun and a small bag of shells. "It's loaded. Now we'll see what that red bone buzzard was blowing that horn about, I reckon. I think I'll blare it at these varmints right before we jump 'em, put the confusion inta' 'em. Don't let it scare ya none."

"Well, I'm used to some mighty fine horn playing down in the French Quarter, you know."

"You was."

"Yeah." Josh was tightening his girth strap and strapping down the tops of his saddlebags. The horses were nickering and signaling with their ears like they heard something up ahead in the dark, as were the mules. Suzette was rolling a small snarl from deep in her throat, her nose sticking out from the saddlebag flap.

"Alright," said Josh LaPoint. "When we get a bead on them, I'll go for the left, you go for the right, then both move our fire towards the middle…we'll give them four barrels then switch to pistols if we need to. Stay close, huh?"

"Alright, lead on with those keen eyes o yorn, I'll take both mules, then leave 'em on the trail when we need to…."

Slowly they proceeded, scanning likely spots for ambush, their ears all tuned to danger sounds. They had traversed the darkened road about a mile when Josh saw movement in the shadow of a thick clump of pine trees. He clicked a danger signal to Gabe, and hissed low like a cat.

While the bushwhackers waited around in the dark for everyone to get ready at their ambush spot, LaPoint and McBride, their horses pacing at a steady controlled walk, quietly approached until they could hear the robbers' voices and see more movement in the shadows. They had both taken big nips of Cypress Sally's night aid potions, and were alert with keen hearing and eyesight in the dark. Eventually Josh spotted a group of riders in the trees, and Suzette heard the horses and went to steady snarling.

"I see them, to the right there, in that dip," said Josh as he reined to a stop. Gabe spoke to Josh in a low whisper. "Alright, I hear 'em getting ready to jump us, and I kin barely see 'em. Let's go straight at 'em on the fly and unload these heavy barreled things on 'em before they got time to think, then go to pistols."

"Alright then. Stay close so we don't get separated in the dark, I'm shooting everything that moves. Ready?"

Gabe swung the cow horn around on it's leather thong and held it to his lips with one hand, the shotgun in the other, the reins looped on his saddle horn.

"Let fly," said Gabe as he released the rope holding the trailing pack mules and took off through the tall pine trees on his line-back dun stallion. He gave a long wailing blast on the cow horn then let it slide back on it's thong while raising the shotgun.

Not to be outrun by his competitor Buck, LaPoint's stallion Scorpio bolted forward and accelerated past the dun as both men readied their shotguns and headed for the cluster of ambushers beside the road ahead. Rapid and scattered movements ahead indicated they had the element of surprise and the advantage. Both stallions began to change leads with a random pattern, dodging and skipping under the shadows of the tall trees, making their direction unpredictable.

Flashes of fire erupted from the darkened shapes of the bushwhackers, and bullets were whizzing by as they dodged branches and rode right at their targets, with Gabe now blowing the horn in stuttering blasts. The stallions accelerated in curving arcs towards the bushwhackers. At thirty feet distance from the dark shadows belching fire, the shotguns began to roar in a methodical rhythm as all four barrels sent tongues of flame and lead shot towards the clumps of panicked ambushers, knocking them to the ground. Smoke belched out of the barrels and obscured vision even further as it lingered in the trees. Shouts of pain and alarm erupted as Josh and Gabe made an abrupt turn and went behind thick timber to reload, then came bursting out again into the panicked robbers, picking them off one by one with reverberating shotgun blasts.

The bushwhackers who could still move took off in different directions, many wounded and carrying pellets of hot lead, while three of them lay on the ground full of big holes, running dark blood, and not moving much. Another wounded bushwhacker fell from his bolting horse directly into a pine tree trunk and died on the spot. The acrid smoke from the shotgun blasts was hanging heavy in the air under the spreading branches of the thick woods. The only sound was of horses fleeing in the dark and the mules were braying like lost sheep back where they had been left on the road. Gabe went back for them while Josh reloaded both shotguns and checked the bodies laying on the ground. One was dead still, one was writhing while he bled out. They had both taken blasts in the body, and were both finished, pouring blood that looked like black ink in the moonlight. The third man was motionless at the base of the tree he had crashed into headfirst.

Josh dismounted and stood over the still one in the moonlight. Suzette, who had burrowed deep into the saddlebags in terror at the shooting, stuck her nose out of the flap and began to growl again, then whimper as she felt Josh dismount.

It was the first time Josh LaPoint stood over a man he had killed. There was another dead body in the shadows beside the first. LaPoint felt no regret at this killing, no sinking in the pit of his stomach, only exultation at his own survival, and a readiness to fight again if need be. He peered around the dark woods looking for more attackers as he pushed Suzette back down into the saddlebag and fastened the flap.

One of the dead men still clutched a New Model Army Remington metallic cartridge .44 cal. revolver in his hand, and LaPoint wrenched it free and stuck it into his belt. He rode back to the bushwhacker's camp and saw piles of loot they had accumulated. He left the dying bushwhackers to bleed out, their dark blood seeping into the ground in the moonlight as one of them called for his mama, and rode back to where Gabe had gathered the mules and was calming them. There they sat mounted side by side, in the shadows reloading their weapons.

"So what's the toll on highwaymen, did we get many?" asked Gabe.

"There's three dead or dying, and the rest scattered, for now. Let's go now before they regroup. Quite an action, with these shotguns, huh?"

"They work pretty damn good in the dark, don't they?"

said Gabe. "I know I got at least two."

"Yeah, they do. Never really appreciated a shotgun until now. Don't have to aim much. Well, let's go. Give me the lead line for Leon, we'll make better time if we both have a mule. Ready?"

"Lead on, LaPoint."

They went at a fast walk and cleared the area without further incident. Even the mules were anxious enough to leave that they had slack in their lead lines. The smell of blood and gunpowder had the stock spooked, and the river crossing into Texas was left behind as they hustled up the rise out of the river valley onto the prairies. Within a hour they were out of the strip called no man's land, the disputed territory.

So they traveled on through densely forested East Texas, taking back-roads and side-trails, camping in thickets, still fearful of patrols and bushwhackers, with guns ready at all times. They kept moving at a steady pacing gait, traveling mostly at night and hiding out during the day for rest and grazing. Supplies were hard to replenish, but the silver coin they carried spoke volumes when it came to store keeps with too many folks on credit, and they managed to keep eating and keep moving. The countryside changed from the tall and thick pine forests to more open country with clustered post oak mixing in with the pine and the cypress in the river bottoms.

Avoiding the sounds of groups of riders, hiding when they could, making steady time, they aimed towards traversing the nearly three hundred miles to the small ranch in Texas, at the crossing of the San Antonio river on the Indianola road, purchased decades before by Mister Alex. It was from this ranch that the several cattle drives to New Orleans had taken place years before, with Gabe riding scout and Josh tending the remuda. It was there they hoped to start over.

The weather stayed wet and cold, especially on the moon-lit nights when they traveled the darkened trails in the gloomy pine woods, their dark silhouettes marking the ground below with strange shadows. They wore coats of sheepskin turned wool-side in that had come down from the Taos trading outpost in the early days, covered with oilcloth rain slickers. When the rain wasn't too thick, Suzette rode up on Josh's lap, but she slipped back into the saddlebags when the drops got larger. In this way they steadily slipped through the dark miles in the cold March weather, fording high streams when they could, riding ferries otherwise.

At dawn they would find a hiding place in some draw or creek-bed or thicket festooned with draperies of Spanish moss where they could hide four big animals and take turns resting. The little dog was superb at listening and helped whoever stayed awake with her alertness and the direction of her pointed ears. The scattered forest cover provided hiding places when they needed them.

With Gabe's consummate woodsman's skill and LaPoint's keen hearing, eyesight, intuition, and cunning they were able to slip by mainly undetected, often swimming their mounts and mules to avoid bridges and ferries where groups of horsemen checked the traffic. They crossed the Trinity River above Houston at a ford they discovered, after deciding to avoid the town. The horses and mules had some difficulty with the strong current, and drifted downstream a ways while the riders swam alongside, hanging on to a short line on the saddle horn. The riders grew chilled after the soaking on a cool windy day, and were hoping for river ferries on the next crossings. About a day later they crossed the Brazos at Mosley's ferry, with no problems and warmer weather.

Josh was grimly silent most of the time, only speaking when necessary, remaining hyper-vigilant. Gabe realized that he was grieving over his mother and the lost horse farm, as he had greived for his lost woman decades earlier. The thought of killing that captain who led the marauders flashed through his mind, but he remained silent. The older man had spent much of his early scouting years on long rides alone, so he dropped into his stoic plodding mode. His mind ranged over the years he had spent in the west as his stallion walked at an easy pace.

The countryside became drier as they moved into stretches of rolling prairie and mixed forests. Then they entered forests of very tall pine again, with refreshing scents on the night breezes. With less marauding patrols they made better distances in each stretch of travel, spending less time hiding out in thickets, deep woods, and swamps. LaPoint began to enjoy the countryside of Texas from atop his spirited mount, and was relieved to leave the wet dripping past behind, hoping for a fresh start where he could make his own life.

Chapter Five: "Tickanwa-tic"

After several days riding through scattered clouds and sunshine, they began to travel in the early morning and at twilight again, enjoying the views of tall dry waving grasses mixed with good timber in along the creeks and scattered across the range. Increasing the pace of their riding, they both were uplifted in spirits by the new land, with its grassy prairies mixed with wonderful groups of trees, elm, cedar elm, blackjack oak, post oak, live oak, Mexican plum, Chickasaw plum, green ash, and hack-berries, many covered with mustang grape vines. Gabe knew them all by the bare shapes and bark, even as some just began budding for the new spring, and pointed each out to Josh as they rode through meadows of dry grasses, the little blue stem, wild rye, and inland sea oats. The horses and mules stayed well fed on the wild grasses, for the riders often stopped to rest and scan the countryside with field glasses. The feeling of close pursuit was not as intense with them, but they were still wary. The swelling around Joshua's eye was going down, leaving several shades of purple and yellow.

When they finally approached the Colorado river in central Texas, from a small rise above the valley they could see it was swollen and swirling sandy brown from recent rains in the west, and they were hesitant to try and swim it with all the sand and current, as well as the occasional snake washing down. They began to deliberate what to do as they slowly moved down the hill towards the river valley, their stock as tired as they were.

Riding down the small hill to the river, Gabe talked of a river ferry near La Grange, a few miles to the south, but was wary of a direct approach to it with their full party. They rode to the river to check it out and to use the timber alongside to hide in. The river flow was lapping the banks and rushing fast.

They hid the horses on the banks amidst oak, pecan, small leaf cottonwood, and hickory trees, while Josh climbed some pecan trees high enough to shake loose lots of nuts, which they ate with bread and cheese and boudin, on the sandy bank of the Colorado as they watched the brown river roll by, carrying trees and branches and other flotsam, full of foam whirlpools and swirling leaves.

"Lucky you can climb like a cat, and the squirrels missed

some," said Gabe.

"Pecans are great if you can avoid that bitter part between, huh? Except they're just making me hungry, being as how we haven't eaten much for miles."

"Damn right. Kinda like life in general, avoid the bitter part. Don't know 'bout swimming this river, though, Josh. Here, have some more bread, might as well finish it off 'fore it gets any greener. I cut the mold off. "

"Yeah, thanks, from above you can see how much junk is in that dirty water, branches and whole trees coming down, plus some snakes."

"Don't I know....I got a bad feeling bout trying to swim this one, Josh," said Gabe as he spit out some of the bitter inner liner of the pecan. "It's a mite different that swimming a sluggish bayou, or that fording of the Trinity. Like you say, it's full of stuff. It ain't as red as them last two rivers, but it'll do."

"Looks pretty thick."

"To do a crossing right we'd need to take off our clothes and boots so they don't fill with sand, and it's a mite cool for that. And my neck hairs are bristling like thar's Comanches around, or somebody chasing us. How's about I go down to that blockhouse by the crossing at La Grange and sniff around, see if there's Federals around, see if we can use that crossing, if the ferry is running?"

"Good idea, I guess. This water ain't too cool. I'm gonna wash this lampblack off me and Scorpio and shed these travel torn clothes."

"Sorta cool for that."

"I'll build a little fire of dry sticks in those trees to warm up. No smoke."

"Alright, then Joshua. Stay alert. Keep that dog on lookout."

"Don't call me by that name anymore, Gabe. Call me Jacques LaPoint."

"Alright then, Jack LaPoint it is. Be back in a while. I'll be glad to see that sweat streaked black mess gone off ya too. You weren't much of a convincing darkie anyway, with them blue-green eyes. You scared the heck out of that ferry crowd. You want me to bring you some rum if they got any? You feeling better now, huh? Up ta beaver yet? Ya ain't said ten words in the last day or so."

"So?"

"I'as figuring you's feeling bad about those ambushers killings back in the no man's land, the strip. Ain't no great loss to tha world, them goin' under, ya know."

"No, just seemed like a time for quiet. I guess the shock was how much it didn't bother me. Seems like it's kill or be killed now. I'm not aiming on killing anybody, but I'm not drawing back from necessary shooting either. And now I shoot for the heart, not like that duel."

"Duels of honor is finished with. That ferry crossing was set up to put us under and get our plunder."

"Well. Nothing but ashes behind us, and a new start in front, if we can make it. I got a new Remington revolver out of the scrape, and an extra cylinder full of slugs, which should come in handy if I can find more metallic cartridges latter on. So sure, Gabe, bring us back a toddy and we'll toast to a fresh start in Texas."

"That there sounds more like your old self, Joshua. And thirst, I got. "

"I'm not who I was. I've killed several men."

"Waugh....some days it's kill or go under, huh?...Killing those that need it ain't no problem ta fester over, especially when they'd aiming to do you in. But I remember how it gets to ya at first, turns ya inta something else, someone ya don't know."

"Yeah, you hit dead center there."

"Yep. Ya just larn ta let that bear out when needs arise. Like iffen we come across that captain again, provided ah don't get him first."

"Yeah, that I will. Seems like they left me no choice. And I'll kill that captain if I get the chance."

"Ya can't let it drop?"

"No. I can't. I'd kill him right now with this knife if I had the chance."

"Wal, so would I. I guess one of us will if we ever get the chance. Marauders like that invites killing, though, and somebody might beat us to it. Now I'm off ta see what I can rustle up."

An hour later Gabe returned, walking his dun stallion in his usual manner, slow and quiet under the huge live oak and pecan trees, and whistled to alert his young friend upstream. Josh had been busy washing himself and the horse, then changing clothes and eating some dried sausage. He stepped from behind Scorpio when Gabe rode under the spreading tree branches.

"Damn if ya don't look a site better, with the carbon black off, both of yal. Couldn't get used ta ya as a darkie. Scorpio neither. And danged if he don't look lighter than he was."

"Yeah, I thought so too. He's turning lighter now, going into dappled gray. Hopefully they'll be looking for a black guy with a black horse while we both turn into white Texians. What did you find out?"

"Wal, hits a long story, but anyways, we can't cross on the ferry, Federal patrol down thar right now, and they got a list of people to look for, so long yore name mightn't even be on it, Josh. But why take the chance, huh? If we don't cross at a ferry, there won't be no record of us progressing further west, if they are hot after you still. Right now I figure they're watching who crosses the ferry."

"Well, we'll have to find a better place to try and swim it."

"That's the way my stick floats too. Supposed to be a possible crossing upstream a bit, place called Woods prairie. Dang, you sure look better, think I'll wash up a bit, water looks sandy but it's better than nuthin'."

"Please do, I've been nervous your smell would give us away plenty of times."

"Damn, it's brown as adobe with all that silt and sand," said Gabe as he pulled off his shirt to prepare for washing.

"Oh, that sand was great for scouring off that black, and smell too. Uh. You're supposed to be calling me Jack, remember?"

"Aw hell, I ain't gonna be able to do that without slipping soon as I get a drink or two in me. How bout Josh, Josh LaPoint?"

"Josh LaPoint. Alright, good enough for now. New man, new horse, new name. Let's get across."

"Wait, I want to wash up a bit, and I got some rum." Gabe walked naked onto a gravel bar, sat in the rushing current, and scoured himself with a rag, then moved quickly out of the water and toweled off by the fire, the scars lining his belly and chest standing out from the cold.

"We'll drink a toast on the other side when we make a successful crossing. I've got sort of a bad feeling too, like hair on my neck sparking. Let's get it done, and tighten up the girth straps and be ready to run."

In a few moments Gabe had dressed and put the fire out. Then they loaded up and moved out of the shelter of the trees, walking the stock upstream. Wary of the federal patrol in La Grange, they followed the stream bed, checking for possible fords. The countryside was alive with birds and deer, with plenty of squirrels in the trees.

They held a northwesterly course a bit off the riverbed with its adjacent grassy prairies bordered by huge oak and pecan trees, spotted by the tall dark conical cedars. Soon they cut through a wide prairie to a spot below a sharp bend in the river where they saw a series of gravel bars and islands that made a ford possible, though some swimming would be necessary. They took their outer clothes off, as well as their boots. Gabe wrapped the greased parfleche bags carrying the ammo as tight as he could and placed them high on the pack mules.

"This is it. Woods prairie crossing. Gonna have a wet Whitworth and Sharps when we're done, repeaters too, have ta oil 'em right away. Pistols too, likely."

"Wish I had more metallic cartridges now," said Josh as he tied short lines to the backs of their saddles, for the riders to hang onto when the horses had to swim. Gabe remounted, and Josh quickly jumped on Scorpio, intending to go first.

"Okay, let's go," said Josh as he edged Scorpio to the stream.

"Not to get too pushy, but lemme go first. I done had lots more experience crossin' Texas rivers." Gabe pushed his golden dun colored horse in front of Scorpio and Josh.

"Alright," said Josh with a small smile. "Hope your old stick floats."

"Alright then, be sure to let off and let the horse swim until their feet touch again, then pull yourself back on the saddle," Gabe said as he spurred Buck into the murky current after sighting upstream for debris. Josephine followed tight behind, her lead line tied to Buck's saddle, braying as her big feet clopped into the water. Leon brayed back at her and Scorpio paced in place, ready to plunge, but Josh controlled him and waited to watch.

It was shallow and they made easy progress til one deep

spot between the opposing gravel bars, but they all swam it well, with Gabe hanging off the side of Buck and swimming along. They drifted perhaps ten yards downstream in their swim, but as soon as Buck made footing on the bar, Gabe slid back into the saddle, and emerged in good shape, the packs still secure on the trailing jenny.

Josh moved upstream a bit and then repeated Gabe's moves with Scorpio and Leon the big jack, and they all swam the deep portion well and emerged ready to run in the sun to warm up. Gabe had his buckskin shirt on by the time Josh dismounted and began to dress.

"Watch out, Gabe, the mules may try to roll in the sand with packs on."

"I got 'em. Here," said Gabe as he pitched another buckskin shirt from the greased parfleche to Josh. "My belly is too big for that one now, it's yorn. My Ute squaw made it for me, long time ago." He was putting on his pants and boots as he spoke. "Hold still, Leon," he said in his firmest voice, as he nearly tripped putting his clothes on.

The shirt was smooth and soft as butter. Josh put it on and laced the collar. "Muchas gracias, amigo. I'll treasure it. Ute squaw? Thought you said it was an Arapaho squaw. No fringes, huh?"

"Naw, they don't do worth a crap when they get wet. I had on buckskin pants crossing the Red River onct and they stretched ta nearly double their length 'fore I was done gettin out of the quicksand. Best thing is don't get 'em wet iffen ya can help it. We got good slickers now, when we need em."

"Well, that crossing wasn't so bad."

"Yeah, but I still got hairs pricklin' on my neck. I heard there whar Comanches around west of here, chasing stragglers from the southern buffalo herd. Just ta hear 'bout 'em again makes my scars twitch. Son's of bitches sure know how to put the terror inta a man."

"Never seen you terrified, Gabe, though you looked pretty grim right before you sat in that cold river. You have one big mess of knife scars on your front."

"I ain't terrified, but I'm damn sure wary, and them scars is part of the reason why. They ain't ever gonna get aholt of me alive again. With Comanches ya gotta save the last bullet for yore-self. We need to get to a place where we can fort up and oil our weapons and check the ammo parfleches, and rest and feed. Maybe find a log jam at a bend or side creek. We gotta have dry powder and workin' weapons in Comanche country."

"Yeah, let's go, I got my boots on," said Josh as he sprung back onto his mount, a white man in buck-skin and wide felt hat. A few miles downstream they came upon a dense thicket of oak and pecan bordering a side creek that held a log jam of sorts. They immediately oiled their weapons and checked the ammo parfleches, which were dry. With weapons ready, they relaxed some and forted up with the driftwood.

They were able to build a camp behind the logs with the stock hidden from view, and actually built a small smokeless fire and heated grub for the first time in a long while. The hunger they had stirred up with the pecans returned in full, and they took to piling in the fuel. Then after they ate heated sausage, beans with wild onions, and bread with cheese, they had a drink to celebrate their escape to Texas.

"I hope thar's no Comanches around, because I'm too tard ta move to another camp to rest. 'Sides that, this here is the best fort we could arrange, ain't gonna find no better. Put the fire out now."

Gabe poured rum into two pewter mugs and handed one to Josh. "This here's my toast. To Josh LaPoint, a new man for a new land, nuevo hombre para nueva terra....and the horse herds we're gonna build on that old Rio San Antone." Josh gave his first smile since the killing had begun at that remark, and they clicked glasses, locked eyes, and downed the brandy.

"Here's to you, ole Texian. You know I wanted to go to Texas with you ever since I was a kid, don't you?"

"Hell, when I come back I warn't in no shape to return for quite a long while. But we done right well on that cattle drive when ya showed yore wrangling skills. And here we are again. "Cept I ain't a Texian no more, now we're Texans. Republic days are over. They done succeeded from Mexico and got swallowed by the United States, along with the rest of the southwest."

"Yeah, I noticed the US wasn't opposed to secession so long as it increased their territory, like Texas."

"Sure glad we made it ta Texas."

"Well me too, old scout."

"Wal, wish it coulda been in better circumstances, but here we be, gave 'em the slip so far, still alive and kicking.

Here's to ya." They downed two shots of rum in their small celebration. Then they shared some of the old timer's special kinnickinick and tobacco in the old pipe. They enjoyed a mellow mood for the first time in their long flight, feeling secure behind the driftwood logs, away from their troubles in Louisiana.

The thicket and log jam was the best hiding spot they had found in a while, so they decided to take turns resting up there before continuing towards their goal. A fair breeze blew from the south, pushing fast-moving but scattered white clouds against the blue sky, and the air was warm enough to shed coats for the first time in a while, as the sun broke into their sheltered location. It felt like a new spring was on the way in a beautiful rolling prairie countryside.

Josh sat enjoying the security of the thicket and logjam while the small fire of dried sticks burnt down to ash. The breeze easily dispersed what smoke the fire made through the branches of the tall trees lining the creek. He noticed how much driftwood, including big logs, was caught up in the upper branches of the trees, indicating powerful floods at times.

Gabe had dozed off, and Josh was feeling sluggish after their first big meal in a while. After an hour of sitting watch he arose to take a dump in a dense thicket apart from the logjam. The constant riding and irregular hours had made him constipated, and the big meal, rum, and smoke had brought on a good relieving squat and dump in the thicket, which he buried, using his big knife as a dirt scraper.

It was while returning from the thicket that Suzette started her low snarling and he saw the mounted Indians come riding up in a group of about seven riders, and a wave of terror rolled through his gut. Running low through the thicket, he jumped the logs back into their little fort.

He got out his telescope and hissed at Gabe as he scanned the approaching riders. Gabe lay snoring still, so Josh pitched a chip of bark at him and hit him in the belly, which drew him awake with his hand on his knife immediately. Josh gave a hand signal for intruder to Gabe, who crept to the logs to look for them.

"Comanches? Gol-dang I knew we shoulda left the fire camp to rest."

"Don't know yet, I don't think they saw smoke, they're not looking this way," said Josh as he drew the ammo bag for the

Whitworth rifle from his saddlebags, pulled the ramrod, and began to load it.

"Should we try to run for it?"

The Indian horsemen were on a slow tracking approach through the high grass of the riverbanks, studying the trail left by the little cluster of horses and heavy laden mules.

"To where? We ain't gonna find a better fort than this. We could stand off a tribe here with these logs for cover, at least for a while. Give 'em more losses than they're willing to take"

They both took Spencer repeaters with the Whitworth and Sharps long rifles they hunkered down between two huge driftwood logs, with solid wood above and below the six inch rifle slit provided by the jam. From there Gabe studied the Indians with the field glasses as the wary riders slowly trailed along the trampled grass. Josh readied the heavy Whitworth, with it's elongated octagon slug and huge powder load.

"Hold on," said Gabe as he peered through the field glasses. "I think they be Tonkawas, unless the Comanche taken to wearing army hats and pants, and doing a lot of tattoos."

"Army hats...from killing soldiers?'

"Naw, from being scouts for the army. Lemme study them a bit more with these here glasses. Hell, they got Confederate and Federal caps both. Lot's of tattoos. Yep, Tonkawas, there's one of them got boots with the bottoms cut out on his legs, like them scouts used to do. Turn good boots into leggings, damn fools. Can't stand nothing tight on their feet, I suppose. Oh, they got their ways, alright."

"So what about these Tonkawas? You've had dealings with them before?"

"Oh yeah. Tonk scouts rode with the rangers, couldn't find Comanche without 'em, I reckon. I scouted with plenty of 'em, and good scouts they was, too. Taught me a lot about tracking Comanches."

"They're looking this way now."

"So they are. Yep. Tonkawas. Tonkawas is a Waco name for them ah reckon, means those who stick together. Ah reckon they have too, since the other tribes hate em. Let's see now, ah reckon they call themselves Tickanwa-tic, the people of the wolf or some such. They ain't farmers like some of these eastern tribes, they're hunter gatherers who got run out of the buffalo plains by Comanches, along with the Apaches and everyone else. Might be lucky for us."

"So they're friendly to whites? I hope so because they're heading for us."

"Sometimes. Hard to say, after over a decade of being gone. Long as we got 'em outgunned they may not want to risk a killing fight."

"The leader is pointing this way."

"Might not have to fight. But they are tracking us, hit's for sure, and are comin' in."

"Another killing fight?"

"Sorta iffy. I been right friendly with Tonk scouts, when I rode with the rangers, ya know. They hate Comanche so much they sorta don't mind having some enemies of the Comanche around. Sorta like that general you was telling me about that time, said 'the enemy of my enemy is my friend.'"

"How do you plan to convince them of that?"

"I might have ridden with their kin when I was with the rangers chasing after captives. I'as known as Top-hat Comanche killer back then, by the Tonks."

"Yeah, but over dozen years ago. These all look like hungry young bucks to me."

"Campfire talk among the Indians takes the place of newspapers and chatting at the Cafe Du Mode. The scouts knew how many I kilt because they feasted on them and went delirious drunken crazy with it. These be younger braves, but they probably heard of me from the old timers. Stories get repeated over and over, and get bigger."

"So what are you intending, Gabe?"

"Ride out and parlay if they keep coming in, which it looks like they will, seeing what a trail we left with these loaded mules. They're after whatever easy pickin' they can find. They look lean and hungry enough to eat our mules on the spot. I aim to dissuade them of any such notions. They know we got four loaded mounts, I aim to convince them thar's four good shooters here, forted-up."

"And what am I to do, exactly?"

"You get that Whitworth and the Sharps both loaded and ready and keep a close eye on them with the field glasses. Lay out the Spencers too, all ready to fire, which gives ya fourteen quick shots after the long guns. Revolvers ready too, with extra cylinders out and ready to go. Keep the stock hidden back behind those trees, so they think we're four riders. They gotta believe we got more shooters than we are, if the fat hits the fire. They likely won't risk a fight with good shooters forted up in a logjam like we are. Thank the lucky stars for this log jam...and all the firearms we got with us. And the wet weather, got . everything too damp for em to burn us out. "

"Yeah, I got everything but the part about how you're going to convince them..."

"Wal I'm going out to make my show as top-hat Comanche killer....they mighta heard how I escaped the hand burning and scalping 'cause a few of them Tonk scouts that rode with the rangers was there at the rescue, when Mr. Alex and them rangers came storming into their camp, so I'll tell em I've come back with a crew of shooters to wipe out the Comanche."

"Sounds too risky, Gabe. Let me..."

"Naw. Listen. I'll tell em I hate the Penataka more than them, and have come back for vengeance because of them burning my hand and trying to scalp me, not to mention destroying my homestead on the Blanco. This used to be their land til the Apache and Comanche sorta drove them into the arms of the white man. Now a lot of 'em are whores for candy, frying pans, cooking pots, geegaws, and whiskey. They all love coffee and sugar and tobacee too. I'll ride out and give them some gifts for crossing their range while you draw a bead on the buffalo shield with the red cross on it. Can't miss that, can ya?"

"Why hell, I could miss anything on a given day," said Josh while peering through the telescope resting on the log.

"Well put off missin' til another day. Just get missin' outa yore mind entirely. If I raise this cow horn I got from that old varmint at the ferry and blow it, then you go ahead on and use the Whitworth and put a hole through that shield without hitting the man holding it, if you can. If that don't stop 'em, grab the Sharps and put a hole through the brave with the shield, the dark one covered with tattoos, with the army hat."

"Alright," said Josh as he slipped the long heavy barrels through the slot in the logs and rested each on a broken branch nub. "I'm ready. Go on ahead, do what you're gonna do. You're the one that knows these Indians."

"Ya sure you got no more questions?"

"It's your play, ole Texian, I'm backing you."

"Just a second now, gotta get suited up for the show,"

said Gabe. "And I told ya, we's Texans now, republic is over, done tole ya, got swallowed by the United States, along with the whole southwest."

"Yeah, I got it, but what are you up to now?"

Josh glanced over and saw that Gabe had put on a ratty old silk top-hat that Suzette was attached to as a sleeping nest, having retrieved it from Josh's saddlebag. Suzette was on the ground, snarling a low growl and looking agitated.

"How do I look?"

"Comical, but I've just seen you in a leather apron for years."

"Aw hell."

"Looks like you're ready for the quadroon ball in New Orleans. I haven't seen you wearing that since I was a teenager. What's it for?"

"It's the hat I used to wear, got it when I rode with the rangers at the Plum Creek fight, with their headman, Placido. We had over a dozen Tonks and the chief himself in the Plum Creek fight. I got it from him on a trade, actually. Might bring back memories for 'em."

"Brings back memories for me. You wore it to cover the nasty gash in your head when you first came back from Texas with Mister Alex. It always struck me as strange that an old beaver trapping mountain man would have a silk hat instead of beaver felt."

"Waugh, 'til that li'l bitch took it over for a sleeping bag, and I come upon it by fate, I reckon. By the time I got that hat, silk hats had ruined the beaver trade. So it was a good fit, 'til that lil dog got it."

"I guess she liked your smell." Both men stared at the Indians through the binoculars and telescope as they conferred. They were still tracking and heading towards their hiding spot.

"Yeah, ah ain't too sure ah likes her's, but it won't be for long. Now listen. We gonna need a fine shooting demonstration to get their respect. If it looks like it this palaver might work and they need more convincing I'm gonna fling this hat on the ground and you're gonna shoot it. Just to impress 'em that we are what I claim we are, Comanche killers with the big guns. So wait 'til it lights and I rein Buck outa tha way, take a steady bead, and don't miss."

"Alright. But don't let it get covered by the tall grass.

Fling it in one of those bushes where it's high enough to sight easily."

"Alright, I'll make a point of placing it on a tall bush for you, if they don't mind. Excuse me gentlemen, while I seek out a tall bush, is what ya reckon I oughta tell 'em, huh?"

"Well, you said don't miss. What if they just ignore your show and start shooting at you?"

"If hell starts popping, I'll be running back here fast as I can while you use the long rifles ta put one inta that shield and the first pursuer. If that don't work then lay into them with tha repeaters when they get close enough."

"Alright Gabe, I don't like it, but can't think of any better plan."

"Waugh. Had years of riding with Tonkawas. I'm pretty sure I can convince 'em, or I wouldn't be trying it. Never seen a Tonkawa wasn't wild for coffee and sugar and hating Comanches."

Gabe quickly grabbed some coffee and sugar sacks from the saddlebags, tied the canvas bags together and strung them over his saddle horn, then strapped on a revolver and checked the repeating rifle in his saddle scabbard. He grabbed one of his handmade layered steel knives from the saddlebags, then thinking the better of it, put it back. Instead he grabbed a pouch of tobacco and stuffed it into the top of the coffee sack. That being done, he scurried around to the other side of his horse and began checking the shotgun, then tightening his girth strap."

"Decided against trading off one of your knives, huh?"

"Wal screw 'em if they don't like the coffee and sugar, I ain't giving up a handmade layered steel knife to some scraggly mule-eating Tonkawas. I put in some tobacco instead. Usta be able to buy em with foofaraw, afore they got spoilt."

"Taking the ten gauge?"

"Yeah. Got it loaded and hung on the other side of my saddle there. I'm a damn riding arsenal. Should impress em, if talk don't work."

"You know their language?"

"Some, and plains sign language, enough ta get by, hoping of course that they speak Spanish or English some."

"Sure you don't want me to ride out with you? Scorpio could impress them with rearing up and kicking."

"Naw, you don't know nothin' 'bout Indians 'cept the ones

that treated you well. These is rascals, takes some learning on how ta read em. They see Scorpio do his warhorse routine and they'll really want him."

"Hey, give me those glasses," said Josh as Gabe was about to mount up. "I like them a bit better than this telescope."

"Oh yeah," said Gabe as he put the binoculars up once more to sight the Tonkawas before handing them to Josh.

"Alright, here they are, in the clearing now, good spot in that prairie to confront 'em, clear view from here, keep a sharp eye on me and hit that hat the first time."

"Don't let 'em get too close, Gabe, I've already lost enough family. I remember that story about the trapper having the Apache grab his hand to shake it and them tomahawk him."

"Aww hell, like I ain't dealt with Tonkawas before. Whose the gol-dang ex-ranger round here, anyway? Hey, whars the leather string I usta have on this hat?"

"Why hell Gabe, Suzette chewed that off years ago."

"Wal shit fire," said Gabe as he pulled the hat down snug on his head, the tattered brim resting just above his eyes. "The sum bitch has ta stay on my head while I ride out. Can't have it blown off. Damn, it shore smells like dog."

"Well, I guess you better draw a deep breath and swell your head up to make sure it stays on, Gabe."

"Now that's the Josh I remember. Just let fly with the witticisms whilst I head out to parley with a bunch of cannibals," Gabe said as he jammed the hat down onto his big head.

"Don't let 'em get close, Gabe. You look tasty, like aged beef."

"I don't aim to. If things go bad these sonsofbitches will be feasting on our carcasses tonight, no fooling."

"What. For real? I thought you were kidding, you told me that the cannibals were the Karankawa."

"Naw, Kronks was rubbed out early for their incorrigible man-eating ways, by the Austin colonists, back when I was just a teenager and up in Taos, I reckon, for they'd had kinfolk kilt and butchered when I got ta Texas. If it was Kronks they'd be sending arrows in from two hundred yards with six foot bows."

"Not a part of the Karankawa tribe?"

"Nah sir, not Kronks, Tonkawas...these Tonks are ritual cannibals from some whar's upcountry, originally, not part of the coastal Karankawa tribe.., which is rubbed out anyway."

"But they still eat human flesh?" asked Josh as he watched the slowly approaching group through the glasses.

"Yep. The scouts for the rangers used ta cook up Comanches after we killed 'em and have a big party with the meat, regular Saturday night social, dancing and all. It's part of their religion, 'cording ta what Placido tole me, gotta eat the heart of the warriors they kill, gives 'em big medicine."

"Now there's a discomforting notion," said Josh as he studied the warriors through the binoculars. "The better I fight, the more they want to eat me?"

"Hell, all them religions are a bunch ah crazy talk, iffen ya ax me. According to theirs, they's trying to soak up all the courage of the warrior they was eating, I reckon, and not let his spirit go to their happy hunting ground. Comanches believe mutilation dooms them to the netherworld as ghosts or suchlike."

"Damnation through consumption, that's a new one, or maybe real old. They're still coming this way."

"Yep. Hell they kept me awake with their singing and feasting all night long up at the Lone Man creek battleground after we chased Comanches all day from the Plum Creek fight. Sorta went crazy drunk when they partook. Wanted me to, but I'd done spent my spleen on 'em and wanted no more part, specially not their flesh."

"They cooked it?"

"Aw yeah, they'll cook ya up right fine, medium rare iffen they got time. Course, probably not the intricate New Orleans French Creole meals that ya usta have, like that garlic roast beef at Two Jacks, but fair middling for camping out," Gabe replied with a grin this time, as he finished tightening up the girth-strap on his saddle. Then he began to methodically check his weapons while watching the riders slowly approach.

Josh stared though the glasses at them. "Still coming in slowly, reading the ground. It's sort of friendly Indians, huh, want to have us over for supper?"

"Yep, Texas is a whole new situation."

"Kill their enemies and eat em, huh. That's not going endear them too much with the other tribes, I guess. They're still headed this way."

"That's sorta why I figure they ain't made no good buddy pacts in the interim I been gone. The red man's tribal memories is strong. And Tonks hates Comanches with a passion.

Comanches done rubbed out and run out the Tonks and Lipan Apaches from these parts, and every tribe has a medicine man who stands around the campfire rousing them up over something."

"Cooked up medium rare and eaten, huh? Well, now there's some impetus to hit what I aim for, huh?"

"Wal, it's a site better than Comanches, being tortured for a day or so, then chased down through cactus, dismembered, scalped, then cooked and eaten while you watch. Best keep the last slug in the navy colt for yourself when the Comanches come for ya, pard. "

"Okay, if I miss then I get eaten or shoot myself, that it?"

"That's it in a nutshell."

"So this is part of what you didn't mention about this route. Cannibal Indians in cutoff cavalry boots and blue breeches, with slouch hats, some of them. Could be hostile, maybe not. Sorta disquieting. If they ate me they would damn sure get indigestion, with all the acid churning in my stomach right now."

"Welcome ta Texas, LaPoint, and watch out for hostile Indians and rattlers," said Gabe.

"I've only known two Indians well, and they taught me horse care and tracking. I'd just as soon not get to killing Indians. My mother was part Carib Indian, which makes me part Indian, along with parts of a lot of other things."

"Wal, I'd just as soon avoid it as not myself. There's plenty better ones to kill. We should be able to bluff these outa a real fight."

"Alright then, let's get this done without it, but if it's us or some cannibals, rather them go down."

"A lot depends on my palaver, and on you making a good shot, again," said Gabe with a grin.

"Now I'm glad we did all that practicing."

"Yeah, me too. I'm counting on you now."

With that comment and a grin, Gabe mounted and spurred his dun stallion and bolted out of the brush with a long and startlingly loud war yell, heading straight for the group of lean looking Tonkawas. Josh watched in amazement as Gabe pushed Buck into a laid out run for the Indians, whipping and kicking his mount to full speed while breasting through the tall grass, yelling like a banshee from hell, in a mixture of Gaelic,

English, Spanish, and some Indian language, looking like he was fixing to whip the whole Indian nation. Josh fixed the glasses on the Tonkawas as Buck leaped small bushes in his furious charge.

The Tonkawa braves looked as startled as a pack of napping coyotes when they heard and spotted Gabe riding at them at breakneck speed. The ones on horses began milling and circling, gesturing with weapons aloft, while the tracker got up from the ground where he was peering and tried to mount his fractious horse. Two of them had on white man's clothes, and one brandished an old pistol. Several readied bows and arrows, and one began to load an old musket.

The one on the ground studying the grass finally mounted up as they readied for whatever the crazy white man was bringing. They spread their horses in a semicircle and waited with long cedarwood lances topped with buffalo bone points. Some had bows and arrows drawn and pointed at Gabe, some with old carbines, while the one was still loading his old musket as his horse milled and impeded his efforts.

At about fifty yards from the Tonkawas, the speeding Gabe drew up hard and skidded his big line-back dun stallion to a grass churning stop. Josh drew a sigh of relief, for Gabe was all he had left of humankind in this life, and he didn't want to see the old bull charging into a mess of savages and get whipped in a lopsided fight.

Quickly the old Texan spun the horse in a circle one way, and then the other, yelling the whole time. Then the stallion reared up and stood facing the Tonkawas, snorting steam and dripping saliva, flailing his hoofs in the sky. Gabe walked him forward on his hind legs a few feet, then brought him to a standstill, but still pacing in place. Joshua smiled as he watched. Then Gabe began to yell something at the Tonkawas and make signs with both hands as the golden tan stallion paced closer.

Josh watched nervously through the field glasses, the objects of his focus being at least two hundred yards away on the flat grassy prairies by the river. The dried grass had silvery stems and russet red tops and waved in the breeze like the waters of Lake Pontchartrain.

Josh gauged the wind from the movement of the grass, and set his sights on the primed and ready Whitworth long rifle.

Then he focused through the glasses again. A large warrior wearing white man's pants with dark tattoos all over his upper body and face rode out about twenty yards ahead of the others, carrying the round shield with the red and black cross. He seemed to be the leader, and wore cavalry boots cut off as leggings, with a cavalry cap. He gestured with the shield at Gabe while shouting.

Gabe had ridden closer and was showing off his scorched and scarred claw of a hand, holding it low in front of him as he turned his mount sideways to them. He definitely had their stunned attention, as Josh watched intently with the glasses. He took off the top-hat and pointed to his scalp scar, rubbed it with his clawed hand, then put the hat back on.

They seemed impressed, as near as Josh could tell in the field glasses. The big brave covered with dark tattoos was gesturing and talking to the other braves as Gabe continued his presentation. He pulled out his big knife and waved it back and forth while he yelled at them. They settled down a bit and watched him.

The old scout talked to them with signs and shouted words for a couple of long moments. Then he swung the two bags holding coffee and sugar, which he had tied together and strung over his saddle, down to the ground in front of him. The lead brave made a sign with his shield arm, bringing it in to his chest, then away.

At that gesture, Gabe wheeled his mount in a complete circle, gave another loud yell, and cantered back towards the thicket where Josh waited behind the sights of the big Whitworth. After Gabe had progressed perhaps twenty yards he wheeled his horse again and faced the Tonkawas, yelling and gesturing at them again, pointing at the bags on the ground.

The big tattooed brave detached from the group and rode over to where Gabe had dropped the coffee and sugar. As the warrior leaned down to pick up the bags, Gabe took the top-hat and held it in his hand down low. The brave picked up the two bags and examined the tops. Then he raised them and yelled something at Gabe. At that Gabe yelled something back and flung the top-hat into the top of a small bush off to the right side, and wheeled his horse away while yelling and pointing at the hat. Josh drew his bead as soon as the hat lodged in the bush, judged the wind by the flow of the wild grass tops, then let loose with the Whitworth and watched the hat fly off the bush and the shocked Tonkawa brave whip his horse back.

Gabe yelled and wheeled his horse once more, facing them again, rearing his dun stallion so that Josh saw the dark line on his back through the glasses, and pointed at the hat. The lead brave wheeled his small pinto mustang twice, and then approached the hat at a trot. He leaned over and grabbed the hat from the bushes as he rode by it, promptly examining the hole, then put it on his head, and circled his horse again, staring and shouting at Gabe. He took his bow and quiver and laid it on the ground, circled again, yelling something, and rode off towards his companions with the hat nearly swallowing his head, waving the bags of loot he had acquired. When he reached his companions, they had a short parley, then all turned and trotted off in the direction they came from, whooping and hollering.

Gabe rode to where the warrior had dropped the weapon, leaned from the saddle and picked them up, then rode back up smiling. When he arrived at the small log fort in the trees he had a big grin on his ruddy face, and said, "Wal, guess I still got the touch."

"Or luck of the Irish. Amazing, actually. He gave you his bow and arrows. Let me see them."

The bow was about four feet long and made of hickory wood strengthened with sinews laminated to it, with a several ply string of buffalo sinew and a tightly wrapped leather handle. The quiver was of buffalo leather with the hair on, and the arrows were smoothed and tipped with exquisitely sculpted flint tips.

"How in the heck did you get his bow and arrow from him?"

"His notion, actually. Yeah, he recognized me, said he saw me as a kid. His daddy was a ranger scout that rode with me when I was with Captain Jack Hays. We called him Coffee John on account a his damned name was so long and hard to say. So that's his boy, a halfbreed Spanish, name of John's Son, believe it or not."

"You ole coon. It sure worked, looks like, unless they circle back." Josh kept the binoculars trained on the departing riders.

"They ain't coming back. They heard of me for years. I was friendly with their chief, Placido, who just went under a while back, when all the other tribes ganged up on them at the reservation up north, on the Brazos. Or so they told me, I think, near as I can recall the words of their language. He was throwing a mixture of three languages at me all at once, and all I been hearing for a dozen years is Cajun French and English. But I think I got the most of it. I hate to hear ole Placido's gone under, though. He was a good man."

"So your fame has lingered?"

"I guess so, with those that still scout for the whites whenever they can."

"Did any of them scout with you?"

"Naw, but they heard of me. Some of their band, including his daddy, was scouts when I rode with the rangers in the early forties. Mr. Alex used some Tonkawa trackers when I got captured by the Comanche, and they helped track 'em down and led him and the rangers to bring help in 'bout the time they lit that fire under my hand and proceeded to whacking at my scalp."

"So maybe you owe your life to Tonkawa trackers?"

"Maybe. His daddy was a great tracker, rode with me when I scouted for Captain Hays. He was a breed, part Lipan Apache and Mexican, I think. He loved that sugared coffee for riding all night. Used ta carry a canteen full of it. So we started callin him Coffee John, scout for John Coffee Hays, as a joke, but it stuck. So he went under on the Brazos too, and this here is his son, John's Son. He likes coffee too, I reckon."

"Damned lucky. Your scent has lingered."

"I reckon they heard stories of me round the campfire, the top-hat ranger who rode with Placido, the old red-haired Irish-man who kept his scalp, ole burnt hand, scar-head, Comanche killer, whatever way the story growed around the campfire. Dang I hate to hear Placido's gone under."

"Placido. You knew him?"

"Yep. That man could outrun old Bill Williams, I recall he run thirty miles with his hand on the rump of Burleson's horse before the Plum creek fight, never seen the likes of it. All his scouts too, they came afoot with Burleson, then got horses by killing Comanches off of 'em and leapin' aboard. We had 'em tie white rags for headbands or neckerchiefs so's we could tell em apart. They was killing Comanches on a rampage, I guarantee ya, after trotting all that way on foot. Tonks can be mighty fierce in battle. Glad we didn't have to fight these hungry bucks."

"So what did you tell these guys to get away scot free?"

"I tole 'em I'as come back to wipe out the Comanche onct and for all, and gave 'em gifts to honor those that helped save me, coffee for their dead chief and my friend, Placido, and told 'em the best long shooters alive was back here drawing beads on 'em, in case they wanted to die today."

"Let's see, that'd be me and Suzette?"

"Right! But what got 'em steered right was when I told 'em I wore the top-hat given to me by Placido himself during the Plum Creek fight when them scattering Comanche were flinging loot left and right. That's when I found out he went under."

"You got that silk hat from their chief?"

"Yep. Placido had two top-hats he scooped off the ground at a full gallop after killing the Comanche who carried them, stuck together they was, that being after the first skirmish when we jumped the Comanche at Plum creek after the big Linnville raid."

"Loot from a warehouse?"

"Yeah, at Linnville, the harbor warehouses. So when we stopped to water our horses and ourselves and reload, I traded him a woman's corset which a buck had hurled back at me as I shot him, which the chief thought he could make into good body armor. It was too small for him, though, so I got the better of the deal. I wore that hat in my Comanche killin' days."

"They're still making a slow approach. Whalebone corsets and top hats, sound like quite a sight."

"Oh it was plenty of that, like to bugged my eyeballs out when they came riding up that Plum Creek prairie in a long stretched out line. Lots of 'em had dresses, and a whole bunch had white linen dress shirts on. Some had long bolts of material tied to their horses, flapping in the wind and dragging in the grass. And a huge horse herd to manage."

"Sounds like you jumped them at the right time."

"After we jumped 'em, them Comanche were trailing so much loot it was all over the ground, while about three thousand horses bolted for hell and back. It was my first fight with revolvers, and what a damn difference. Before that a bow and arrow set, like this Tonkawa one here, in the hands of a good warrior could unloose twenty killing shots by the time we could get off two shots, iffen we ever got the second one loaded with arrows whizzing in. The tables turned that day when we charged 'em a horseback with pistols blazing. It was McCullough that talked ole Huston into the charge, instead of an infantry stand."

"They busted and ran when you charged?"

"They sure did, like bamboozled drunks. They mighta been an organized war party when Buffalo Hump brought 'em down for the raid, but after looting the warehouses and getting all those horses they were just like a gaggle at a fandango, with lots of 'em drunk as skunks and playing the fool in white folk's garb, formal coats and dresses on painted savages, footwear ta beat all hell, shore was a sight. Comical even, scared as we was. So we got our chance to lay into 'em with revolvers, and put 'em on a fright. Anyway, it was the first time we felt the upper hand."

"So how did it turn out."

"Wal, I musta put a dozen on the ground, and we chased and shot 'em all they way up to the hill country. Trailed 'em to a little valley off the Blanco, named it Lone Man Creek. We put a lot of them under that day."

"Walker Colts?"

"Yep, heavy ole Walker Colts. I had two good ones, and lots of ammo. I killed my first Comanche's in that scrape, and it went on from there."

"Well, better them than us, and you talked our way out a fight today."

"Sure sorry to hear ole Placido went under, though. He was a good ole hoss, despite his eating habits. He said he'd never eat me, though, said Irishmen tasted like pickles from too much tangle-foot in their blood. Don't know if he made that up or not, but I never rode in front of him during hungry times, about like Bill Williams, come ta think on it."

"Hell, I never knew Suzette's sleeping bag had such a history. I might have missed it had I known."

"Yep. Damn glad you hit that hat, 'cause they was hot on getting our mules with loads and all. They're desperate. They've had it bad since I left Texas, said they nearly got wiped out a few years back, up where they'd got penned up on the Brazos reserve, so the remainder come down here to try to survive. They made the mistake of siding with the Confederates before their last massacre, and every tribe in the territory jumped on 'em in the reserve without no protection from the Federal troops. They're out trying to gather food for their starving relatives now, looking for tracking jobs, buffalo, deer, rabbit, snake, mule, whatever they can get. They say all the immigrant Indians make the buffalo scarce now."

"You learned all this with a few words of Tonkawa?"

"Aw hell no, that leader spoke some English and Spanish. He's a breed, for his pap was part Mexican, I think. Calls himself John's Son now. He's trying to get a scouting job with the rangers, asked me to put in a word for him. He was scouting for the Confederates, but that sorta ended."

"I'll say. Who wiped them out?"

"Who knows? Comanche, Kiowa, immigrant Indians from back east, they say, along with just about any other Indians that was around. The Tonkawas ain't got too shinin' a reputation amongst the other tribes, on account of their eating the warriors and all, and scoutin for the Texans."

"So they've been laid low."

"Yep, more than half gone under. In addition to tha smallpox and cholera that's been rubbing 'em out for years, and horse thieves stealing all their mounts, a mixed bunch jumped on 'em,"

"Sounds like they've been losing for a long time, huh?"

"That's for certain. Why this country was full of Indians until the first European brought our diseases, wiped most of 'em out in tha ensuing years. And then the Comanches come down and pushed 'em outa' the buffalo grounds. That's why my palaver worked with 'em. Killing Comanches is high on their wish list. Course, yore good shooting didn't hurt, neither. Not that two hundred yards is that much of a shot, but still...thanks pard."

"Well, alright then. Here's to ya, old timer. I thought you were going to get killed and you came back with a bow and arrow. What was that about?"

"Said it was for killing Comanches, trade for the hat of Placido. But really I think he wanted me to put in a word for him to get hired as a scout."

"First Indians we come upon in Texas and one wants a job reference from a ranger who's been gone twenty years?"

"I reckon so, which proves my contention that ya just can't never tell what's gonna happen."

"I'll say. You left a strong scent here. That was, as you say, 'shining.' First scrape in Texas and we come out smelling like, like hot coffee and tobacco, without a drop of blood spilled. You're not a bad ole pard to have around. And here I was thinking you were just that old grouchy blacksmith hammering away and muttering to himself out back, arguing with the mules all day."

"Waugh! I kept my powder dry," replied Gabe, tapping his forehead and smiling. "But just to be safe let's move on a bit further so we ain't inviting trouble. A new camp away from the river, and we'll try to mix up our trail somehow."

"Alright. But Suzette ain't gonna be happy we left her sleeping bag."

"Waugh. Too bad for her. That hat gotta stay right where it is, on John's Son's head. That's part of the legend now. The word will spread. Here, my French knitted cap for her, the little bitch, best watchdog I ever seen, with the weather warming up now I don't need it so much. I'll cut holes for her legs in it and she can wear it like a sweater 'til spring."

He took out his small bone-handled patch knife and slit leg-holes in the hat, and a hole for her head, and slid it onto her. She struggled against it at first, but then seemed to like it once she had it on. Excited now, tail wagging and pointed ears with bright eyes, she scrambled into the saddlebag and left her head out as they prepared to depart. Gabe put on a wide brimmed hat he pulled from the mule pack. Josh fed the mounts and pack mules by hand while Gabe readied his gear.

Then they quietly rode away at a fast walk, heading west away from the river, through rolling prairies, with a mixed forest of tall bare post oaks, and spreading thick branched live oak with leaves just starting to fall, and clumps of blackjack oak, and tall dark cedars scattered about in the lower areas. As they headed west, the wind from the south increased in gusts, and white puffy clouds went scudding across the wide blue sky overhead. Gabe peered at the sky, scowling. "I might have been mistaken about the weather. This hard wind from the south means a norther is up there somewhars, coming down. We could be in for a blow and a temperature drop. We'd better find some shelter to weather a storm tonight."

They picked up their pace and rode into the freshening breeze through grassy meadows spotted with good patches of timber. Gabe kept peering to the northwest when they topped the rises. Suzette began to get her nervous look, for she heard the distant thunder, and hated storms. Soon Josh heard the distant rumblings and saw flashes in the west. They hastened their pace against the increasing south wind that blew dead leaves and grass into their faces. The mules became nervous and sounded off with rattling brays as they hurried southwest.

Sure enough, within an hour they saw a dark and massive blue gray line of clouds off to the northwest horizon. Streaks and flashes of lightning crackled all along the tall line of thunderheads, and the line seemed to approach very rapidly, though the wind along the ground was gusting towards the front, and gray clouds were speeding low overhead towards it as well.

They rode south at a lively pace about five miles until they came to a likely spot to weather a blow, a small rise above a little creek beside a grassy meadow, the knob covered with thick brush and trees, with a small depression on the southeast side, where they quickly built a small oak and mesquite fire, using sandstone rocks from a loose strata on the hillside to shield it from the coming wind.

"Wal, here's our first home in Texas. I name it Escondito, little hideout. Let's get the stock secure and a shelter up, quick" said Gabe.

Then they gathered brush and fallen branches and made a wind shield for the stock. Josh rubbed and calmed the nervous horses, then fed them by hand with grains while thunder rattled in the west. Gabe hustled about making a shelter, a very low lean-too made of the tarp stretched over a rope strung between two trees. He put warm bedding underneath, sheepskin coats and a buffalo robe, and secured the tarp all around with stakes and tie-lines, arranging it where it could be lowered or raised with tension on the rope.

Josh went to heating food and boiling water for some hot drinks while Gabe did his expert job on the makeshift shelter in the lee of the hill. About the time the small fire had burned down to a thick bed of coals while they finished eating, the huge line of dark towering clouds was just a few miles away. Dried leaves, dust, and twigs were stirred up by the gusts and began to shower them with debris in their faces. Lightning and thunder got closer as they did their best to secure everything and shelter the stock.

Then the wind shift hit them with a mass of flying forest litter, and cold air from the north shrieked through the branches overhead. The air suddenly turned white with sleet driving down at a hard angle, pelting their faces, and they crawled under their tarp and buffalo robe. With the ground turning white with the bouncing white ice pellets, they saw that the stock were huddled together with their heads sheltered, and both of them huddled under the tarp and robe, pulling the tarp down tight to weather the storm.

The wind increased to a steady howling gale and the ground turned solid white as they huddled under the protection of the tarp and robe, with Joshua cradling the nervous Suzette in his belly. Pellets of ice bounced off the trees branches overhead and dropped helter-skelter onto their tarp. Soon they turned to hail as big as eyeballs and began to knock down dried twigs and leaves as they came hurling into the little woods. There was nothing to do but rest while the wind raged, and they lay still for a while, glad to be warm and secure after the long day.

Gabe actually began to doze and snore as the weight of the hail increased on their shelter. The temperature dropped thirty degrees in an hour, and the sleet began to mix with driving rain. A crackle of nearby lightning was instantly followed by a booming crash of thunder that caused both of them to jerk and cringe in terror reflex.

Gabe sat up quickly at the boom, his hand jerking to his knife as his head pushed the tarp up, dumping a load of ice from it. "Damn, that was a loud one, thought I was at Monterrey with the San Patricio boys, with the artillery going off."

"It was close, too close."

"Raining now, huh? I'd like to have some coals in the morning, be right back," Gabe said as he rolled to his side and stuck his head out from under the tarp.

"You're not going out there?"

"Whew, now thar's a cold Texas baptism," said Gabe as he stuck his head out. He got up quickly, stooping low as he ran and grabbed a saddlebag with more rum in it, threw a big barked log on the fire and dove back under the robe.

"Brrrrr, this here's what we ole Texans call a norther. Welcome to Texas, mister LaPoint, sir. If ya don't like our weather, wait a while, it'll change."

"I've never seen the weather change so fast so hard. Damn frigid blast like it's coming from the north pole."

"Yeah, and it's gonna howl all night. Nuthin to do but wait

it out and hope the stock does all right. Least wise we don't have ta worry about Comanches attacking. They'll be hunkered down too. Here, want some tangle-foot? I need a shot after this day."

They both partook of a small snort while the wind rose in fury above them. Josh couldn't help but notice a change in Gabe, though he was obviously very tired, there was a lightness to him Josh had not seen before. Josh had only known him as a grumpy and pedantic teacher who had retreated to the LaPoint Plantation to lick his wounds. The man who confronted the Tonkawas on that day was a different man, someone reborn from long ago. They both were becoming different men than they were in New Orleans. But in Gabe was stirring an older self that was tied to this land.

"Damn, it's been a day, that's for sure. I had just taken a good dump when I spotted those Tonkawas trailing us," said Josh.

"Good thing. I ain't gonna tell ya how close I came ta doing the same while I was whipping ole Buck out to meet with em."

"That was a sight I'll never forget. You shocked the hell out of me. I didn't know you'd go screaming like an Irish banshee at them riding full bore. They'da shot you if they had not been so shocked."

"Yep, I learned long ago it's best to come at them 'bout like this blue norther hit us."

"Blue norther, huh? I didn't know these blizzards came this far south. It's been howling and spitting sleet and hail out there for a solid hour with increasing speed and bigger hail. I'm worried about the horses," said Josh.

"Wal, yeah, 'cept this ain't no blizzard, like I told ya, it's a Texas norther. That hail hurts worse than snow, I'll guarantee that. The stock should be all right if they keep their heads together in that shelter. But go ahead. Go on out and check 'em, for that Josie might be knocking things down with her worrying. Hand me that jug back. I'll maintain a warm spot here. You'll be wishing it was a snowy blizzard when them hailstones hit yore face." Gabe was well lubricated with the rum and worn out from his encounter with the Tonks, and was not about to shift from his warm nest. He looked more contented than Josh had ever seen him.

"Well alright," said Josh, and he jammed on his big felt hat and left the shelter to make sure the horses were secure from the wind and driving ice pellets. The shelter they had fashioned was doing the job, providing a place for them to huddle together out of the blast and flying hailstones. He spoke with each in turn, secured feed bags on their noses, and rolled another two logs on top of the one Gabe had put on the fire.

Then he scurried back under the tarp, after being pelted by ice the whole time. "They're okay for now, but the ground is white, covered with sleet and hailstones. Never seen white ground before."

"Waugh. This ain't nothin' compared to getting caught on the staked plains. They got blizzards up thar that kin shore kill ya quick. I woke up with three feet of snow on me onct. Without buffalo robes I would have froze up plenty of times. I onct knew a fella fleeing from the Kiowa who crawled into a buffalo carcass to hide out in a warm spot, up on the Canadian in '33, but it froze solid and trapped him in thar for a day or so. Now that thar's a blizzard."

"What were you doing out there, anyway?"

"Why, I was hunkering down, like now, ya danged wolf pup."

"But how did you come to get out there in the first place? Seems like I've been hearing about this Llano Estacado, the staked plains, for years, but I don't know how you got there."

"Wal, I ran away from Harlan county Kentucky in1828, after my seventeenth birthday, when I was a dang fool kid, with dreams of being a free trapper, a mountain man. Went up ta St. Louie and later down the Sante Fe trail. I'd been apprenticed out to a blacksmith for a couple of years by then, and had 'bout learnt all he could teach me. So I lit out for the shining mountains, which I had heard about all my life."

"Didn't that put a worry into your folks?"

"Naw, not really. They sorta expected it, I reckon. I was born during the big New Madrid quake on December 16th of 1811, and Pap always said that quake gave me itchy feet, all that pitching' and shaking. They say the Mississippi ran backwards on the night I was born. I never took to living in houses much, I reckon. I spent most of my growing up time roaming the hills with a long rifle. Had to start providing meat for the family at ten years old, and when I was twelve I won me a fine weapon, a

Deckard long rifle, at a shooting contest, that was deadly accurate. I gave away my smooth bore and started out knocking squirrels out of tall trees at a hundred yards, moved on ta deer and bear. Only came home to bring tha meat in and rest. Old Pap knew I would go west someday. He wanted me to, for thar was old blood feuds thar in them hills, going back ta Megregors and Campbells, I figure, in the highlands of Scotland. He wanted me to be shed of that, afore I got inta it. Then a drought and a depression caused by them Whigs and their shenanagans forced my folks to apprentice me out to that blacksmith."

"I'd like to have seen you as an apprentice, like I was to you."

"Yeah, wal I took all of him I could take after a couple o years, when he didn't have nothin' else ta teach me."

"So you lit out to be a mountain man. What gave you that idea?"

"Wal, my ma was an educated woman and insisted we learn ta read and ta memorize stuff, so she used ta read ta me in the evenings, by the light of homemade candles. Of course she read the Bible to me, which I always considered pretty good fiction, but lots of other things too, from the classics and such, which she had sent from the tidewater area of Virginia. It was from a book on the Crusaders that I first larn't 'bout Damascas steel, when them Syrian blades chopped the Crusader blades in two with the first blow. One of the things she read was the report of the Lewis and Clark expedition, and that musta stuck in my head, them shinin mountains out west. So I larn't up all I could about it growing up, after I could read on my own."

"And you took off without telling anyone, like I tried a couple of times and you fetched me back?'

"Yep, wal, sort of, the feuding come close, a cousin of mine got kilt, and hit was either get inta it or skedaddle, so I left a note, then went up ta Saint Louie. Got a job black-smithin', mostly working on wagon wheels and gear, but learning how to fold steel for knives too, for they had a book in the library on it thar, but I couldn't perfect it then. By and by I got hired on to take care of the wagon wheels on a trading caravan to Sante Fe, and later for hunting when they saw how I could cut sign and bring in meat. So I worked my way west, to Bent's fort, and then Sante Fe."

"What's a bent fort?"

"The Bent brothers set up the early trading posts out west, on the Red River and the Arkansas, near the front range of tha stony mountains, which is whar I worked. Big adobe compound, tall walls, forted up. Used ta play pool with Kit Carson thar. Hunted for meat with Ceran and Britt, supplied the post and the travelers on the Sante Fe trail. After a couple of years thar I moved on down tha trail to tha stony mountains."

"So you settled around Sante Fe and started trapping?"

"Naw. We had a heap o troubles in Sante Fe with the Spanish officials, and their Popish ways, so I went to Taos, 'cause I heard it was a better place for white trappers to engage from. They was sorta hostile to trappers at the time in Sante Fe and corrupt as all hell. Most everything went out in bribes that didn't stick. Then as soon as Mr. Alex would get one set of officials bribed, then here'd come another whole new set."

"That sounds familiar after these years of dealing with the federals in New Orleans, quibbling fussbudgets, always with an eye out for graft. So did you do your beaver trapping out of Taos, and find out how your old stick floated?"

"That's right, Hoss. Went with a party of trappers up the Rio Grande into Ute country, shining tall mountains up thar for shore, but we didn't make it out with our beaver plews, so it was a bust that first year. Some Utes got our plews. I was able to trade a fella more desperate than me outa his Hawken rifle, though, so it warn't a complete loss. And just being alive up in that valley was an experience to remember, I tell ya."

"How'd you make your way then?"

"Oh, this and that, whatever I could scratch up. Hunting for fresh meat for ta sell. Shooting cougars and wolves that was killin' stock. Trapping for a while, but I never made more than a grubstake at that, so I headed back to Taos, where the winters was snug and easy, got me a little blacksmith shop thar, started farrier and wagon work, and went ta perfecting my techniques on the knives. I larned about tempering it by plunging it inta a sheepskin with special solutions in it."

"Then you made Taos your home base, like Mister Alex?"

"First couple of years thar, well I rode with the Ciboleros, hunting buffalo meat for the folks in Taos, for their winter food supply, dried buffalo, best winter food in the world. I also tracked elk and mule deer in the mountains, sold the meat in town or at the Pueblo. Did some hunting of cougars for the pelts as well, since they was akilling sheep and goats around Taos and needed to be rubbed out. Got about a dozen good cat pelts. Alex bought lots for his place."

"When did you get involved with the Comanche?"

"First time was at the Taos trade fair, where they brought in the best finished buffalo robes I ever seen. Then later we ran into Comanches out on the staked plains but they was usually friendly 'cause they been going to the Taos trade fairs for decades. Seems like long ago they come to an understanding that ready trade with the settled Pueblo folks had advantages over raiding, and buffalo meat and robes was highly valued in a place where beans and corn tortillas was the daily fare and the nights was cold."

"How'd you learn to deal with them, communicate?"

"Wal, there a plains sign language for simple stuff and barter is pretty straightforward, this for that. The Pueblo Ciboleros helped me out with that. I had a pretty good knack for tongues too, so eventually I learnt some of several, Spanish, Comanche, Ute, Arapaho, a bit of Navajo, some Cheyenne and Kiowa. Then I got into trading with the Kotsotekas, the Penetakas, the Nakoni, the Yamparika, for buffalo robes and skins. Quohadis are conservative though, don't want no truck with whites, 'cause they seen how it weakened the southern tribes, with disease and whiskey."

"So the Comanche had the best robes to trade?"

"Oh yeah. Comanche women finish out buffalo robes better than anyone. We're snug under one right now. Best product of expert craftswomen. Nothin finer in a norther."

"It is awfully warm."

"Want some more this tanglefoot? Sure makes a warm spot in the belly. Oh lordy, I'm back in Comanche country again. I knew this day was a comin'."

"You surprise me, you actually traded with the Comanche?"

"Shore nuff. When I was a Cibolero we hunted buff together with them, using a twelve foot lance like some of them did. Thar weren't nothin' like it for a young fella seeking adventure, running the herd with them lances at the ready, coming up on the side of a fat cow and ramming it through that certain spot behind the last rib into the heart and watching it tumble in a heap.   Now that takes some real skill and daring. I got pretty good at it back then, though I did some tumbling too."

"Hunting from a running horse with a lance! Why you're about half Comanche yourself, aren't you?"

"I could have lived thar and had a good life with them. They admired my lancework, and I showed 'em how to fix a knife blade to a lance. They make lances by taking the long narrow lower branches of the cedar tree, actually a juniper tree that folks calls cedar, and smoothing 'em down with knives, making a light strong lance about a dozen feet long, with a sharpened buffalo bone for a tip. Mighty fearsome weapon if handled correctly. Put it in a spot on the left side of a buffalo behind the last rib at a full run, then cut away as it tumbles head over heels and hope it don't hook your mount. I doubt I could do it today, but onct I was young and agile like you, believe it or not."

"I think I do. So did that ferryman with the shotgun, and that snake on the post."

"Yeah, anyway...It was with the Ciboleros that I got in good for the buffalo robe trade. Onct the Comanche seen us hunt buffalo in their style, they accepted us as equals in their eyes, ya see. So we got sorta friendly, and I traded with 'em for buff robes twice a year when we went out for meat. They loved my knives and traded lots of robes that were really well done, horses too. And I always had a good time bartering and smoking with the northern Comanches. They could be a jovial bunch."

"Amazing to hear that. So it was part-time on the staked plains and part-time in Taos."

"With hunting the mountains in between. I finally set up a big blacksmith shop behind my adobe off the square thar, and made knives to trade and metal repair in general, mostly wagon repair and farrier work. Had me a still for grain liquor too, Taos Lightening, we called it. Thar was lots of ways to make a living if a fella was willing to hustle any opportunity that presented itself. And thar was quite a few trappers around, ole Bill Williams, Kit Carson, the Robideaux brothers, and such like fer company and news of where ta hunt and trap."

"So you did black-smithing in the winter and shacked up with a pretty senorita, huh?"

"Yep, the lovely Lupita, and she whar a dang good cook and good in bed too. I shoulda stayed with her, I guess. I can still see them dark shimmering eyes. Lawdy."

Gabe took another drink and closed his eyes. "Them was shining times, but for beaver trapping I didn't know much, so I had to go with old trappers like Williams and the Ashley bunch ta learn. Keepin up with Bill Williams burnt all the baby fat off me, I'll guarantee ya. No man can move through the mountains faster than that long gaited man. But I kept up with him."

"Bill Williams, where have I read that name?"

"Fremont expedition of 18 and 48, durn fools tried to force a snow march through the upper Rio Grande valley and over the divide in the dead of winter, for the danged railroad route, through the most tangled mountains around. Williams was the guide, but it whar impossible what they tried, and come starving time ole Bill was suspected of eatin' some folks when they got lost in the La Garita mountains. Lots of 'em died in the snow."

"That's right, Fremont's forth expedition, pushed by his father-in-law, Senator Benton and the railroads, to find a way through the high Rockies in winter. It was a disaster, if I remember right."

"Yep, I turned 'em down for the scoutin' job, for I felt that Fremont was a bit reckless, always willin' ta take tha slim chance too much. So did Lucien Maxwell, and then Dick Wooton quit when he saw the snow in the Sangre De Christos and told 'em it was a fool crazy idea in that deep snow. But the worst of it was that Kit didn't go, but stayed home with his new wife in Taos. Without Kit, Fremont was in trouble, tryin' ta make a name fer himself by pushing a winter passage, without the tools ta do it with. A good scout knows when ta turn back."

"But Williams took the job?"

"Yeah. I guess the only guide Fremont could find that was desperate or foolish enough to try the crossing in winter was old Bill, who was drinkin' pretty heavy by then, having fallen off the Bible-thumping wagon he was usually on. Now Bill was a hell of a mountain man and knew his passes and trails, but them upper Rio Grande mountains was heaped with snow too deep to travel or even recognize anything. There is a trail over the divide in summer, at the head of the Rio Grande valley, over the pass into the valley of the Los Animas River, but they didn't get that far."

"How far did they get?"

"Fremont got the bit in his teeth and demanded to push

on to a pass called Cochetopa, inta tha valley of tha Gunnison, but Williams figured only another pass to the south, the Canero, could be forced. It was the worst winter for snow in decades, with avalanche danger high. Williams got lost up in them twisting La Garita mountains, got plumb flummoxed on Mesa Mountain, nothing but row after row of white mountains, each taller and whiter than the last, snow upon snow, ice upon ice. They got bogged down trying to climb in deep snow, pounding paths on their hands and knees up steep slopes. It got about as bad as it could, and the few survivors limped back to Taos. I'm thankful Kit didn't go, 'cause they most of 'em went under."

"I'm glad you didn't go, or I wouldn't have had you to hector me like an old hen all these years. So you kept trapping and hunting around Taos then?"

"Waugh. Yeah, but I never walked in front of Bill Williams in starving time. Went out to the Gila one year, got some plews, lost 'em, came back broke and hungry. The next year I trapped beaver in the San Luis valley, up to the headwaters of the Rio Grande where those fools got snowbound up thar, and up to tha great Pagosa Hot Springs in the mountains. I was led in thar by some Ute friends, and I got me a Ute squaw for a while, right pretty gal. Got over as far as the Piedra river, with some box canyons thar that could raise the hair on yore neck. I did alright for a couple of seasons. Traded my plews to Mister Alex for good prices."

"Not much Indian trouble?"

"Naw, not in the mountains so much. I was friendly with Utes and Navajos and Jicarilla Apaches at that time. Us ta bath regular in a little pool we made by the river for the hot springs to mix with that snow melt San Juan River from the tall mountains thar. That steaming hot water comes out of a bottomless well beside the river thar, stinking of brimstone and steaming away, nearly boiling, so we'd make mud bath pools with it and clear pools mixed with that ice-melt river water. It's quite a spot, all the tribes know about it and use it. They call it tha Great Pagosa."

"Gabe, I always sort of assumed you hated Comanches, for the torturing and all. You never wanted to talk about it much, except to say you were scalped and tortured."

"Wal, I didn't start out hating 'em, just the opposite back in them days. I was a squaw man for a time, lived like an Indian in a buffalo skin lodge. Of course, I ain't too fond of the ones that did the torturing, nor the ones who burned me out, and might drop a hot galena pill in them someday."

"But before that you traded with them, slept in their camps?"

"Why hell yes. Comanches got a hospitality custom that made us feel safe there, under the protection of the chieftain we was bartering with. We traded for years, and they made us welcome in their camps. Comanche ain't bad folk if they ain't on a raid. Lots of these German farm kids they steal end up becoming big warriors, and never want to go back to slopping pigs on the farm. They use their drive to get ahead."

"Because they're outsiders, I can believe that."

"Truth is, white boys just ain't naturally lazy like red men, and they try harder to advance. They are all tough and good on horseback, 'cause it's a warrior society, and everyone has to be to tough to survive on the plains, but they treat each other decent, just like any other folk. It's a society like the old Spartans, the boys trained to be horse hunters and warriors from birth, and the women got plains living down to an art. Riding out for Buffalo or Apaches, same thing to a young warrior, a way to gain ranking in the tribe."

"The Comanches, they always ruled the plains?"

"Naw, they came down and took over in the middle 1700s, from what I gathered. Ran the Apache and everyone else out of the buffalo grounds by 1800. The Apache planted corn, squash, and beans in settled rancheros near a water source, which they learned from the Pueblos in times long past. That made them settled targets for the Comanche raiders, and Comanche's are the best horse raiders. The Comanche's conquered everyone, except the Kiowas, who they allied up with. They raid down to Mexico for horses and slaves too."

"The Apaches are supposed to be pretty fierce, but they couldn't hold off the Comanche?"

"Naw. Comanches don't plant crops and settle, making it nigh onta impossible to raid 'em. Most can't find the Comanche camps, for they move too much, and the Llano Estacado is wide and trackless."

"So they're totally dependent on horse and buffalo?"

"That's about it. And knowledge of the good watering spots in the upper canyons of the Red River, and great memory and star reading for traveling the staked plains. They can go deep into Mexico on information memorized about the landmarks and stars and such, passed down through the generations."

"You do that pretty well yourself."

"Not like them. They can do just about everything with all the parts of the buffalo, I can tell ya that. We had right friendly relations then, never had to deal with thievery or insult like some other redskins, Kiowas, for example. Probably less violence and crime in their world, cause they turn it outward, on other tribes. They was fierce on raiding and stealing horses. Like I said, they done run the Apaches out of the buffalo plains in the early days, the 1700s. Comanche don't settle anywhere where they can be found, so it's hard to match 'em in a hit and run war. So they ended up ruling the buffalo plains, allied with the crazy superstitious Kiowas, and we ended up being the main trade outlet for their pelts for a while.

"I'm amazed, you trading with the Comanches. I thought you always hated them. Now it sounds like you knew them well enough to find their camps."

"Wal hell, jus' cause I taught you everything you know that don't meant I taught you everything I know, Josh. Hell, I was conferring with Houston on trying to get a line established between tha buffalo Indians and the settlers, but he couldn't get it through the legislature. Anyways, in '32 I hooked up with Mister Alex to deal off all my pelts."

"Then how did you do?"

"That's when I started to do well, money wise. The boss, Mr. Alex, had a good market for plews and robes for a while, and with his persuasive ways and business sense and connections, it freed me up to do what I did best, bringing in pelts."

"What's a plew?"

"Finished out beaver pelt. We did pretty well for a few years there, had regular trading parley sites along the Canadian and other places. But officials in Taos were always asking bigger and bigger bribes, so we started using Bent's fort later on, around 34, I reckon, for transporting robes back up the Sante Fe trail to the St. Louis offices. So I hunted fresh meat for them as well, out on the Arkansas. I had a cache of silver buried in the hills where nobody could find it at that time, and every season I'd add to it, amazing to think of it now, broke as I am."

"We've got plenty of silver, Gabe. Enough for a fresh start. I've been hoarding it for years."

"Yep, I figured there was some reason why that saddlebag was so heavy. Not to mention yer guard dog in it."

"Well, how long did you trade with them before things went sour?"

"Let's see, I joined the Comancheros whole heart in 1832 when the bottom fell out of the beaver pelt market, and my dreams of being a free trapper went sailing off with the wind. I'as working for Mister Alex full time by then, and he saw the market crash coming and steered me onto buffalo robes. Most of the easy beaver trappin' already been done anyway. It was a shinin' time but in the end I barely broke even on it, and lost as many plews as I brought in."

"But the robe trading was a different matter. We'd head out from Taos through the Cimarron canyon, then down the Canadian, several times a year, to trade with the Comanche for finished robes, both with hair and without, and ta get buffalo meat as well. My gal would dry the buff meat and we'd have meat all winter to go with the beans and corn. Or if I got it from the Nokonis, their woman had it dried perfectly and done into a powered form that you could just add to yore stew. I did venison hunting on the side, cougar hunting, and some guide work, and translating. And I always had the black-smithin' when I settled inta Taos for the winter."

"I see, Taos, you and mister Alex were bringing in the buffalo robes and keeping warm in winter, huh?"

"Yep. By '33 we had a pretty good holt on the market and were collecting robes by the hundreds, spring and fall, with me making really good money first time in my life, thanks to Mister Alex. I had me a little adobe in Taos with a Spanish gal in it to winter over, a thriving blacksmithin' business, plenty of Taos lightning, good smoke, plenty of good grub, hunting in the most beautiful country the Creator ever put a hand to, and fandangos."

"Sounds like tall cotton, wasn't it?"

"Yassir. Them was shinin' times for me and yore Pa. Mister Alex was the cleverest man I ever met, as far as making the most of the situation. The Robideaux brothers was swarming all over the mountains with traps then, so 'fore long Alex had them Spanish customs officials believing he was a

Robideaux brother. Robinoix. Robideaux. Sounds pert near
alike if you say it fast with a French accent, huh? Like
Bobidough and Robinoix, huh? He kept 'em confused,
blabbering Cajun French and Creole Spanish at them lickity split,
then change trading locations, change his appearance, change
his tactics. That's when they ever saw him, which wasn't much.
He kept a low profile and made money, that man, I swear. I
always said he was one of a kind, 'til you come along."

"Where did he stay, in the mountains? He told me once
about an underground house."

"Yep. Had him a dugout north of Taos that was a regular
underground house, had some Pueblo Indians build it for him out
of rock and adobe and big Ponderosa logs for the ceiling, then
covered it with earth and sod, right in the side of an arroyo whar
nobody would see it lessen they was searching for it, and maybe
not then. Had him a corral in that arroyo where he kept the
stock he traded, underground caches for pelts and ice storage,
gals to run the house and gardens, and his own still. Kept a keg
of cold beer on tap for the free trappers he traded with. While
the Robideaux brothers was gettin' drunk in the Taos cantinas
and shooting their mouths off, ending up getting their pelts
confiscated more often than not, Mr. Alex laid low and traded
hand over fist, sending big loads back to St. Louie and to Bent's
fort and then down the Arkansas river to New Orleans. Hell, he
told me they was ending up in Paris, France, where he ended up
sending you for book larnin', I recollect. If he ever got in a bind
with the Alcaldes, he'd bribe those Spanish officials with fine
brandy, ceegars, silver, or Andalusian horses, which nobody else
could match. That man could talk the Alcalde out of his pistola if
he put his mind to it. We traded for hundreds of fine buff robes
every year with the Comanches on the Canadian."

"And what happened to turn you against the Comanche
so hard?"

"Wal, Comanchero business was always sorta risky.
Even though we were friendly with several bands, there was
always the chance of running into a rogue raiding party, or the
damn Kiowas, or Spanish officials who'd confiscate all your
goods and money. They even confiscated my knives once, said
I didn't pay the tradesman tax. Fuggin' thieves in fancy-pants is
what they are. They was shore 'nuff prejudiced against white
trappers."

"Give a fool a uniform and he thinks he's meant to issue orders and take what he wants," said Josh.

Gabe took another snort. "I'll drink to that. Oh yeah, dealing with them Spanish officials was always a chore, though Mister Alex usually took care of that end. But it was always touch and go. So I began ta saving my money to get me a place of my own. I tried to get one outside Taos, near the Ranchos, but them Spanish is so danged quirky and persnickety against American trappers, and ya never know where ya stand with em. Mister Alex told me ta stay thar with him, but I wanted a place of my own, outside of the range of nosy Spanish officials."

"So, lets see, long about 18 and 38 I went down to south Texas to help drive a herd of steers to New Orleans for Mr. Alex, and on the way down there I spotted a place in the Blanco River valley, northeast of San Antone about fifty miles, by a big spring at the base of a tall limestone cliff, surrounded by them huge-butted cypress trees with their roots all coiling round the rocks, gushing the clearest water you ever seen, with good grass along the river. It seemed like a spot right out of my dreams, and Texas was no longer ruled by Spanish officials like Taos was, so I went ahead and bought it with money Mr. Alex loaned me, which I paid back later when I dug up the silver cache outside Taos."

"And you stayed in Texas then?"

"Waugh, wish I had. Not then. I hired a Mexican couple to build a jacal and raise some goats there, start a garden and such. The next year after a good trading season I went down with my earnings and built me a little stone homestead out of the rock on the place. Gathered it off the property and drug it in on rawhide travois skids pulled by mules. Got lime and cement from New Braunfels and sand from the riverbed. Built a proper double rock walled cabin, and a solid stone barn. Got me a German gal from a farmstead on the Guadalupe, and settled down raising stock and vegetables there until 1840, when the big Comanche raid on Victoria and Linnville happened."

"That ended it?"

"Yep. It was a short shinin' time, probably the best in this ole coon's life. That gal was tough as rawhide, worked dawn til dusk, and durned pretty too. I had a smith shop, and extra work from Alex driving herds from south Texas ta New Orleans. We made a go of it thar, and it was mighty nice, living on that clear gurgling water with the big spring just a boiling out of that cliff."

"Sounds like a fine place."

"Shore was. That Blanco River was lined with pecan trees, I was able to hunt buffalo up north of Austin, and we had a good couple of years there with the gardens and stock, but that raiding Buffalo Hump ended it all."

"But how did that raid affect you up on the Blanco, isn't it far north of Linnville? I thought all that took place in south Texas, closer to where we're going. Town of Victoria, I thought?"

"Wal yeah, most of it did, but Buffalo Hump gathered up over twelve hundred warriors up on the Llano Estacado and led them down the Blanco valley to make the raid. It's a narrow valley without too many settlers at the time, so they tried to sneak down that way, with lots of good springs for drinking water."

A flash of lightening struck, followed immediately by a crackle and boom that made them both cringe.

"Damn, that was close," said Josh.

"On the hilltop, one o them tall trees, I reckon. Why we're here in this hole."

"What set them off on this big raid, anyway, since yal had friendly trade relations with them up north?"

"Wal, they didn't come to hate Texans til around 18 and 40, I believe it was. Til that time they sorta liked the Texicans like they did the Mexicans, as folks to grow livestock for them to steal. They was getting back at the Texans for the Council House fight in San Antone, where a bunch of their sub-chiefs were killed at a parley over captives."

"How'd that happen?"

"Wal, lemme recollect the particulars now, gotta get this right. Don't want ta leave nothin' out like some do.'

"Well?"

"The southern Comanches was supposed ta bring in all their white captives and they only brought in one pore disfigured and bruised-up lil gal with her nose plumb burnt down to the bone from fire sticks, and said they trade captives one at a time, and 'how do ya like that answer?" They was talking through an interpreter who fled the room after relaying that answer. So that riled up the folks in San Antone, seeing that Matilda Lockhart gal like that, and hearing her tale of prolonged abuse and torture with glowing coals, and anyway the Penatekas was supposed to bring in all the captives. Matilda told the women thar about plenty more in the camps, and horrible abuse. She tole Mary Maverick and the women who attended her."

"What did the Texans do?"

"Hell, this was under Lamar's government, and he already hated Indians, far as I can figure. They tried to clamp down on all the sub-chiefs that came to parley, hold 'em hostage to get the other captives back. Some wanted to kill 'em on the spot for what they done to that lil gal. The Texans was feelin' plumb wrathy over it on account of figuring all the captives was tortured like tha Lockhart gal. Of course these sub-chiefs only came in for presents anyway, and tried to bolt rather than get jailed, fighting with their knives. A Comanche will never surrender. Once tha fight starts, hits to the death."

"So they tried to fight their way out of a building?"

"Yep, drew knives and tried it, and died for it. A close quarters fight ensued, with point blank firing, the end result was a general slaughter of the Comanches and a couple of white men killed too. They kept the woman and kids who came in and traded 'em back for white captives, later on. Anyway, the whole Comanche nation hated Texans from that day, and lots of captives were tortured to death in revenge."

"Was this Buffalo Hump there?"

"Hell no, he already hated the whites, and wouldn't meet with 'em. Buffalo Hump had big medicine then, already railing against the whites. and just looking for a reason to unite the Comanche against them. The northern buffalo Comanche done seen how contact with the white man had decimated the southern bands, with diseases, whiskey, and all."

"What was the upshot of the Council House fight?"

"Wal, it warn't good...and hit resulted in lots of captives getting' tortured ta death in revenge. After the council house fight, that Buffalo Hump ranged all over the Llano Estacado, rounding up a whole bunch of raiders to go down and drive out all the whites in a general war, burn the coastal landing spots, take the land back. He considered it a betrayal for Texans to kill Comanches who went to a parley. Just like I considered it a betrayal for Comanches to burn me out after treating 'em fair for years as a Comanchero. Like you felt about them federals. Betrayal draws the deepest revenge, seems ta me. Sorta like a dog biting the hand that feeds it."

"I know what you mean there. So they just happened to pick your valley to come down out of the hills?"

"Wal, I reckon so....same reason I did, springs and grass. That Blanco river valley is lined with springs and good campsites in tiny side canyons. Seems like the underground is full of creeks too, so thar's lots of springs, and a big spring comes busting out of the ground at San Marcos that you won't believe the size of until you see it. Comanches know all the springs and watering holes over all of Texas and northern Mexico."

"So of course they all came to the big spring and pastures by my house, probably been stopping there for a century or more. I always knew it was a risk living that far north of San Antone, but I figured I could parley with any small hunting parties, with all my experience as a Comanchero, and knowing the customs and lingo a bit. Little did I imagine that the biggest war party of Comanches ever assembled would come right by my homestead. They wiped out everything, kilt my wife instead of taking her captive, kilt my helpers, and all my stock, even my milk goat, left me smoke and ashes, like you was done to back in Louisiana."

"They burnt your stone cottage?"

"Wal, the cypress shake and timber roof I suppose, to drive folks out and kill 'em. The rock walls had all cracked and turned black and pink from the heat of the timbers burning. It whar a gruesome sight ta come home and see."

"Where were you when they attacked?"

"I was out chasing stock in the canyons on the other side of the ridge at the time. When I got home and saw what they done, I hightailed it over that ridge called the Devil's backbone into the Guadalupe valley and headed south as fast as I could to try to warn folks. I hit the prairies a bit east of the German settlement thar, New Braunfels, and then headed southeast to try to cut ahead of them. But they was moving fast and was ahead of me when I got to the San Marcos river, so I followed 'em down and tried to raise the alarm when I could. The trail was so huge it was hard to believe. Nobody had ever heard of a raiding party that big. Nobody believed me at first, 'till they saw for themselves. Buffalo Hump was intending to kill all the whites with every warrior he could recruit."

"How could you take on so many?"

"Revolvers and ranger horseback attack. When we

finally got enough help together, with a lot of them Tonkawa scouts, at least a dozen of them, including the pap of John's Son, ole Coffee John, and lots of others, we jumped 'em on their way back from looting Linnville and capturing all the horses around Victoria, at Plum Creek, where I got the top-hat."

"I see, then you started killing Comanches? To get back at them for burning you out, killing your woman when you weren't there to protect her?"

"Wal, yeah, my blood was up for killin' 'em then, and I swore I'd put that Hump under, for what he done, and the rangers needed help tracking, which I was pretty good at. Of course, I was always a fair shot and could work on most anything metal, guns, wagons, horseshoes, what-all. So I joined up in San Antone and rode with the rangers a few years, mostly around San Antone and north of thar, the hill country, and finally up on the plains, hunting raiders and rescuing captives. Since I knew the whar-abouts of the good water on the staked plains, they came to me for scouting up thar after captives. Lean years they was, though."

"But I rode with some mighty good fellas, one name of John Coffee Hays was especially shining. Captain Jack. Not much on the big talk, but damn cool and effective when it came time for action. And he was a man who did his preparations and thinking on time. He trained us in horseback fighting before we went out, that's how I got to be a good pistol shot from horseback. But it was mighty risky all the time. Came close to being wolf meat plenty of times. And I did lots of Comanche killin' then. I got my fill of it. But there weren't no future nor profit in it 'cept venting my rage, and I finally tired of it after several years. Living in a rage is the worst thing that can happen to a man. It kills all the pleasure in life. I reckon I vented mine. And thar got to be too many massacres to stomach, on both sides."

"I got a feeling there's still quite a bit inside me, though it was hard to stomach being a sniper. That's when you went back to Taos and the staked plains?"

"Lets see, I recollect that I took part in the battle of Salado, fighting a Mexican invasion army, in September of 42, outside of San Antone, scouting with Captain Jack Hays, then rode with some other outfits that was not up to his standards for a few months after that. I had a couple of wounds bothering me then, slugs moving near my heart, so I packed it in and went to

San Antone to get the lead cut out. That was the end of my rangering days, and I was laid up thar for a while, then headed back north for them shinin' mountains."

The lightening and thunder had moved on as a steady rain pelted the little tent. "Can I fix you another hot toddy while the coals are still warm, Gabe?"

"I'd shore appreciate another, they's mighty good ta settle my nerves. This is the first time I've been in the old Comanche stomping grounds since they had a holt of me, ya know, and it's stirring up some old memories that sort of wrench my gut and make me nervous. Sons o bitches takes such pleasure in torture, never could figure that. Each one of them would come take a little slice on my forehead while my hand was over them gol-danged coals. Now them's the guy's I'd like to introduce to my blade, I guarantee ya." The grizzled mountain man took out his knife and sharpening stone and began rubbing the edge with it.

"I can understand that now. So how did you end up in their clutches again? That was back up on the staked plains, wasn't it?'

"Yep, up on the Canadian, heading back for Taos with wagon loads of robes."

"You went back up to Taos?"

"After we rescued some captives, a couple of young gals name of French, up on the Llano Estacado, and failed to save some others." The old weathered face wrinkled into a grimace.

"I saw one massacre too many, and I had to get away from it for a while, and I went on back up to Taos and hooked up with Mister Alex again, got back with my senorita Lupita, and got my smithin' going again."

"What massacre was that?"

"Some so called rangers after plunder wiped out a whole Lipan Apache village, mostly woman and children. A lot of white border trash took the Indian wars as an opportunity to massacre and plunder. They was as bad as the savages."

"So....after several years of killing Comanches you went back north to trade with them?"

"Yep, different bands though. I did a lot of scouting and hunting for meat back then too."

"Scouting for who?"

"Army, wagon trains, Rangers, miners heading west, you

name it."

"You kept scouting for Ranger parties up onto the staked plains?"

"Wal we was tracking and killing the ones that raided the settlements and carried off captives. The Comanches of the Llano Estacado weren't doing that at the time. They was living their old life on the plains, just them and the buffalo and their horses. So lets see, it was fall of '44, and I engaged in the Comanchero trading business again, gathering buff robes by the hundreds from various bands. That worked out pretty well for a few years, and when things got risky thar I went to guiding miners to California in '49 and '50, and then some up into Colorado."

Gabe took another long draw from his pipe and continued. "Then I guided some traders in the spring of fifty, out onto the staked plains, and I got caught by a rogue bunch of Penetakas and Kiowas out on the Llano near Tule Canyon, and you know the rest of the story....it's whar I got this hand crippled up and tha head scar, plus a few others."

"I know they tortured you, but you never told me the details."

"Waugh. You'd might as well know now, and understand why lots of old timers carried a cartridge filled with arsenic. They just beat me with their bows and lances the first day, then started the slicing the next day, on my belly and head. They was slow scalping me while they built a small fire under my left hand, then started dropping hot coals in it. They told me they wasn't gonna burn my feet because I would be doing some running later on. They'd done tortured me for about an hour that morning when Mister Alex busted into their camp with guns a-blazing and saved me right when they was about done slicing my forehead to pull my red haired scalp off. The bucks had gotten half drunk on some whiskey other traders had lost to them,and was gambling with each other on who would get it, being as they prized red hair and I had a bushy mane back then. Since I could talk the lingo they delighted in telling me what else they were gonna do to me, involving cutting a slit in my lower belly and pulling my guts out it to wrap around my head after they scalped me, or cutting my prick off and stuffing it into my mouth after they done run me down on horses after my footrace, nice sorta stuff like that, trying to work up the fear spirit so they could steal my power."

"They shore was carrying on about who was gonna get my red scalp for their lance, though. Yassir. One of them got too close and I got my raw-hided hands around his neck and strangled him to death before the others could get me off him. That's bad medicine for him."

"Hellfire, Gabe. Were you trying to get them to kill you?"

"Why hell yes. I'd rather they scalp me after I'as dead."

Josh burst out a chuckle at the old mountain man. "They admired your red scalp, huh? I barely remember copper colored hair in it when you came to Louisiana. I was scared of you back then."

"Oh it turned gray pretty quick after that. I won't have made it if it weren't for Mr. Alex. I owe him my life. They had ridden for two days of searching and skirmishing by the time they found us. He shot a buffalo calf and gave me the warm milk from the stomach to keep me alive. He took me in to Bent's Fort, then back down the Arkansas to the plantation when I could travel that far, down the river trail in a bumpy wagon, I'll never forget that ride, and we met while yore ma was healing me up. You was a smart little schoolboy in fancy pants back then. Then he set me ta teaching you. And I been badgering you ever since, huh?"

"Damn. That's for certain, and a good job of it you did. Quite an adventurous life, Gabe. I just thought you were a grumpy old blacksmith and shooting master. Ran away to the mountains at 17, huh? I remember you talking me out of running away when I was about that age. You did what you wanted to do, I did what Alex wanted me to do. I thought you were old time Texian, at the Alamo and all that."

"Waugh. Alamo was before I got thar. I knew more about fighting even back then ta avoid getting stuck in an ole church with the Mexican army on its way. Of course the fools failed to have scouts out to realize they was coming."

"And for all these years you never told me about being a Comanchero."

"Wal, people has heard some bad things about Comancheros, so I didn't advertise it too much. I never done anything I'm ashamed of as a Comanchero, but people hears about trading guns and whiskey to the Indians and stuff such as that. Hell we traded foodstuffs, cooking utensils, livestock, and knives for buffalo robes, and ended up helping to find and rescue lots of captives. Never sold no guns nor whiskey to the Indians. They was getting guns from some-whars else, up north I think. Mostly worthless smooth-bore guns anyway, compared to what they do with a bow and arrow. And the last thing we wanted was to get 'em liquored up while we was in their camp trading, or after. If they got drunk they'd like as not ride in on ya and steal back everything they traded. No-sir, Whiskey plumb ruins Indians, and I never done gave 'em any. Robinoix Company has strict rules against it too, not to mention what Mister Alex would do if he found out."

"Gabe, I've got to say, you really impressed me today, with the show for the Tonkawas, how you buffaloed them. And now I think I understand you a little better, after what you just told me. I knew you'd spent time as a mountain man, from all your beaver-trapper slang, but never knew the whole story. You got burned out like I did."

"Yep, just like, and I know what you're goin' through."

"And you know a lot of trails that I haven't been on yet. And I'm sure glad we threw in together for this trip. Nobody I'd rather take on Texas with."

"Me too, pard. Looks like it was meant to be. LaPoint and McBride. Now let's get some shuteye so's we can make some miles tomorrow. I'm bout talked out."

"Alright then, why don't you quit sharpening that knife and relax?" replied Josh as he rolled to his side and began to doze off while the wind howled around the little knob they sheltered behind.

"Hell, that's what I'm doin'. I relax best with my blade sharp." Gabe was soon snoring. A steady cold rain pelted the shelter all night.

They slept like well-fed babes in a nest with their cozy bedding, Josh curled up around the warm little Chihuahua, and awoke to a clear sky and diminishing wind. The wood was all soaked, but a few coals glowed under the logs they had thrown on the fire, so they had a bit of hot coffee and warmed some grub, while the stock grazed the wet meadow. The leaves and twigs had been freshly rearranged by the rivulets of water coming off the hill. After the horses were well cared for by Josh, Gabe had the mules packed with all the possibles, and was ready to go.

They headed southwest across muddy fields, a cool breeze blowing steadily from the northwest, keeping them huddled in their sheepskin coats. Since they were leaving deep tracks, Gabe insisted on sheltering in woods to watch their back-trail at times.

The air was sparkling clean after the storm, and they felt glad to be alive on the rolling prairies. The Texas countryside was beautiful grassy range-land with scattered timber, with enough roll to make them a bit wary of who was hiding behind each small hill, but they pushed on to the southwest with the steady breeze blowing in their eyes. Gabe rode in the lead, trailing Josie. After a couple of hours Josh rode up beside him in a clear meadow.

"So how far you figure it is to the Guadalupe?" asked Josh.

"If memory serves, nearly forty miles. Prettiest river I ever saw. You will shore be surprised when you see it, though it may not be all clear and cool green like I described it to you yesterday, 'counta the storms....might be on a rise."

"But the ferry ought to be there still, huh?"

"Ah reckon."

They made good time but couldn't help leaving a clear trail on the soft ground, which tended to make Gabe nervous and more vigilant than usual even. Around noon the came upon a wide prairie that was well watered by joining streams, and they saw their first buffalo.

"Alright then, buffalo, feast yore eyes, thar they are, best meat in the world, and likely buffalo Indians could be close. Keep a sharp eye out, you got those glasses handy, let's get on the little rise upwind of 'em and look around. Don't top the hill, though, we'll leave the stock in that little draw and crawl up for a look-see."

They did as Gabe indicated, and took a good while scanning for movement in all directions while Gabe filled his pipe and lit up a smoke.

"Well, I wanted to see this all my life, or at least since you moved in and started telling me about them. Do you think this is part of the big herd?"

"Probably just a small bunch, stragglers on their own hunt for grass. Oh boy, if this don't bring back memories of Cibolero times. 'Cept I ain't gonna use a lance or even that bartered bow.

Get the Spencer. We'll just pick off a fat cow for meat, replenish our supply, nothing to it. Do it from here. It ain't but a hundred and fifty yards to them cows there."

"Alright, I'll get it while you scan the area for riders."

"Alright then, and get that whetstone, would ya? We need to make a quick job of skinning and quartering up the meat, then move on a ways to build a fire and dry it while we rest the horses tomorrow. I'd like to get it done and get across the Guadalupe by evening camp."

Josh fetched what they needed while Gabe kept scanning in all directions with the binoculars. When he returned with the Spencer repeater, he had a metal shooting rest and the whetstone as well as the bag of ammo.

"Here, let me load yer first for ya, hot damn, you gonna get yer first buff. Take that cow on the edge of that bunch thar. The one turned sideways. Put it in behind the last rib thar, angle it into her heart. We don't want to do no chasing."

Josh took the Spencer and laid down the buffalo cow with ease. The rest of the group hardly took notice. The shot echoed off the rolling prairie and they held firm and scanned for riders for a few minutes. Seeing none, they went down and quickly skinned and quartered up the meat, packing it all onto the mules after the small herd browsed off.

Gabe was really nervous and moved quickly with his freshly honed blades, and in twenty minutes they were packed and heading southwest towards the Guadalupe. The mules were not happy with the huge load of buffalo meat added to their packs, and did some protesting. Josh was nervous because Gabe was nervous, but he tried to hide it.

"Shuddup, ye ornery mules, that's what we got ya fer, to haul stuff. Damnation. I'm glad we didn't run into any Comanche, hunting that bunch of buffs. It's just a separated fragment of the southern herd, I reckon. But whar thar's buffs, you can be sure thar's buff Indians, specially in winter when there's still grass down here. Hell fire, Josh. We got enough meat to last for a while if we can get to a place to dry it out. This cold air should keep it from spoiling 'til we do," said Gabe. "And we can have fresh buff hump and tongue for dinner.

"We're gonna get across the river before camping, huh?"

"Yep, I reckon, if we can."

They continued on across the rolling prairies in a

southwesterly direction until they approached the small but old town of Gonzales and the Guadalupe River. Bypassing the town, they headed out for the river crossing, noticing that the ground was not as wet here, as if the big downpour had bypassed it. The tall prairie grass had been laid down by the wind, but the footing was better, and they made easier time with the mules fully loaded with fresh meat. A line of huge trees, pecans, oaks, willows, and cypress lined the big river, which they could see from a distance.

They got to the river ferry around sunset, paid a man named Duncan in silver coin, and crossed over without problems. The water was not red and cloudy with silt like the other rivers they had crossed, but just a pale green color with a little bit of turbidity from recent rains upriver. The riverbank was lined with huge trees and thick brush, and the water looked inviting to the grubby travelers.

Pushing the stock a few more miles south, they found a likely spot for a camp with plenty of grass and a draw to fort up in, at the headwaters of a seasonal creek. The wind had let up to a slight breeze by the time they made camp, though the temperature was dropping rapidly, so they made a lean-too with a fire facing it and had a hot meal of fresh buffalo meat and bread in relative comfort. They slept behind logs laid with a rifle slit in between them.

The next day Gabe awoke early and made a dutch oven full of sourdough biscuits, which they had with the last of the coffee and buffalo tenderloin. Then they rested the stock and let them graze while they sliced and smoked the meat over a fire of oak and pecan wood. The pecan gave off a delicious smell and a good taste to the dried meat, according to Gabe. By careful attention to their racks and the heat of the fire, they were able to accomplish a lot of meat curing. Gabe was of course an expert in this, and took the lead while showing Josh how to do it.

After their evening meal they settled back for a hot rum toddy and sharing a smoke from Gabe's pipe filled with his special kinnickinnick.

"Well, a whole day of travel without a scrape, then a good day of resting the stock and jerky making...and I got to see buffalo and shoot one the first time. We're doing alright," said Josh.

"Shore nuff. I guess I should have gone inta Gonzales to

get some more dumplin's dust and such, but my mind was sorta reeling from old memories, so I took my druthers and just forted up here."

"Never a careless moment, eh old timer?"

"Carelessness weeds out the fools in Indian country."

"So what happened to you here at Gonzales?"

"Wal, I told ya about the big raid in 40, when Buffalo Hump came through the Blanco River valley and burnt me out thar by the big springs."

"So that battle's been preying on your mind?"

"Naw. That was a battle we won. But the thing that was festering in my mind was remembering having ta tell my wife's folks that she'd been put under by Comanches. They lived in Gonzales thar, and hits a painful memory of seeing her ma just crumple when I had ta go in and tell her. Woman never was the same after that. That's when I took a vow to finish Buffalo Hump or die a-tryin. "

"But you never caught him?"

"Naw, I never. Hunted him for three or four years til I had my fill of killing Comanches. Rescued a few captives though. But I never got to that Buffalo Hump's band. That warn't his name anyhow, white folks didn't want to translate his real name, which means man with a hard-on that won't go down."

"Chief Hard-on?"

"Yep. He had a hard on for raiding after that Council House fight, that's for sure. I still might kill him if I got the chance, never know. Like you with that Yankee Captain, I ain't clinging to the thought, but I'd stick a knife into his heart without regret. Son of a bitch, I didn't have nothing to do with the Council House fight, I was up trading friendly with the Comanche on the plains at the time. But he'd set his teeth on wiping out all the Texans. If they hadn't been so greedy for horses, mules, and loot, they might have pulled it off. But they was an undisciplined gaggle loaded with loot and spread out with a giant horse herd when we jumped 'em at Plum Creek. That's the reason we whipped 'em, that and charging with revolvers."

Chapter Six: Helena Hand-basket

They stayed in the hidden camp and rested their horses while drying the buffalo meat over mesquite fires for a couple of days, taking time to explore the countryside and take swims in the clear Guadalupe river. Josh loved it there, the lush river valley and the refreshing water that was not murky and stagnant like the bayous he grew up with. Gabe seem preoccupied with old memories, tending the meat and the fire.

After getting lean from the long ride with not much to eat but dried sausage, cheese, sometimes beans, and bread, they obtained more supplies in Gonzales and feasted on sourdough biscuits with real butter and honey, black beans with pork seasoning, real eggs, buffalo meat, canned peaches and pears, and sugared coffee.

 For the stock they obtained more grains and molasses to make the strong feed that supplemented the grass and kept them going strong. Joshua spent lots of time currying and caring for the horses, tending to their sore backs and minor scrapes on their legs, being thankful to them for their long and strenuous trip. Gabe noticed that whenever Josh became inactive, a sad look overtook his face, and he went to care for the horses. He determined to kill that captain who murdered Josh's mother, if he could, so Josh could let it go.

Leon the big jack mule had stone bruises on his hooves, so Joshua doctored them with some of his mother's healing salve. The big jack, who liked to annoy Gabe, responded to Josh with affection. The older scout spent his time around the fire, tending to the smoking meat, and sharpening his knives on a piece of green Pennsylvania sandstone he carried. It was a good camp for recovery, with no intruders or sign of Indians, but on the morning of the third day they were well-rested, and they headed out southwest as the sun rose to their backs. The chillness of the earlier days had been replaced with a mild south wind. They felt fresh and provisioned with plenty of good buff jerky.

Gabe rode in the lead, trailing Josie, his senses alert for any sign of riders. He figured there was about forty miles to the little ranch near Alamita, on the San Antonio river, a long day's ride. Josh rode along about twenty yards behind, trailing Leon, who wasn't sure he liked traveling again, laden with buffalo meat, after the nice rest. Leon liked to bray and heehaw until Josie joined in, then he settled down after a few minutes of raucous noise and did his job.

The rolling prairies were fairly clear and grassy except for scattered oaks and thick forests along the creeks. They saw no Indians nor buffalo, only a group of five riders in the distance once, and they laid up and rested until the dust was settled, then headed southwest again. At sunset, with the easy pace they had taken, they had gone around twenty miles and found a floodplain around the junction of two creeks that was full of good grass for the horses, and trees to hide in, so they made what they hoped would be their last camp on the ground. Josh tended the stock while Gabe made a hot fire with dry oak and mesquite branches and prepared dinner.

Gabe pulled out his dutch oven and made biscuits again, and they had another big meal while the stock munched away at their new feedbag mixture. After dinner and dessert of canned peaches, they doused the fire and watched the stars for a while. Gabe pulled out the whiskey bottle he had acquired in Gonzales and put his special kinnickinnick mixture in his pipe. Taking a draw from each, he passed each to Joshua in turn. In a while they where feeling pretty mellow after several days of having no trouble, and their goal within a day's ride. The night was clear and only a little cool, and the stars seemed just a few feet overhead.

"I don't know what you got in that pipe, but it sure relaxes me. So, how far do you figure it is to the ranchito?" asked Josh.

"Wal, in a free country like Texas a man's smokin' mixture is his own business, ah reckon. Ain't far now, 'bout twenty miles or less. I figure we'll go to the Alamita crossing to get over the river if it's up like the rest have been. Thar usta be a lil Mexican town and trading post thar, 'cause it's on the cart trail from the coast to San Antone, and on the Chihuahua trail. I'm sure hoping Pancho is still there at the rancho; last I heard of him was when Mister Alex brought that herd from here in 60. He and his little woman Rosita had the place fixed up nice then, 'cordin to Mr. Alex. Course, I ain't seen Pancho since '44, when I headed back to Taos."

"But you spent time with them back then, when you were in Texas?"

"Oh yeah. I used the ranch for a sort of headquarters during the several years I rode after Comanches. 'Bout the only safe nest I had back then. We built a small place out of boards split from post oak trees. It was sturdy enough. Not a bad spot...'cept for the damned rattlesnakes. Lost two horses to rattlesnakes, and had to cut the heads off of several inside the jacal. Later on we built a tighter building with material Mr. Alex got sent up from Indianola, the port down south. And we made a big corral to hold the horses and mules in. The herds we gathered in a big pasture down by the river."

"And this Alamita, it's the only town nearby?"

"Wal, no, come ta think on it, Mr. Alex told me thar was a new Polish settlement nearby, across the river, I think he called it Panna Maria. Bunch of Catholic Poles trying to escape the Prussians or some such, settled thar in the mid fifties. They was having a tough time of it, he said, so they may be gone by now. That was years ago, and they had a bad drought. He said thar was another town started up too, on the cart trail. Can't think of the name of it, though."

"So how will we get supplies when we need them?"

"Wal, like I said, the ole cart trail from Indianola to San Antone runs right by thar, and connects to the Chihuahua trail nearby, so it ain't all that isolated. San Antone is just about sixty miles north."

"Alright. I'm looking forward to getting there. This here is beautiful countryside. I could have settled right by that Guadalupe river without much trouble, if we didn't have this rancho to go to. One more day of riding sounds just right for me, my butt and the horses' backs need more rest."

"Yeah buddy, my ole butt ain't what it used ta be for these long rides. I'm ready to take a little rest myself."

They both lay back and stretched, comfortable on their buffalo robe pallets, relaxed and silently staring at the stars overhead, each wondering what they would find at their destination, until sleep overcame them.

When Josh awoke, Gabe had breakfast ready, buffalo steak and sourdough biscuits, with the smell of fresh coffee wafting over the little camp under the spreading live oaks.

"Morning, Gabe. Smells good. Biscuits already done, how long you been up?"

"Too long. Hell, I drank too much whiskey and woke

early with the need to piss, which I did. You'll understand when ya get ta my age. Then I was too worked up in the mind to get back ta sleep, so I tossed for a while, then got up and made biscuits. How do you want your steak?"

"Just like you made it last night. That coffee sure smells good. You're a wonder round the camp, aren't ya, ole coon?" Josh knelt by the glowing coals and used his glove to handle the metal coffeepot, pouring himself a cup and re-filling Gabe's for him.

Gabe was intent on frying two buffalo steaks to just the right condition. "I'm getting back in the swing of things after living under roofs for over a decade. The sooner we get thar to the rancho and hole up for a while, the sooner I can relax a bit."

"So this caretaker couple, Pancho and Rosita, they have no idea that we might show up, fugitives from the law?"

"Naw, not a clue, 'cept it wouldn't be the first time I darkened their doorway unexpectedly, and it's always been 'mi casa su casa'. So don't concern yourself bout that much. Pancho and I was tight back in the forties, and he rode with me after captives a couple of times til his esposa put her foot down on that. That was after she overheard him thanking me over and over for saving his life as we polished off some tequila after a long hunt. Don't worry. They'll make us welcome."

"Will there be enough room for us?"

"Oh yeah, it's a good sized house, three big rooms. We made it out of lumber, there being no rock around thar worth usin'. Mr. Alex got the lumber on a trading deal, got it hauled up from Indianola and hired a crew from San Antone to build it. Also got a small pole barn and a couple of jacals, which we stayed in during the early times. Full of rattlers, though. Never killed so many snakes in my life."

"So that's where you got your snake chopping practice, huh? I was impressed with that swipe you took at that cottonmouth back after the ferry crossing on the Sabine, chopped his head off in one lick."

"I keep a sharp knife and dry powder, always have. Careless means disaster for a scout. Here, put yore plate out, here's yore steak, and the biscuits is in the oven. Thar's some of that honey for them from Gonzales too, and sugar for the coffee. And for desert I got some hot peaches to put over the biscuits. Eat up, it's gonna be a long day with a cold lunch. After yore grievin' time is done, ya got ta put tha past behind, and look upstream."

"I intend to." Josh dug into the hot food with the vigor of a young and hungry man, while Gabe watched and grinned. Finally he spoke, as Josh finished his steak.

"Hey, LaPoint, you used to smile at times. We doing alright so far, huh? Still alive, ain't scraped up against federals or Indians we couldn't face down."

"One more day."

"One more day, and we gotta stay sharp. Anything could still go wrong. Comanches might be down this far after the southern herd remnants that are wintering down here. Keep a sharp lookout, stay strung out, don't raise much dust, and don't top the rises."

"Alright Gabe, steady on. Sharp lookout, stay hidden. I got it. Good food. Remind me to take you if I ever go camping again, huh?"

"You can count on it, pard."

After they ate, the sun was lighting up the eastern sky a golden orange color that lit the passing clouds in brilliant yellow, and Josh tended to the horses while Gabe packed the camp gear on the mules. With a light breeze from the south they plodded on towards the southwest, with Gabe in the lead again. He no longer used his compass to chart the path, for his old memories of roving Texas were revived, and he knew the way to go, creek bed to riverbed.

They set a faster pace than the day before, both of them excited to get there. The Andalusians both had a smooth and comfortable fast walking pace, but the mules had to be towed with some difficulty, for they did not like to walk that fast, especially laden with buffalo meat as they were. They would go a certain speed, above which they would start balking and braying. The constant tugging was tiresome, so both men were ready to take a lunch break and rest a while by the time the sun got overhead. The sun had warmed the air into the fifties, and sprouts of green were showing up in places. The trees begin to change from broad leafed shade trees into smaller mesquite trees and scrubby sticker bushes with tiny leaves that did not give up much moisture to the constant wind. And the wind was constant, blowing gusty from the south.

Joshua noticed that a lot of the trees and bushes had

thorns on them as they moved into dryer country and the wind picked up. Soon the winds were rolling tumbleweeds across their path, making the horses nervous as dust and dry grass stung the eyes of the riders. When they crossed a small creek, they saw a whole swarm of baby cottonmouths nearby, coiling around in the warm sandbank. Josh nudged Scorpio into an instant full gallop, tugging hard on the tow rope to hurry the mule. After they cleared the danger, Josh caught up with Gabe in a flat prairie area to talk.

"That nearly pulled my arm out of socket, tugging on a panicked mule. What a nest of snakes!"

"What's that?"

Josh rode alongside so he could speak into Gabe's good ear. "Say, you already mentioned rattlesnakes, cannibals, and Comanches, and now I see the trees are turning more towards thorn bushes in spots, and a hundred cottonmouths down by the creek. Anything else you didn't tell me about this place?"

"Welcome ta South Texas, son. Lots o biting snakes and stinging insects and thorny bushes down whar we be goin'. Just be thankful it ain't August and over 100 degrees with a hot wind blowing a prairie fire at us."

"Well, I guess I am. You still aiming for that Alamita crossing and trading post?'

"Yep."

"Well, let's try to get some better liquor than that swill we had last night. I'll treat us to the best we can get, in celebration of journey's end. How about New Orleans Sazerac brandy? Didn't you used to sweeten alkali water with that on the staked plains?"

"Wal, we shore did. I guess you listened some. But you ain't much of a drinker, Josh, what'd you care?"

"I think I might just get drunk with you when we finally get there, Gabe. It's been quite a journey. Longest I ever made. And lots of it in the dark and rain, with dim prospects of surviving."

"Speakin' o rain, think we're in for another shower."

"Yep, that's right. Time for oilcloth again."

"So this is yore longest trip, huh? I reckon so. You was in on moving that herd from Galveston when you was a teenager, and showed what you could do with a remuda, but this is further. I figure we come over five hundred miles, in about forty days, give or take a few. And that was filled with night riding and hidin' and stoppin' and backtrackin' who knows what all. Not bad for an ole fart and young whipper-snapper, huh?"

"You kept track of the days?"

"Yep, sorta, that is, I mark 'em in a journal"

"I started a journal too, of life in Texas."

"Yep, I seen ya scribblin' in it. I got aholt of a newspaper at Gonzales. We left the Teche that dark rainy night round the first week of March. This is the middle of April. Spring coming soon, and it gets hot down here by June, I mean really hot. Ain't gonna be easy, starting over, ya know."

"Yeah, but I'm a free man, the first time in my life. I've got no master setting a course for me now. I'm ready for a fresh start, no matter how hard it is. We lost a hell of a lot, losing LaPoint horse farms. I aim to build another one."

"Wal then, let's get 'er done, now drop back and spread out like I tole ya, and don't raise much dust, I gotta spooky Comanche feeling starting ta creep over me, and I don't know if I'm just too tired and imagining, or if it's real." Josh did as Gabe told him, and became hyper-vigilant again, for the old man's hunches were usually right. Suzette seemed to sense his mood and wanted to climb onto his lap and sniff the air, which she did. Scorpio and Buck were pricking their ears in all directions with nervous alertness as well.

Within an hour they came around a small rise and spotted more buffalo, a small herd of perhaps forty animals, shaggy in their shedding winter coats, grazing on the tall dry golden grass with reddish tops. Gabe quickly backtracked and urged Josh to spin around and follow him, his face flushed and his eyes bugged out, his forehead pouring sweat as he jerked on the lead line pulling the balky Josie.

"Get out of sight, I think I saw a hunting party, need to get out the field glasses and take a peek."

They put their stock in a little copse of trees and crept to a small rise to look through the field glasses. Gabe was right, for there was a band of horseback Indian hunters on the other side of the small herd, preparing to run them and gather meat. The sweat was pouring from his brow onto the glasses, and he had to keep wiping them with his bandana. They watched from their hidden spot under a low creeping mesquite trunk as the Indians expertly surrounded the back end of the herd with riders. Then at some signal they all charged the herd from the back, got them running in a mass, and began to take them down around the edges, as the small herd took alarm and began to run with a sound like thunder.

It was fascinating to watch as the expert horsemen took down one animal after another with a well placed lance or arrow, or both. As soon as the buffalo went down the women came scurrying up to begin the field dressing. Within five minutes there was ten buffalo on the ground, with the herd thundering off west, raising a column of dust, being followed by the team of hunters, who were still taking them down in sprawling rolling heaps of fur and dust.

"Damn, that's some great team hunting, huh?" said Josh. "Really impressive. Arrows and lances into the heart, meat processing starts immediately, they got it down to an art, huh?"

"Oh yeah, Comanche is the best at all things connected with buffalo. They had a hundred years or more ta get their techniques worked out. Their dried buff powder is the best protein a man can carry horseback. And they usually know where buff will be at each time of the year."

"They're Comanche? You can tell thru the glasses?"

"Yep. And my neck hairs is bristling while my stomach churns. Josh, for now I seen enough. It reminds me of the time I was a Cibolero and used to hunt with 'em, and I want to be down there with a lance, but I know that will never happen again, and it's a sore feeling to be locked outa a joy because of hatred, but that's the way it is. Right now I feel fear, envy, and hatred, and it's a bitter mix. So let's go. Now is the perfect time for us to detour south and get the hell out of here. Let's go while they're busy getting their larders full. They probably won't have riders out, since they're all needed for the hunt."

Josh had never seen Gabe acting so nervous, his ruddy face covered with sweat on a cool day, so he quickly complied. Gabe rode fast as he could tow Josie without her balking and braying, and Josh noticed the hand that held the lead rope was resting on his pistol. They backtracked for a while and then headed south for a few miles before turning back west. Gabe was grim-lipped and silent when Josh rode up beside him for a while, so Josh dropped back and rode on in silence, tugging at Napoleon to get him to keep up with the fast pacing Scorpio. If Gabe was nervous there was reason to be afraid.

In the afternoon they passed by several big creeks lined with trees, then saw the San Antonio river off to their right, defined by dense vegetation, so they followed it south. It was late afternoon when they approached the San Antonio river crossing where Gabe had remembered a Mexican trading post. Instead there was a town of board lumber, with a main street of false front retail establishments, and the muddy thoroughfare busy with wagons and mule trains. Gabe called a halt and sat on Buck with his hat in his hand, scratching his scar as Josh rode up.

"Is that Alamita?"

"Hell no, Least I don't think so. I figured it was a couple of miles further, by a little creek. I could be lost, but I don't think so, 'cause we been following the river. This here must be a new town, a white man's town, from the look of it. Wasn't here when I made tracks in these parts. Probably got lots of supplies, maybe even good whiskey. What say we ride on in thar and get a meal and a drink or two, maybe a bath and bed, find out the local news?"

"Take the mules and all, just ride into town after we've been avoiding them all along?"

"Yep. Can't avoid towns forever, LaPoint. And we're both sick of camp cooking. They ain't no fuggin' federals lookin' for ya here. And I tell ya what, I'd rather sleep in a hotel and put the stock in a livery than go messing around in the dark in this rattlesnake country. I got ta remembering tripping over them varmints in the dark. I'd rather approach in daylight, if possible. Hell, I'm tired."

Josh sat silent for a moment, peering at the little town from under the great sweeping boughs of a live oak where they had stopped. He had been in wilderness for over a month, hiding out, on the run, wary, always scanning the horizon for riders. Now Gabe wanted to ride into town. He knew that Gabe was exhausted and shaken from the earlier brush with the buffalo and Comanches. He had never seen a look of fear on Gabe's face like he saw that day. And he was tired too.

"Alright. I'm game for a town if you are. Not that I'm tired of your cooking, but a sit-down meal with a beer would be nice. And something besides boudin, buffalo, biscuits, and beans would be a treat. And I'd rather sleep in a bed than on the ground with rattlesnakes. How far is the rancho from here?"

"About two miles to the river crossin', I figure, then maybe three miles back upstream, maybe less."

"So if they've got decent accommodations and a safe place for the stock, we'll stay the night in town and head out in the morning light?"

"That's how my stick floats, pard."

Josh laughed, the first belly chuckle in a long time. "Alright, lead on, float that durned stick on in there, ya old coon."

Gabe turned and gave him a tight grin. "Now that's more like it, LaPoint. Enough of the grim faces."

They headed out of the shelter of the oak into the darkening twilight towards the town. As they got closer they could see carts and mule trains jostling around in the main street. At the outskirts they came upon a nicely painted sign on a square wooden post, painted white with black trim, that said, **"Helena"**. It had several large caliber bullet holes in it. Leon began to bray like he smelled other jacks, and Josie soon joined in. Scorpio began to step lively and pulled up beside Buck.

"Say Gabe, did you know Helena was the mother of Christianity?"

"Nope, can't say as I studied that one. Nor care to. I leave that to them thar continental educated New Orleans gentlemen, products of the 'lightenment. Come on Josie, ya done stretched my arm a foot with yer balking, get moving. If she was the mother, I hope she knows her offspring didn't turn out so well."

"Oh yeah, Helena spawned a murderer of the worst sort, killed his family and founded the Roman church, is what I read."

"Nothin' worse than that, I reckon. This here is a lot bigger town than Alex mentioned, musta growed."

They rode on into the raw-boarded little town as the sun set in their eyes and lit the scattered rainclouds purple and magenta, and a light mist settled on them from a cloud overhead. The town was on a prairie with the river vegetation in the background. Fresh board lumber and even some brick buildings lined the street, including a post office and courthouse.

The main street was a muddy quagmire, but they slowly rode down it, into the first town they had been in together during their long trek. Their fine animals drew appraising stares from the various drovers and teamsters on the street. There was plenty of mule-drawn wagons and mule trains in the streets, but no striking Spanish stallions with high arched necks and ornate saddles like Buck and Scorpio.

The sound of mule voices provided a constant backdrop to the clopping of their hooves in the muddy street. They saw several livery stables and selected a well-kept one to rest their stock. They unpacked and unsaddled the stock, then Josh rubbed them down and hand-fed them while Gabe secured a lockup for their saddles, packs, and gear. Before they left the livery, Josh grabbed the saddlebag with Suzette and the bag of silver coin in it, and together they walked stiff-legged up the main street into the little town. The intermittent rain had them still in oilskins, and a slurry of muck smelling of animal manure clung to their boot-heels.

Wagons and carts and mule trains cluttered the street, a regular traffic jam at spots, with braying mules and snorting tired horses, and even an ox or two pulling older run-down wagons. Teamsters were cussing and popping bullwhips, coming in and heading out. The smell of fresh-cut lumber and animal manure mixed with the scent of cooking and beer, overlaid with scents of outhouses and cheap tobacco. They spotted a bar and grill in the bottom of a small but nice looking hotel, scraped the mud from their boots on a scraper by the door, and went in for dinner and a beer, their first in over a month.

"Damn," said Josh. "Crossroads of the world, huh? Haven't seen so many mules in a long time."

"I'm amazed myself."

Muldoon's Bar and Grill was about half full when Gabe and Josh walked in and found a table. There was a sign over the bar that said "Cash Only, No Confederate Script."

They were still clad in wet oilcloth jackets and sheepskin vests, both dripping moisture, and their entry drew stares from the teamsters and assorted drovers who lined the bar and filled the tables. Some older men playing cards and dominoes glanced at them cautiously.

"Looks like them boys been through rain. Which way yal come in?" asked a burly teamster-looking guy in canvass clothing.

"From Gonzales way," answered Gabe as they walked into the big room to find a place.

"More mud ta tramp through up northeast, huh. Just my luck. I'm waiting til morning, Karl," said the fellow to his drinking buddy.

"Dat goes fer me too."

There were no Mexicans in the bar, which struck Gabe as odd, since there used to be a Mexican settlement here. It seemed strange that there were none of the old Mexican ox carts that resembled the Comanchero carts in the street either, since they were in full use when Gabe was in the area before.

A card game was proceeding on a table covered with green felt-cloth at the back of the large room. The man obviously running it was well dressed in a suit with shiny flowered waistcoat, while the others looked dejected and about half asleep. Gabe chose a table near the side wall, away from the door and the bar. They took off their oilcloth jackets, revealing their tie-down pistol rigs and big knives strapped over their sweat-stained dirty buckskins, which drew more stares, chuckles, and muttered conversations at the tables and bar.

"Hey old timer, where ya get that Bowie knife, from old Jim?"

"Who farted that sour smell?" said another wise acre.

"Ain't no Bowie knife, pup. It's a McBride, the kind Kit Carson carries," replied Gabe with a stern look. He did not draw the knife.

"Kit Carson? You come out of one of them there dime novels, pops?"

"Leave 'im alone, Ralph," said his pal, with a wary look at the travelers.

Josh hung his coat on the back of an adjacent chair, then draped his saddlebags over the arm of the chair, and Suzette stuck her little snout out of the corner under the flap and sniffed the air, which drew a smile out of both of them.

"What a gal, five hundred miles in a saddlebag, always on alert, don't eat or shit much, no unnecessary barking, no complaints. Wish I had a gal like that back on the staked plains."

Josh laughed and petted the tiny head of the alert Chihuahua, causing her to make a peculiar snorkeling sound in pleasure. She had been a patient and valuable traveler, always alerting them to danger, saving them from groups of riders with her sharp hearing, keeping him warm at night, and Josh was very grateful to her.

There were three gals in fancy dresses tending the bar, flirting with customers, working them for drinks and conversation to ease their loneliness, or something better upstairs if the right bargain could be struck. Then there were gals waiting tables in calico, who only worked downstairs, it seemed, from their spurning of drover advances. They were all kept busy by the crowd.

"Wal lookee thar, a light rise in the trail, even for an old timer. I hope you brought that sheath with ya, never know about these bar gals."

"You're just assuming I'm going to bed one?"

"Wal, ya been away from yore New Orleans gals for quite a while, I reckon it'd be a safe bet. Just wear that french sheath, as a favor to me. I seen a guy go crazy from syphilis, and it ain't pretty."

"Alright, I will, like always, if the occasion arises."

"Oh, I reckon thar'll be a risin', alright."

They laughed together and looked around the room. The pretty gals were a sight for sore eyes after constant peering for hostile riders across the horizons.

Silent and watchful stood a thick-bodied bartender who leaned back motionless behind the bar with his brawny arms crossed over his thick chest, only moving when required to pour drinks, which he gave to the waitress or slid down the slick bartop with practiced skill. A lovely older gal named Delores ran the bar front with him, and smiled and joked with the guys, keeping a mellow mood.

An upright piano sat against the wall nearby, and the bar had a brass foot rail and polished mahogany top. There was a long mirror behind the bar, and big paintings of plump inviting female nudes hung on the walls. The place was surprisingly clean and well furnished with round tables and brass spittoons. The gals were all becoming lovelier as they watched, and the air was warm from the big pot bellied stove in the front. The smell of good food and beer filled the place.

"Damn," said Gabe. "A regular town done sprouted up here, fancy saloon, bath-house, hotel, and all."

"I'm amazed," said Josh. "Seem's downright civilized. From what you told me, I expected to find a jacal with some fermented Spanish dagger juice to drink, what do they call it, pulque?"

"Gonna be good whiskey here, I reckon. And maybe even cool beer."

They both sat with their backs to the side wall and looked around. The denizens of the bar were an assorted lot, the younger braggadocios with pistol rigs and wide brimmed hats standing at the bar with their loud talking and expansive gestures, and the older men drinking quietly at the tables, some playing dominoes or cards, some playing at a billiards table, most just sitting back chatting in European-looking clothes.

The stout Irish-looking bartender with a long, full, and well waxed auburn mustache and bald head was eying them, and he nodded to Gabe when their eyes met, then sent a pretty young blond woman in a blue calico dress to take their order.

"Cash only, no Confederate script, I'm required by Muldoon to say. So.....What'll it be, gents?" she said.

"Howdy ma'am," said Gabe. "Yore a sight for sore eyes to this ole coon. We'd like some of all ya got, dinner, beer, then whiskey, a hot bath, and a place for us to sleep. And we pay in silver."

"Silver makes Muldoon light up like the sunrise. Some of all we got, huh? Well, we got all that you mentioned and more, 'cept it'll take some time ta get your room ready, 'cause the maid quit and we're running behind. Delores has got a gal up there cleaning now, won't be long. Want me to take your saddlebag on up there now?"

"No thank you," said Josh with a slight smile. "We're famished. I'll eat the dinner special just so yal can get it out to us sooner." Suzette had pulled her head back under the leather flap when the waitress approached. Josh took his hat off, revealing that his hair had grown out some and was light colored again. Gabe left his hat on, so as not to provoke stares and questions about his scalping scar.

"Me too, I'll take the blue-plate special with beer as soon as ya can get to it. Say, lady, last time I was thru here, this town wasn't here. Usta be a place called Alamita round here, but it was mostly some jacals and such, maybe an adobe or two, nothin' like a town of board lumber. When's this place sprout up?"

"I believe it was in the early fifties, around fifty two. Some merchants named Ruckman and Owings, proprietors of that store across the street, tried to start up a nice town, made it the county seat with a courthouse, schools, church, gristmill, post office, and what all, but it's gone downhill since then, on accounts so much riffraff moving in, the cart road trash, we call 'em. We're on the cart trails, you know, some go east, some go up to San Antonio, some to Chihuahua, but all just passing through, like you, I guess?"

"Wal, we hope ta stay a night, at least, then head for our ranch nearby."

"Did they name the town after Helena, the mother of Emperor Constantine"? asked Josh.

"Emperor who? Folks round here don't cotton to Emperors, especially in Panna Maria, where they mostly came to get away from the Prussians. They named it Helena after Owings' wife. Why, it's been here over a dozen years, growing like a bad weed. So you haven't been around in quite a while, huh? Alamita went the way of the Mexican carters, I've been told. I'm not from here. I'm from San Antonio, came for a teaching job, but the priest didn't like me, and fired me. Do you want me to get some bath water heating? There's a tub room down that hall. Not to be rude, but the sooner yal get a bath, the better we'll all feel. Yal are sorta fragrant, or maybe it's them ole buckskins, don't see them too much any more."

"Yes ma'am, I know the smell yore talking about, it's closer to me than it is to you, and been close for too long..got real strong when I saw them Comanches today...it's fear sweat soaked inta buckskin...but we shore do need some good vittles first. The smell of good cooking got a holt on us now. And that beer, please, ain't had a cool beer in a month. And tell 'em ta start heating the bathwater."

"Comanches? Which way? Was it a raiding party?"

"No ma'am, just hunting buffalo up on the prairies to the northeast. Feeding their families, I reckon. No cause for alarm."

The waitress left with a worried look and told the other gals about the Comanches. The news moved throughout the bar, causing worried comments and consternation on the faces of all.

"Mud and Comanches up north and a bad stink," said a teamster. "Yal bring any good news?"

"The way it is...is the way it is, ain't it?' asked Gabe.

In a few minutes the two weary travelers were eating a full meal, on real china plates overloaded with pork chops, cabbage, black beans, cornbread with butter and molasses, and canned peas with corn, with cool beer to wash it down. After a month in the saddle and scanty camp food, they enjoyed themselves thoroughly by stuffing their bellies while sitting at a real table, using clean tableware. When they were finished eating and left a good tip in silver coin, the same gal who served them brought them a bottle of the best Irish whiskey in the place, and they proceeded to take a few drinks, toasting their successful journada.

Leaning back in his chair, Josh looked finally relaxed. "Wal, I'd say we're finally back in civilization, and hits a surprise to me," said Gabe. "Be sure and tip them good, that was fine vittles, and lots of it, with good service too, and all them gals is sure a sight for sore eyes, huh."

Josh nodded. "I agree. I'm amazed. I thought it would be cold biscuits and jerky tonight, with rattlesnakes for dessert."

As they were just getting fully relaxed from the whiskey and thinking about heading down the hall to the bath house, a group of wagons pulled up outside and a loud gang of teamsters came clomping in, six burly and dirty guys, tramping mud all over the just swept floor and making a lot of unnecessary noise. They called for a bottle with cards and chips for poker, and took a table beside Gabe and Josh. They were all acting rowdy and shoving each other around, grabbing for chairs, talking loud as if they were yelling at their mules. There was one chair nobody touched, which was obviously for their leader, a big fellow who spoke up loud and hoarse as he draped his coiled whip over the arm of the chair.

"Come on now, get that bottle over here sweet patootie, I got money to make from these suckers, and I'm gonna spend it on one of them cute little gals!" The fancy gal in a pink satin dress he had pointed to rolled her eyes and walked away. The waitresses scurried with trays carrying bottles, cards, chips, and glasses, and pretzels, to keep the big fellow from making too much of a commotion. He was obviously used to people jumping when he said frog.

He was a very large and dark skinned man with a protruding belly and huge chest, shoulders, and arms, and a scraggly black beard stained with tobacco juice that drooled from the corner of his mouth. His teeth were broken, stained brown, and jagged against puffy red lips, and his nose was crooked from a previous busting. He had the stub of a cigar, unlit and chewed on the end, stuck in the corner of his mouth. His face was pockmarked and splattered with tiny bits of mud.

The others found great humor in his muttered comments about the gals, and took to guffawing and giggling as they surrounded the table, scraping chairs around to fill it. The waitress brought a bottle and set it with glasses on the table, then swatted at the hands reaching for her butt as she walked away in a huff.

"Ronald Bartelske, dammit, I warned you to make them boys behave," she said over her shoulder. "Yal can get your own from now on. I ain't serving you."

"Awww, baby-doll, you should be glad they're grabbin' at your ass, someday nobody will want it, huh?" More guffaws arose from the teamsters. Gabe scowled and LaPoint felt trouble coming.

"I am just a waitress, Ronnie, and you know it."

The bartender spoke up. "Ron, better behave. Fair warning."

The muddy crowd circled the table beside Gabe and Josh's, but were short a chair, and the biggest of the burly crowd, the one called big Ron by his gang, turned towards Gabe and Josh's table, after getting no reaction from the waitress with his comment.

"We need another chair here," he looked at Gabe, then at Josh, then back at Gabe.

"I said we need another chair, boys."

"Good luck to ya on that," said Gabe, with an upward glance at the man's eyes. "We ain't had chairs to set on in a long time and don't aim to give 'em up."

The tall heavyset man looked back at Josh, with a bit of wariness in his eyes, as Josh put his hand on the edge of the saddlebag.

"You wood ticks the one's with them Spanish tooled leather saddles on them little Latino Stallions out there?"

"You might say that," replied Gabe.

"Mighta known. Ya talk like hicks from tha boondocks, and smell like woods-rats. Lookee here, fella, how bout you get to movin' yer saddlebags and coat offa this chair pronto so we can use it. We don't hold with no Mex lover's round here."

"No, that chair is being used," replied Josh in a quiet voice, briefly glancing up into the fellow's eyes. "You'd best find another."

"Yeah, aw, time's up, boy. I axed ya nice, didn't I? Wal, you'll find out I don't ax twice. Now I'm taking that chair, Meskin lover," replied the big fellow as he reached for the tooled leather saddlebags.

In a flash of quick motion, Suzette's head popped out of the saddlebag as she lunged for the big hairy hand of the teamster, snarling with tiny white teeth exposed. She snapped twice at him, nearly too quick to see. The teamster jumped back, startled, and barely missed getting bit hard, suffering only a nip which caused him to put his hand to his mouth and suck the finger. Suzette kept snarling, rising up in the saddlebag with the cover flopped back, guarding her little home as if she was a lioness.

"What the hell is that, a rabid rat?" asked the teamster as he spat on the floor. "A Mexican dog! Lucky it didn't draw much blood, or I might jus' beat you ta death with tha limp body."

"Lookout Ron, you gonna get rat-bit," said one of his buddies who had taken a chair at the other table.

"Yeah, by a danged Chihuahua too. That'll take the cake. Getting bit by a Mex dog after grinding all them Mex carters."

"Hey yeah, Ron, cut her in two with yore spoke saw, like ya done them cart-wheels."

Embarrassed by his startled reaction, the teamster hitched up his pants and flopped the pistol and knife holsters against his belly while doing so.

"I'm taking that chair," he said.

"The chair is being used" Josh LaPoint said in a calm measured voice. "I'm keeping it. I told you to find another. Don't bother us any further."

"Further? I ain't your gol-dang farther, sonny. I"ll show you further."

"Yeah, show 'em, big Ron, saw their spokes off!" and similar calls came from the group at the table, with their glasses filled now, ready for the show.

Gabe was partially amused, and started laughing. "Wal hell mister, what'd ya expect? That's thar's a Chihuahua, ain't this the Chihuahua trail? We thought we's supposed to bring a saddlebag full of Chihuahua when we came down ta the Chihuahua trail. Ain't that right? You ain't tellin' me yal don't have a Chihuahua for the Chihuahua trail. I thought it was required by statute?"

That drew a loud protesting response from the table of loud freighters, who began to deride the whole idea of required Chihuahuas in profane terms, with garbled speculating on required statues. "Ain't no chihuahua statues round here, not since the cart war. Mexican's done been run out," said the tallest.

"That Mex dog wouldn't be the first greaser I stomped," said Ronnie. "Now move it or lose it."

"Now... Listen here, Sir. We ain't givin' up tha chair. Have one of your pards belly up to tha bar until somebody vacates a chair, and we'll buy him a drink, huh?"

"Chihuahua my ass, you Mex-lovin skunks. You guys are way behind the times, ya smelly old woods' rat. We done run all the danged Chihuahua lovers out of here with the greaser carters. Ain't no Chihuahua gonna mess up my card game. That chair is what's *required by statue*, by God. So don't get your sour old stoved-up ass in my way, ya broken down old fart, or I'll make a statue out of you, on the ground."

"Whoa boy, here it comes, Ron gonna make statues of 'em."

"Yeah, statues layin' out on that ground," said another.

Gabe turned his gaze up to the man, and said. "Don't ya know son, it all came up from Chihuahua to San Antone, from the early day Spanish."

"Shut yore trap, greaser lover," said Ronnie.

"Don't disturb my dog, she's had a long trip, and don't talk to my friend that way," said Josh in his low and steady tone.

"You really don't want that chair, mister," said Gabe in a mild tone, while staring at the dark eyes of the teamster.

"Yeah, well tough titty, I just had a long trip too, down from San Antone, and got a long haul to go to Indianola, dodging Comanche the whole way, and we been looking forward to this poker game for hours. Now get that danged Mex dog off that chair or we'd do to yal what we done to them other greasers back in the fifties. The gol-danged lil Chihuahua tried to take my finger off. Oughta cut tha little Mex-rat's head off and stuff it, is what." With the last statement he put his hand to his knife scabbard and stomped his big muddy boot on the sounding floorboard. "Come on, get moving ya balky mule, gee, haw, gee, haw. Get going afor I take ya out in the street and bullwhip ya like I done lots of Mexican lovers. This here ain't no place for

Mexican or Mex lovers, we done won that war."

"Yeah, remember the Alamo, and Goliad," said a fellow at the table.

"I do," said Gabe, which brought a round of guffaws from the freighter crowd, while some of the older men were leaving the saloon.

Gabe slowly shook his head with a grim smile, poured drinks for Josh and himself, then addressed the surly fellow, who stood waiting like he wasn't used to any lip. "Now listen to some good advice from someone old enough to be yore pap, mister. We're sitting here mindin' our own business tryin' to relax after a long ride that's got my back aching, my old cracked butt sore with a nasty rash, and my temperament cross and cranky."

"So?"

"So I'ma sayin' I already had a chapped ass before you started disturbing me, and it's really getting chapped now. But I'm still feeling kindly enough to ignorant strangers to warn 'em offa danger. So I'm tellin' ya once, as a favor to ya. You best not mess with this man right here, or his dog. You'd best just back off while you still can. And don't go ta threatening me or mine with no piddly little toad sticker of a cheap ass trade knife that even the Tonkawas would laugh at."

A worried crease showed on the teamster's brow as he glanced over at the big knife on Gabe's belt, then to the well-armed LaPoint, who sat with his weight resting on the balls of his feet and his pistol holster ready with the gleaming blue black navy colt. These were no meek religious foreign-jabbering farmers from Panna Maria who went out of their way to avoid trouble. They were well armed strangers in town, an unknown factor, but possibly hired guns brought in to settle some dispute over loose cattle, or land.

Josh kept staring the fellow in the eyes, silent and motionless. He was sorely disappointed in the situation. After being hyper-vigilant for five hundred miles, they had finally relaxed in a town to enjoy some of the comforts of civilization, and this had to happen. He was not pleased, and strongly resented the man's verbal abuse of Gabe. He felt his blood start to simmer, ready for action. He thought of the federal captain who burned down the plantation and killed his mother, and all the other miscreants who went unpunished. A killing rage began to envelope him, rising hot from his solar plexus. He steadied his breathing. He waited for the man to step just a bit closer.

Suzette kept a low snarl going, then she raised the pitch and temper when the teamster stepped up close and again reached for her.

In a flash of unexpected motion Josh raised his big spread-open hand towards Bartelske's face, fluttering it like a hawk after a mouse and flinging a deck of cards at him, completely catching the attention of the dark and bloodshot beady eyes and causing him to jerk his big head back, while Josh simultaneously swung the sharp point of his riding boot against the side of the big man's knee, sending him to the plank floor with a yell and shriek of pain and a crash. The booming of the rough planks increased as the big man pounded the floor in agony, grabbing his knee with the other hand. Josh settled back into his chair as the teamster writhed around on the dirty floor, holding his knee and cussing up a storm, unaware of what caused the pain in his knee.

"Ya stinking buckskin bastards, you're dead. You're a dead man, both of ya, gonna slice you and spill your guts, ya damned old shit, kick me from behind..." he moaned as he kicked out with his other leg and knocked Gabe ajar in his chair, causing him to spill his drink.

"If you try it, I'll be the last bastard you see," said Josh.

"Alright then, that tears it, ah heard 'bout nuff o foul talk," said Gabe as he glanced at Josh.

"Boys, grab the young one while I finish off this old fart," bellowed the downed teamster. The chairs at the other table started to scrap along the boards as they began to get up.

"Nobody move," said Gabe as Josh threw a quick glance their way, then looked back at Gabe to see what he was going to do. At first nobody in the bar moved, then within a few seconds the older wiser men began to slowly get up and step back. In a short time it was a regular procession out the door, slowly clearing the bar of farmers, loungers, idlers, diners, and gamblers. The girls all headed out through the door into the hallway and out of sight. Muldoon was left standing behind the bar, shaking his head in a grim manner.

"That worked well," said Josh, smiling until he saw a flash of grim anger replace the amusement in Gabe's face, and knew a stern chastisement was coming, so his own hand went to his belt by the big Colt Navy pistol as he shot a glance over at the other guys while the sounds of chairs scrapping and people exiting filled the room.

The bartender had not moved except to reach his hand under the bar, but kept watching and slowly shaking his head as the older customers filed out the doors and the younger ones pulled back to watch big Ron kick another guy's ass. The teamsters at the adjoining table were held in check by the threat in Josh's glances, and the gun on his hip.

"Come on, help me kill these low down Mexican lovers!" yelled big Ron through splayed teeth. He continued to pound the floorboards in pain as he spoke.

Two of the other teamsters had risen from their chairs and were watching, not too sure whether to join in, since the biggest teamster of the gang was rolling in pain on the floor, clutching his knee and grimacing with a steady drool, seemingly put down by what looked like a scruffy gray-bearded old man in worn and smelly buckskins, like something out of a dime novel about the old time mountain men.

Gabe got up, sliding his chair out from behind him, finished his drink with a slam and set the shot glass on the table, then pulled his 12" Damascus steel knife with the elk antler handle, and stepped over the teamster, who was rolling over towards him.

"Gol-dang, he's gonna gut Ron," said one of the boys at the table. Without a word Gabe dropped his full weight and landed with a pointed knee on the thick man's barrel chest while smacking him in the mouth with the thick butt end of the knife, the gnarly part at the base of the elk antler, knocking a number of teeth out and starting the blood gushing from splayed lips and gums. A large pee spot appeared at big Ron's crotch as well. His yelling turned to guttural moans and he rolled in pain.

"I won't abide a foul mouth," said Gabe. "'Specially in front o gals."

The teamster bellowed in pain mixed with surprised rage, and rolled to his side clutching his mouth with one hand and his knee with the other. Bright blood was dripping all over the floorboards and spraying out when he yelled and sputtered in rage. Josh remained still while throwing glances at the table of teamsters, who had quieted down by then, their main activity reduced to holding very still and beading sweat on their foreheads. Josh had his hand on the dark cherry-wood butt of the big Colt pistol by then.

Gabe reared back and kicked the big fellow hard on his broad rump, rolling him over. "This here is the sound of an old woods' rat kicking yore ass," he said. Enraged, the teamster raised to one knee and tried a lunge at Gabe across the dusty board floor, bellowing like a stuck hog, but Gabe sidestepped him with a quick step like an Irish gig, grabbed the man's coat at the collar and jerked hard to continue his momentum into the chair, and whacked him on the back of his head as he went by, again using the big elk-antler butt of his long and heavy knife. This put the teamster out like a light, and Gabe bent down and took away his pistol and knife, setting them on the table.

Then Gabe examined his knife butt to make sure he didn't chip it, glanced around, then stood erect and took a deep breath while looking at the table of teamsters. "This is tiresome, fellas," he said. "I hate tussling on a full belly. Yal best behave or I'll really cut loose on ya."

Then he looked back to check on Ronnie, who had no movement other than a slight tremor in one leg. Gabe toed that quivering leg with his boot.

"I tole ya ta leave us alone, now, didn't I sonny?" Gabe poured drinks into their tiny shot glasses, and raised his towards the other guys at the table.

"Ya reckon ya can do that now?"

No reply from Ronnie. LaPoint stared at the teamsters. One fellow, the youngest looking at the table, said, "We don't want no trouble, mister."

"Wal, good for yal, and here's a toast to you, big fella, yore the biggest fool in the place." The big teamster was out cold, the blood pouring out of his mouth onto the floor into a dark pool. His other leg began jerking spasmodically as Gabe and Josh threw back their drinks. Another fellow at the table spoke up.

"Hey, yal can't jus come into town and put Ron Bartelske down like that. This here is our town. We could just fill ya full of holes, the five of us, right now. Or maybe tie ya up into a Helena knife fight. Yal..."

Josh had risen from the table and turned towards them, his hand on his holster, staring each one in the eyes in quick succession, reading their faces. The barkeep had brought out a short double-barreled shotgun and held it on the bar.

"Whoa boys, don't turn a mishap into a disaster," said Gabe. "If you boys like breathin', then pick up your friend here and take him to the wagon and get out of town right now."

A few seconds passed as LaPoint stood motionless staring at them, then they all trooped around to pick up the heavy man and carry him like a giant sack of potatoes out the door. He dripped a trail a blood as he went, and they nearly dropped his heavy body at the door. Gabe poured them another drink while Josh glanced at him with a barely suppressed smile.

"Welcome to Helena, all the accouterments of civilization," said Josh as he raised his shot glass.

Gabe shook his head with a sour look. "Helena hand basket, is what."

"This used to be a nice town, believe it or not," said Muldoon. "Girls, come on back and clean up this blood before it sets in the floorboards."

They clicked shot glasses and had another drink. The door opened again and a young fellow from the teamster crowd stepped in.

"Sir, what about Ronnie's pistol and knife? If he wakes up without them, there'll be hell to pay."

Gabe picked the heavy old Walker Colt and short knife off the table, peered at the colt for a while, then casually dropped it into a spittoon near the wall.

"You kin tell 'im I cached his nice old Walker colt for him right thar. Now this thing he calls a knife." Gabe peered at the little trade knife and shook his head in disgust. "This here thing's gonna let him down in a pinch someday, so I better get shed of it for him, since he obviously ain't got the sense of a sorry mule."

Gabe took the blade and stuck it in one wide crack that appeared between the floorboards, then kicked it and broke it in two, shunting the handle off under the piano, then pushing the blade down through the floor with his boot. "Cheap trade knife, made to swindle the ignorant. Now clear outa here and let me finish my sit down in peace. And tell Ronnie I done saved his life, when he wakes up. He was messing with the wrong fellow. Tell 'im in the future, he'd best steer clear of us."

The young teamster glanced nervously at LaPoint, who met his gaze and remained silent, forcing him to turn away. There was a piercing beam coming from his light colored eyes, and the teamster couldn't stand the steady glare from his wide-set brow. And the big pistol was unhooked and ready for action, with his hand nearby.

"And who might yal be, mister?" said the youngster as he glanced down.

"You's lookin' at LaPoint, and I'm McBride. Now get going, and don't stop til yal get in sight of Matagorda bay, on accounta I still got a chapped ass, and might come after yal when my dinner settles."

"Well alright, but there'll be hell to pay down the road. Ronnie ain't gonna take kindly ta..."

"Ronnie's lucky he's still breathin', and he'd better learn to let a sleepin' dog lie," replied Gabe as he poured another round. "He could be full of holes with his scalp missin'. Lookee here," said Gabe as he pulled his hat off to show them his scar. "What do ya think I did to tha fellas that tried to take mine, huh?"

The youngsters eyes bugged out and he backed out the door. Josh poured them another whiskey and clicked glasses with Gabe. It wasn't great whiskey, but better than they had been drinking on the trail, and they relished it for a while.

Gabe looked over at the bartender. "Sorry for the disturbance and mess, buddy."

"Hell, I'm sorry you didn't show up a few years ago. Don't worry 'bout the mess, it's less than usual for that crew. Good riddance. If I could have shot him with this shotgun without making a huge mess on my new wallpaper, I probably would have done it already."

One of the bar-gals sat down at the piano with a glance in their direction, and opened the lid from the keys. A young maid came in with a metal bucket of steaming water and went towards the blood on the floor.

"Lisa, I told you to use cold water on blood stains, didn't I, like a dozen times at least?" said the bartender, never moving from his spot.

"Oh yes sir, but I didn't heat it for this. It was already hot for the baths."

"Use cold water, works better, hot water sets bloodstains, so save the hot for bathing and washing all these glasses."

Lisa trooped back into the hall with her bucket and returned with cold water and a brush and rags, then went to cleaning up the blood.

Then the waitress came up to their table.

"Well, now that yal cleaned the riffraff outa this joint, I guess yal are ready for your baths now? They're a steaming."

"Why yes mam, we shore are. Let us pay ya for the food and drinks right now, and get the other later when we check out. Yal got any clean rooms ready?"

"Well, with Ronnie's crew gone, I guess we got several. They will be ready enough when yal are done bathing. We got two tubs ready for you now."

"Well," said Josh. "There's no shortage of chairs now. Sorry about the mess, ma'am."

"Ronnie always makes a mess, but usually it's the other guy's blood. I don't see how yal took care of him so quick. He's been throwing his weight around here for years, trying to run every Tejano out of town. It did my ears good to hear him hit the floor like that. Wasn't it a loud boom, though?"

"Teamwork, ma'am," said Gabe.

"Yeah, shuffling that deck of cards into his face didn't hurt any. Yal go on down and have your hot soaks."

The bathhouse was at the end of a darkened hall, and was warm and steamy with two big full tubs. The stripped out of their stinking clothes and put all but the buckskins into the trash barrel. They both had long soaking baths and sipped on the whiskey in the warm bathhouse while they relaxed.

"Well, old Hoss," said Josh with a smile. "You've done it again , saved me from getting in a scrape. Here's to ya."

"Oh yeah, I suppose the big fella just tripped in front of me, huh? I saw that Chinese kick ya whapped his knee with.

"Not much family left, Gabe."

"Wal, yore right about a toast to young Helena...it's in order after that fine dinner. What's a little scuffle compared to a good meal with cool beer and a good bath and bed, huh?"

"You reckon he'll be back?"

"Not for a while, I reckon. I believe he's got a busted knee and a busted rib or two, not to mention a sore mouth and head. I shore liked that sparrow in the face with the cards flying as you cracked his knee. Talk about a flummoxed ox. Oughta learn him a thing or two, huh?"

"Maybe, but he got manhandled by one old hoss in front of his friends. That can't sit too well. I should have done it, I suppose, but you had that stern look."

"Wal, we'll see. Usually a big ole bully boy like that picks on easy targets and don't mess with those that hold their ground. But if we see a shabby bear with no teeth and a limp come hobbling up, we might pay heed."

"I guess time will tell," said Josh. "Say, I see a mirror on the wall there, I think I'm gonna shave and wash out this stinking sour buckskin too. Gotta figure out a way to wash that stench off them. I'm sure tired of smelling myself."

"Wal go ahead on. Not me for the shave. Having this gray beard makes 'em think I'm an old codger, til they find out different."

Josh shaved and changed into clean clothes, noticing his face was much leaner and more suntanned now, then washed and toweled off Suzette while Gabe finished soaking. After soaking both buckskins and rubbing them in soapy water, he squeezed the water out and wrapped them together. When they walked back into the bar it was nearly empty, and the gal at the piano was still playing "Clementine".

Josh felt a wave of sad nostalgia as he heard the tune, one he used to hear in better times in New Orleans. He stood behind the gal listening until she finished and slowly spun on the stool to face him.

"Well, you sure clean up nicely. I don't smell those sour buckskins either. Did you like that tune?"

"Yes, it brings back memories. And you play so well. We didn't expect good food and good music and beautiful women. Didn't even know this town was here. My mother used to play that tune."

"Do you play?"

"I used to, a bit."

"Sit down here and play one for me. What do they call you?"

"They call me LaPoint, but you can call me Josh. And your name is?"

"Delores Delmonico. I help Muldoon run the bar and hotel. And no, I'm not Irish."

Josh laughed and sat beside her on the piano bench. He began to play on the bass keys while she played the other end, and they played "Stewball", "Old Dan Tucker", and "Cotton-eyed Joe". While they were playing the "Sourwood Mountain", Gabe ambled in to the barroom and smiled when he saw them playing together. He casually walked over to the bartender and spoke.

"Yal got two rooms?"

"Yep, now we do, after ya run all the freighters off. Small loss, they usually break and tear up more than they pay for. Here's two keys,12 and 14; the rooms are ready, up the stairs. What'd ya say your names were?"

"McBride, and he's LaPoint. You ain't got a newspaper, do ya?"

"Yeah, maybe. Yal come up from Indianola, bring any news yourself?" The barman rummaged around looking for a newspaper while he spoke.

"Naw, we come from Gonzales way. Say, what is the date today, do ya know?"

"Why, it's April sixteenth. So you come overland, ya ain't heard bout Lee and Grant, the war news? Can't find the paper, somebody musta took it. Damned teamsters steal it for the outhouse."

"Was it recent?"

"Oh yeah, fresh news off the telegraph and into print, I reckon. Yal ain't heard?"

"Naw, 'cept I heard in Gonzales that Lincoln got installed with a nice ball where he danced with his crazy wife and everything was real nice. It didn't say whether any one-legged soldiers were invited to the dance, but I'm sure all the railroad gang was thar. Mighta got a bit crowded if they let in the amputees. Does the paper come up from the coast, or San Antone?"

"This one was from New Orleans. Yal been out of touch, huh? War's about over."

"Ya don't say. They burying the tomahawk, huh?"

"Well, there's still lots of fighting going on, mostly won by the federals, but the Galveston paper said Lee surrendered to Grant at Appomattox Courthouse last week, and Sherman has left a scar across in Georgia. What else?.... lets see now, oh yeah, the federals done occupied Richmond and the Confederate congress done adjourned and skedaddled, along with ole Jefferson, who's on the run. Or maybe he's caught one of them stinking camels he brought through here a while back and is riding it west across the desert. It's all over but the shouting, looks like. Stupid bloody war anyway, ya ask me. I got no slaves nor cotton either, though tons of it been coming through here. It was out of the frying pan into the fire for the

South, trying to fight a big industrial state that filled the army with conscripts and Irishmen fresh off the boats for cannon fodder. Say, ye wouldn't be confederate congressmen hightailing it from Richmond, would ya now?"

"Nope, we're mustangers and drovers. Got a rancho across the river, heading there in the morning, after a good night's sleep in a bed."

"You're the ones who have the Spanish stallions and big mules in my livery stable, eh?"

"Your livery? Well, you doin' alright for an Irishman. Yep, that's our stock, pretty good livery too, from the look of it."

"My stable-man says he never saw such well behaved stallions, easy to handle. A dappled gray and a sort of golden colored horse?"

"That'd be Buck and Scorpio."

"Scorpio? You guys believe in that astrology stuff?"

"Naw, we don't hold stock in any religious palaver, to speak of, 'cept we're thankful fer being alive."

"Well, if I didn't believe there was a better world than this mess, it'd be hard to rise in the morning. You don't share the beliefs of the folks who go to church at Helena then?"

"Naw, I get's up early ta make biscuits and grab a good holt on tha day. Ah reckon what ya see is what ya get, when it all boils down. Mostly we believe we got ta stay alert and look out fer ourselves, 'cause ain't no other big spirit gonna take time off and do it for us."

"Well, that often seems to be the case around here, though I often pray it's otherwise. Rancho across the river, huh? Most of the ranchos round here folded their tents during the drought a few years back, along with lots of those stubborn farmers at Panna Maria. But we always had the trade on this road to help us survive the tough times, and the Indian raiders don't like to raid towns full of repeating firearms in the hands of young hellions. This town filled with gunmen during the cart war, and some stayed on to rob and bully their way around here, and try to run out all the Tejanos."

"We're hopin' them raiders feel the same way bout raiding ranches with lots of firearms. We can shoot. We don't stop shootin' when the bullets fly."

"Where is the ranch, exactly?"

"Directly across from Panna Maria, all along that side of

the river, for a ways."

"Let's see now, that might be the ranch of Don Alexander Robinoix, right? Pancho Menchaca's running it for him?"

"By golly, you hit that nail on the head. Is Pancho still around?"

"That he is, saw him last Sunday at mass in Panna Maria. I watch his box at the post office for him, after he got into too many scrapes in Helena. Got mule-whipped by that Bartelske bastard you manhandled, once, actually. I just check his box on Sunday morning and take whatever he's got, hardly ever anything, to church at Panna Maria."

"So they got a going settlement over thar, Polish folks?"

"Oh, those poor Poles. Best I could say is they're surviving, and it's a bloody miracle. They went through hell over there, got so mad at one point they tried to hang the priest that brought them here, the poor gullible peasants. Hard workers though. They were anxious to get out of Silesia, where the Prussians wanted to use them for cannon fodder, and the revolutions and all, and they heard how well the Germans were doing in Texas, so they sold their land in the old country and came over, dying of yellow fever on the way. Now they have to contend with the hellions from Helena instead of Prussians."

"Had a hard go of it, did they?"

"Nobody told 'em it ceases to rain here at times, and won't support farming in dry years, nor that it's hotter than a furnace in summer, nor about the unceasing wind blowing prairie fires, nor the land they settled was a rattlesnake breeding grounds, just crawling with mean vipers, nor the Indians would come in and take everything as soon as they got some accumulation of stock."

"Seen the elephant?"

"Aye laddy, they was trampled by the bloody elephant, but it's a long way back to Silesia. Hell the first bunch landed ignorant with nobody to meet them at Indianola and walked all the way to San Antonio, dying off with yellow fever along the way. Then they had to turn around and hoof it, some of them barefoot and sick, right back another sixty five miles to the rattlesnake plateau over there, with not even a shack to shelter in. First few years they all carried hoes and sticks with em for the daily serpent smacking. Killed a few folks, too, those rattlers. Some big ones there, five and six feet long. Put up a good fight for their turf, they do. "

"I remember that," said Gabe. "Lost two good horses to tha varmints."

"Oh they're sent from the devil, always lurking around my livery stables," said Muldoon.

"I guess the snakes figured it was their home, not some rosary-fingering foreigners with fat calves. Sorta like the Indians, need constant persuasion to get outa the way."

"But the Poles were between a rock and a hard place, no place to go back to."

"Wal, folks is always trying to get away from a bad situation to make a new start, and Texas is an open country still. I read a lot in the paper 'bout those overbearing Prussians over thar, and I can't blame them Poles for wanting a new home. I ain't been here in nigh on a dozen years, and it sounds like a lot has happened. Heading over thar across the river in the mornin', but I need some rest now, little fracas and then that hot bath got me plumb tuckered."

"Well, I hope you have a good rest. You done damned good, taking that Bartelske down. He's a tall pile of dung, that one, always throwing his weight around, pushing the racist line. I hate ta see him come in, except without teamsters, I'd have no business. I didn't see how you took him down, exactly, and I've seen a lot of bar fights."

"Yeah, I think maybe he slipped up or something. Them big fellas is sorta clumsy on their feet sometime. He seemed to get the point, though."

"Yeah, well I seen that Ronnie take his bullwhip to a fella in the street and cut him all to shreds. He especially likes to pick on Mexicans. Seen him ruin my chairs for years breaking them over guys' heads, not to mention the stabbing and slicing he's done with that knife of his. Never seen him shoot that heavy old colt, though, just whack guys over the head with it. And he treats Mexicans like dirt, pulls out his mule whip and starts to popping at them on sight. Did some vicious cutting on Pancho when he used to come in to check the mail and get supplies. "

"Wal, that makes me feel better bout gettin' his attention, like it warn't just wasted effort."

"Right you are, but you were lucky he didn't get the upper hand. Not an ounce of mercy in that one, just extra pounds of meanness. But he won't be back tonight, I figure, with what you did to him. But that won't keep him from back shooting you later on, and never get in range of that bullwhip. Personally, I really enjoyed seeing an older Celtic gent, like myself, take him down. Your room is on the house, Mr. McBride. Have a good rest."

Gabe took the keys and strolled over to where Josh was still with the lovely gal playing piano tunes they both knew. He set the key on the piano in front of Josh, smiled, and said, "I'll see ya in the mornin', Hoss."

Josh smiled and kept playing with Delores, who played and looked and smelled divinely to his famished senses. He had at least lived a life with female companionship in New Orleans, and had just ridden five hundred miles without it.

"Delores, would you like to join me for the evening?"

"Well, I don't work upstairs. Like I said, I help run the place. But I would like to join you for the evening, as long as you understand, it's because I want to, not my job."

"Well that makes it considerably better," replied Josh.

After a few more tunes they both went up to his room, where Josh took his mind off his recent troubles with an hours' lovemaking with the beautiful Delores, after which they both slept soundly til morning. When he went downstairs, leaving Delores asleep in the feather bed that was strung over horsehair ropes, he found Gabe having coffee with the barman.

"Morning, LaPoint,"said Gabe. "Coffee's hot, over there, gotta serve yourself, nobody up but us ole Irishmen. This here's Muldoon, come up from San Patricio in 53, owns this place and the livery we put our stock in. He tells me lots of fighting been goin' on here in the interval since I been gone."

Josh poured himself a cup of coffee and took the pot over to refill the other guys' cups. "Fighting, you mean like last night?"

"Wal, lots of that, but they was having a regular war here between the Mexican carters and the whites, in the mid fifties, not that long ago. These white teamsters, led by the likes of that hog Ronnie we whupped last night, decided the Mexican carters was undercutting their hauling charges, so they went against em. Started off with tricks like sawing the wheel spokes so they broke down on the trail, ended up a shooting war with general mayhem on Mexicans till all the Mexicans carters up and left to work the Chihuahua trail. That was after about seventy of them were put under. Law sided with the white carters, ignored the crimes. Then the Mexican government complained to Washington, which put pressure on the Texas governor, and some hanging of night-riders was done at the big hanging tree at Goliad. The change had already been wrought, though. Nothing but whites hauling now. And of course, freight prices went up after they got shed of the competition."

Josh took a long drink of coffee and replied. "Oh, well, times as they are, not much surprise there. People use race as an excuse to stomp on other people. Seems like there's wars and troubles everywhere. Mostly they're about territory, race is just an excuse to raise a mob. What about the rancho, and Pancho and Rosita?"

"Muldoon here says they're still around, but they don't show up here much any more, since Mexicans get treated poorly. He thinks they trade at Panna Maria some, since they go to the Catholic Church there. He get's their mail from here and takes it to them at Sunday mass, and supplies sometimes."

"Panna Maria. Virgin Mary?"

"Musta been raised a Catholic. Knows his Latin," said Muldoon. "They're a bunch came over from Poland in the early fifties, and later, settled on that rattlesnake breeding plateau west of here a few miles, made a start, then the drought hit em, and things went bad over their union sympathies, and being Poles, and being Catholics, and having good looking blond daughters they won't allow to be abused by Helena toughs. So they've been exchanging shots. It's right across the river from the Robinoix spread, actually."

"Damn," said Josh. "I thought we were coming to a wilderness, sounds like it's civilized as all hell."

"Yeah, more organized warfare rather than just your piddling bandits," said Gabe.

"Well, I guess we'll see how this all fits together somehow, but now I'm anxious to get to the rancho, and we're burning daylight. Let's eat and go see what the situation is . I'd like to get saddles and packs off these animals for a few days, let their backs heal up. Mr. Muldoon, what do we owe for the rooms and bath, and breakfast?"

"You don't owe me nothin'. On the house, 'counta my fellow Irishman McBride here. You're riding with a good man. His name is still known in these parts. I still can't figure how he manhandled Ronnie so easy like. Ronnie's whipped many a man in this town. Sum-bitch went down like a sack of corn."

"Yes-sir, ole Gabe's a curly wolf still, I figure. Smells a lot better this morning, thanks to your bathhouse. I'm learning more about him every day."

"Oh yeah, like what?" said Muldoon.

"Well, on a day he's seen Comanches, best not to rile him, no matter how big you think you are."

"You saw Comanches yesterday?"

"Yep. They was on a buffalo hunt, about twenty miles northeast."

"Didn't look like a raiding party?"

"Naw. Meat was what they was after. "

"Well, I guess I witnessed the truth of the Comanche statement, LaPoint. What else did you learn about your feisty friend here?"

"Well, if you ever need a room cleared, just have him say, 'Nobody move.' When he said that last night about a dozen of your more refined type of customer shuffled out the door."

"Wal what 'bout you, stood up like ya was gonna fast draw all five of them boys. How long since you practiced a fast draw?"

"Never," said Josh, which drew a round of chuckles. "But I was pissed off enough to give it a go by that time. It would have been two against five, right?"

"Aw yeah, I'm 'bout as fast on the draw as a possum in daylight. Lucky they had lost their nerve by that point."

"You reckon that had anything to do with your whipping big Ron's ass?" said Muldoon with a smile.

"Maybe so. He durn sure needed it."

"He sorely needed what you gave him."

"Wal lets eat and get going afore my head busts from swelling up on praise," said Gabe with a twinkle in his eye.

They ate another big meal with real yard eggs that had huge orange yokes standing up like a Texas sunrise. After chatting more with Muldoon about local conditions, they headed down the muddy street to the livery stables and collected their gear and stock, then rode out, heading southwest towards the San Antonio river crossing as the sun lit the sky crimson to their backs.

The crossing was just a shallow ford with a firm bottom of large gravel, but they swam it without much problem, then

headed upstream towards the rancho, riding east into the
brilliant rising sun's rays. A Mexican eagle seemed to follow
them from the river ford, soaring in lazy circles overhead, seldom
shifting his wingtips. The green live oak trees were full of
rustling birds as the sunlight stirred them into song. The grass
was damp with the intermittent rains overnight, and there was
white mist in the draws. Within a quarter hour they crested a
small rise covered with big live oak and mesquite that
overlooked the river meadows of the rancho, and saw the house
in the distance. There was smoke coming from the short
chimney, somehow a welcoming sign. The eagle circled above
the ranch house. They had their destination in sight, at last.

Chapter Seven: Rancho Escondito to Eagle Ford

They rested on a slight rise under a spreading live oak tree, the stallions standing with sweat shining on their layered chest and shoulder muscles, saliva dripping from their blackened steel bits. LaPoint stood in the stirrups with his field glasses and scanned the scene. He first sighted in on the eagle, which had landed in the top of a tall mesquite tree. When he focused on the regal bird, it stared back at him, then took off and rose to make lazy circles above the ranch buildings. After correcting his focus, LaPoint surveyed the rest of the rancho, which stretched along the riverbanks, under the shadow of the swooping eagle, a land of scattered brush and grass, with large live oak and mesquite trees scattered about.

The small white stucco house had a low gable roof of sheet metal, with a rough rock chimney at both ends. A larger stream of smoke was starting to rise from the front chimney as well as the back. The outside of the cottage was smoothly plastered and painted white, as were some outbuildings. The yard was fenced and lined with flower bushes, with a small fire circle of sandstone rocks in the yard, and a hand pump. They saw several horses in the corral, and one of them was a fine looking tall thoroughbred mare, a chestnut with black mane. She nickered and swung her head up and down when she noticed their approach, and both stallions answered, which set the mules to making their braying racket. Scorpio and Buck took an alert interest in her, and perked up their ears and their pacing.

"Dang it's hard to move quiet with these mules. Sometimes I feel like wrapping their noses," said Gabe.

"They'd just eat the wrappings," said Josh. "You never hear them heehawing at me. They just like to confound you, to get a rise."

"Like you, ah reckon. I wonder which taught who?"

"Or vice versa?"

"Yeah, vice and versa, comin' ta call. Hush, and come on."

Gabe led the way from the river plain up the slight rise to the house, where a windmill with the name Halliday painted on the vane was just starting to creak and turn as the first breeze from the south stirred the smoke column. A big plastered stone tank stood below the windmill tower, full of water. Gabe halted there and let his horse and mule drink while he stretched his back in the saddle, and waited for Josh to come alongside.

"Back bothering you, Gabe?"

"Yeah, that and my chapped ass. I think that bed had too much sag in it, made my back worse. Needed the ropes tightened."

"Sorry about that. Slept like a babe myself."

"Slept with a babe, didn't ya, all soft and warm, didn't ya? Left me with yore little dog. Just as well, I was a tired ole coon. And they say sleepin' with a chihuahua cures rheumatism, which I still got from workin' them mountain streams."

Josh just smiled and nodded his head. He moved closer to let his animals drink at the tank while he looked up at the windmill. The eagle that had started following them at the river ford was making lazy spirals overhead, scarcely tilting its wings to ride the thermals effortlessly.

"Lookee here at this setup, they got a bored well now, with one of them wind pumps on it. Mister Alex is always up on the latest stuff. No more drinking cloudy river water, with sand in your teeth."

"That's what I was thinking it was. Never seen one like this, except for pictures in Harpers Magazine. So that wheel drives a sucker rod up and down some well casing, huh?"

"Ah reckon so. Pulls the water up each time it rises. They got it cemented in the hole thar. That's about like Alex, ain't it? Bored well with a wind pump. That's shore gonna change things, if a fellow can get the wind to pump water. Plenty of wind, that's for sure. Why hell, that means settlement ain't tied ta natural waterholes any more. Folks can settle anywhar with one of these, and water their stock in different pastures."

"Maybe so, if they can afford a well driller and the cost of one."

"Plenty of good German well drilling rigs around the hill country, I reckon. Hit's these clever inventions that's gonna change things."

"You're right. It will change where folks can settle, especially a dry country like this. Look around this place. What a change from wet Louisiana, eh? It's amazing how many of the trees and bushes have stickers here, sure a thorny place, Gabe.

I haven't seen any rattlesnakes yet. At least that infernal wind isn't blowing like the last several days."

"Wait 'til the sun warms the ground a bit. Better trail back behind me so we don't look like a big clump of riders, so as not to spook anybody. Pancho don't have the greatest eyesight. With all this cart war between the races around here, he's apt ta be spooky too."

Josh dropped back again as they plodded off towards the house, still a quarter mile away. The stock was starting to hurry a bit, like they were heading towards their own barn. They heard horses calling from around the barn pens and from down by the river. Scorpio was all ears and stepping lively with his big head held high. Buck took a notice and began to prance as well.

When they came around a clump of mesquite and huisache brush they saw a woman milking a goat on a stand, in a small shed near the house. She was focused on her work, her bright shawl over white cotton dress, centered in the inviting scene of the flowered yard with the stream of smoke out the chimney. It reminded Josh of his early childhood on the plantation, before he was sent to board with the orphans, when they got fresh goats' milk every day. He felt a deep sigh of relief.

They kept their slow approach, rounding a big live oak in full foliage with low spreading branches that nearly touched the ground. An old longhorn bull was resting underneath it, and did nothing but twist its head and watch as they rode by. He had a spread of massive shiny horns at least four feet across, with a brindled hide of brown and white.

When the woman saw them a moment later she quickly stopped milking, grabbed the bucket, and left the goat crying like a baby on the milking stand as she ran for the house with tiny steps so as not to spill the milk. She entered the house and slammed the wooden door behind her.

This caused Gabe to stop, raise his hand to signal Josh to stop, and then motion him to stay as Gabe slowly plodded in towards the house.

"I think that's Rosita, and we spooked her," he said over his shoulder to Josh. He proceeded slowly forward on Buck, who was ready to be there and had to be restrained. Both stallions were alert to the piles of hay and the beautiful thoroughbred mare nickering at them. Before the old scout had gone twenty steps he began to sing "Danny Boy" in a strong if creaky Irish baritone. The closer to the house he got, the louder he sang. Josh had never heard him sing before, other than the low drunken chanting of some mountain man ditties, and was amazed again at the hidden talents in the old Texian.

The front door opened and a small man in white cotton clothing with a large double barreled shotgun emerged from the door and took a position behind the woodpile with the shotgun laid on top and aimed at Gabe.

"This is the ranch of Don Alex Robinoix, and the mare belongs to him, and you are trespassing! Don't be coming here singing Danny Boy, damn you...." he shouted.

"Don't ya know me, Pancho?" said Gabe in a loud voice. "Who else would be singing "Danny Boy" to ya at this hour of the day?"

"Eeeejo-de-lachingada-pincheputa-cabrone!" I think you jus pretending to be my friend, but he is dead, so you are some malo animus or a Helena-sonofabich. Begone. You trespass on the land of Mister Alexandre Robinoix. I got a scatter gun on you."

"Yore sitting thar aiming a shotgun I gave ya back in 44 at me when you should be offering me hot coffee. And me with a chaffered butt too, and ya remember how that makes me behave."

"Stop talking and vamoose, cabron!"

"Gol-dang, clean out yore weak eyes. It's me, Pancho. Gabe, Top-hat McBride, they ain't kilt me yet. Me and Mister Alexander's boy done rode all the way here from New Orleans, just to taste Rosita's enchiladas, not yore buckshot."

"Senor Gabriel? Gabe McBride? This cannot be. You went under. They tole me you was tortured to death by the Comanche. The Tonkawa scouts told me. But it sound like Gabe McBride."

"Wal, them varmints had a go at me 'til Mr. Alex rode in and laid waste to em. So here I am. You know them Tonks get everything all mixed up."

"They said you were dying as Senor Alex pulled you off towards Bent's fort on a travois. They said you had no blood left."

"Wal that whar about the size of it, til Alex shot a buffalo and fed me the stomach milk and the blood. Brought me back to life."

Pancho took a few steps away from the woodpile, peering at Gabe as he nudged his horse from a stop and rode a few steps closer.

"Eeehualachingaaada...It is you! Alive!....and you gotta gray beard and a fine Spanish buckskin stallion. Muy macho ahora! Gabriel McBride! The Irish ranger. The pipes, the pipes are calling....We been sending prayers for your soul in purgatory for over ten years, and you still alive, and riding a golden stallion, like Senor Alex used to ride! Climb down off that fine horse, Gabe McBride. Rosita," he yelled. "It's Senor Gabe, the ranger. It's Senor Gabe."

"Purgatory, huh? Wal I see you're still hunkered down, hidin' out on the Escondito."

"Thas right. Welcome to our little hideout."

Gabe climbed down and Pancho rushed forward in his bare feet and jumped on him, clasping him in a tight abbrazo that lasted almost a minute. Josh decided it was time to continue and nudged his animals forward at a slow walk. Rosita came out of the house crossing herself repeatedly, gave a slight scream running towards Gabe, and began to cry while she hugged Gabe and Pancho together. Suzette started a soft whimpering as Josh approached.

The mule was tugging on Gabe's arm as he held the lead line and was swamped with abbrazos, for Josie had spotted fresh feed by the goat shed, and was tugging to get to it. The milk-goat was still protesting loudly, sounding like a baby crying, and Rosita broke away to go attend her as Josh slowly plodded up. Josie started her hee-hawing at the feed pile, and Leon, not to be outdone, joined in, both tugging at their leads. Scorpio showed his excitement by starting to pace proudly, raising his front steps a little higher and quicker.

When Josh and Scorpio got a few feet away, Pancho broke his embrace on Gabe, and stared at the approaching rider on the magnificent dappled blue-gray and white stallion. The pungent fragrance of mesquite smoke wafted from the chimney and the rooster started crowing as Josh rode to a stop and tipped his hat. That got the mare to nickering again, and the stallions alert and answering her.

"This here is Joshua LaPoint, the son of Mister Alex. We're riding together now."

"Eeejohuala! Seguro! Mister Alexander's son! Yo

compredo ahora! Con mucho gusto. And another fine stallion, tambien. I thought you were a ghost too, you look so much like Mister Alex when he was younger. Welcome, senor LaPoint, Mi Casa Su Casa."

Josh swung his long legs down onto the packed dark earth of their destination, then took a deep breath as he patted his horse on the sweaty shoulder. Scorpio looked at him and grinned with a nicker, then shook his neck flesh and his head. Then Josh stepped forward to shake hands with Pancho, and to meet Rosita, who had returned from tending to the goat, which she had left feeding.

Josh shook hands with Pancho, who held his hand limp and weak in the younger man's big strong grip. Josh released the pressure of his hand when he felt Pancho's small hand, which did not return his firm grip.

"Con Mucho Gusto, Senor Robinoix. Welcome to Rancho Escondito."

"Con Mucho Gusto," said Josh in return, smiling with his eyes.

"Que Bueno, Senor LaPoint. Mira Rosita, he's got the same eyes as Senor Alex. Gabe McBride and de ejo de patron. Que bueno! I can hardly believe this. So many time we wish you were here, Gabe. I never see you long time, since '44 when you went back up to the Llano Estacado, and then I heard the Comanche put you under, from some lying Tonkawas. I'm so glad to see you here, right now. You and Mister LaPoint must come in and have coffee while Rosita fixes breakfast. My boy will tend to your animals for you. We got a shed for your packs and saddles by the corral. Come in, come in."

"Yore boy?" said Gabe with wide eyes.

"Yeah Gabe, I got a boy Jesse and a girl Rosa, 16 and 12 years old. You been gone long time," replied Pancho as he ushered them towards his home. He raised his voice and yelled towards the house. "Jesse, andale, come out here, some old amigos del corozon have arrived from a long journada. Go tend to their animals."

"Yes papa," said a slender and wiry teenager with a short clipped haircut who emerged from the kitchen in sandals and clean white cotton pants.

"You speak English to your boy, Pancho?"

"Si Senor Gabe, English is the language of the future.

Around here they disrespect Tejanos now, even though my family, the Menchacas, were among the first settlers here. Both our kids go to school at Panna Maria, and learn proper English with the Polish people, who hired a good teacher, from the German colonies. They both can read and write in English and Spanish. And they got a Catholic church, which we attend also. We only go to Helena when we have to, for supplies. It's a rough town."

"Wal, I'll be. Settled right in and making a home, that's shining'. Yal done real good. Place looks good too, sight for sore eyes after a long ride ta get here. We seen a windmill and well on the way in. And chimneys too."

"Seguro. For sure. A chimney of bricks and a wood stove, and two more coats of plaster. No more cold nights, Gabe. No more snakes underfoot in the morning. Mr. Alex hired an Alleman well driller from San Antonio, and he came down and hit good water and put the wind vanes up, so now we don't have to use the river water for drinking, and the corral has a trough so we don't have to haul buckets, and even a pump in the yard and the kitchen. Mr. Alex like to fix everything nice with the latest things, you know. The plaster stucco, me and Jesse did it. Mr. Alex sent me money to buy lime cement and I covered the boards with tar paper and chicken wire, then plastered every little hole to keep the chigada rattlesnakes and scorpions out. Remember that time you had the little rattlesnake in your boot, Gabe? You jumped so high you hit the door-frame with your head!"

"I shore do. I remember you frying him up too, after I chopped his head off, but I wouldn't eat 'im. When did ya last see Mr. Alex?"

"Oh, I never see him, long time, but he sends me letters and instructions sometimes, or he used to. I never seen him since before I last seen you, maybe in '43 when they gathered the herd here. But he sent men down to gather and drive more herds a few times during those years, and he sends my pay and instructions regular for many years."

"Wal, that's what I was hoping, to find yal still here in his employ."

"But ahora, no se, I doan know. Now, I not hear from him for nearly two years, so I don't know what to do. I was thinking maybe he dead like I think you was dead, but you alive, so

maybe he is tambein. Chansa? Maybe so? When I saw you
both riding up from the river on the fine Spanish horses with
good mules, out the glass window there, I thought it looked like
you and mister Alex, but maybe ghosts, because you both dead.
But you alive, Gabe, alive! Que Bueno! Come sit down for
coffee. Come. Come into my home. Welcome to the little
hidden ranch."

They all went into the house and sat around a long table
on hard red and yellow mesquite planks while Rosita filled coffee
cups and her shy young daughter washed some dishes at the
indoor sink with a hand pump. Josh untied the saddlebag and
let Suzette out. The youngster cooed at her and squatted down,
which caused Suzette to run to her for petting.

"You must eat with us, you must be famished, tengo
hambre, eh?"

"Naw, gracias just the same, we stopped at that new
town, Helena, last night, had a sit down dinner, a bath, and a
bed. Had an early breakfast too, at Muldoon's Bar and Grill,
eggs and pork chops with cornbread. We'll just have coffee and
jaw with ya. I saw you had a fine mare out there in that pen, and
a nice little bunch of mustangs too, down by the river."

"Si. Que bonita, no? That's the mare I got on the
instructions of Mister Alex, after he sent me the money and told
me where to go to get it. It was down at Indianola, waiting when
I got there, a pretty little skinny chestnut filly, and she turned into
a beauty. That's the last time I heard from him, in 62, and I fight
hard to keep that horse, as everyone wants to steal her now that
she has turned into a prima caballa. Especially those malo
hombres in Helena who treat Mexicans worse than dogs. I think
your stallions noticed her too, eh? That mare, she's a beauty."

"Oh yeah, they was feelin' frisky 'bout her right away. Still
are, from the sound of it."

Josh sat quietly by the window and sipped his coffee, but
kept glancing out the window at the boy tending the horses. He
noticed how attentive Scorpio and Buck were towards the mare,
in an adjacent pen to where they were being unsaddled.
Pancho noticed, and spoke to him.

"Senor LaPoint. If you wish to attend your horse, you
should feel free to do so, since you have already eaten, it won't
insult our cook. I see that you are like your father, a man who
cares for his horses. Perhaps your stallion is used to special

treatment? They carried you a long way, no?"

About that time Scorpio stood on his hind legs, milling his front hooves high in the air, with his long pink cock out, and screamed his mating call to the mare. He walked on his hind legs towards the fence nickering to her. Josh got up quick holding his saddlebags, not sure where to deposit it. "Yes. I'd like to go rub them down now that he's got the packs and saddles off, if yal don't mind? They're both hot for that mare. She must be near her time."

"She could be. Do as you like, Senor. You may put that saddlebag you brought in beside the bed in the back room, the one on the right has a chest you may stow your gear in. I hope you intend to stay. You are welcome for as long as you like. This is the ranch of your father Mr. Alex. My house is your house."

While Pancho was talking Josh looked through the wavy window glass and observed Scorpio back up on all fours as if he was going to jump the corral fence, while Jesse tried to deter him by flicking a lariat in front of his face. Buck, who was tied to a railing, was ready to follow, and tugging on his tie-down. Jesse was flustered, trying to handle them.

"Thank you, I'll just go talk to Scorpio for a while, get him settled in." Josh quickly stepped out the door, whistled very loud and shrill, then quickly walked to the barn to tend to his horse and chat with the boy, Jesse. Scorpio settled down and watched Josh approach.

After Josh stepped out and headed for the barn, Pancho spoke to Gabe about him. "Aaaaiiiee, Gabe. Bueno Caballero, no? I saw you from the window and it looked like an old Gabe and a young Mister Alex. The glass is wavy to look through, so I thought it was making a fool of me, for my old worn out wishes. He looks so much like Mr. Alex. And the last time I saw you there was a copper colored beard on your face, now it's almost all gray."

"And Josh is handsome like his Papa, tambien," said Rosita. "Wait til the guerra girls in Panna Maria see him, and the teacher. He's a Catholic tambien, si?"

"Not no more, I reckon. Not fer a long time, actually. More of a free-thinker type now. Says he don't see the hand of no merciful God in this world, and neither do I, Rosita, so don't waste any more time on that. He's well educated, even went back East and to France and England for schooling."

"And a horseman like his Papa, verdad?" asked Pancho.

"Yessir, even better, seems like. He larned from good native horsemen, then a man his pap brought over from Spain, then at the Riding school in Vienna, Austria. He can train horses better than anyone I ever seen. He seems to feel a way into their minds. He'd be with them most of the time if he had his druthers. 'Specially that stallion of his, Scorpio."

"Es magnifico caballo, muy macho, like the rider, eh?"

"Yep," said Gabe.

"Gabe. Yo tengo nueva bueno idea. I got a strange feeling that Senor Alex had me get that mare for your stallions, Gabe. He never told me why he wanted that expensive mare here, but he had a strange way of seeing the future sometimes. He always look a long way ahead, like you say, like the aguilar, the eagle, no? Did he send you here?"

"Naw. But an eagle followed us from the ford, come ta think of it. Ain't seen him since spring of 61, when he left Josh in charge of the business in New Orleans and vanished."

"Josh, he is so young to be in charge of that business. He must have his papa's brains, no? How in the world did you ever end up in New Orleans?"

"After Alex rescued me from that torture he took me back to his plantation to heal. Josh's mother was a healer."

"I think you still got angels looking after you, Gabe, like Rosita says, to live through all that. Can I see the scar on your head where they try to cut your red hair off?"

Gabe took off his hat and showed the scalping scar on his forehead, then his burned hand. "That's what the Comanche done to me. They about half scalped me and burnt my hand."

"Aaaeeeiii. Mira, Rosita. It's a big scar. Can I touch it Gabe?"

Rosita replied, "Esta muy duro cabeza."

"For good luck. Shore. My ole head ain't as purdy as it used to be with that shock o' red hair, huh?"

"At least you got some skin on top to cover it. I saw a man named Josiah come through Helena who had been scalped and lived, and he didn't have no covering on top, just a little cap."

"Oh yeah, I heard o him. Sure glad they never got ta rippin' mine off."

"Senor Gabe! Senor Gabe is here!...the top hat ranger jefe, back in Texas! This is a very good day. We been having all kinds of trouble round here, Gabe. We need help from a man like you. Rosita was praying last week to the archangel Miguel that a man like you would show up to help us. She says that God has sent you to protect us in battle, against the wickedness and snares of the devils from Helena."

Rosita looked over from the kitchen where she was busy cutting onions, her eyes running tears, crossed herself, and kissed her fingers. "Es Verdad. Es Verdad." She broke into real bawling, and turned back to her breakfast making, while her daughter Rosa stared at the strangers with big dark inquisitive eyes, holding Suzette close to her chest. Suzette was in heaven in the little girl's arms, and snorkeled her funny little pleasure sound. She had found a new home, Rosita's kitchen with the girls and the delicious smells.

Gabe laughed. "Wal, I sorta doubt that, but we been dealing with some mean devils, that's for shore. What kinda troubles yal been having?"

"Well, you know about the Indian raids we used to have sometimes, that wasn't so bad for a while, during the drought, because there was not too many healthy horses to steal, but then they had the cart war and started killing Mexicans. All of a sudden, Mexicans were no good anymore, except for target practice. Even the early settlers at Alamita left,...oh yeah, malo tiempo for muchos anos aqui, Gabe, lots of problems with the rough men in Helena, so we quit going there except to trade and go to Panna Maria now, when we can get across the river. But I got to check the mail for letters from Senor Alex, so I go on Sunday mornings now, when all the borochons, the drunken ones, and otra malo hombres are asleep."

"Had some scuffles in Helena, did ya?"

"Oh si, si. Todo tiempo, much trouble. Helena is el pueblo del malos hombres. The white teamsters hate all Tejanos now. Some of the merchants are decent to us, but the freighter are always disrespectful. They insulted my wife there and threw mud and dung all over me. One of them bull-whipped me as he rode by splashing mud all over us. And now they are after the mare, I think. During the cart war they stole anything a Mexican had, and got my remuda more than one time, many times."

"Tres," said Rosita.

"But now I think they want to try to steal Senor Alex's good mare. We had disturbances at night several times this spring, and I think they will come to take her, now that I got her bridal broke. I got a shotgun and an old pistol that might work sometimes, but you know I am not a good shot like you. You the best shot, Gabriel. I remember, you don't shoot fast, but when you take good aim and shoot they go quiet."

"Wal, maybe the time of hunkering down is over when we start shooting back. Speaking of shooting, I guess now's the time to tell ya. We been in some shooting scrapes ourselves. Had a little bar-room scrape in Helena too. But we had to leave Louisiana because we made wolf meat of some federal boys, put 'em under. One was in the city, New Orleans, when Josh caught some riff-raff soldier boys raping a yellow gal and let his stallion kick 'em ta pieces. Josh's ma was what ya might call a 'yalla-gal' herself, though he's a Creole with all kinds of blood running through him, mostly French, but some Spanish and Irish and even Carib Indian."

"Anyway. We hightailed it out of New Orleans, and when we got to the home plantation on the bayou Teche, and we found it burnt out and his mom and several others kilt. We found out who done it from a boy that survived, a little cousin of Joshua's. So after some maneuvering he took down two of the killers. First killings for Josh, though he winged a fella in a duel over a woman onct before. So that is why we run ta Texas, hopin' yal was still here, after these twenty years or so. Had ta kill some bushwhackers at the Sabine too."

"He jus' kill several Union soldiers? Aaaiiieee! No bueno, Gabe. They no chase him?"

"Maybe, but they're busy, and he ain't easy to catch. We traveled by night for the first part of the trip."

"So they have the posters, the wanted posters, with his name and picture?"

"Naw. Not really. But now he's going by the name of LaPoint, 'cause he was well known in New Orleans as a crack shot, and they did put a warrant out for him with the wrong name on it, but now he's LaPoint, not Robinoix, to be on the safe side, and he's trying for a fresh start. Ain't no federals around here, huh?"

"But they been here, Gabe. In 62 the Union gunboats

shelled the port on Matagorda Bay, at Indianola, what they used to call Karlshafen when you were here, where the German's landed, your wife's people, may she rest in peace. You remember, we called it Indian Point before that. They took over the town and looted it, and came back and did it again the next year."

"Damn, are they there now?"

"No, they left again, I think. But they could come back any time."

"Is thar much of a town there now?"

"No se. I think so, but maybe the ship cannons broke it down. The last time I was there was when I got the mare. It was a big town then. A few years before they had a herd of those Arabian beasts with humps come through there, and we saw them on the trail. It spooked my remuda and took me all day to round them up."

"You talkin' bout camels? I heard of that. I think it was one of ole Jeff Davis's ideas. Scared the crap outa every horse that smelt 'em."

"Si, that's it. Camels. A very strange sight."

"I never seen one, 'cept in books Josh showed me. He's always been one for the library ta larn about stuff. We'll steer clear of Indianola and other big places where the federals might go til we see how the dust settles. So for now, hit's time to forget the name Robinoix and just call him LaPoint, savvy? When this war ends, which ain't gonna be long, his misspelled name might be on a long list they're searchin' for, but we'll stay out of any nets they throw. They ain't taking him in for rubbin' out those murdering scumbags while I'm alive."

"You both come to the right place to lay low and start over, Senor Gabe," said Pancho. "We call it Rancho Escondito, because it's our little hideout. Is Josh good with the pistol, like his papa and you?"

"Wal, he ain't no fast draw artist, not yet anyway, but he can shoot the eye outa a baby frog at a good pistol distance. He just winged that guy on purpose in the duel, coulda put it dead center in his forehead if he so desired."

"Bueno. So he is a pistolero like you."

"More of a rifleman right now. Hell, he was just a target shooter til he took down them murderers. But he's a natural dead-eye. I never was fast with a pistol anyway."

"But you always hit because you take aim when bullets are flying."

"Wal, that was when my eyesight was better. Josh is a better shot than I could ever hope to be, and he is accurate with every weapon from rocks and bow and arrow to sharps long rifle or repeaters."

"A better shot than you, I don't believe it. Not under fire."

"Hell yes, he is and will be. Oops. Pardon my French, Rosita."

"Oh Gabe, es no le hace. But you tole me your mama don't like you to cuss."

"Sorry. Well it's a fact he's the best shot I ever seen. Josh don't never miss with a rifle, not in years, and he's powerful accurate with a pistol, not to mention his throwing arm. I seen him blind an alligator when he was a kid by throwing pieces of brick at his eyes, then wrestle him in the swamp water and hogtie him. And his ma made all kinds of gear outa the hide, too, boots, bags, shoes, and such. She was some woman, a first rate healer, and I owe her my life."

Tears formed in Gabe's eyes at the thought of the murder of Josh's mom, for the ride back to Texas had stirred scars of his own. He too had lost the woman he loved to foul murder, and lived with the regret of leaving her unprotected. He knew that Josh had been torn away from his mother at age four because Mr. Alex's sickly white wife had wanted to sell him, and from then on he lived at the orphan school. Since Josh treasured the limited contact he had with his mother, Gabe knew how it tore a hole in his heart to lose her. He paused in his story, took several deep breaths to steady his voice, then started again

"Los siento mucho, Gabriel," said Rosita.

"I'm very sorry, Gabe," said Pancho.

"So, like I said, Josh learned to hunt deer with bow and arrow from the Attakapas before I got ta teaching him firearms and knives. He can flick a cigarette outa my mouth with a bullwhip too. He kin put a ball dead center in a melon from 700 yards every time with a Whitworth rifle, and I seen him do it at over a thousand yards with a scope. And he's always been quicker than me with a knife, even as a kid. He ain't afraid to practice for long hours. He gets sorta fixated on practicing 'til he gets it down, I expect so as ta shine for his Pa, who weren't around much."

"So you were his good teacher, the legendary Top-hat McBride as a schoolteacher, that's muy rico, Senor Gabe."

"Yep, and he's a quick study with the self discipline to practice until he was a crack shot. But he warn't the man-killing type til they kilt his ma, and then he had to bite the bullet and take them varmints down from a distance with the Whitworth rifle, which sorta went against his grain. So he's still recovering from losing his ma, getting his horse barns and his pa's plantation burned down, and his first killings. Hit sorta changed his manner, quieted him down, put him in a funk. I was worried bout him for a while, but he's weathered it. You know what I mean by that, Pancho."

"Si Gabe, you was with me when it happen to me. It was a hard time."

"Yep, right after I gave you that shotgun you had leveled at me by the woodpile. Anyway. Speaking of shotguns, we got a couple of ten gauges ourselves. Which we had to use in the dark to kill a few more bushwhackers at an ambush on the Sabine. That was during the last full moon, I reckon. Not rightly sure how many we put under thar in the shadows of those tall pines and cypress, maybe three or four."

"Aaaaiiieee," said Pancho, and touched Gabe on the shoulder reassuringly. Rosita crossed herself again and started praying louder. She sent Rosa from the room and tried to send Jesse, but the teenager refused to leave.

"So we been on the run for more than a month, sorta touch and go, a few scrapes, but here we are, alive and well, 'cept for a chapped ass and stiff legs. We even soaked ourselves clean and burned our riding rags at Muldoon's bath-house last night. We rode for over forty days and nights too, sometimes, creeping inta tha bushes when we had to."

"So you stayed at Muldoon's after your journada, a good choice. I like Muldoon. He goes to mass at Panna Marie, and is always kind and respectful, not like the Helena bastardos."

"Aaah, Pancho, I tried not to use that word around Josh. He used to be pretty sensitive about that as a kid. Remember, Mr. Alex had a sickly white wife, and he never married Joshua's ma, even after his wife went under. But he shore loved her and stayed with her for a quarter century."

"Oh si, pardon. Repete no mas. I not say it again."

"Your mama told you no cussing, Gabriel," said Rosita.

"no more chasing after los Comanches either."

"That's right. It ain't no hanging matter, Pancho, but really, being born a bastard ain't no kid's fault, eh. Why heck, I've known some bastards that was great explorers of the West, for that matter, like ole Fremont. It ain't like Josh's ma was a whore or nothin' such-like, she was the only woman Mr. Alex ever loved, far as I ever saw, and she ran that dang plantation better'n anyone else could of. She had a regular bounty of a garden there, richest soil you can imagine with lots of rain, plenty to eat with a mixed cropping, slaves wouldn'ta run away if ya paid 'em. Anyway, I try ta use another term," Gabe said with a smile.

"Se, I understand. I'm the same way with Muldoon. They say he's the bastardo son of that priest who baptized everyone to get them into the Austin colony in the old days. Padre Muldoon. I don't know, so I just take care around him, like I will around Josh."

"Wal alright, then."

"Senor Gabe, we are so glad you are here. The times are crazy now, muy malo, muy loco, and we have been living in constant fear, and sometimes terror. Los Indios, Lipan Apache we think maybe, came through, stole my cousins down at Refugio, and tried to steal Jesse too. If I had not plastered the house they would have burned us out, but with the metal roof and plaster, their torches wouldn't light it. The Helena outlaws try to burn us out too. I put buckshot in them if they get close."

"So you're hunkered down on the Escondito. We gonna change that. We'll put a stop to raiding."

"Muy Bueno, mi amigo. Further north the Comanche are trying to take the land back, with the soldiers gone for the big wars in the East."

"You no chase Comanche, Gabriel McBride," said Rosita as she crossed herself.

"Ah reckon ah'm done with that," said Gabe.

Pancho continued. "The Helena toughs and night riders want to run all the Mexicans out of the country. 'Back to Mexico' they say. I never even been to Mexico. I am Tejano. I was born here and schooled by the monks at Bexar, before they arrived. My family married into the family of Eraso Seguin, the first land grant holder here."

"They'll play hell driving us out, we're 'bout fed up with

running. Mexico's a mess anyway."

"Si! The French have taken Mexico for bad debts, anyway. They got an Austrian running it. Me go to Mexico? No! I am a proud descendent of the first Menchaca settlers, raised in San Antonio and taught by the friars after Indians killed my people, I know nothing about Mexico. This is my home, a Spanish land grant, and we were the first on it. I can read and write better than most of them. I am no savage to be pushed out. We are the people that make a place civilized and peaceful. With you here, we have a chance to stay. After the cart war, there's not too many Mexicans left."

"Wal, I reckon they'd play hell tryin to run us off. We done run all we gonna, and we shoot better than most. You needn't worry 'bout that with yore old amigo around, savvy? So, eeerr, whar are me and LaPoint gonna sleep?"

"In the back bedroom on the right. Jesse can sleep in Rosa's room, and she will bring her mat into our room, no problema. There are two beds and chests there for you. Make yourselves at home, then we will go look at the place, okay?"

Within a half hour Pancho's family had eaten and Josh had doctored the sore backs of the mounts and mules, and had gotten them fed and rubbed down.

Gabe and Pancho came strolling out and took a walking tour of the place with Josh, who has secured Buck and Scorpio in a small pen while letting the mules into a small river pasture with hobbles to graze. Josh was already imagining a house addition, blacksmith shop, and more horse corrals. After looking over the barn, sheds, and pens, they stood to admire the chestnut mare.

"She looks to have a lot of thoroughbred in her. Look at those long legs, looks fast in a long race. Where is she from, Pancho?" asked Josh.

"I think she come down from Kentucky on that big river before the Yankees block it off. But I don't know for sure. She was long-legged and skinny when I got her, but now look at her. Que bonita, no?"

"She's a beauty, good spirit in the eye too. I think we should breed Scorpio to her when she's ready."

"Seguro, for sure, Senor LaPoint. That's what I think. And I heard my cousins, the vaqueros, say there's more like her coming through Helena from the coast, headed for sale in San

Antonio and the German towns up north of there."

"Wal, did you discuss tha breeding situation with Buck any?" asked Gabe. "Looks ta me like he's mighty interested too."

"No, I didn't. Either one, or both would be alright. We could let them both have a shot at her. And I could start buying more mares to breed right away."

"Now yer talkin', and may the best cream rise to the occasion."

"Alright, that's settled. And we can race the horses to see who goes first, later on when they're well rested. What about that other bunch down in the river pasture. I think I counted three dozen at least. They saddle ready?"

"Que Lastima, no. No. They are wild mustangs and crossbreeds. They could make good cow ponies. Some local jefes are starting to talk about big drives. After the drought broke and the rains came again, the horse and cattle multiplied like rabbits. I could sell them if they were saddle broke. But I have a hard time by myself with them, and Jesse is in school. Can you break them to saddle, Senor LaPoint?"

"I'd like to try to make saddle mounts out of them. I'd need a round pen for training."

"Round-pen? Redondo? Por que?... Why?....we got that corral there for breaking them, that's what the caballeros always used, tie them to the post in there." Pancho pointed to the corral that held the stallions, a stout one made of upright mesquite posts with cedar railings lashed on with thick strips of rawhide, then pegged with huge square nails. It held a tall post in the middle with rope burn marks on it.

"No. I don't break them the old way. I don't tie them and break their spirit. I run them in a smooth circle until they want to come back to me. I need a round pen without the post in the middle."

"We not got one, Senor LaPoint, lo siento mucho. Es problema?"

"I'll build one then. And call me Josh when we're among friends, alright? LaPoint among strangers, okay?"

"Okay, Josh. How you gonna build it?"

"Well, I imagine the same way the square one is built, mesquite posts with the lighter cedar railings."

"We got the mesquite, for sure, but we had to get the

cedar rails from freighters last time. It grows up in the hill country, up north of San Marcos. We could get a load down from San Antonio, if you got money. I used up the money Don Alex sent for corrals."

"Alright. We'll do that. Do you have a post-hole digger?"

"Oh si senor, we gotta good one that Gabe made long time ago, steel handles, can't break it like the wooden ones. But it's very heavy."

"How about a crosscut saw and ax?"

"Yes, by the woodpile."

"Well, how about this idea. I'll get the wood and build the pen, and I'll pay Jesse as my part-time helper to load the posts and sink them while the load of wood is coming from San Antonio. Meanwhile I can get to know those mustangs in the pasture. With your approval, I'll make a deal with Jesse for work after school and weekends, helping me work the posts. How does that sound?"

"Es okay with me, Josh. Es good, but you gotta take a shotgun with you for snakes when you go cutting posts in the brush. They coming out to warm up on sunny days now. And the wagon is old, not so good anymore, loose wheels. Maybe senor Gabe..."

"Good. We'll start tomorrow. Eh Gabe? If you'd be good enough to make further inventory of what we're gonna need, then go order it in Helena tomorrow, I'll get the cash for it ready tonight. Now I think I'll go meet that bunch in the lower pasture. What about that old longhorn, he isn't going to come try to hook us with that big spread, is he?"

"Oh no, senor. He don't leave the shade of that tree. He's the old viejo who led the herd to Indianola twice, so Mr. Alex retired him here. He don't do nothing but chew and get up to make manure sometimes. He's got a bell on, but we don't hear it ring much."

"By the way, Pancho. What do you call this place?" Josh inquired.

"Ranchito Escondito."

"That was what Gabe called our storm shelter back at the Colorado River. Why that?"

"Little hidden ranch. Because we been hiding out here since the times got hard on Tejanos, since the cart wars. But it's really your ranch, Senor."

"Alex Robinoix's ranch, you mean."

"Yours too."

"Well perhaps it is time to rename it. Maybe we won't have to hide out if we have enough ammo."

"Well, I for one am done with hunkering down and hiding out," said Gabe.

"Right," said LaPoint. "We aim to build something here, and fight if we have to. Maybe we should name it for the eagle that's been following us since we forded the river. He's up there still, see him?"

"Eagle Ford Ranch?" asked Gabe.

"Sure, why not? Might be lucky someday, eh?"

"We'll be lucky to be shed of the rattlesnakes."

" And how big is it, Pancho, what are the boundaries?"

"It's 2640 acres of the Erasmo Seguin grant, from the ford and all along the river on one side, and I show you the other boundaries tomorrow when we go riding. I go with you to Helena, ok?"

"Over 2600 acres! Small? Another surprise, Gabe. You always called it a small ranch. Seems more like rancho grande than ranchito."

"It has to be big, for a dry country. Eagle Ford suits it better than Rancho Grande, believe me. Thar's spreads down south that make this one seem tiny. Anyway, that's what the vaqueros called Alex, El Aguilar. The Eagle. Maybe yore right, new name might bring good luck."

"Oh yeah," said Josh as he looked around the scattered sticker bushes with a wry smile, "in about a century and a half."

"Wal, we got time to make something now. And I think I'd better go into Helena alone tomorrow. I'll check that mailbox for any letters from Mister Alex. Could be some hangover from a little scrape we got into, and I'd rather just have ta lookout for myself 'til I get the lay of the land."

"Okay," said Pancho. "I just wanted to check the mail and get corn flour and beans anyway."

"That's what I figured. I'll take care of it for ya."

"Alright then, we're set. Set us up a new mailbox for Eagle Ford Ranch, a big one."

"Oh yeah, a big one fer all that mailbox money we're agonna get..."

"Gonna need that wagon in the morning," Josh said with

a smile.

Gabe smiled and nodded his head. "Alright, LaPoint of the Eagle Ford Spread, you keep that smile coming from now on, huh? Ain't seen it much in the last five hundred miles. Even killers smile, ya know. Here, look at me, I kilt more varmints than I got teeth," Gabe showed a broken and gaped front set of yellow teeth, which brought a full laugh from Josh.

"Es verdad, very true he speak. He shoot more Comanches than he got teeth," said Pancho.

"Now there's an old coon grin if there ever was one," said Josh, chuckling. "Looks like he's been chewing horseshoe nails too long. A kisser only a mother could love."

"That face used to be the Comanches' nightmare, amigo," said Pancho.

"Gabe, you no chase Comanche!" said Rosita.

"Ah ain't, just horses."

"I think he's telling the truth," said Josh. "He hightailed it when we saw some."

"You saw Comanches, raiders?"

"Naw, meat hunters," said Gabe. "Still, Ah did skedaddle, like he said. Ah'm done with chasing Comanches."

"Good. Let's chase horses, the countryside is full of them."

"They don't chase back, either," said Josh.

"Waugh," was all Gabe replied as he chuckled, remembering the cold sweat that seeing the hunting party had put him into.

Josh looked fully relaxed and happy for the first time since the journada began, and he walked with a light step over the dirt of his new home to the corral, grabbing a small bag of his special grain and molasses mixture as he did. He looped the bag over one shoulder so that it hung at his chest as he approached the stallions.

Buck and Scorpio stood admiring the mare in the adjacent pen, about ten yards away, both pawing the dirt with ears pricked towards her. The mare was prancing around and snorting at them, and they were very keen on her every move. Josh whistled to Scorpio and the glistening stallion wheeled away from the mare and came over to where Josh stood, the big muscular neck arched up high and proud. The Andalusian had lost weight like the rest of them on the long ride, and this accentuated the rippling muscles in his chest and shoulders. The stallion stepped up and gently touched noses with Josh, then they inhaled each others breath for a few seconds. Speaking softly towards the horse's front pricked ears, Josh let him eat from the feedbag at his chest while rubbing his head. Buck joined them, and they felt home at last.

Gabe smiled and shook his head in affirmation towards Pancho. Opening the gate, Josh let the big dappled gray and white stallion out and sprung up on his back without saddle or bridal. Holding onto the thick dark mane that had grown out again during the preceding forty odd day trip after being cut, Josh signaled Scorpio with his legs and feet and hands on his neck, and they cantered off towards the small herd of horses in the river meadows below the house.

Pancho smiled in amazement at the gate as Josh rode off. "Eeejo-huala. I seen bareback with a hackamore, but not bareback without no bridal at all. He is primo caballero, no? How long he train that horse to be able to do that?"

"He raised that horse from the day of its birth. Trained him a little every day, I reckon. Didn't use a saddle on him for the first year of riding. When he first started riding like that he pulled on the upper mane to bend the horse in either direction. Now he uses signals from legs and butt and feet and hands. It still amazes me, though I seen it many times."

"He's better than a Comanche, even they use a hackamore."

"You ain't seen nothing yet. Lets go watch what he does with that bunch down below. You sure that ole bull ain't gonna charge us?

"Si. I'm sure. The kids play with him. He's tame."

"Yeah, well he knows the kids, he don't know me."

"He's old and lazy, Gabe. No worry. We call him Way, because he used to lead the way, but now there's no way he's gonna get up out of the shade."

As he had moved to the herd, Josh had rubbed horse sweat all over him. The big stallion cantered into the herd. The horses broke into a run, and soon Josh had them circling the meadow in an accelerating pace, at first running behind them, but later running with them. They went around to the right for several times, slowing a bit with each circle, until the horses began to tire of their flight and put their heads down and show their teeth, chewing and licking. Then Josh rode Scorpio away from them, to the center of the meadow, and dismounted, pulling Scorpio down on the ground immediately thereafter in the smoothest of practiced motions.

Scorpio lay there with an occasional nicker, watching intently as Josh walked towards the herd while spreading the horse sweat all over him. The herd had stopped running and were walking and milling, some starting to graze again, some just working their mouths and walking, eying him warily. They settled, and he moved towards them again, steadily and very slowly, while they watched.

When Josh got close enough for them to start to shy away, he turned sideways and stopped moving, whistled, then slowly walked away from them. He repeated this several times. Each time they seemed less inclined to shy away, and more curious. A sturdy mare came to the fore and watched him closely. The forth time he did it, the lead mare followed him, and he stopped and held his open palm with aromatic feed mix out to the side, holding his body sideways to her and slowly leaning out in the offering. She took a few steps towards him, cautiously, sniffing the air. He remained motionless with the feed held out. She moved towards it and he pulled it in to his chest again, turned away from her and took two steps. She stood watching, sniffing, ears pricked forward. He took two more steps away. She pawed the ground, her ears still pricked forward. He looked over his shoulder and spoke to her. She slowly walked up and put her head on his shoulder. He remained motionless for a few seconds, then slowly turned and guided her head to the pouch of feed on his chest. He stroked her neck while she ate, as calm as a barnyard nag.

"Eeeee-juala" said Pancho. "Es magico. Gabe, the prairies southwest of here are full of wild horses. Together we can catch them and this magico hombre can tame them for us to sell to range bosses for the cattle drives. We can get the best mares and breed them with bigger horses, tambien?"

Gabe gave an appraising and thoughtful nod. "I expect so. He can calm just about any horse that ain't been ruint."

When the mare joined Josh, the other horses began to approach as if he was just part of the herd. Josh slowly turned with his hands stroking the mare's lips and muzzle, and kept feeding her from the feed bag at his chest. Scorpio got up after dusting and strolled over, grazing as he came. Within a moment Josh had all the horses gathered around him as he fed each one, rubbed it, talked to it, then moved to the next. When he got back up on Scorpio they were all grazing peacefully around him, having finished up the feed bag mix.

"I cannot believe what I am seeing, Gabe. The only way I can get close to those loco mustenos is rope them after a long chase. He is magico, no? El brujo de caballeros, si."

"Wal, you said it. He could be. Both his ma and pa carried peculiar talents. And I reckon when he got shunted off to that orphan school, about the only friends he had were the horses for a few years. He would lay in the pasture for hours watching the horse herd. He lived with 'em and learned how ta get close to them."

"Es verdad, seguro. We got a whole pasture of crossbreeds and mustangs for him to train."

They watched as Josh remounted and rode down to the river, where both rider and horse entered for a wash. As Gabe and Pancho turned to head back for the house, the old longhorn came moseying up to Gabe, his bell clanging and his boney ass swaying. He paced right up to the old Texian, swaying gently, one creaky step at a time, and touched his nose to the surprised man's chest, with a soft bellow.

"He never done that before," said Pancho. "This is an amazing day. It's a new beginning."

"That's for shore. Hey. I know that bull, it's the one we used for a lead with the herd drives. That's ole Plunger. We chose him at the first river ford, when he plunged in without stopping."

"Si. El Plunger. The old lead bull that Mr. Alex held in con mucho respecto. It's like a miracle seeing you together. Look at him sway those horns, like he used to do with the herd, to hook any cow that tried to pass him. Rosita prayed for help from St. Michael to save this rancho, and here you are. Sometimes I think a holy woman has the most power of all."

"Waugh. Don't we all wish that? If wishes were horses, huh? Didn't save some of 'em from being drug thru hell by the Comanches at times, though. Nor save Joshua's mother. Woman need protectin' with guns around here. And the main reason we finally got here is 'cause we got driven out of whar we was. But we'll durn shore make a stand with ya here."

"It's a new day, Gabriel. We gonna make a horse ranch, the best in the country, and to hell with the Helena bandidos."

"Yep. LaPoint and McBride are here now, so thar'll be no more hidin' out from varmints."

Chapter Eight: Mustangs to Saddle Mounts

The next morning Josh got up before dawn when he heard Gabe arise to relieve himself and start puttering around in the kitchen. They had coffee with goat-milk, and Josh hitched up the mules after feeding them, then took the repaired wagon and sharpened cutting tools out to a thicket where he had noticed straight mesquite posts were available. The mules had not pulled a wagon in months, and were not too keen on the idea, with a few loud protestations and variations on the heehaw as they rattled down the bumpy little rise towards the dense mesquite and live oak thicket. Josh took a shotgun and his pistol belt with his big revolver.

At dawn he entered the mesquite thicket and began clearing out underbrush with the freshly sharpened ax to start cutting with the bucksaw at the base of some oak and mesquite with post-like qualities. Gabe was the past master at putting a sharp edge on, and the ax worked well on the bases of the bushes. Most of the bushes had various kinds of thorns on them, some long and deadly looking, some short but hooked like cat claws. Josh wore his leather gloves and buckskin shirt when handling the thorny branches. A quick moving bird with mixed brown, black, and cream color ran around spying on him like a scout.

As the sun rose, the songs of birds began in many places. A few coyotes were yipping up the draw a mile or two away from the river. Huge flocks of dark brown birds were nesting in the treetops, and they all began to stir as he began the crosscut work. Soon he saw deer flitting by, and a couple of coyotes slinking along, eying him warily. He kept up his steady chopping and sawing, pouring sweat, forgetting his past losses in the exertion that required total focus to keep from getting snagged by the sticker thorns protruding everywhere. Losing himself in his work, his mind quit tumbling the painful events of the recent past.

Within an hour, he had four stout mesquite posts, around ten feet long, and the day was warming up nicely, the suns' direct rays drying the dew. He was sweating in the moist air, with the intense effort of sawing near the base of the tree, and it felt good to him to be doing something constructive and engaging after the long tense journey that got them there through their dark ride of mourning.

After another tough hour of difficult sawing and chopping he had ten posts with a big pile of branches for other uses. He glanced towards the house when he heard the door slam and saw Gabe mount Buck and head out towards him. Josh took a water break and wiped the sweat from his face with a big bandanna as Gabe rode up and pointed to the eagle circling above them.

"Thar he is again. Aguilar."

"Nice morning to get started again, huh?"

Gabe slid his battered felt hat back and scratched his scar, took an appraising look at the pile of posts, and gave a low whistle before he spoke. "Wal, yore makin' beaver, I see."

"No beaver here, trapper."

"Got ya a biscuit with and egg and pork in it, thought ya might be hungry now."

"Thanks pard, you headed for town?" Josh chomped down on the breakfast biscuit. Gabe's sourdough biscuits were a mainstay of his diet, and they always tasted good, warm or cold. These had spelt flour in them, with high protein like the Roman soldiers had used, and were dense enough to last for a while.

"Yas-sir, got a long list, got tha silver, got my head on straight, got my gun and knife, gonna get some more household food with the change if it's alright with you, fill the larders round here, for that Rosita can do wonders if she's well supplied. The pantry is a bit bare for guests."

"For sure, get what we need, load up the pantry and make them glad we're here. 'Seguro', as Pancho says. Is he working with the mare?"

"Yep, got a bridle on her right off tha bat. I'm gonna look around in Helena for more mares, I expect."

"Scorpio behaving?"

"Wal, he's been talkin' at her a lot, but he don't look like he's ready to jump the fence. We oughta put some more stout rails on that pen too, when we get the cedar. It ain't built for no jumping Andalusians, 'specially with that mare in the next pen."

"Yeah. We will. Be careful in Helena. Somebody might like to take down the ole codger who took down big Ron, notch his stick with it."

"Yas-sir, I reckon so. I'll just tell 'em it was LaPoint that took him down. La point of yore boot, to be exact. Don't fret bout nothin, just enjoy your work. I'm awake and well armed. Hell-in-a-handbasket ain't nuthin' new ta me."

"I guess not, you seemed quite accustomed to the ways of civilization the other day, you did. Don't forget metallic cartridges for that new Remington."

"Yas-sir. Be back this afternoon with what I can carry in my saddlebags. Hell, now that I've seen yore silver pouch, I'm gonna order a whole wagon load of cedar rails, plenty of use for them. Gonna get some lime for plastering too, new trowels, another shovel; that stucco makes things fireproof and tight. Hits a good idea for sealing out the snakes and scorpions. Gonna get a lot of rope too. Feed corn, more coffee and grain and a new grinder. Hope to find a blacksmith shop for some more tools, and maybe the use of it at times, eh? Jesse and Rosa done crossed the river in a little boat and went ta school in Panna Maria. We could lash a rope across there, and maybe think about a dam to deepen the swimming hole. Jesse be back to help load all this around four, good Lord willin' and tha creek don't rise."

"Well alright, I haven't heard so many yes-sirs from you, ever. Lets make a horse ranch, Ole Coon," said Josh with a smile as he wiped his face with a towel. "If the creek rises, I hope it floats your stick off so I don't have to hear about it any more, waugh!"

"Dang-it, I tole ya 'bout that. I did not learn to talk in a school; I learned in the mountains. I warn't no educated company factor, neither."

"Well, the beavers are gone, and this ain't the mountains...this place is sort of a sticker patch with a lot of rough stock in the neighborhood, but I expect we can make a horse gathering ranch out of it, being as it's all we got."

"That we will. It's warming up Josh; watch out for rattlesnakes. Keep that shot gun ready."

"Isn't it their custom to warn you first, coil up and rattle furiously?"

"Sometimes, lessen ya startle em. But ya gotta watch out for other pit vipers too. Cottonmouths, you already know what them varmints look like, by the river and wet draws, also ya got copperheads, sort of olive and rust cross-patterned, sort of pretty actually, just about anywhere, especially under logs and river-side rocks. Oh yeah, and another bright colored lil sneak, a coral snake, deadly poison, some Indians use it on their arrows. It ain't got the viper head or long fangs, just a pretty slender little fella with bright colors and tiny fangs that kin kill with a scratch. Red and yella and black, hit resembles another harmless snake with a different order on the colors. Red and yella kill a fella. Iffen you see red and yella together on one, hits a coral snake, with the worst poison of all, drives ya crazy as it kills ya. Red and yella, kill a fella. Sorta like with redskins, if ya show yella around 'em, they'll kill ya quick. Could ya repeat it after me, sonny?"

"Go on now, and be careful, ya ole coon. Don't get too drunk. Just make sure you remember the way back."

"Come on, like repeating yore shooter's procedure in the old days. Red and yella.."

"Hey, I had enough of that. After listening to yal I'm ready to jump back at the sight of a garden snake. You be careful. I heard that little Rosa thanking the Virgin Mary for sending you this morning. Don't overload Buck on the way back, we can take the wagon in later for the big stuff. Seems like you fixed it well, but we haven't hauled a load up the hill yet."

"It'll hold for a while, I reckon, el Jefe. Could use a little blacksmith shop in that shed thar, or a new shed with one in it."

"Yeah, I figured that was coming. I'll throw in with you on that. We'll need your farrier skills for the wagon and all these horses we're gonna gather and shoe."

"Alright then. Skookum."

"Gabe, listen to me. I mostly don't like you going in there alone right now. You by God better be extra alert, and watch out for back-shooters in Helena. I haven't been praying to the Virgin, but I've grown accustomed to your biscuits."

Gabe chuckled, nudged Buck forward and chanted in time to the rhythm of the stallion's pacing, "red and yella, kill a fella."

Josh entered the thicket with ax and bucksaw, cut and piled all day, forgetting himself in strenuous and productive labor, forgetting the loss of his mother and home, the loss of his old self. Instead of his losses, he focused on the fact that for the first time in his life he was free to follow his own bent, to build his horse ranch from the ground up. For hour after steady hour he just engaged in hacking and sawing to build a round-pen and fulfill his dream of working with horses, all the while alert for rattlesnakes and Indians.

Through midday he hacked and sawed in the dense thicket as the day grew warmer, all the while making plans for the future as the sweat burned his eyes. He only saw snakes leaving the area, probably because he was always making noise and picking posts from the edge of the thicket. Once he saw a small herd of javelinas scurry by along the riverside below him, but he ignored them and kept a steady pace. The eagle overhead was joined by another, and they cruised the river banks looking for prey.

In the warm afternoon a large rattler threatened him and Josh whacked his head with a post after a risky fight with him. He threw the still moving body off as far as he could after rendering it harmless by slicing the head off. One of the quick ground birds came out and grabbed the writhing body, began to tear it apart and eat it. Another soon joined it, and they feasted in the sun, while Josh kept working. The eagle made a low pass over the treetops, eying the snake carcass being consumed by the piasanos.

By the time Jesse returned from school, ate, and was ready to help, Josh had a wagon-load of posts ready to load. Together they loaded the dense and heavy red mesquite timber, strained the mules a bit hauling the full wagon up the rise to the barn, and unloaded them near where the round-pen would go. Josh noticed that Jesse was very strong, agile, alert, and knew how to work together, anticipating the next move and making himself ready for it. He had an easy-going and eager-to-learn attitude that made him fun to work with.

Gabe returned as the sun was starting to set, and Josh was starting to worry about him. Rosita was cooking dinner of enchiladas and Spanish rice and beans, the glorious spicy smells filling the yard. The smell of various peppers and garlic cooking made Josh think of his mother. Buck was laden with full saddlebags and ropes. Gabe nearly snagged his foot on a stiff coil of rope as he dismounted.

"Opps, tangle-footed again." He'd had a few nips, by the sound of his voice, though he wasn't really tipsy. " Wal, lookee that pile o posts, yal done good, huh?"

"Yeah, no problems. Only killed one snake. Jesse's a

good helper, and Pancho's got the mare doing really nicely. Did you smell that food as you rode by the house?"

"Smelled it a mile away, and I'm drooling. I told ya bout Rosita's enchiladas."

"Any scrapes in town?"

"Naw, smooth as a french silk top hat, thank ya. Had lunch with Muldoon, learned the war news, all bad. Or good, considering it's hastening to an end. Found a blacksmith that's gonna let me use his shop on occasion 'cause he was drooling at my knife and wanted to larn how ta fold steel. Ordered all our stuff. Got you a heap o metallic cartridges."

"What about horses for sale?"

"Seen some mares for sale that you need to look at. Found some bargains on grain and some lime, so we gotta go back in tha wagon within a few days for big bags of stuff. My saddlebags are full, and I got fresh ropes, as ya kin see, so here's another thing for ya to master, roping from a running mount, with an expert ta teach ya, ole Pancho, who's among the very best at mustanging."

"Excellent. Great day. Snakes all skedaddled without much fight so far. No problems with the posts, and Jesse helped lift for the loading. Got a big pile of stove wood too. Jesse learned about fractions in school and made some pocket money too. He's a smart helper, strong too. We're heading for a wash at the river. Want to join us?"

"Naw, Josh. You kin have that cold water, spent too much time in cold water in the mountains already, picking up them floating sticks. Rheumatism would kick up. They got a tub hanging on that shed wall behind the yard pump. I'm gonna have a hot bath with this pine tar soap I got."

"You sure? They got a nice little swimming hole."

"You and Jesse go on, watch for snakes."

Scorpio nickered and showed his teeth, and then Josh bridled him and carried Jesse bareback down to the river. Since they had no saddle scabbard, they did not carry the shotgun, but Josh had his pistol belt on. His shirt was off in the warm spring air and he shone with sweat as Scorpio broke into full run for the river bottoms.

The riverbanks were thick with trees and brush on the other bank, with a gravel bar on this side for water entry. Many of the trees were sprouting fresh greenery, lending a verdant feeling to the swimming hole. The water was cool and not too muddy, and they found enough deep water to stroke a bit. Josh rubbed the course sand over his body to remove the grime.

"Keep a lookout for the viejo grande snake, Senor," said Jesse as he swam.

After bathing they were putting their pants back on when they saw the cottonmouth, a big one coming towards them along the bank, his tongue flicking out from his big jawed head as he moved right at them, swimming gracefully in an undulating line of S-curves.

The gun belt with the new Remington he had acquired was now filled with metallic cartridges in loops around the back, and he had practiced enough with the long barreled gun to hit what he aimed at. The loaded weapon belt was hanging on a branch stub several yards away, and Josh was barefoot with blisters from his work in the underbrush, so instead of going for the gun he grabbed a rounded river stone and nailed the head of the snake at ten yards with a sharp throw, when it was obvious the slithering big-headed serpent was coming for them. That stopped the snake and turned it into a writhing coil.

"Chingado! You hit him first shot," said Jesse. "Bueno Pistolero! You gotta teach me to do that. We got lotta snake trouble here. He's still alive though."

"Well I can see that with all the twisting," said Josh as he stepped gingerly on the gravel bar to where his pistol belt hung. "Ouch, damned blisters, riding boots ain't worth much for crawling under brush and cutting. Got my feet tender as a babes."

"How you learn to do that, Senor?"

"Practice. That's my only secret. If you want to be the best, you have to do it the most. That one's sure making a coil, isn't it. Look at him writhing, gives me the gooseflesh to watch."

"Oh, I've seen them keep twisting like that long after the head is chopped off. But this one is striking still. Look, it's gone loco, striking everywhere. Shoot him, Senor LaPoint. Shoot him. Kill him. He tried to own the swimming hole for long time, always chasing us. Now's our chance to get rid of him."

"Yeah, they can be damned aggressive, especially in water when they can go under and latch on. Been killing them since I was six, just to keep my swimming areas safe." Josh drew the revolver, stepped behind the low sweeping mesquite branch, braced the pistol on it, and blew the snakes head off with one shot at fifteen yards.

"Senor Josh! One shot! Bravo Pistolero! You not waste the bullets. I will feel safer when we swim now. See our little boat in the brush there? It's made from the cypress planks, with canvas and pitch. This is where we cross, and that big cottonmouth is always coming for us. I learn to paddle fast because of that snake. He is, how does the viejo Gabe call it, 'put under' now?"

Josh smiled, nodded to Jesse, and was flooded with nostalgic feelings when he saw the small boat, a tiny canoe with canvass-covered ends that resembled the pirogue he paddled for hundreds of miles as a child on the bayou. "I believe Gabe would say we made wolf meat of him. Want me to take him away and throw him in the brush?"

They looked at the snake in the twilight and saw it still slowly writhing, without its head, which lay still with the white mouth open and fangs bared. Josh spotted the eagle swooping low along the water's edge.

"Let the eagle and buzzards and coyotes have him. Or the javelinas. He will be gone in the morning," said Jesse. "That eagle has been around all the time since you showed up."

"Yeah, I noticed that. He followed us from the ford, and he's been around since then. The vaqueros used to call Mister Alex El Aguilar. We renamed the spread, Eagle Ford Ranch, no more hiding out at the Escondito."

"That's a good one. I'm tired of hiding from bandits. I want to learn to shoot, like you. Look, the eagle is coming back; he wants that snake. Mr. Alex Robinoix is your papa, no?"

The eagle made a low pass over the snake and flapped upstream again, followed by it's companion. A great blue heron passed overhead, then cruised low along the top of the water, seeking fish.

"So it's said. He never actually claimed me, but he got me educated and put me to work for the trading company. Then he disappeared."

"But he didn't raise you?"

"He was never around much. He spent most of his time out west, with the fur trading business. I got sent away to a mission school when I was young."

"The old ranger, Senor Gabe, he is like your papa, no?"

"About as close as it comes, I guess. Look, the eagle's circled back again."

"If we go away he will get that snake."

"Alright, food for better creatures, come on, let's go eat. They'll be wondering what the shot was for."

"Do you think your true father, Senor Alex, is still alive?"

"I don't know, and I can't waste time worrying about it. This ranch is all that's left, so I aim to build it up. Let's go." As Josh mounted, they saw a quick and elegant looking bird go running by.

"Hey, I saw that little guy before, kept coming around all day, what was that? A fast running bird, look, there he goes."

"Es piasano. El chapparal bird. The white guys call them Roadrunners. Es a good sign, Senor. They are snake killers, very smart and quick. They circle the snake and make him strike, then they will peck his head with the hard point of their beaks. They gotta funny little snake dance they do, to confuse the rattlers. Muy rapido, like you. Sometimes two of them kill the biggest rattlesnakes, the one drawing his attention while the other attacks. They bring good luck. Very good for the ranchito. It's a good, how you say ...Omen? in English. The times are changing now for Texas, Senor LaPoint. Better times coming, I can feel it. El Rancho del vado de Aguilar. We gonna be lucky now."

"Yes. Omens, my mother used to call them. Come on, lets eat." Jesse mounted Scorpio, who was wet from his dip in the olive-green water, and they rode in to dinner and made the females happy with news of killing the big snake. Rosa crossed herself and went to pray at the little alter to St. Michael she had made. Josh stayed at the barn to rub Scorpio down and feed him. Jesse told his papa about Josh's accuracy with stone and pistol slug, which pleased Pancho greatly.

"We finally got some sharpshooters around here, eh? Muy bueno. You guys are so much better a shot than I can ever be."

"Wal, I recollect ya ain't too bad with a shotgun when there's Comanche coming at ya, and that's pert near good enough. One thing ya could teach us both is roping those running horses. I ain't seen a better mustanger for cutting out good stock with a riata. You gotta teach that to LaPoint. I never taught him, warn't no good compared ta you. He can throw a loop, but nothin' like you vaqueros."

"Oh Senor Gabe. De nada. I learned riding and roping as a kid, from the real experts, my father's vaqueros, before I went to San Antonio. I got a riata as soon as I could walk, and it was my main toy growing up. I roped everything. But I not a good shot, you know that. All I got is the shotgun, and an old pistol with the trigger broke."

Later the men sat on the porch with drinks and smokes after dinner and watched the rising of the moon. It was a good beginning, and they all felt good to be together, combining their skills to build a ranch. They slept well on their mattresses stuffed with Spanish moss and cedar bark, slung over horsehair ropes threaded through cedar post frames. The colorful bantam rooster awoke them early with his incessant celebration of dawn.

That morning Josh wanted to learn to use the riata like Pancho, and asked for lessons. Pancho had hung a heavy weight from the tallest tree to straighten the new coiled rope the night before, then showed Josh how to handle it. They worked for an hour on it, but the new rope did not respond as well as Pancho's horsehair or rawhide riatas, and Josh realized he would have to keep working on it.

Then, as the sun rose in the clear blue sky and heated the spring day, Josh again took the wagon down for more timber. He got into a new thicket in a draw and there he saw rattlers, lots of three-footers and some as long as he was tall, over six feet, with big knobby heads and huge fangs that folded out ominously when they felt threatened and buzzed their rattles. They did not want to leave the area either.

There was a certain beauty and fairness to the coiling and rattling a warning, in Josh's mind, and he didn't want to kill them indiscriminately, but some of them were clinging to the best timber area, and he had to get rid of them.

Instead of using the shotgun, he decided to practice a smooth fast draw on them. By hitting them in the head he could save the skin for tanning, instead of blowing it to shreds with the big shotgun. Shooting at them didn't scare them away, only seemed to bring more out of their holes. It took killing to get shed of them. So the next few days were full of sporadic pistol fire as he worked steadily, accumulating a big pile of posts by the barn, with Jesse's help. He was even able to make some curving rails from some of the tough sweeping branches. The snakes came out every day when the sun warmed things up, never fazed by the death of their kin on the previous days. They were always ready for action.

Josh, an excellent marksman with many weapons, had never practiced the actual art of drawing fast and shooting accurately, since dueling in the south only required a steady hand and good eye with a long barreled pistol, and he'd only been in one duel over a woman. He found it quite difficult at first, since he was used to shooting from a rest most of the time. He decided to start slowly, just get the motion down pat and combine it with an accurate shot, then start to speed it up. By the end of the week, perhaps a hundred shots later, he could usually hit the big knotted head of a rattler with two out of three big slugs from the Remington New Model Army .44, at around twelve to fifteen yards or closer. He didn't like to get too close to the big ones, for they could lunge from a coil and strike nearly their length, sometimes six feet.

Hearing of Josh's practicing his fast draw with the pistol, Gabe modified Pancho's broken Remington .36 caliber revolver, a lightweight pistol with a three inch barrel and metallic cartridges. Gabe removed the broken trigger and did some alterations on the mechanism in his blacksmith shop. He took the gun apart and filed away the trigger mechanism entirely, then loosened the tension on the spring, producing a trigger-less gun that would fire quickly, simply by drawing back the hammer and releasing. Gabe taught Josh the practice of using the second joint of his thumb instead of the ball, on the smoothed down hammer, with a close grip as he drew.

Then Josh learned the art of fanning the hammer for maximum speed, and with a built in hammer ledge, the gun could carry six shots safely. The result, after hours of practice, was a much faster first shot and faster stream of fire for the remaining five. It wasn't as powerful or accurate as the new Remington .44 long barreled cartridge revolvers they had both started to carry, but was very smooth and quick to draw and fire accurately for short distances.

It was tricky to learn at first, but with plenty of aggressive rattlers to practice on, he mastered it to the point of delivering six slugs into a tiny spot in a matter of seconds. Josh liked the altered pistol and began wearing it, trading another revolver, a '51 Navy colt .36 caliber with a long barrel to Pancho for it.

Gabe had suggested that gun would be better for Pancho, with its lighter load and less kick. Everyone was happy with the trade, and Josh also began to teach Jesse and Pancho his shooting techniques with the big Remington cartridge .44 caliber pistols and the Spencer repeater rifle, with its quick loading tube of seven shots. Josh took to wearing a weapons belt with the fast draw .36 caliber Remington in a tie down rig on his right, the big Remington .44 caliber long barreled pistol in a backwards holster on his left, and a knife behind the big pistol. When he was cutting wood he just wore the .36 and a big knife.

With four armed men to defend the rancho, the raiders stayed away. As it became well known as a safe and friendly place, a lot of the Tejano rancheros and vaqueros began stopping by to visit. Since the cart wars, there were very few ranchos where they felt welcome and safe, so they soon lent their skills to the horse work. Many an evening were spent watching horseback contests between expert riders who could pick up a bottle from the ground at top speed, and rope a running mustang with ease.

The rattlers were a constant menace around the house, and sharpened hoes were left near the cottage door and the barn for dealing with them. One warm afternoon Pancho came around the chicken coop and spotted a big one trying to get in. Gabe and Josh were nearby, working on the pens by the barn. With the lariat he carried, Pancho quickly doubled the line with a big knot on the end, then furiously pounded the snake with it over and over until it was reeling in confusion. The hens and rooster went into a squawking uproar as the flailing increased in fury and a cloud of dust rose up from the fray. Pancho was cursing at the snake as he whipped it in a fury.

"No vive aqui, es me casa, chingada! Vive in brasada o no vive. No vive aqui, chingada! Combate aqui, si.si.si."

Gabe and Josh had watched with admiration from the makeshift blacksmith shed they had constructed, adjacent to the horse pens holding four half-wild mustangs who were getting alarmed and starting to skitter around. Pancho, usually mild and relaxed, was thrashing the coiling snake like a drummer, never giving the reptile time to recover from the last blow before the next one hit it, usually on the head. The rattles were giving off sporadic buzzing as the big knot of a head flopped around from the constant pounding by the heavy knot on the end of the doubled riata. The dust being raised was drifting over to Gabe and Josh, and smelled of chickenshit and horse urine. The chickens were fluttering around, shedding feathers, and making a big squawking ruckus.

Watching the mustangs began to circle in panic over the affair, Josh spoke up. "I can't shoot him with these spooky horses in this half repaired corral, they'd tear it to pieces."

"Wal, they got to get gunshot broke at some point."

"Yeah, well not now, they're fixing to tear down the rails." Josh grabbed his mortar mixing hoe from the tool room to go and help Pancho.

"Don't worry, he got that snake down anyway, with his riata. These Tejano vaqueros learned how to deal with this country long before any white man set foot on it. Just watch..."

They watched as Pancho rendered the snake into a helpless writhing coil, striking blindly when it could. His arm was whirling that rope like a dervish through the rising dust, smacking it over and over before it could recoil and strike. Soon it was reeling, unable to strike while the knotted rope pounded his head repeatedly. Gabe spoke again as Pancho relented with the thrashing.

"I told ya he's a good man with a lariat, huh? I seen him do that on horseback, in a pinch. He can put that rope anywhere he wants, like you can put hot lead. "

"Boy, I know that's right. Yesterday I saw him lean down and bounce a loop off the ground to catch a steer by the back foot, and now this. He can do just about anything with that rope. I've got lots to learn from him about that."

"I reckon it's time for a good knife about now," said Gabe. "Then I got to go butcher that young steer he brought in. Waugh. Wish it was a buffalo."

Josh stayed to calm the mustangs while Gabe gripped his knife's antler handle and started strolling over to where Pancho was finishing up. He pulled his gleaming razor sharp knife, stepped on the writhing coil, and cut the battered head off.

"Now there's a fine skin for somethin' or 'nother, huh?" he said, holding up the writhing body. "We could put some of that fang juice on them arrows we got, if we's a mind to. Never know when a silent poisoned arrow might come in handy, eh?"

"I think you hunt Comanche's too long, and you start to think like them," said Pancho.

"Maybe so."

With the mustangs circling in flight but not seeming ready to tear down the railings, Josh walked over to the chicken coop. "Damn, Pancho, that was something. Looks like you've had a lot of practice at that. Beats firing off guns and spooking these horses, huh?" said Josh.

Pancho smiled. "You gotta fight for this land if you want it, they want it too. Especially Rosita's chickens. But they got the brasada, and can't live here."

"I know that's right," said Gabe.

They always skinned the snakes they killed and Gabe taught Jesse how to stretch and dry them. Then Rosa treated them with special oil solution and sewed them to strips of deerskin for hatbands, sashes, belts, and bag handles. Jesse sold them through Muldoon to the traffic in Helena, for spending cash. They kept the rattles and tied them to a gourd, which gave a terrifying sound when shaken.

In two weeks of working the brush, Josh accumulated nearly a hundred usable posts and rails, lots of firewood for the stove and fireplace, and 21 rattlesnake skins with the diamondback pattern. The mesquite and oak wood was very dense and heavy, and difficult to handle, and the constant exertion helped him keep his mind on the present and future instead of the past.

Often in the early morning or near twilight, after the shooting stopped, Josh would see the roadrunner bird dart by, stop abruptly, scan the terrain with top-knotted head jerking this way and that, then take off in a sprint again. He grew fond of the sightings, and named the bird Lucky. Soon after that Lucky seemed to find a female friend, who ran with him and helped in snake attacks, the first bird attracting the rattler's attention while the other attacked from the blind side. The vaqueros called them paisanos, and whistled to them for good luck.

After skinning and barking the posts, Josh had Jesse help him swing a circle with the new lariat, which he had also learned to handle passably well by copying the motions of Pancho. They drug a stick on the ground at the end of a loop, the large size Josh wanted his round-pen. Then they swung the radius length of rope around the circle eight times and marked points on the circumference. They marked the points with the post-hole digger, made eight more marks dividing the first eight by swinging the radius arch again, and Josh proceeded to dig sixteen equally spaced and deep holes for the posts, which he had soaking in grease to waterproof the bottoms. This took many hours of steady pounding work, jamming the blades down, scooping the loose stuff up. At first the soil was loam and not too tough to dig, but at the bottom it was a crumbly cream colored rock that Pancho called caliche, and very hard to penetrate. At the bottom he used a long steel bar with wedge point to break it up, then scooped it up with the post-hole digger. Each post hole took hours of pounding, and the work stretched into weeks.

After a constant effort at this, his already leaned-down and substantial upper body was rippling with muscle like Scorpio's, especially his arms and shoulders, with bulging deltoid muscles that looked like he was wearing padded jackets when he dressed in the cool evenings. His mood brightened as the corrals grew from their combined efforts, and the blacksmith shed was beginning as well.

After they had settled into a work routine, Rosita thought Josh should go to Sunday mass with her at Panna Maria, mentioning the pretty blond Polish girls there, but he politely refused and instead rode over the ranch with Pancho and Gabe. When he needed a woman, he rode to Muldoon's alone and had one for the night, usually Delores if she was around, returning early in the morning for Gabe's biscuits.   Since Delores did not go upstairs with other customers, she was usually very glad to see Josh.

On their long circle rides, they saw several groups of wild mustangs, some of them good looking, some of them sort of degenerated and spavined looking. Scorpio and Buck did lots of calling with sharp screams and nickers at the stallions running the small herds, but they did not chase them, just learned the lay of the land, which ran along the river through rolling meadows of live oak savannah and mesquite thickets in the draws, much of it rich with grass, though lots of it was patterned with cactus and sticker bushes. Deer were thick in the brush along the river, and healthy looking, their white tails flashing as they bolted through the brush and meadows at high speed. The air was full of birds, with lots of hawks hovering and diving for rodents and snakes in the grass.

The ranch building progressed steadily, and after the weeks it took to build the round-pen structure of posts, Gabe and

Josh took the wagon to town to get the load of cedar rails and posts which had arrived and were waiting at Muldoon's livery. The town was full of teams with wagons, mules and oxen defecating in the streets while teamsters drank and ate in the wooden buildings.

While taking a meal at Muldoon's they learned that Abe Lincoln had been shot in the back of the head by an assassin, and they both felt shocked and saddened by the news. Though Lincoln had been relentless in his war on the Confederacy, he had also expressed a spirit of reconciliation near the end, and they feared what would happen to the South now that he was put under. Muldoon was chagrined and depressed by the news as well, carrying on how it would be like the Irish living under the heel of the British after that foul stroke of fortune.

Josh deplored the assassination, and remembered the soldier whose head he had blown apart at the plantation on the Teche again, ruining his mood. Disgust with the worsening effects of the war, disdain for what he had been forced to do, regret at the marauders killing his mother as he went to rescue her, all this resurfaced in his mind, where they had been submerged by constant focus on his ranching goals. But jumping back into working from dawn until dusk always provided a refuge from rambling thoughts of the painful past.

They had no scrapes in Helena on that occasion, though Josh did bump into the lovely Delores, who was very glad to see him, and immediately took him to the bath house and then upstairs. They spent the afternoon up there, following which mellow endeavors, a smiling Josh joined Gabe and headed off with the braying mules, and were back at nightfall with a full load of supplies and the long tough cedar railings for the round-pen.

Within another few days the round pen and another pen were built, and the old pens were repaired with the railings raised when possible. Pancho had begun plastering the outbuildings after Josh assigned him the job for extra pay, with Jesse's help. The chicken coop was repaired and stocked with fresh layers, and the windmill serviced by Gabe, who could figure out any mechanical device and fine-tune it. The shed for the blacksmith shop was completed.

The ranch was in top shape when they readied to head out mustanging, on the morning of May 12, 1865, the day of the last land action of the civil war, at Palmito ranch, on the banks of the Rio Grande. They hired a Tejano man, an old vaquero of local renown, to come and stay with Rosita and help with the stock. He arrived the night before they left, and squatted there in the corner of the house in white cotton clothing and an ancient leather-collared and cuffed riding jacket with big conchos for buttons, cradling an ancient rifle that he had brought for "gatos grandes", as he called them, and the "malo hombres de la Helena."

Josh had awakened early that morn, excited to be heading out to fulfill his dream of a horse ranch, and smelt the hot coals of mesquite and oak wood from Gabe's small fire out in the yard, and the delicious smell of coffee and fresh biscuits.

"Well, good morning, Ole Coon. I see you beat everyone to the breakfast fixing. Took to the yard for making biscuits, huh?"

Gabe poured Josh a cup of coffee and refilled his own as he fiddled around the fire.

"Oh hell, been up for hours, didn't want ta wake Rosita up and get her fluttering round her kitchen, so I just come out ta tha yard fire, watched the moon. We're headin' out to tha buffalo range, and I always get my hairs on end when I step into Comanche lands."

"Why, I'm the one should be nervous, now that my hair is grown back out."

"Yep, that sun-streaked mane would look nice on some Comanche's war lance. You oughta get yorn done up like mine, if ya don't want it ta look good to a Comanche. I got a sharp knife right here if ya want me ta..."

"No thanks."

"Mighta known. Biscuits is done, come and get 'em. I'll go wake up Pancho now. Me and him stayed up drinkin' after yal retired, so he's still snoring. That horse of yorn shore looks lighter in the sunrise."

"Yeah, he's turning white now, going to dappled and then white, I imagine. Getting to look like that silver moon over there."

The big moon was setting as Gabe set aside two big greased and loaded Dutch ovens of his prized sourdough biscuits, one for breakfast, and one batch to carry for snacking on. The morning dawned bright and warm, and they knew the summer was coming. Everyone was chattering and scurrying around, eating and getting ready. The old peon named Jorge could not get over how good Gabe's biscuits were. He had never eaten sourdough biscuits before, only corn tortillas. Gabe told him, "It's in the starter, gotta age it right. Brought mine from Louisiana."

Breakfast done, they filed out the door and mounted, leaving old Jorge standing with his rifle in a military pose. They were all happy and excited to be finally after wild horses, and they headed west to where they had spotted the small herds before, trailing the mules laden with supplies. The big Texas sun was rising warm at their backs, throwing long shadows as they headed west.

Breaking into a run for the fun of it, they raced west with the sun spreading heat on their backs as they headed for where the mustang herds had been sighted lately. The coyotes scattered as raucous crows burst from the bushes at their approach. They searched all morning as the sun warmed the day, bringing the temperatures into the sixties with a light southern breeze sailing the white clouds across the blue dome of the sky over the broad rolling grassy prairies. While seeing lots of wild longhorns, javelinas, feral hogs with huge tusks, a few slinking coyotes, and lots of roadrunners looking for snakes, they failed to find quality herds of mustangs, so they drifted southwest towards Oakville along a creek that smelled and tasted of sulfur.

It was in the grasslands of the creek bottom that they encountered a quality herd of mustangs led by a small buckskin stallion and a dappled gray mare of good conformation. They selected the best stock they could from this herd, most of them about fifteen hands high and fairly narrow chested, and began their remuda with them. Pancho showed tremendous skill on his well trained mount as he cut out the best stock with his riata and pulled them away from the small herd to hobble. LaPoint began to ride beside him, imitating his moves, and slowly mastered the lariat.

At one point the stallion in charge of the small herd decided he was ready to fight for his mares, but Buck and Scorpio were rushed at him, and he changed his mind. He stopped about twenty yards away on a small rise, but Scorpio got very aggressive at that point and charged him at full speed. The other stallion high-tailed it with what mares were left to him, glad to have escaped without injury.

The wild mustangs were mostly descendents of Spanish horses with Andalusian blood, mixed with runaway cow-ponies and nags. Sometimes they were sorry looking animals, but some groups held finer stock, great potential cow ponies, and mares for breeding saddle mounts who could live on grass if they had to. Also roaming the prairies were small bachelor bands of young stallions, not ready for their own bands of mares. From these they selected the best looking horses.

They were small, around 15 hands, but hardy, and could live on range grass and scarce water like the buffalo and wild cattle that shared their range of wild grassland scattered with sticker-bushes and trees. Josh was improving from constant practice with the lariat, and with Jesse and Tom already proficient, they did well at capture. Gabe was not a good roper, and mostly used the quick-turning Buck to herd them. Soon they had a good sized group in a corral improvised from brush and ropes, which Gabe rode herd on while the others chased horses. Gabe was also expert at hobbling and tying animals to hold them safely, and took over that part of the job, as well as erecting brush and rope corrals.

By the time they made camp a few miles northwest of Oakville at sunset the third day, they had over two dozen good horses captured and corralled in a rope and brush pen. The clouds in the west were turning scarlet, pink, and purple as the mesquite and Spanish oak smoke from their dinner fire wafted off in the breeze. Buck was tied to a tree near the fire while Gabe worked on a shoe that was coming loose, while Josh and the vaqueros drank coffee.

When they were settled down for the night with grub cooking they heard a rider hailing the camp. His voice sounded weak and weary.

"Hello the campfire, can I ride in?"

"Hello the rider," yelled Gabe.

"That's a weary man," said LaPoint, as he grabbed his canteen. "Call him in."

"Shore, slow and easy," yelled Gabe. The rider plodded in, his horse displaying the gait of a jaded mount with a stagger. He looked worn down to the bone, covered with white dust. He dismounted his weary mount and nearly stumbled into the small fire. Gabe grabbed a hold on his shoulders and sat him down on the oak log they were using for a bench. Josh took his horse and watered it, then slipped a feedbag on it. Pancho brought the stranger some hot rum, lemon, and sugar, and a plate of grub, with a canteen of water. He poured some water from the canteen into an empty tin cup and handed it to him.

"Take it slow, Senor. Despacio. Slowly," said Pancho. Josh went and unsaddled his horse, rubbed down its sore back, watered it and fed it grain. After consuming a plate of food and a half canteen of water, without touching the rum toddy, the fellow finally took a deep breath to speak, as Josh approached the campfire again.

"I sure do thank you kindly, for the grub and seeing to my horse. Tom Jackson's my name, is this your outfit?" the stranger said as he extended his hand to LaPoint, who shook it.

"Yes, I'm LaPoint."

"I stumbled upon yal in the nick of time. I was about dried down to an old hide. I feel pert near alive again. Been lost a while, looking for my brother. His name is Hoseah Jackson. He came down from Lockhart area over three weeks ago, where we have a small spread on Plum Creek, looking to sign on to a cattle drive. We ain't heard of him since,and he's supposed ta send me word, so's I could maybe hire on too, so I been looking and looking, but I'm bout give out, with no success. I talked to the range boss, Old Uncle Willy, that he was coming to see about the job, and they never seen him. Could be some of that Helena riffraff bushwhacked him. Something happened to him, and I don't know if he's alive or dead."

"Wal hell, that's no good. Sorry fer yer troubles, it's hell to lose family and get lost lookin' for 'em. I hate that part. It leaves a damned bitter taste. Yore welcome to spend the night in our camp, if that sits right with our jefe. I been to Plum creek myself, back at the big battle with Buffalo Hump in 18 and 40. When did yal settle thar?"

The weary rawboned rider looked at Gabe in surprise and admiration, his eyebrows raising and blue eyes widening. "My folks settled there when I was a kid, twenty years ago. My brother and I each got pieces adjoining theirs. You fought at the battle of Plum Creek?"

"Yep, shore did, alongside Ben McCullough and Matt Caldwell and lots of others, including lots of Tonkawas, even ole Placido, a hell of a fightin' man and tracker."

The bone weary man got up and stepped over to the fire where Gabe was squatting to offer his hand.

"I'd be proud to shake your hand, sir. Without you guys, we never could have settled there at all. We got there a few years after that battle. Folks were still talking about it all the time. I growed up listening to stories about the great Linnville raid and the battle of Plum Creek. Our place is a few miles west of the prairie where yal jumped them. They say yal chased Comanches all the way to the hill country, blowing them to hell with new revolvers. My name is Tom Jackson." He offered Gabe his hand.

"Pleased to meet ya, Tom. My name is Gabe McBride, and this is the LaPoint outfit, and that there is Pancho Menchaca, and his son Jesse back thar eatin' still. We're out mustanging for saddle horses ta sell to the cattle drives." They shook hands all around, Jesse keeping his plate of food in his left hand, shaking while chewing.

"Gabe McBride," said Tom Jackson. "Gabe McBride, him that rode with Captain Jack Hays in the forties? Top-hat McBride the Comanche hunter, the ranger scout.?"

"I did a few years of cuttin' sign on ranging searches. Back then a few called me Top-hat. But I gave that hat away lately."

"Well I'll be jiggered. I recognize you now. I saw you once when I was a kid, riding with Captain Jack Hays down main street of Lockhart. You had that flaming copper hair and beard back then. Yal was a heading for that fight against the Mexican army on Salado creek. Both of you rangers have been sorely missed around here. There's some guys rangering now that have gone way overboard in slaughtering the wrong Indians for not being able to find the right ones, if ya ask me. But Captain Hays was the best, and you were a legend for tracking and scouting back then, and rescuing captives from the staked plains. Then you were gone. What happened?"

"Wal, I got a belly-full, seen too many massacres, killed too many people without finding that gol-damned Buffalo Hump, took in too much lead, and went back north ta Taos, in the shining mountains, hoping to get back into some peaceful trading and buffalo robe business. And I did some scouting for the miner's road to California."

"Up on the staked plains? I heard you knew the plains

like the back of your hand, and that's how they got back those French girls, on accounta your tracking and knowing the watering spots."

"Yeah, that one was a success, finally. Had some luck. Mostly we couldn't find em. I knew the Llano Estacado pretty well back then, and I got to trading for buffalo hides again. Then I got caught by a bad bunch, cut up pretty bad, and went ta Louisiana to heal. We got burnt out there and came here."

"Gabe McBride. Wait till I tell 'em back home who I met. Why, the old-timers still tell stories about you in the saloons and at the mercantile. And that blacksmith in town is full of stories bout Gabe McBride and his knives, and finding Comanches. If we had a scout and tracker like Gabe McBride, they always say. It's a real honor to know you, sir."

"Likewise, Jackson. But them saloon stories grow like mushrooms spouting from bullshit, ya know. You never answered my question 'bout the army. Yal take a French leave of your units.?"

"No sir, Hoseah and me, we mustered out on parole after the surrender of Vicksburg, in July of 63...walked home 'bout half starved, eating anything we could find along the way. Got home in October of 63, been there since, trying to survive the rustlers and hard times."

"Yal was at Vicksburg? We heard that was bad."

"Well, if ya call constant shelling and no food bad, and the damned ground explodin' under ya from an infernal sapper's tunnel fulla black podwer like hell itself opened up to swallow ya, bad?, ...yeah, it was bad."

"Tunneled under the lines and blew ya up, huh?"

"Yep, after starvation and shelling, had tunnels all around, constant shelling of the city overhead, I'd hear 'em digging and try ta tell the officers, but they didn't do nothin'. I had a good sniper's rifle and was putting some slugs in the arms and shoulders of federals when it all blew up, dirt flying everywhere. Threw me back twenty feet from the blast, but I landed in soft dirt and didn't break nothin', though I could not hear for a couple of weeks after."

"Hell of a thing, what Christian men will do to each other, huh?"

"You got that right, sir. Weren't no relief from prayin', so I spent my time doin' my job. Shelling and starving a city ain't nothing ta Sherman. After the ground exploded out from under us, we heard that they had tunnels everywhere, ready to blow, so we gave it up. After we surrendered, we was so hungry guys was just keeling over as they marched out to stack their rifles. Sherman took one look at us, a bunch of walking skeletons, and let us go. Most were too weak to fart. Sherman paroled us to get shed of our hungry bellies and our wounded. Hell, we mostly surrendered so we could eat. I'da just as soon gotten blown up as listen to my growling belly and count my ribs. He didn't want to have to feed us, so we got to walk home with some hardtack, sorry sonofabitch."

"Sorry for yore troubles thar, we heard it was awful. Some folk from our area was thar, and come home crippled up bad, the ones that got paroled. Shows yore tough just survivin' it. So you ain't wanted by no officials, got your parole papers and all?"

"Yes-sir, got it in my saddlebags, I can show you..." said Tom as he started to rise.

"I believe ya, never mind that. What are ya going to do now that you can't find your brother, give up the search and head back to Plum Creek?"

"I can't do that."

"Sometimes ya got to, I done it many times myself, so did Jack Hays. This is a hard country ta find folks."

"I know that, but I can't go back home empty-handed. That won't do much good. The reason Hoseah left was that we was broke and needed cash to keep things going, what with the drought and the horse and cattle thieving and all. With him not making no money to bring home, it falls to me, I reckon. I'll try to get a job on a trail drive, I reckon. I heard a fellow named Mathis was gathering a big herd on the Nueces, maybe he'll hire me on, if I can make it that far. Do you know how far it is?"

"Lemmi think, 'bout a long days' ride, twenty five miles, I reckon, down to Roughtown on Lagarto creek, just this side of the Nueces River. You done much cattle driving before?"

"Well, yeah, sort of. We had a dozen head with a few calves 'til they rustled em, so I know how to work cattle. Fair hand with a rope, and Pokey there is a good cutting horse, though he's ganted down now. Mainly worked my own place. Never been on a long drive and took another man's pay, though. Have you?"

"Only to New Orleans a couple of times, for this man's father. He was a young fella when he went on one and learned to handle horses. I don't like cattle, sorta ornery and stupid animals ta herd, ya ask me. Them longhorns taste like an old boot too. Gemme buff meat any day. But I reckon it's 'bout the only way to make a living round here right now. After the drought they had, these wild cattle and horses proliferated like rabbits in the rainy areas. We seen beaucoup wild cattle while we been ranging about for horses."

"Yep, they're being gathered all over, lots of fighting over them too."

"I hear tell these fellows are heading up north ta Kansas. Water's liable to be more of a problem on that stretch, not ta mention Comanche, Kiowa, squatters, rustlers, gyp water, and quicksand at the river crossings. If yore green, they'll put ya ta riding drag and you'll sweat mud from the dust, cough up mud-balls, and black tears from yore sore eyes, and round up straying cattle that is stupider than the rest, which is already pretty stupid."

"I reckon that's true, but I gotta have a job for now or go under with my little spread. These droughts have been hell on planting corn or cotton and growing stock. Only cash crop we got was watermelons this year."

"Can ya handle a rope from a running horse, and put a loop around a mustang? What about collecting and driving horses, mustanging, are ya interested in work like that?"

"Well hell yes, working with you guys? Riding with Gabe McBride? Damn right. Sign me on. I don't know that much 'bout mustanging, but I'm game and hungry and willing to learn. I'd be proud to ride with Gabe McBride, that's for sure. It'd be something to tell my grand-kids, if I live that long. I'll make a hand for ya."

"Ya got no sidearm on, I see. Nor saddle gun. Ya ever been in shootin' scrapes, aside from the war, with Indian's or bandits and suchlike?"

"I got an old Walker colt in that saddlebag, but it needs fixin'. My brother had our Spencer repeater, only one we could manage to get our hands on after the war. I could shoot that Spencer pretty well, being as I was a sharpshooter in the war. As far as shooting scrapes, I ain't never had occasion, other than shooting at rustlers in the dark as they drove my cows off. I winged one."

"How about scrapes with Comanches, ever fought with them?"

"Well yes and no. Never met them on the plains, though my mom tells me I came close to being a Comanche in a scrape once."

"Waugh. How's that?"

"Well, when I was a toddler some Comanches, three bucks and a squaw, came to our cabin on Plum Creek while my Dad was in town selling some horses. They came in the house and the bucks demanded grub from my mom, so she started cooking them up some salt pork and eggs and coffee. The squaw picked me up and began to play with me, but then the bucks grabbed me. Now my ma was a right feisty old German housewife who was boss of that kitchen, and she sorta grew heated."

"I reckon so, tha varmints. They was seein' if ya was worth stealin'."

"So ma says they started shaking me and pitching me back and forth between them, getting rougher and rougher to see how tough I was. Then they started throwing me up in the air to see if I got scared easy. The squaw got mad at them and tried to get me back, but the meaner of the bucks pushed her down. Then they started throwing me up high. Mom says I never got scared, 'cause my pa used to do it outside for fun, and I used to giggle when he did it. When they hit the ceiling with me, my ole German mom threw hot pork grease and eggs on two of them, right in their faces, then grabbed me, and started beating the buck who was throwing me with the hot frying pan."

"Hot damn," said Gabe with a laugh.

"Then she grabbed the coffee pot and sloshed steaming hot coffee over them. She ran them out the door about the time Pa and his drovers came riding up, so they hightailed it, muy pronto. Pa used to say that ma was the only woman who scared even the Comanches."

"Damnation, she got hell ta popping on 'em, do you remember any of it?"

"Sounds like my grandmother," said Jesse.

"No, but I remember my mom never backed down from anything, mules, bulls, pecking roosters, biting dogs. She'd whip what gave her problems, and chop the head off a pecking rooster and make stew of him."

"Yep," said Jesse. "Abuela Maria."

"Wal shit-fire, yore blood can't be too thin with a mom like that. I'm for hiring ya on. We got a saddle gun you could carry for just in case, a Spencer seven shot .52 caliber."

"That's what we had, I can shoot a Spencer pretty well."

"Good, you may have to, never know. We got coyotes all around the herd right now, listen to 'em, hungry sounds. But I'm just the segundo. This here is Mr. LaPoint's camp, LaPoint's drive. What do ya say, El Jefe LaPoint?"

"Hire him on, boss," said Jesse.

Josh nodded and gave a rare grin. "Yes. Tom seems like he'd make a good hand. We need another drover if we're gonna try to run down that herd we spotted at sunset and keep these contained. We've got more horses than we got hobbles or brush corrals now. That's a good campfire story too, maybe he's got more. Or more about you."

"Wal, welcome to tha LaPoint outfit, Tom Jackson," said Gabe, with general agreement all around. They all shook hands.

So they worked out the necessary pay agreement and signed on Tom Jackson, from Plum Creek. Josh made him an offer of wages by the day and a portion of the profits at the end. Tom was happy with the offer and threw in with the LaPoint crew of mustangers. The next day Tom proved his worth by showing expertise with the rope and good riding skills, though his mount was still a bit worn down. He switched over to one of the extra mounts, a recently saddle-conditioned mare, and did well with her. In the evening when coyotes gathered to harass the horses, Tom took out their leader with well placed rifle shots and proved his statement about being a sharpshooter with the Spencer.

Many of the small herds they encountered had lots of degenerated horses, and the time it took for selection of good mares increased, despite the extra help. Within a week of selecting carefully they had over fifty mares of good quality and at least ten colts from bachelor bands, and were driving them up towards the ranchito, reaching a prairie about fifteen miles south of Helena, when sunset overtook them, and they found some grass and water to settle the herd down for the night.

When they had made camp and eaten, Pancho and Gabe drew first watch at night-riding, and they went off humming and singing to circle the herd. Scorpio had been turned loose with the herd for the night to replace the stallions they had been taken from. There was no stallion on these prairies that would challenge Scorpio for the mares. On his hind legs he was too fierce a fighter, and he could spin and kick in a blinding whirl. Josh and Tom were alone in camp drinking rum toddies with lots of lemon juice, when two riders approached.

"Hello the campfire, got any coffee?"

"Nope, coffee is for breakfast," replied Josh.

"Can we ride in friendly like?'

"Alright," said Josh as he strapped on his pistol belt. "Friendly like?" said Josh to Tom. "Something's not right with that voice. Something false. Stay alert. We've been told of lots of horse thieves and cut-throats out here." The strangers rode into camp and sat on their horses, looking things over. They rode good mounts, with saddle guns in leather sheathes and full saddlebags with slickers draped over them. They dressed like drovers and were covered with dust and sporting fancy tie-down pistol rigs.

"Howdy, fellers," said one of them. "Looks like you fellas are mustangers, like us, but with better luck, judging from the size of that herd out there. I hear an Irish ditty and a Mex song. How many night-riders you got out there?..., cause we could help out for very little recompense."

"Enough," said Josh.

"Enough, he says. Sorta twilight reply, neither daylight or dark, huh?"

"Twilight is coming on now," said Josh.

"Sure is. Cooling off fast like, too. Well, if yal got enough riders would yal mind if we sit by yer fire a while, been a long ride and it's gotten a bit chilly for the last mile or two. Any hot grub ya got would be appreciated too. We been smelling biscuits and beans, seems like, and meat too, riding in from downwind. It plumb took a hold of our noses a mile back or so."

"Sure, no problemo, sit by our campfire and take the chill off. There's beans in that pot and some appalos of pork and venison on those sticks there, laying on the lid of the dutch oven. Fresh out of biscuits til morning though. Help yourself."

The strangers kept their hat-brims down and partook of camp food without introducing themselves. They hunkered down on the log by the fire and shoveled in the food, half turned away from the camp residents.

Josh had an uneasy feeling about them, and kept sitting on his saddle leaning against an oak tree, watching them while Tom got up casually, stretched by the fire, glancing at the man who had done the talking, then leaning by the fire as if to warm his hands, and looking back again, directly at the man's chest, then said, "Want me to grain your horses, mister? We got an oat and corn mix with molasses."

"Why I sure would. Go on ahead while we chow down here. We could even eat those half et biscuits ya set down there. Ain't et nuthin all day but jerky and dry tortillas."

"Those biscuits have previous claims, I reckon," said Josh as he sat quietly staring at the two men. The younger of the two seemed very nervous and spilled his bean juice from his plate of food with a trembling hand.

"Suit yerself, but like I say, we ain't et much today," said the stranger in a more surly tone. "Been smelling them biscuits for a while as we rode up. Smells like good ole sourdough."

"They're for the night-riders."

When Tom Jackson walked over to grain their horses, he saw that his brother's saddle was on the man's horse, with the initials that they had burned under the cantle with a hot wire. And the saddle gun was his brother's too, likewise marked. A hot flash ran through his neck and face.

That confirmed what he was thinking when he looked closely at the man in the campfire light, that the man was wearing his brother's tan leather vest. Tom Jackson had no working pistol, and both strangers were armed with well used tie-down pistol rigs. The younger of the two men seemed diffident and failed to look up at all. Tom thought he also spotted a belly gun under his bother's vest on the man by the fire.

By then his heart was pounding, but he casually walked over to squat by Josh and get himself a bit hot water and lemon into his hot drink, getting his head close to Josh's ear. He whispered to Josh, unheard by the strangers who had thrown wood on the fire and gotten it crackling to drive the chill out after their long ride in the cooling air.

"Hey, that guy's got my brother's vest and saddle, and his carbine on the saddle. Will you back my play?"

"You sure of that, Tom?"

"Damned sure."

"Alright, then. Yes. Confirms my hunch. But....It's my camp, my play," said Josh.

"What's that, yal wanna play some whist or poker?" asked the stranger who did the limited talking, the other being silent as a post so far, as he wiped the dust off his meat and gulped at it. The dirty cowboy spoke over his shoulder to Josh as he gnawed on some of the meat. "I didn't catch that, did ya say I could have them biscuits after all?"

"I said it's my camp, my play. I'll lay it out for you, Mister. Tom here's been looking for his brother who disappeared a while back, and he spotted his brother's saddle and carbine on your horse, and his brother's vest on your body. So. There it is. You got some explaining to do, right now."

The stranger spat out a hunk of gristle he had been working over with yellow teeth, set his metal plate on the ground, and stood to turn and face Josh, who rose at the same time, still holding his plate. "And just who are you to be asking me about my saddle and vest like you was the boss of me?"

"I'm LaPoint. Boss of this outfit and this camp. Who are you?"

"Never heard of ya. I'm Ike Covington, and this here is Ben Burnett, the Lagarto Kid."

"Likewise," said Josh. "Never heard of you or the lizard kid."

The younger stranger put down his plate and stepped away from the fire towards the nearby darkness. Tom Jackson picked up a Spencer repeater he had used to shoot coyotes and was just finished cleaning, and leveled it on the younger man, saying, "That's far enough. Not another move. Now you by the fire with my brother's vest, who come into camp riding my brother's saddle, you start talking, real friendly like. Tell me what happened to my brother." Tom jacked the lever and loaded a cartridge into the chamber as he spoke.

The man by the fire replied while staring at Josh's gun-hand close to the small Remington. "You're plumb loco. We ride for J.R.Northern, got a big spread over by the three rivers, west of here, past Oakville, and I got that saddle from his tack room. Ain't your brother's saddle, that's a cheap common saddle, lots just like it. And this here is J.R.Northern range, which I'm in charge of, and I'm well known in these parts. You could ask anyone in Oakville about me, they'd tell ya..."

Josh cut him off. "You're lying. You'd better tell him what he needs to know."

"I done told ya, it's a goddamn common saddle. I got it at the J.R.Northern ranch tack-room."

Tom spoke up. "Oh yeah, its a cheap enough saddle, and common too. Except for the initials burned under the cantle, my bother's initials. On the butt of that saddle gun too. I don't give a damn about the saddle. I'm looking for my brother. Where is he?"

"You're barking up the wrong tree, mutt. Go chase a squirrel. Don't know nothing 'bout your gaddamned brother, but nobody pushes or pulls on Ike Covington without regretting it, 'cept those that die too soon for regret. You'd best back down while you got the chance to walk away."

"There'll be no backing down on it," said LaPoint. "Tell him now."

"You may think you can plug both of us with that repeater, but you can't. We could kill both of you with fat slugs before you can cock that Spencer again, and there's two of us with fast draws. You're on our range now. We didn't get hired to ride for J.R. Northern for our good looks, you know. We're hired to take care of range rustlers like you."

"I think you're the range rustlers," said Jackson. "And I think I can pump seven slugs from this Spencer before I fall."

"Wait," said the younger man. "I ain't a part of this..."

"Hell-fire, settle down." said Covington. "We ain't looking for trouble with yal after eating your grub. We got places to be, men to meet up with south of here. Now yal relax and we'll just ride on outa here real easy like. You fellers is too touchy. Settle down, back off."

"Not likely," said Josh, his gaze boring into the man's eyes, reading his intentions. "We've got no branded horses in our herd. You got his brother's saddle and a bad odor about you. You're lying. I'm saying this for the last time. You'd better start telling us what we want to hear within ten seconds."

"I got nothing to say about it, don't know nothing, and you'd better take it up with J.R. Northern and his crew at the Bar-N spread. I ain't got the time ta fool with ya, we're just gonna...."

"You've got ten seconds to tell him."

"Hold on there, you goddamned bastard, there's no point in....that's a common saddle...J.R. Northern's the one you should be talking to."

"Five."

The dusty stranger started to draw his big Army Colt .44, but Josh had been practicing on rattlesnakes for weeks and was much faster, firing two shots from his trigger-less 36.caliber Remington into the man's right thigh and gun arm before the stranger had cleared leather. He went down yelling in pain, on his left knee, rolled to his belly, then pulled and lifted a palm pistol, a Derringer, to try again with his other hand, which was shaking and swaying.

The man faltered as the blood poured from his wounds, going white in the face with wide eyes glazing, his arm starting to drop. Josh aimed but did not fire the finishing shot, so Tom Jackson fired the Spencer repeater into his chest from a few feet away, blowing a hole out the back of his dirty shirt with the big slug, and Ike went down flat on the dark ground with a grunt, his leg jerking nearly into the fire, his shirt shredded and bloody where the slug came out.

Clouds of gun-smoke made a haze in the firelight, the smell pungent with the smoldering from the half scattered fire. The young Ben Burnett started a run for the horses during the commotion, and Josh heard the horse herd start to run.

"Stop or die," said LaPoint, bringing the lad to a quick halt.

"Lord God don't kill me, I seen what ya done. I don't want no part of it."

"Dammit, there go the horses. Keep a bead on that one,Tom. I have to go help Gabe and Pancho. The horses will scatter to hell and back if we don't stop them quick. Keep this guy under guard or hobbled. This other is finished with that Spencer slug through his heart. He isn't even twitching anymore, nor pumping blood out the holes in him. I'm going."

"Alright, I got him, go," said Tom with the rifle leveled on the guy, who had stumbled over a log in the dark and was trying to rise.

"Stay down or die now, Lagarto Kid."

"Don't kill me. I ain't no Lagarto Kid, that's just something they made up ta trifle me with. Name is Ben Burnett. I didn't have nothing to do with killing your brother, I swear. I just started riding for this outfit, I didn't know what they was like. I just had ta have a job."

Josh grabbed a rope and took the stranger's horse, galloping off into the starlit night towards the sound of the running herd. He wished he had Scorpio to ride for this dangerous run, but he was on a strange horse with stirrups a bit too short, and took his chances. Soon he was breathing the dust from the running herd, and catching up, straining the cow-pony into a lather to do so. The horse was a strong bay gelding over sixteen hands high, with longer legs than Scorpio, but with the rider and saddle, he was soon panting and lathering trying to sustain an all out run. Josh saw it would be a difficult feat to catch up, then leaned over the gelding's neck and began to stroke it and talk to the horse, garnering even more speed out of him.

By the campfire, Tom got closer to the man, keeping the smoking Spencer trained on his body.

"Alright, get up and go sit by the fire."

"You said stay down and I will, Mister. Just let me go. I ain't no killer or gunman like that LaPoint fella nor Ike. Dang. He got off two shots before Ike cleared leather."

"Yeah, did you notice that too? Too bad Ike didn't know about it before he came in to bushwhack us." Tom prodded him again with the Spencer barrel and got him sitting on the log by the fire. The stranger was terrified and started to tremble as he saw his riding companion dead in a bloody heap by the fire. The pants leg on the dead stranger was scorching and starting to burn.

"Drag him away from that fire before he scalds. I don't want to smell him burning. He's bad meat."

The younger stranger did as he was told. "I know he is. He got what he deserved."

"Now start talking or I'm gonna start shooting holes in your boots, one after another."

"Mister, he wasn't a friend of mine. I'm glad to be shed of him. I took no part in what they done to your brother."

"Who did? What?"

"Well, this fella yal just kilt was the ringleader, that's why he got the saddle and vest. Another fella got the carbine, on account of Ike already has a Spencer rifle, or he used to."

"This man killed my brother?"

"Him and some others from the saloons of Oakville. They got a regular gang of rustlers over there to scour this range for drovers and the mustangs or cattle they got. They let other folks round up all this wild stock, and then they steal the herds. I took no part, but I seen it."

"I'm glad I shot him. How'd they kill my brother?"

"They come into his camp friendly like, south of Oakville, coming back from Rough-Town down on Lagarto creek where we delivered a remuda to some drovers, which is all I hired on for, then two of them roped him and proceeded to drag him through cactus. I didn't know they was meaning him harm attal. All they been doing was stealing horses from other mustangers up to that point, to sell down south where drovers are gathering a big herd of cattle to drive north. I just hired on to help drive a bunch down there, which they had already gathered."

"You're telling me this sonofabitch dragged my brother through cactus?"

"Yes-sir, I'm afraid so. First they got two loops on him and took off fast through a big cactus bed, through them prickly pears with the stickers, like them over there."

"Damnation."

"Then they'd pull in opposite direction, sort of a tug of war, when one got him by the feet in a loop. It was powerful cruel, like Comanches, and your brother fought like a wildcat to escape, but every time he came near getting untangled, they'd spur their mounts and jerk him down again, or somebody would throw another rope on him and there they'd go again."

"Murdering varmints," said Tom as tears flowed down his dusty face.

"They was. I never seen anything like it. Wasn't what I signed up for, but I ain't no gunman, despite this borrowed rig, and I couldn't stop them guys. Damn, did you see how fast that guy drew? Who is that guy?"

"He's LaPoint. So they killed Hosea by dragging him through cactus?"

"Well, yes and no. They drug him for a while, like ta shredded his clothes and got him all scraped and stickered up with cactus thorns, pouring blood, but he was still struggling. Then Covington here got a rope round his neck and shoulder and drug him through a field of them big Spanish daggers several times, swinging a wide circle with him, 'til he hooked on a mesquite tree and broke his neck, broke the rope and all, come near breaking his girth strap and unhorsing him. It was godawful. I couldn't believe my eyes. I was thankful when the poor man died, to tell the truth, just to end it, but I threw up everything in my belly after it was over. It was the worst I seen, and I seen Injun fights too. I seen several men killed before, but for some reason or another. This was mad loco killing, like Comanche torture but worse, cause these was white men. Your brother didn't even have any horses to steal, other than the wore-down mare he was riding."

Tom Jackson stood with stinging salt water streaming from his eyes. "So when did this all take place?"

"Maybe thirty miles south from here, hard to say. That-away. 'Bout three days ago. It was a powerful shock to me, learning what types I'd thrown in with. I been tryin' to figure how to get away since then, but Ike's been known to back-shoot anyone tries to quit. I hired on to round up wild cattle and horses, but all we done since we delivered that herd of horses is steal other fellow's stock after they rounded 'em up."

"That's what LaPoint took a notion of when he heard that man's voice hailing the camp."

"Well, he was just checking yal out, and planned to go back to Oakville and get more hands, depending on the size of your bunch. I already told him I wouldn't do it, and was ready to quit if I could draw my pay, but they said I couldn't quit, on account of I owed for use of the saddle and gun rig. There's a nest of them guys at Oakville that ride with him when the job's big enough to pay, and they all back his play."

"So they go around killing guys for their outfits and herds?" asked Jackson.

"Yeah, if the guys don't let 'em have the stock they want. They don't take it all, just the best, call it a range tax. When they killed your brother, I knew I signed on with the wrong outfit, but it was hell to pull away. Ole Covington was half crazy, could turn on anybody in a second. He's killed a lot of men, so many he got to thinking nobody could touch him for speed and daring. I'm glad yal killed him."

Tom Jackson stood clench-jawed and crying in the campfire light, the Spencer leveled on the young man's chest, in a struggle with his trigger finger on whether to kill him. The brass side-plates of the rifle glittered in the firelight as the young man started to sob.

Tom choked down his sobs and spoke. "Murdering

varmints. To think we made it through the whole goddamned war only to come home and get murdered by polecats..."

"Please don't kill me, mister. I'll repent. I swear to God. I had no part in his killing. I'm the one who gave your brother a decent burial."

"Assssssghiiii. You're lucky I got more than my fill of killing in the war, boy. Where?'

"Awww hell, I don't know. South of here 'bout thirty miles I reckon. They run horses over it to hide it. No marker. You'd never find it, nor could I. There wasn't any rocks around ta mark it or nothin'. They mocked me for burying him, told me ta leave him for the coyotes. Please don't kill me, I wouldn't been riding with them 'cept I was desperate for some kind of work. We been starving since the drought and Mexicans stole our stock."

"How old are you?"

"18 in May, sir."

"You'd better mend your ways if you want to see 19. You stay put there by the fire while I have a drink to sort this out. I just might not kill you if you sit there quiet."

Out under the starlight behind the thundering noise and billowing clouds of choking dust, Josh had nearly caught up with the herd on the strange horse and was quirting it to catch up with Gabe who was near the head of the herd on the left, following close behind Pancho, who was moving into the front of the herd with his riata coiled in one hand, whipping it aloft. Running behind the herd through all the dust, noise, and heat was intense and difficult in the dark, but so far they were running in a bunch rather than scattering, so the riders had a chance to recapture them.

The ground was dark bushes and tall grasses, and uneven in spots, and the best choice was to let the stranger's horse pick his way, with plenty of chances to tumble. The big gelding was of good cow-pony stock and did not stumble as they strained to move up on the herd. Josh spotted Scorpio running near the middle of the herd, and whistled, then called to him. The powerful gray stallion finally heard him and began to work his way over, shouldering his way through the running herd amidst the dust and thundering noise. Scorpio used his powerful broad based neck to muscle his way through other horses, one by one, as Josh pushed his new mount towards the lead. Soon they were running side by side on the left leading edge of the small horse herd, and almost up to the front and even with Gabe, who trailed Pancho. He called to Gabe, who glanced over and nodded.

"Let's turn them into that little valley," Josh yelled and pointed when he had pulled even with Gabe.

"Turn them," Josh yelled again, louder, pointing right. Gabe nodded, Josh pounded Scorpio on his rump, sending him into the herd behind Pancho and into a diagonal, and Pancho rode alongside, already aware of Josh's plan, whipping and twirling his riata over his head, and they pushed in on the front runners of the herd, turning them into a circle, aided by Scorpio, who had raced to the lead and was neighing and turning the herd as it's lead stallion, his voice stronger than the others.

They kept bending the wild herd in the dark, with Scorpio snorting and neighing and plunging ahead into the lead, followed by Pancho with his coiled riata twirling, and LaPoint, calling to them in his horse language.

Scorpio leaned his powerful neck against the lead mare, turning her down towards the creek meadows. It worked, the lead was bent to the right and the herd followed, the horses circled into the meadows and slowed as the circle tightened, milling in on themselves and breathing their own dust and aroma until they stilled to a tired but nervous walk.

In ten more minutes they had the small herd pacing slowly and grazing in a meadow surrounded by creek brush, and the stampede was over. The only sound was the two vaqueros singing smooth ballads, and a few nervous whinnies and snorts.

Josh called Scorpio, led him back to the camp, saddled him, and rode out to join Pancho in singing to and calming the horses. Gabe went back to camp, tired out from the run in the dark, for Buck had nearly stumbled and thrown him twice as he broke into the herd for the lead, jarring Gabe to the bone each time. It was a bumpy straining ride for everyone, but Gabe was an older man and needed a rest, and when he dismounted in camp he saw the dead man on the ground and Tom holding the other down with the Spencer.

"So that's what started it, huh? A shootout in camp. Company fer dinner, I see. I guess I forgot to mention about not firing off rifle shots to echo down that draw and start a gol-danged stampede while I was on night-rider duty, huh? What the hell happened here, Tom, and why you so worked up and drawing a bead on this young fella?"

Tom was still standing in a muttering rage and crying freely, tears rolling through the dust on his face in muddy rivulets that glistened in the flickering firelight. "The dead one there was wearing my brother's vest and riding his saddle. I asked the boss to back my play, but he said it was his camp, his play. That dead fellow there wouldn't abide being questioned and drew down on LaPoint, who shot him before he cleared leather. Then the sonofabitch was gonna shoot again with a belly gun and I killed him with this repeater here. I thought maybe LaPoint was blinded by the campfire and didn't see the belly-gun."

"I get the picture. And shed no tears over killin' a varmint who comes into our camp and draws down on us, not to mention riding your brother's saddle. Use our firearms whenever ya need to. I can fix your Walker colt when we get back to tha rancho. Go ahead and put one through his head to make sure if ya feel the need."

"Thanks Gabe. Proud to ride with you. Like I said the other day."

The old scout stepped near the body. "Waugh. That one ain't even running blood, heart stopped when that slug hit it dead center. Sheeit! Shot in the leg and arm before he cleared leather. I reckon they'd better larn not ta mess with LaPoint."

"With that small gun he's very fast and accurate too. Not many are both. They were pretty close, but with darkness and blinding firelight, and Mr. LaPoint could have shot him anywhere easy, and chose the thigh and then the gun arm, shots real close together. Damn he's got really fast hands. Never seen anything like that. And the second shot so fast after the first."

Gabe examined the body. "Practice. That hole in the inner thigh woulda bled him out quick if ya hadn't stopped his heart. Josh hits what he aims at, always has, and now he's fast."

"Damn right, a good skill at times in this country. But it's a sorry note to go off and fight a war for three years and come back to get kilt by riffraff like this. My brother deserved better out of this life."

"Yeah, so did them that went down in that unnecessary war. Wal did ya find out for shore what happened to your brother?"

"Yeah I did, that's why I'm crying, not 'cause I'm upset for

killin' that sonofabitch. That man and others drug him through
cactus, then broke his neck against a tree. This young fella here
saw it all. They tortured him to death."

"Awww hell. Sonsobitches. Ya gonna kill him too?"

"Much as I'd like to, no. Killing one varmint was enough
for me. He claims he didn't partake in the killing, and I tend to
believe him. Don't know what to do with him. Hoping you might.
My arms getting tired of beading down on him, and I get the urge
to shoot him when my mind turns over what they done to
Hoseah."

"Hmmm. Don't shoot him if he didn't do the killin'. You'd
regret it later. He's just a pup anyway. Here, I got some fresh
made hobble thongs, I'll tie him up til morning, then we'll turn him
loose barefoot. It's just about twelve or fifteen miles or so to
Oakville. He'll make it. Give him time ta repent."

Gabe got leather thongs and started in on wrapping the
guy tight, arms and legs. His hands were well wrapped
individually, then joined together behind his back, pulling it all
tight.

"Hey, take it easy there, old-timer, that's damned tight. I
didn't do no killing and didn't know I was riding with killers either,
'til they done the deed."

When he protested too much, Gabe stuck one of his
smelly socks that he had earlier hung on sticks by the fire to air
out into the guys' mouth, rolled in a tight ball, wrapping the fella's
own bandana tight around with a good knot in it to shut him up.

"Thar ye go, how does that taste, a little cheesy? Wal,
so's yore palaver", said Gabe as he tugged and stretched the
leather to get a tight fit.

"Hell, he'll be begging you to shoot him after having your
sock in his mouth for a while, won't he?" Tom started laughing
through his tears, and Gabe grinned back at him. "Now that's
some sour dough, huh?"

"A sad fate for sure."

"I washed 'em last night in that sulfur creek, so they
should taste good, remind ya of the smell of brimstone, which
yore gonna be in iffen ya don't change yore ways, young fella...."

The young man grunted and shook his head, looking truly
sorry. Then Gabe laid him on his belly over next to the dead
man, pulled his hands taut behind him, and tied them to his feet.
Satisfied with the hog-tying, he went and poured himself a rum

toddy with lots of lemon and honey, and had a smoke by the fire in his old pipe. Smoking his special kinnickinnick always seemed to relax him. They could hear the beautiful high voices of Pancho and the other vaquero singing some Mexican lullaby while Josh sang softly on the other side of the herd.

Tom stood up, walked to his horse, then turned to face Gabe. "Sorry that my troubles came into your outfit, Gabe."

"We ride together now, Tom. Your troubles is our troubles. Get on now and relieve Pancho, he must be tuckered after that run. Send him on in for a rest. I'll be back out there with him at two. You got a watch, huh?"

"Yeah, thanks a lot, watch broke a while back. I'll just keep an eye on the big dipper as it wheels around for time. Gabe. I ain't gonna doze after all this anyway. You don't know how long I rode, searching in vain, lost, trying to resolve this, worrying 'bout the ranch busting out, worrying 'bout my brother. I figured he might be dead, but it feels better to know, instead of always wondering. Sonsobitches. There's some mean sonsobitches down here. Makes it hard to build a decent life. I ain't sorry I shot him."

"Me neither. Gotta do what ya gotta do. Ya done your duty, Tom. But like I done told Josh several times, don't dwell on it. Put yer mind to yer work, and don't dwell on it. It's over now, forget it, and we'll hide his body in the morning. I'm shore sorry bout you losing your kin, but not about yore using my rifle to kill him who done it. Throw some more wood on that fire to keep the coyotes from coming in and gnawing on the carcass til morning."

"Alright then, thanks Gabe."

"Shore, pard. Have a nice night-ride. Them mustangs likely worn out, ain't gonna run no more. Pancho was hobbling that lead mare when I left. And we didn't lose more than a few, who might drift back."

"Alright then, Gabe. Thanks again. And I got to go thank Mr. LaPoint. He called the guy out on it, faced him down, and pulled and fired that small pistol faster than anybody I ever seen. Damn. I hardly could see it, actually, his hand moved so fast. The stranger never cleared leather til he pulled a belly-gun. LaPoint couldn't see him pull it, with the fire and the shadows, or so I thought, 'cause he didn't fire again. So I blew that hole in him and finished him, and I feel satisfied about it. Whew. Glad that's over. Have a good rest."

"I might if ya'd quit dwellin' on that killin', tha danged stampede was bad enough."

"Alright then, I'm done, and glad of it."

With that Tom Jackson rode out to join with Josh in night-riding the herd, and Gabe went back to his pipe and rum. That night the coyotes came in and gnawed on the body a bit, but Gabe threw chunks of firewood at them and ran them off. A while later he started feeling sorry for the young stranger and went to piss nearby where the youngster lay hogtied on his belly.

"Now, I'll take that sock outa yore mouth if ya keeps quiet." No noise emitted from the hogtied body, so Gabe grabbed a hand-full of hair to lift the head and pull the sock out.

The next morning Gabe awoke early and made biscuits and breakfast, using the last of the coffee. When he approached the dead body, they found where wild hogs had been eating on it and tearing up the ground around it. They got the blanket from the man's saddle and wrapped him in it. Then they slung the blood caked body over his own saddle-mount after breakfast and headed northeast with the herd, after turning the younger guy loose without pants or boots, pointing him towards Oakville.

Within a few miles they found a draw and dumped the murderer's body in while the herd grazed and watered on a small creek-bed, and Tom kicked dirt over him from the silt walls of the draw. Tom got about a half-foot of dirt over the murderer, then pissed on the grave and called it done.

"Anybody want to say a few words?" asked Tom.

"Another varmint bit the dust," said Gabe. "Hope you didn't bury him so deep that the coyotes and hogs won't find him soon."

"Rot in hell, you murdering buzzard bait," said Tom.

"Yeah," said Josh. "I can't think of a better epitaph for a rustler and murderer. I'd like to say that you get that murderer's horse, which is a good mount, surefooted and fast. That will give you two good mounts and time to rest your first one. And that Spencer rifle is yours now, seeing as how you shot to save my life with it. Also that was quite a shot on a moving horse that killed the coyote yesterday. I want you always well armed when you're riding for me. We got more rifles."

"Well alright then, boss. Thanks. Nobody I'd rather ride with. I gotta ask. Did you see that man reach for the belly-gun?"

"Yeah, but I didn't think he could use it with his left hand. I was considering another shot to kill him, but really didn't want to if I didn't have to."

"Well, ya ain't put out that I did, nor going to hold it against me?"

"No. We did what needed doing. Turned out it was best for you to finish him anyway, on account of your brother and all. Now let's keep on doing what needs doing, with this herd."

"Yes-sir, Mr. LaPoint," said Tom as he nodded and mounted the big bay horse of the dead stranger.

An hour later they were heading north for the Eagle Ford Ranch with their herd of potential saddle-horses, mostly mares with selected young males added for their size. The best mares would be bred by Buck and Scorpio, with others turned to saddle mounts and sold. Josh rode Scorpio in front, leading the herd, while the rest contained the herd from the back and sides. With the two stallions front and back, it was not that difficult to control the herd. Soon they found other bachelor bands and selected the best from them.

By sunset they were driving the tired herd into the river meadows below the ranch on the little rise. Pancho led the cantering herd into the pastures by the river. Jesse was running out waving his hat in the air as he ran with the long rope to pen them into the meadow. Their first mustanging trip was a success. They had found plenty of solid mares and many firm colts from a bachelor band they encountered on their way back east. Many of the mares were suitable for breeding, and Josh had his plate full of training for a while, making him quite satisfied. They also spotted horses for sale in town, larger mounts for crossbreeding.

LaPoint paid Tom in cash, the first he had seen in a long time, and he returned to his place on Plum creek, promising to come back for the next roundup and stay longer, after he took care of pressing matters at home. Tom faced the grim task of telling relatives of his brother's sad demise, and left carrying a long face with that in mind.

The effects of the shootout with Ike Covington were varied. Ben Burnett, surviving his barefoot walk without pants, soon spread the word on LaPoint's lightening draw in Oakville and later in Helena. Soon guys with tie-down rigs for their big .44 Colts were daring each other in the saloons to throw down on LaPoint. On the other hand, the thought of two slugs going into a fast draw artist like Ike kept a lot of would be fast-draw artists a good distance back, more in the imaginary stage of risking a shootout. There was talk around the saloons about some of Ike's gang planning to back-shoot LaPoint, but they never got him. And rumors swirled of a raid on the ranch, but nothing came of it.

The need to avoid would be shoot-out artists was an annoyance to LaPoint, but he used various stratagems and slipped around town when the toughs were sleeping off hang-overs to avoid them. Mostly he avoided Helena and stuck to his work, spending as much time training horses as he could, for that was what he loved to do.

LaPoint used the round-pen to tame the first herd, after which Pancho took them out with saddle to teach them herding and cutting with the small group of cattle they rounded up from the western meadows along the river. LaPoint's round-pen technique was the same with every horse as the one he started with, the lead mare. At first he stood in the middle, squarely faced the horse, and flicked a rope with a knotted end behind them to get the horse running. They always circled the pen as he faced them squarely, urging them on with continual flicks of the knotted rope. After circling the pen a while the horse would begin lowering his head and opening his mouth, moving the lips, then chewing. At that point Josh discontinued squaring off with the horse, and turned sideways to it, which seemed to slow the horse down and draw it in to him.

After a few rounds of this the horse walked up to him and they went nose to muzzle for a few long moments while he spoke softly and lightly traced his fingers over'her nose and head, after which Josh stroked the horse all over, first with his hands, then the saddle blanket. Josh explained to Pancho and the ever curious Jesse that he had to run them a certain distance before their desire to rejoin a herd took over from their flight instinct, and then he would let them return to the fold again by imitating horse body language that he had learned with careful observation of lead mares. He had learned this as a boy from a Chickasaw Indian, and from long hours of laying in the tall grass and watching the small herd at the orphanage.

Within an hour after the first bonding, Josh was on her back, using a softened rawhide hackamore bridle, gently guiding her around the pen. After that it was easy for Pancho and Jesse to break them to snaffle bit bridle and saddle, making neck-reining cutting horses out of them in a few days each. If they got too nervous Josh took them again and tamed them by the same process. This was the work Josh LaPoint excelled at, and what he loved to do. The initial bond of trust and affection he established with the horses made them the best saddle mounts possible.

With their combined efforts and skills for several years, the Eagle Ford Ranch became the best horse outfit in the area for producing steady saddle mounts, with two round-pens and more outbuildings adding to the operation. They turned out eager, spirited, and co-operative saddle mounts for drovers, very quickly. They first sold a remuda of fifty to Uncle Billy Ricks, who was building a herd of longhorns to run north to the rail-head at Sedalia. Uncle Billy wanted Josh to go along as horse wrangler, but he refused, and stayed to build the ranch. By that time the corrals were filling with pregnant mares, and geldings roamed the pastures by the river, waiting for saddle training. Josh trained Jesse in horse taming while Jesse trained Josh in vaquero skills of roping and gathering mustangs, so one by one the horses were conditioned to bridle and saddle.

After that first big sale and division of profits, and the return of Tom Jackson, they quickly returned to the prairies for another mustang gathering and drive, and performed the same feat again, selling this remuda to a trail-boss gathering a big herd of 1200 or more near the joining of the three rivers, Nueces, Atascosa, and Frio. The drovers liked the mounts and the news spread to other trail bosses.

In the sultry heat of July they had received word from Muldoon in Helena that a trail boss named Winger had heard from Uncle Billy of the quality remuda they had delivered, and wanted a remuda for his own late drive. It was over that herd that LaPoint had his second pistol shootout, in a dispute over unbranded stock which had been running the coastal prairies during the cool fall of '66.

The incident occurred after they had just camped for the night on a little creek that Jesse called the Coleto. Jesse and two vaqueros were out watching the herd of nearly thirty horses. The twilight chill had LaPoint squatting on the ground, building a fire for camp. Tom Jackson spotted them first, coming in out of the brush alongside the creek, from downstream. "We got a group of riders coming in, boss," he said.

"Better remount and go see what's up."

The riders, numbering about eight, spread out and cantered towards the herd, where Jesse and two vaqueros rode the first night-watch. LaPoint and Jackson remounted and rode out fast towards the strangers, and their leader reined in with two other riders to confront them as they approached.

"We're cutting this herd for our horses, bub," said the leader with a double pistol holster, tie-down rigs with Army Colts.

"You can take a look, but these are all unbranded horses," replied LaPoint as he reined Scorpio to a quick stop about ten yards away from the man, who sat on a large bay gelding. Jackson stopped as well, about ten yards towards the herd from LaPoint, with rifle out, but balanced over his saddle.

The jefe turned his horse towards the herd. "They're not all mustangs. Some of them's runaways from our range. Our horses."

"They're all unbranded, every one, and we aim to hold on to them."

"Likely die trying, I reckon, being outgunned and all," said the man, with a smirk.

"No. It might cut both ways. No use anyone dying over wild horses, for the range is full of wild stock, there for anyone willing to work for it, horses and cows both," said LaPoint. Scorpio began to sidestep away from Jackson and the herd, quickly moving with stutter-steps to the right, then accelerating on the diagonal in an instant and running full speed into the side of the leader's mount, knocking them over into the other rider beside them. The first horse went down and the second bolted off and nearly threw the rider. The rider was agile and was up on his feet in a flash, disengaging himself from the struggling horse and reaching for his right gun.

"Don't," yelled LaPoint. The man continued and LaPoint drew and shot him twice in the chest, knocking him down. The holes were near his heart, and he was dying fast. The gunshots spooked the other man's horse into bucking him off into the dust. The other man threw up his hands while LaPoint put a bead on him, forcing the other riders to come in. Jackson held a bead on the group with his repeater.

"Don't shoot, I ain't drawin'," said the shaken man.

"You can leave or get shot here and now. Take his body

and get out of here, for these are our horses, and we'll take you down if you try to take them. That man with the rifle there can pick off all your pals before they get back here."

"Alright, alright, Lefty, come on in, they done kilt Bart!"

The group of strangers wheeled around and walked their mounts back towards the fracas.

"Pick up his body and get out of here or the coyotes will have a big feast," said LaPoint.

"He mean's business, Lefty," said the man on the ground, starting to haul his boss's body up. "He's LaPoint. Come on and help me, and let's get outa this alive. There's no pay nor profit in it now."

Two of the riders dismounted while another collected the man's horse. They wrapped the man's body in a tarp, tied it on the saddle, and departed, soon spreading further word of LaPoint's fast draw among the rustler crews that had dominated the brush country counties. The LaPoint outfit drove the herd to their ranch and finished them out to form a remuda for Bud Winger's drive north.

The next fast draw incident occurred in Helena, over nothing much, a year after the first. LaPoint had just gotten a bath and haircut when one of Muldoon's gals came in and told him that a gunman had grabbed Delores and gotten into a scrape with Jesse over it. Pulling the barber cloth and wiping his face with it, Lapoint emerged from the shop to see Jesse being confronted by a gunman near the livery. The gunslinger was standing ready to draw, and was full of racial insults and challenges for Jesse, with his hand near his tie-down gun rig. Then he noticed Josh coming from the barber shop and walking fast across the street towards him.

"Jesse, step aside," said LaPoint, which made Jesse turn and move to the right.

"My fight, boss," said Jesse as he glanced over his shoulder at LaPoint.

"My girl, my fight."

The gunman squared off with LaPoint as he approached with the leather loop already off his small Remington. He intended to talk the fellow down.

"Get back greaser, I'll get you later," said the gunman. Jesse stepped back with his hand out near his pistol, turning and looking at LaPoint, who was a few paces away.

"Now simmer down, wait and live to tell about it," said LaPoint.

The gunman started to draw, without time to think LaPoint had drawn and shot him twice, dead center in his chest, with his small pistol, before the man got his pistol raised. The countless practice draws while clearing the land of rattlers had taken over his reactions to deadly effect. The man died within seconds as a crowd gathered.

The deputy and a few other witnesses declared that LaPoint shot in self defense. The dead youngster was a fast draw artist who had already killed plenty of men around Oakville and Helena. So the reputation for speed and marksmanship increased the need for gun-work, and LaPoint practiced continually to stay sharp, for survival's sake. But he preferred to stay home and train horses. The horses had to be conditioned to gunfire eventually, so sometimes the training went hand in hand.

There were other forced shootouts with rifles on the rolling prairies when rustlers tried to steal the stock, sporadic gun-work that had to be done, often in the dark. Tom Jackson proved a fearless fighter and very accurate marksman with fourteen shots from two repeaters he carried, shooting very well while riding, and better on the ground. His marksmanship, with the fast firing Spencer rifles he carried, proved crucial in the LaPoint outfit's success, and Josh kept increasing his rewards in pay and percentage of profits on horse sales.

In the third year of horse ranching, they had a big remuda delivery to Mr. Winger in spring. Arriving at San Antonio after two days of driving, they left the horses in a brush corral under the watchful eyes of Pancho, Tom Jackson, and another vaquero named Enrique they had hired. The corral was on the outskirts of town, near the river. The buyer's rep was there at the corrals near the old mission rancho, and was impressed with the stock. He gave Josh a paper for stock received, and set up a future delivery point north of town. The meeting to exchange silver and arrange future contracts would be in old San Antonio, at a hotel near the river.

Josh and Gabe rode into the Spanish flavored-town and checked in at the Menger Hotel, a solid two-story establishment about a hundred yards from the Alamo ruins. After cleaning up and taking in the sights, they had dinner at the Menger dining room with a trail boss who was looking for remudas, a man named Jefferson Winger, from a big ranch on the Nueces. He was a tall and heavyset man with a big walrus mustache and brown hair graying at the temples. He wore a tooled leather vest and boots, obviously made in the ornate florid Spanish style by a superior craftsman. Friendly and gregarious, he insisted they have a good dinner before they talked business. He recommended the filet mignon, and they all had one wrapped in bacon, with fresh greens and cool beer. Gabe said it was almost as good as buffalo. The big cowman ate and quaffed sudsy beer with gusto, a big napkin tucked into his collar to catch the drips.

They chatted about rain and grass, about horses, rustlers, bandits, Indians, weapons, and conditions in South Texas during dinner, then afterwards made a deal on the saddle mounts. The well-known, tightfisted trail boss took their first price without any dickering, to their surprise. After paper and silver exchanged hands, the cowman had more on his mind.

"Mr. LaPoint, Uncle Billy Ricks says you provided him with the best string of spirited and willing saddle mounts he ever had. That's why I paid your asking price. I need a scout and a horse wrangler, and I think you're one of these fellas with a smooth way with horses, the right touch for my remudas. I believe in taking good care of my stock. I don't want beat down sullen saddle mounts. I want spirited willing pardners for my drovers, and that's what Uncle Billy said you produced. I got a job for you if you want it, anytime, as horse wrangler on my herds or my ranch on the Nueces. And maybe move up to trail boss after that."

"Why, I appreciate the offer, Mr. Winger. But I'm satisfied with my current situation, and we're building a ranch down south of here, about sixty miles downstream on this river, with a blacksmith shop for Gabe here first on the list, and then an add-on to the ranch house, so I'd have to decline because of previous plans."

The cowman nodded, took a drink of brandy, pulled cigars out of his vest pocket, and looked at Gabe.

"Sul Ross told me you're the best scout for the high plains, and that you scouted for Jack Hays, and brought those French girls back in. That right, McBride?"

"Yep, I know the high plains. Sul Ross? I remember a Shapely Ross from those days."

"Shapely, yeah, old man Ross. He's quit rangering, settled at Waco with a store, postmaster and all. Sul is his son, and every bit the Comanche fighter his pap was."

"Wal I'll be, takes generations to fight Comanches, I reckon. Everybody's been fightin' 'em for bout a century and a half, without much success so far."

"Hell, they've been driving back the frontier since the war with horrible raiding. The confederates did a worse job than the federals at protecting the line of settlements, if you can believe that. If old Sam Houston had convinced the legislature to draw a dividing line at the staked plains, maybe it might have worked out, but it's gone to hell in a hand-basket now."

"Seems like it. So how'd you know who I was."

"Well, this letter about the horses says the outfit of LaPoint & McBride, and my rep down at the pens described you to me. The Tonkawas said you had a scalping scar. Not too many guys carry a scar like that. Of course, ole Josiah Wilbarger was walking around without his scalp for about ten years, they say. He usually kept it covered, thank God."

"Yep, I reckon my hairline gives me away. I keep a hat on it mostly so as not to shock women-folk. But in a nice hotel like this, ya know, ain't polite ta eat with hats on. I got this scar in what I hope to be my last scrape with Comanches, Mr. Winger. I just as soon lay low and mustang rather than get wrapped up in killing Comanche's again. I had more'n a bellyfull of that. I's hopin folks ain't heerd I was back."

"We heard you were back in these parts from a Tonkawa scout that goes by the name of John's Son, or Johnson, whatever. He says he ran into you and another sharpshooter at the Colorado, and you gave him your old top-hat that you got from Placido at Plum Creek. He says his daddy used to ride with you and captain Jack sometimes."

"Wal I'll be. That's right. He's the son of ole Coffee-John, who used ta scout with us when I rode with John Coffee Hays. He liked the captain so he wanted to be called Coffee John, and it stuck on 'im."

"Well, he scouting with the rangers now, and says you're the man I need."

"For what?"

"To scout for herds moving to the rail-heads, to parley with the Indians and talk our way through. The rails are moving west, and will be at Ft. Dodge before long. The trails drives will be moving west with them. I'm told you've got the best knowledge, the best sense for good water and quicksand crossings, the best ability to parley with the various bands. I want you and LaPoint here to scout and run cattle drives for me as they move west, simple as that."

"They're moving the rail-heads west, and the cattle drives too?" asked Gabe.

"That's right. My sources tell me that a man named McCoy is building pens for a rail-head at Abilene, Kansas, for next year's herds, and later on out to Fort Dodge. That means we'll be heading straight north through Austin and Fort Worth and Fort Sill, through the Indian territories, on a route I ain't been on. I'd like to find a couple of good men to scout and help run a drive that way next spring. It's on the edge of Comancheria, and I was told you speak their lingo and can parley with them. You know they been raising hell all along the frontier since the war started, don't ya? Wichitas too, they say."

"So we heard, but they ain't bothered us down on the south San Antonio lately. And we don't want to get tangled in an endless fight with them atal."

"Well, lucky you don't live north of San Antonio. Gabe, you're known for speaking Indian lingos and tracking as good as any Tonkawa scout. As a matter of fact young Sul Ross said he wanted you to scout for the rangers, no matter how old and cut up you were. Everyone says you know the staked plains better than anyone. Young Mr. LaPoint here is already well-known for being a master horseman. And I know by his fine handwriting and business dealings that he ain't an uneducated saddle bum. Yal have any experience driving cattle?"

"Wal, yeah. I run a couple of small herds to New Orleans back around thirty nine and forty. Didn't like it much though. And LaPoint here was the horse wrangler on one, as a teenager, and a good one too. But I don't know that country too well, and we's doing purdy good with horses right now. Yal won't be going up on the cap rock with that route, which is my old stompin' grounds."

"We'll be going by the edge of it, with Comanches and Kiowas to contend with, plus all the tribes in the territories and south of Abilene, maybe Cheyennes, Arapahoes, Wichitas, who knows what all. I need a man who can keep ahead of the herd and parley with the sonobitches and whittle their tolls down without starting a fracas with 'em. I hate goddamned stampedes, and would rather give 'em some beeves, but need somebody who can barter."

"Yep, that's true. But my haunts was further west. I know the cap-rock and the staked plains, as far as the Quitaque canyons, and on over to the Cimarron. I only been ta Fort Sill area once, from the west, taking some captives back. And when I was young I hunted buffalo up north of Austin for a few years. But nothing like the time I spent up on the cap-rock, the Llano Estacado."

"Well, the scout that you are, you'd still be the best man around to pick a trail with good water, avoiding quicksand river crossings and gyp water, and to parley with the Indians. I want you and Mr. LaPoint here to work for me, if you take a mind to it, Gabe. There's a nation ready for beef out there, instead of salted pork, and I'm gonna get it to them, so I need good men like you two. What do you say?"

"We don't want ta get involved in no scrapes with Comanches," said Gabe. "I reckon we'll keep with the horses for a while, got contracts with you, Charlie Goodnight, Uncle Ricks, and the army, lots of commitments. But the offer is appreciated, and one never can tell about the future."

"What about you LaPoint, you must be tired of messing with those gun hands around Helena and Live Oak always trying to back-shoot you?"

"Well frankly Mr. Winger, I am pretty disgusted with the constant wrangle with rustlers and fast draw artists around Helena and Live Oak. The idea of heading north has some appeal, but we are so tied up in horse contracts and ongoing operations that we can't think of pulling off right now."

"Most folks get played out from dealing with those Oakville and Helena rustlers."

"It's been a chore. Selecting the best stock out on the range and rounding it up in rough country is hard enough without rustlers constantly trying to steal the herds. And I'd like to be able to go into a town and sit down to eat without having to dodge some slick draw kid who's looking to get famous."

"Lots of sticker bushes and bad eggs around there," said Winger.

"Thar's liable ta be scrapes with Kiowa's up thar, too,"

said Gabe.

"Yeah," said Josh, "that there is, Mr. Winger, but it's where we are for now, right in the nest of them. And like Gabe says, we have contracts to fulfill."

"Oh hell, the country is filling up with trash rustlers like that. Some of 'em posing as Indians too, which stirs up strikes against Indians, which stirs up strikes against whites. And that damned Baylor fellow with his 'White Man' newspaper, always stirring up hatred against all the Indians, even the tame ones. Turning it into another bloodbath, as if the damned civil war wasn't enough. These radicals are always stirring up wars, the war on secession, and now on the redskins. Makes everything a fella tries to do that much harder."

"We shore been larnin' that without fightin' no Indians," said Gabe.

"Listen. Reliable men are a big plus in this country, now the war's over and the country is hungry for beef, with rail heads moving further west in Kansas. If I can rely on you to build me some good remudas, you can rely on me to pay a fair price for them come spring, every spring from now on. Give me a post office box there in Helena, and I'll contact you in late winter about how many horses I'll need, and when. It'll be at least a hundred mounts."

"Alright-sir, here's my name and address." Josh handed him a small card that he had hand-lettered in a fine style on thick paper. "And my hand. I'll build you good remudas, Mr Winger."

"I know you will, and I'll pay a fair price for them. And don't forget my offer, neither of you. I'd be proud to have yal riding for me," said Winger. He looked down at the card in his hand. "Eagle Ford Ranch, LaPoint & McBride", he read from the card. I'll hang on to this one. But yal remember the offer is always open to come ride for me."

"Well, it could happen someday, you never know," said LaPoint.

"Good luck with the Comanches, Winger, I done had enough of 'em," said Gabe.

The next morning Josh awoke with an idea, and decided to share it with Gabe. When he came down the stairs he saw Gabe sitting with his hat on reading a newspaper in the lobby on a leather couch. Together they entered the dining room and found a table. The waitress was blond and spoke with a German accent, and was very pretty. They had coffee and then started breakfast of eggs, grits, potatoes, and biscuits.

"How's tha biscuits?"

"Not too bad, but I'm spoiled to your sourdough, you know that. That was some news about the railheads moving west, sure going to change things with the tribes. What newspaper did you find?"

"A local, the *San Antonio Herald*."

"Any big news?"

"Veteran's limping home. Reconstruction is what they call the federal occupation now. Renegades and bandits raiding south in the brush country. Rangers fighting bandit gangs down there.   Comanches and Kiowas raising hell all along the frontier. Waugh. Glad we been laying low, just fightin' rustlers. They caught eight of the conspirators in the Lincoln assassination a while back. Louisiana is in chaos, even worse than it was. And Horace Greely says 'go west, young man'. Meanwhile they's hiring China-men to finish the cross-country railroad up north, racing to beat the Irish who are drinking oat water and laying down track in a hurry. So the railroad crowd got what they wanted, a northern route across the country."

"Well, interesting, but not much that affects us, except the rail-heads moving west for the trail drives, huh? Gabe, I woke up with an idea, but I want you to agree only if you feel like it."

"What's that?"

"Well, you said you still owned that land on the Blanco River, north of here, and I thought it'd be nice to ride up that way. I know it's got some bad memories of the raid and all, so if you don't want to, I understand. Still, from what you told me, it's a beautiful place, maybe worth salvaging somehow, huh? I'd like to see some of that clear running water you've told me about. I've never seen a really clear river, you know."

"Waugh. I ain't been back since the burnout, but I've thought of it a thousand times. I'd shore like to see it, but then again I wouldn't. With you along, maybe it wouldn't put me in a lather. Alright. Let's go on up there, sight out the situation."

"Alright. How far is it, do you figure?"

"About fifty miles as the crow flies. But it's further into Penateca Comanche country."

"Alright, let's get the horses delivered and leave the mules with Pancho so we can travel fast and light, then just swing by up there, and you can show me some springs and clear running rivers. I've yet to see a clear running river, except in France. Doesn't the Guadalupe River rise in those hills too?"

"One ridge over, it does. I think yore right, it's time ta shed the past and take a fresh look at that place. It shore was beautiful there, right shinin'. Hills and clear water valleys. It ain't all sticker-bushes and constant wind and humidity, like down south. I'll show you some swimming holes that's make you forget those murky bayous forever."

The next morning dawned cool and clear, and they rode out towards the northwest as the sun rose behind the rolling hills beyond the sleepy town. Moving fast on their spirited stallions without mules to tow, they were at the Guadalupe River valley by noon, despite the steep and rough hills of limestone rock, and the dense oak and cedar growth in the wet creek bottoms. Josh was so impressed with the cool, clear, jade green beauty of the Guadalupe, with it's giant cypress and pecan trees lining the banks, that he stripped down and went for a swim.

"I can see why you fell in love with this country. This is sure a beautiful valley. How far to your old place on the Blanco river?"

"About another couple of hours, I figure. See that tall ridge up north there. We used ta call it the Devil's Backbone. It's over that, in the next valley. We got some steep terrain to get through yet."

After a short lunch they rode towards the ridge and by late afternoon were approaching the big spring near Gabe's old homestead on the Blanco river, a smaller stream than the Guadalupe, but just as clear and beautiful, with gray rocky banks and lush foliage with tall cypress, pecans, and oaks making great gallery forests along the banks. As they stopped above the river on seventy foot stone cliffs and looked down, they saw the giant spring come rushing clear and cold out of the base of the small escarpment.

Finding a narrow trail left by deer that angled down the tall cliff, they walked the horses down. When they reached the clear jade green rushing river they noticed a great blue heron circling back to a nest in tall cottonwoods with fish in his beak. Above that they spotted a Mexican eagle, spiraling down, and a tiny waterfall dripping from a ledge covered in moss, water-cress, and ferns. LaPoint, being the young and agile one, climbed up to the ledge where water was dripping out of a fault line, took a drink from it, then brought some water-cress down to add to their supper.

Above them they noticed curious rock formations, where a veil of water minerals had built up through the ages from the drip, the translucent calcium magnesium like stalactites in a cave, but more like a curtain wall, providing shelter in the overhang behind it. It seemed to reappear in spots along the cliffs, making a sheltered niche in the overhangs behind them.

Bees buzzed around the entrance to a small hole and another great blue heron circled over small whitewater falls and pools downstream. The fast moving river was small and clear with a jade green tint, the springs rushing into it from the base of the cliff enough to increase the size substantially downstream. Three dark cormorants took off across the water, fleeing their approach, paddling and flapping and running on water until they took off and flapped upstream. The Mexican eagle came down and landed in the top of a tall bald cypress that towered above the rocky cliff. They could see fish in the clear water, bass, cat, crappie, and lots of perch. There were several white tail deer browsing across the river, a group of wild turkeys ranged the grass along the shore.

Across the fast river, which was perhaps fifteen yards wide, was a smooth grassy meadow. Beyond that they could see the burned out hulk of limestone walls and chimney that had been Gabe's homestead, under huge pecan trees. Beyond that a huge thunderhead was mushrooming up high into the blue sky, with flashes of lightening crackling through it.

"That storm may be here in an hour or so," said Gabe. "May come a frog floater."

"Maybe. I've been watching it for a while. It's not moving fast this way, mostly billowing up. Could be hail in it, being so high. This is a great place, Gabe."

"I can't go no closer than this here," said McBride. "Don't want to rake those scars. We'll have a dinner down here, by the river, if that suits you. I'd like you to go look it over, and I got a deal to offer you when you get back. I'll get a quick fire going for supper. I got that good German bread from San Antone, beans, jerky, and coffee."

"Alright, Gabe. Isn't that a ford right upstream there?"

"Yeah, you can cross there easy. Lots of fording places

for these horses, without loaded mules. I'll make camp at a bend in the stream, down about ten yards. There's a grassy meadow thar."

Gabe squatted down and made a quick fire of dry driftwood sticks, adding oak twigs and branches. Then he took his hat and boots off and sat on a rock with his feet in the cool water while the fire turned to coals, dipping his hands in the water and splashing it over his face and head. When the fire was down to a small nest of coals he took out his knife, sharpened it a bit, and cut thick slices of the store-bought bread loaf while the bean skillet and coffee pot heated up.

Josh rode Scorpio across the flat stone bottom of the ford upstream about fifty yards, the clear rushing water barely touching Scorpio's muscular chest. He spent a half hour examining the burnt out cottage and the area around it as the thunderstorm slowly approached, then joined Gabe at camp downstream, this time fording across some gravel bars at the bend where the river had braided into smaller streams.

"Gabe, this is as beautiful as you told me. The house is pretty well ruined, I figure. The heat of the fire cracked the stone up pretty good. But I saw ledges of the same stuff out back."

"Oh, thars plenty of rock for rebuildin', if ya was of a mind to."

"It's such a fine place, lots of grass in those meadows, and all these nice oak and pecan trees. A hell of a lot more pleasant than down south, and these giant cypress remind me of my childhood swimming holes. Clear water, good grass, beautiful hills, springs, I can see why you chose this place over down south."

"This was a homestead, the rancho down south was for gathering herds, which is whar we're makin' our silver now. "

"Yeah, that's right, but I'd rather live here, given the choice."

"Wal, that's good. Cause I got a barter to parley with ya. I'll trade you this place, 320 acres along the river here, for equal value in silver and land on the Eagle Ford Ranch."

"The Eagle Ford Ranch isn't mine to trade, Gabe."

"Oh yes it is. Pancho got the papers in the mail four years ago transferring the one half tha deed to yore name, Joshua Alexandre of LaPoint. Mr. Alex done it, but didn't want ya to know unless you showed interest in the rancho."

"Damn. You could knock me over with a feather. How'd he know to put LaPoint?"

"That durned aguilar vision, I guess."

"Well, sure, I'll trade you."

"One condition, Josh."

"What's that?"

"You got ta hire somebody to tear down the shell of my homestead and turn it to ground rubble, use if for back-fill, remove all sign of it, before I come visit."

"Yes. I will do that as soon as possible."

"Alright then. If yore gonna take a swim in that river, ya'd better do it before that thunderstorm comes and dumps on us. It's just twenty miles away or so, and look at that lightening. We need to wrap it up here and find some shelter."

With the deal sealed with a handshake, Josh walked down over rounded gray rocks and twining roots supporting huge buttressed trunks of bald cypress trees to take a swim in the cool, jade green waters, in a deep pool, right below where two Comanches were hiding, with rifles, pistols, and bows and arrows. The Comanches kept down and watched from a sheltered overhang in the solid stone cliff.

Balancing in riding boots on rounded river cobbles big as watermelons, he slowly walked down to the water's edge and stepped onto a big flat boulder by the rushing white water. The rock shifted a bit on its irregular bottom, and three water moccasins came slithering out from under it, coiling and raising their heads a couple of feet from his leg. Lightening and thunder crashed again, echoing off the canyon walls.

The snakes emerging from their den under the big flat stone were agitated, with white mouths open, and their big knotty heads were spouting fangs when the flash of lightening and immediate crash of thunder jarred LaPoint into awareness they were about to strike his leg. Scorpio reared up when he saw them, alerting Josh to their presence. Without pausing to think he pulled his fast action pistol and shot all three, as he had done numerous times before while removing the rattlesnake hordes down south. The bullets ricocheted off the solid stone river bank and went whizzing and zinging past where Gabe was sitting with his feet in the cool water.

"Gol-dang, watch it, lightening, thunder, fuggin' gunfire, what the hell are you firing for?"

"Cottonmouths. Sorry, didn't have time for much else. I stirred a nest of them. It may be beautiful here, but it's still got vipers, eh?"

"Oh yeah, it's still Texas, plenty of biting snakes, damned thunder too, and they get ta movin' when they feel a storm brewing. That storm's getting closer, and it's liable to raise this river. Look up in those treetops thar, at those logs and branches. I seen this river up that high every year I lived here, a good thirty feet above our heads. So get your swim in and lets move downstream and find some shelter. Thar's some barns down a few miles we can hole up in til it passes."

"Alright, alright."

Seventy feet up the gray rock cliff, downstream a few yards, the two Comanche braves hidden behind the fallen roof boulder of their overhang in the cliff watched the white men. Their eyes grew big when they saw how fast LaPoint dispatched the cottonmouths after drawing his small pistol with the lightening bolt. The bigger of the two whispered, "Ekakwitsubaitu!" The other pointed to his rifle, but the big one shook his head in the negative and continued watching. He pointed to McBride, whose white balding dome was marked with the obvious scalping scar. "Ekaa Wasape Nahuu"

The other nodded, then they hunkered down to watch, staring with envy at the fine horses that the two white men kept so close to them.

LaPoint stripped to his tanned skin and swam for a while as Gabe took a bath on the shore while the coffee boiled and beans heated with buffalo jerky in them. Then LaPoint sat in the shallow where a cold spring poured out of the ground. He sat into the whirling pool and lay back in the white water, looking up through the branches of the huge pecan trees, noticing a bunch of pecans still left on them. On impulse he left the pool naked and climbed a big cypress next to the pecan tree, and began to shake the branches, knocking down the shells from last year which winter winds had not dislodged. As he did so, a blond cougar across the river stirred from his hiding place in a deep overhang of the cliff and hurried up over the top of the gray stone wall and away, out of sight.

Above them on the cliff, the two Comanches crept along the gray weathered rock, watching LaPoint climb the tree, dislodge the cougar from its daytime hiding place, and scamper back down to crack the pecans with a rock and eat them.

"Pia-waoo. Pia-waoo" said the younger brave, pointing at the escaping dark coated cougar.

"Pia-waoo ekakwitsubaitu!" replied the bigger fellow, then pointing up to the top of another cypress tree at the Mexican eagle sitting on the top, he said. "Kiwih-nia!" The bigger man, looking like a young chieftain by his adornments of bear claw necklace and eagle feathers in his braided hair, was keen on watching, but not attacking the white men. It was the horses he wanted, and he pointed to them and said, "tuhuya, tuhuya"

The other brave, a well tanned blue-eyed youngster with hair that was sun-bleached blond, gripped a bow and arrow tipped with rusty points cut from a barrel hoop in his hands, and crouched behind a rock and looked at the bigger man with a questioning expression.

At that moment Josh whistled and both horses came to join him at the river, where he used a canvass bag to wash them. The older warrior watched Josh, then shook his head in the negative, and they crept back from the cliff edge and scurried back to their horses, hidden in a small side canyon. They mounted and circled northwest to cross the river upstream of LaPoint and McBride, then headed due north.

A big barn was located down stream that Josh and Gabe utilized for shelter from the thunderstorm that raised the river nearly a foot and clouded the water a bit.

After a peaceful night camping in the old cypress shake barn of the abandoned settler's spread, LaPoint and McBride went downstream until they came to the edge of the hills at San Marcos, where Gabe showed Josh the huge outflows of fresh water that gushed from the ground there and formed a river that joined the Blanco below the town. It was amazing to both of them to see so much clear water gushing out of the ground, and they filled all their canteens with it. There was watercress growing along the edges, which they ate with relish. Gabe had desired to call on and pay his respects to General Burleson there, but found out at the general store that the old Texian had passed on.

After a short visit in a saloon in San Marcos, they rode south down the prairies where Gabe had chased Comanches after the Plum Creek fight, back down to the rancho, their home, where they spent the winter improving the place.

In the mild but wet winter of 1869, furnishing a new blacksmith shop was first order of business, which involved more pole cutting, rattlesnake shooting, and ordering tools and a real anvil in Helena. They had been using short pieces of train rails fastened to mesquite stumps for anvils long enough, was Gabe's familiar refrain as he tried to work on horse shoes with the irregular pounding surfaces.

While waiting for the big anvil and other blacksmith and wheelwright tools to arrive by freighter, they built an add-on section to the main house, separated by a dog run breezeway where they stacked firewood. This they divided into two rooms, to give them private quarters. When they found out somebody had bought the anvil en route, they decided to tackle other projects to ignore the disappointment. When Josh saw a freighter hauling a load of firebricks through Helena, he bought them on the spot and had them hauled to the spread.

"What tha hell we gonna do with all them bricks," asked Gabe as he saw the heavy laden wagon pull into the shed.

"Build Rumford fireplaces that actually work, like in Europe."

"Oh boy, here we go, I told Mr. Alex not ta send ya over thar, ya know."

"Come on, it'll be fun. You got to make me some rasps to grind these brick and a file to put cut lines, and turn some ball peen hammers into rock hammers with the forge. And some wide chisels."

"Such as it is, with no proper anvil yet."

"Such as it is, while we're waiting for the equipment."

"Alright then, you're tha boss."

Together Gabe and Josh built a Rumford fireplace at one end of the add-on out of the bricks and fire-clay mortar, plastering the back with a parging of cement and fine sand. It was a design that Josh had learned about in Europe after standing in front of one and feeling the intense heat. The tall shallow fireplace was scoffed at by Pancho as it was being built, but proved very efficient at throwing heat when finished. It warmed the new addition to a cozy glow in the coldest northers. With two big rooms in it, connected by double french doors, the add-on supplied space for Gabe and Josh to have privacy and return the cottage space to the family of Rosita and Pancho.

Since Helena was on the crossroads with access to

Indianola and San Antonio, it became their supply base for all the improvements, so they often frequented Muldoon's and became quite friendly with him. They usually went in the mornings, when the drunks, would-be shootout artists, and saloon loungers were still asleep and out of the way.

One Sunday morn they checked in at Muldoon's livery stable to find Ben Burnett, the young man riding with Ike Covington, whom they had turned loose pant-less and barefoot on the prairie. He had been working at the livery for two weeks, but didn't particularly like the job, and asked Gabe if there was a chance of him hiring on with the LaPoint outfit. Gabe spoke to Josh about it and got him to agree, so Ben started helping with the horse handling. The youngster proved to be an enthusiastic hand, and slowly won their trust to become part of the crew. LaPoint asked Tom Jackson to take an interest in setting the lad straight, and Tom complied after mulling it over some.

The horse gathering continued, along with breeding of the mustangs to larger stock. After the mild winter in 1870 they had over 80 saddle mounts, their best remuda yet, the larger and sturdier of the mustangs and about half being mixed breeds, with lots of Grullas and blacks and bays from a group of small herds they had found to the southwest. To the south they had also found bachelor bands and selected some colts from them for geldings.

This was the first remuda they sold to Charles Goodnight, for moving herds west across the dry country towards the Pecos and up to Fort Sumner, and the quality of the mounts established a successful long-term connection. The mustangs and crossbred horses could live on the sparse grass of the dry stretches when necessary, and were proving to be excellent cow ponies for the new trails through tougher country. Bud Winger was buying horses with similar desires in mind, for moving north to Abilene, across the dry grasslands of the northern trail routes. Cavalry contracts for horses to range the staked plains became a growing part of their business. The LaPoint outfit worked steadily; all year round they spent gathering, breeding, raising, and training horses.

During several years of building the ranch, LaPoint made many trips to buy thoroughbred mares for breeding to their Andalusians, in order to develop midsized saddle mount which would thrive on grain but could do well on grass when required.

With the twin foals from Pancho's big mare, and foals from the new mares, as well as from select mustangs, they began developing a mount built for the west, with a smooth fast pacing gait and the ability to do well on natural grasses.

The first colt from Pancho's big mare, bred early and often, was growing into a tall gray stallion with a beautiful pacing gait, and Josh was already impressed with its intelligence. He spent a lot of time training it and its female counterpart. The big colt was already taller than Scorpio, but carried the same muscular build and high arched neck. And the filly was nearly as large, with a longer back. There was already an army officer, a Lt. Peter Boehm sent down from General Augur's offices in San Antonio, who had expressed definite interest in both foals, for officer's mounts. Lt. Boehm thought it befit an officer to ride a big horse with the high Andalusian head, like Napoleon rode, but he was searching for a horse with a comfortable fast pacing gate for an officer with a lot of civil war injuries. He contracted for a group of saddle mounts for the army at Fort Concho, and told Josh that he wanted to contract for both big grays when they were ready. LaPoint agree to a contract on the fast growing colt, which he spent a lot of time training.

Scorpio and Buck were kept busy breeding the best mustang mares and larger purchased mares, to produce saddle mounts, and before long the outfit had new corrals for pregnant mares and mares with foals. Soon the two stallions had several other Kentucky mares to breed, and were happy as they could be impregnating mares while Josh built corrals for the new additions. His body grew stronger from the steady work with post hole digger, shovels, crosscut saws, and ax. His deltoids, triceps, and biceps grew as muscular and strong as Gabe's, who had wielded a blacksmith hammer for years pounding hot steel, but Josh kept his lightening speed. Rosita kept all the hands supplied with healthy fresh food, with goats-milk yogurt and cheese along with honey from their own hives to complement the garden fare.

Many thickets of very hard oak and mesquite were taken down and the rattlesnakes therein shot for practice with the fast action revolver. They put three pastures down by the river into good hay and acquired a hay mow and rake to make their own hay for winter. That soon necessitated a hay-barn, which meant more clearing and more rattlesnakes to evict, and more lumber from Helena. For railings they brought down wagon-loads of long cedar poles from the Blanco Valley, and every day LaPoint spent at least an hour or so building.

The land changed from rattlesnake thicket and Tejano hideout to a first class ranch in a few years of unceasing work, with new quarters, corrals, pastures, barn, blacksmith shop, and bunkhouse. No longer "Escondito", the hidden away, the "Eagle Ford Ranch" was becoming well-known for the remudas of fine saddle-mounts they consistently produced. And Josh LaPoint was becoming well-known for his fast and accurate pistol and rifle work as well as his way with horses, among the vaqueros who gathered for horsemanship contests and shooting matches on Sundays, and throughout the surrounding countryside. With Tom Jackson, also renowned as an expert rifleman, in charge of ranch defense, none of the local rustlers wanted to risk a raid on the Eagle Ford Ranch.

Tom Jackson, as well as being a sharpshooter, emerged as a foreman who could direct men of any race fairly and well. Pancho translated his orders to the growing crew of vaqueros, who were already expert at roping and riding. Jesse grew into a first class vaquero and horse trainer, and learned to shoot from LaPoint, with rifle and revolver. Gabe spent most of his time in farrier work, and blacksmithing in general. Everyone spent spare time in target shooting with the latest weapons, or practicing roping skills.

The extra growth of the operation and crew necessitated more buildings at the ranch as well, a bunkhouse, more corrals and sheds, and the creation of more enclosed pastures to hold the wild herds of mustangs they were gathering. After building all the necessary structures for the working necessities of the ranch on the San Antonio, Josh took Jesse and went north to the Blanco valley in '70, where they hired some German masons and built a small ranch house on the land there.

Using white limestone blocks purchased from a quarry near Fredricksburg, the old world masons made a solid double rock walled house, in which Josh built a Rumford fireplace at both ends. After the house was finished Josh hired a crew to help them build corrals, round pens, and herd enclosures of brush along the river pastures. The native oak and cedar provided excellent posts for corrals, but the digging of post-holes proved difficult in the shallow bedrock, and a big steel railroad rod was necessary to chip a hole in the marl below. At some points they had to brace the poles with surrounds of mortared rock to steady them, but the long cedar poles made excellent railings. With a crew of cedar choppers from New Braunfels, they cleared several acres to carry a load of poles back down to the Eagle Ford Ranch on the San Antonio.

Steady work through every season was the rule, and by the spring of '71, they were ranging for mustangs down as far as the Nueces River near Corpus Christi Bay, and filling continuous saddle mount contracts for the army frontier forts as well as the trail drives. With the demand for so many horses, Josh spent most of his time training them for saddle, leaving the rounding up of mustangs to Tom and Pancho with their expert vaqueros who knew the southern brush country so well. But he realized they were clearing the local area of good horses, and had to go further on each gathering drive.

The Helena crowd was known to be grumbling about LaPoint hiring so many 'Meskins' and not enough whites, but nobody there had the gumption to confront anyone in the outfit, for they usually went to town for supplies with pistols and rifles handy, in a group. And the fact of the matter was the vaqueros made a far better horse handling outfit than the white thugs in Helena or Oakville, who didn't want to get up early and ride til late, and who lacked the traditional riding and roping skills of the expert horsemen of Spanish descent. LaPoint had fired a few of the Helena drovers he had hired once, for neglect of their horses, and went to hiring only vaqueros after that.

The new trail west that Charlie Goodnight had blazed was taking steady traffic in beef herds by then, and the LaPoint outfit worked from 'can til can't' supplying horses for Goodnight, Winger, and the army. Winger was still badgering them to head up cattle drives on the new trails further west, across the staked plains, but not wanting to get mixed up in fighting the resident Comanches, they refused the offers. Life around the ranch, with all the rustlers and gun thugs from Helena and Oakville, involved enough gun work, without getting into the Comanche wars, which seemed endless.

Besides rattlesnakes around the southern ranch, and deer for meat, the only other animals they shot and killed were cougars and coyotes. In '71 there was a very large old male cougar that was intent on tearing into the chicken shed. Josh shot him with a Sharps fifty from the front yard of the house, about sixty yards away, in the pale light of dawn, no great feat, except that the shot went in one ear and out the other, which LaPoint attributed to his new brass telescope. Gabe was pleased that the pelt was undamaged, and praised the new telescopes.

The long brass telescope LaPoint had won at a shooting match, over near Helena, in the fall of '70. The match had been arranged by Muldoon, when the renowned black frontiers-man and sharpshooter Britt Jonson came through town on a freighting trip and heard that Gabe McBride was around. Britt was well-known as a scout, hunter, and all around remarkable sharpshooter with the Sharps fifty.

Gabe and Britt had ridden together on the staked plains in successful ventures to obtain captives and return them to their families, over a decade earlier. With McBride's tracking ability and intimate knowledge of the staked plains, the long range shooting skills and language facility of the big ex-slave proved invaluable in dealing with raiders.

Britt Jonson, a coffee colored mulatto of around fifty years, was a big and muscular man with a very sharp and keen eye and a capacity for languages and negotiation which aided in the parleys with Comanches over captives. His eyesight and skill with the old Sharps with adjustable sights was reportedly unmatched by any man in the long shot, where the bullet was arched to achieve great distance. His imposing, fearless, and gregarious presence appealed to the Comanches, and they considered him a great warrior, worthy of respect and camaraderie. He had spent many hours smoking and laughing with the northern bands while on bartering trips, and was well known among them.

Britt was a frontier hero, for he had been instrumental, along with the Chisholms, in returning many captives from the tribes of the staked plains. Together he and Gabe had tracked the raiders with the French sisters in '48 and brought them home before permanent damage had been done to them. In recent years he had been operating his own freighting business, with several wagons, and was on his way up from Indianola with a load of gear to sell up on the plains, his six mules pulling a big wagon heavy-laden with trade goods.

Britt was having dinner at Muldoon's when the bartender

mentioned old Gabe. Having known Gabe in the old days as a great shot with a Sharps rifle, Britt wanted to show him the new models that he had acquired, with long mounted brass telescopes. Muldoon sent a rider across the river for Gabe who found him working at horseshoeing some finished saddle mounts in the blacksmith shop. Hearing that Britt, his big jolly black pal was in town, Gabe grabbed Josh and hustled in to meet with him. Britt got up from his dinner meal and embraced Gabe when he came in the door, picking him off the ground with ease and laughing a deep belly laugh.

"Whar's that copper-red scalp? Ya done turned gray, Captain."

"Hell, they tried ta take it but it stuck on thar, head's too hard."

"Oh lawdy! Captain McBride. Ekaa Wasape Nahuu!"

"Shore glad ta see ya too, ole pard! Tuhubitu papii tasiwoo tenahpu!" replied McBride, his feet above the ground.

"Say what?" said LaPoint. "You guys talkin in tongues?"

"Ah's sho glad ta see ya, Captain, thought ya was rubbed out years ago."

"Put me down, ya big black buffalo bull, glad ta see ya myself."

"Yeah, don't get him agitated," said LaPoint.

"Whar ya been hidin yourself, Captain McBride?" asked the frontiersman as he released Gabe from his grasp and set him in a chair. "Bring a beer for my friends here, Missus, please." The powerful black man sat down and stared at Gabe with a smile. "They tried to lift that copper-wire scalp, huh?"

Gabe took off his hat and bent his head down, showing the scar and scarce gray hair.

"Whoooowee, ah know dat's right! Lookee thar, done put the first cut on dat ole stone-hard noggin of yorn and gave up, did they?"

"They was takin' turns making little slices across the front, and putting hot burning buffalo chips on my left hand here."

"Damn, Captain. Made a claw out of that one. Howdy mister, my name is Britt."

"Howdy Britt."

"How'd you get out o that one, Captain?"

"Waugh. 'Bout tha time they was fixing ta yank my scalp, Mr. Alexander came ridin' in, and hell started poppin'. He put a whole bunch of 'em down, and the Tonkawas got the rest."

"Lucky for them, huh? I reckon you was fixin' ta get mad at em."

"I was, but it was nice to see Mr. Alex."

Britt grinned with big white teeth. "Always. So he set you free before they got the prize?"

"Yep, but I's in bad shape. Then I was at Mr. Alexander's plantation healing, and then in New Orleans blacksmithin' until a few years ago, when I came here. It was this fella's mom who sewed the flap back on my cabeza and got it ta grow back, and healed my hand up too, leastwise where I can use it some. This here is Josh LaPoint, the only son of Mr. Alex, my pard, and the best shot I've seen so far, sides yourself, maybe."

"Maybe.... he says," replied Britt with a wide grin. He extended his huge hand to shake with Josh LaPoint. "Glad to meet you, Mr. Josh LaPoint. You looks like Mr. Alexander Robinoix did when I first knew him."

"He do, don't he?" said Gabe with a little smile. "Favors Alex in a lot of ways."

"Zat so? Gotta be a good thing, ah reckon. Mr. Alexander's word was good as granite, and his aim was always true. I'as proud ta know him, and proud to meet you, Mr. LaPoint. How about yal joinin me for supper? I'll arm wrestle 'Ekaa Wasape Nahuu' for the cost of the food, though I don't eat much," said the huge fellow.

"Oh no," said Gabe, "Last time we did that my arm went out of socket."

"What's that you're calling him, Britt?"

"Ekaa Wasape Nahuu, his Comanche name."

"What does it mean?"

"Aaaaah, means 'Red bear with a sharp knife', I think, something like that."

"Well that fits,"Josh replied. "And what was that Comanche name you had for Britt, Gabe?"

"Tuhubitu papii tasiwoo Tuhubitu ..Black headed buffalo man."

"So they know you both by those names?"

"Right, black buffalo and red bear, we was quite a team among the Numunu, especially the Kotosekas and Quahadis."

"And ya done alright humpin' those Nokoni gals too, didn't ya?"

"Ah know dats right, captain," laughed Britt with his reply.

Josh laughed, happy to see Gabe with an old friend he seemed to treasure. "Dinner's on me, gentlemen. And I'm proud to know you, Mr. Jonson. Gabe told me about you on the ride over. That ornery old cuss doesn't speak highly of too many folks, so I'm impressed. He said without you a lot of captives would not have ever been returned."

"I was able to help a bit," said Britt.

"He's also told me for years I had a good eye for the long shot, but I wasn't quite as good as Britt Jonson yet, so keep practicing. He said you could arch a shot on target with the old Sharps better than any man, and that's how you got those girls back, picking off the raiding party one by one from eight hundred yards."

"Awww, go on now, it's mostly his trackin' and obstinate nature dat got dem French gals back. His scouting hunches are usually right. Is he still stubborn as a bloodhound on a scent?"

"More so."

"Ah knows dat's right. If his sourdough biscuits weren't so good we'd traded him off for jerky, pound for pound. Stubborn as a mule, he was, more stubborn, actually. Which made him a good man with mules, huh?"

"Waugh, look who's talkin', two stubborn, hell-bent-for-leather, bit in the teeth...."

"Aww Captain, go on now. You can come freight with me anytime, drive mules across the plains."

"No thanks, we're doing okay here for now, though LaPoint wants to go ta Taos, get out o this sticker patch for a while and see some shinin' mountain country."

"Taos, old times, Captain. What a gal you had in Taos, lovely Lupita, and such a fine blacksmith shop. Remember we stayed up all night hammering them knives, folding and hammering and folding and hammering?"

"Shore do, shinin' times, and LaPoint and I been don tha same thing," replied Gabe.

"So you got drug all over the plains by this old scout, looking for those French girls?" asked Josh.

"Oh sure. I's ready to quit plenty o times while we was after that raiding party with dem French gals, but he said no, we'd just go on to da next water hole, den de next, den de next til we found em and started picking em off with our Sharps."

"How far away?" asked LaPoint.

"Oh, bout seven hundred yards or so, give or take."

"How many did you get?"

"Why, we got all of them 'ceptin the one that took off with the horses and left the gals behind. I got four, Captain McBride got three."

"You's tha better shot that time, Britt," said Gabe.

"Maybe. But far as trackin' up on da staked plains, dis ole coon heah is de best," stated Britt as he grabbed McBride's beefy arm and squeezed it with his huge hand. "Still a hard ole coot, too, huh?"

"He's an old piece of bull-neck rawhide. What was it like riding with him on the staked plains?"

"We'd ride all day on twelve gulps of water, just scorching up there, suckin' on cactus tunas, right next to the sun on them plains, flat as a table top, that sea of grass and nothin', wishing I was anywhars else. He'd see a little mesquite tree and say tell me, "Hey, buck up, there's got ta be water withing twenty miles, which is far as a mustang goes from water to shit a mesquite bean, so watch the fuggin' birds."

"Wal, that's right," said Gabe.

"Watch the little birds, he says, with a prickly pear tuna in his mouth for saliva, to see how their tiny little beaks sit when they fly by, and what speed and direction, he says, while I can barely hold my head up, crapping dem ole gyp-water farts, running enough sweat to make my saddle slippery, ready for ta turn back to the last waterhole at a moments notice."

Gabe started laughing, his eyes crinkling and shiny at the memories evoked. Britt softly jabbed him with his long black fingers, keeping him going with his belly laugh.

"Naw, I ain't no tracker compared to my ole Captain, Gabe McBride. I never could see nothin' in that wiry mesquite grass, lessen it was a party dragging poles and dropping gear from a few hours previous. Why, I believe he could smell where a squaw peed from the day before."

"Ya could shore see a long distance though, old pard. Yal fellas got that in common, the long view. It's somethin' that fades as ya gets my age, I warn ya. And both of you know how to arch a shot with the old Sharps better than anybody. And thoughts o scalpin' seemed ta drain away when you rode into a Comanche parley, towering over em with your close cropped buffalo hair. One look at you and they figured tha scalp wasn't worth tha fight."

"Ah know dat's right, they wanted your copper-red scalp lots more dan mine, and your knife too. You still carrying that oversized Bowie knife with the big ole elk antler handle, I see."

"Bowie my ass, it's a goldurn McBride, and ya knows it. Bowie weren't no knife maker."

"Naw, he was an artist at forging Spanish land grants, though."

"Yeah, and running slaves."

"Ole Jo use ta dislike him."

"Yeah, he did."

"Who is this Ole Jo?" asked Josh.

"He was slave to that Travis boy, him that lived through de battle. Jo was the one that got away. 'Bout the only time being black ever did ole Jo any good, he used to say."

"Bowie was nothing but a land swindler, a fraud, and a fool. Him and Travis, who had already abandoned his family and a pile of debt to come to Texas and stir up a mess o trouble so he could be a big high-struttin' colonel and salvage his miserable life. Folks tryin' to make 'em hero's now, regular plaster saints. Brave settlers fighting for liberty and justice in the old fortress, what a load of crap. They wasn't settlers, they was the same filibuster and freebooter crowd of glory hogs and land seekers that been coming down ta steal Texas for decades. Houston told 'em to destroy that worthless ruin and keep the cannons out of Santa Anna's hands."

"Why shore, only thing ta do. But Bowie wanted ta stay in San Antone. So they stayed til they got over-run, though I heard lots of them got lanced by Mexican cavalrymen when they tried to run."

"Bowie had been sick for years, but still managing to carouse every night with the boys at the saloon. But when Santa Anna showed, he went to his sickbed and turned things over to that foolish boy Travis, looking for glory."

"He tole me dat too, Captain. Big bad Bowie in his bed waitin for rescue. Didn't have his brother thar ta make up no big stories for de newspaper dat time. I wouldn't ride wif him nor Travis neither one."

"Neither one of them had a lick of sense about fighting neither, or they wouldn't have got trapped and slaughtered in an old church they couldn't possibly defend. Didn't even have rifle loops cut in. If the Mexican army couldn't hold it before, from a bunch of rag tag filibusters, why did they think they could hold out against a cannon siege and a professional army? Silly fools signed their own death warrants sealing themselves up in thar. Only way ta fight an army like that is hit and run, or catch 'em sleeping, like at San Jacinto."

"I wish you hadn't set him off on Bowie, Britt," said Josh with a smile.

Britt burst out laughing, followed by Josh. "Dat gets him every time, doan it, just call dat knife a Bowie knife, eh?" The gregarious coffee colored man slapped his big hand on Gabe's back in a loose fingered way so as not to jar him, then gave him another shake, pulling a chuckle out of him.

"Now I'm sure hit's you, huh Captain? You ole coon, Captain McBride, the scout of the Llano Estacado."

"Whar's the knife I made ya?"

"I lost it in a Comanche scrape, ole Peta Nacona got it and let me keep my horse to ride out of there. He sho prized dat knife. Real good thing I had it to trade, Captain. He wanted my horse. He liked big horses. But he seen that knife you gave ole Para-Coom many a time, and always wanted a McBride. I seen his eyes light up when he spotted it, so I used it to barter my way out of there."

"What in hell were you doing with him?"

"Tryin' ta get dat Parker gal back, back around about 1848 or so it was, right after you was gone out west, guiding to California."

"That'd be spring of '49, right after the French girls."

"Maybe, yeah, das about right. Anyway. I couldn't get her to go with me, though. She wouldn't even look at me, much less talk to me."

"Why hell, ya overgrown brown giant, she's scared of ya, thought ya was some kinda buffalo bull man or such."

"Could'a been some o dat, Captain, but mainly it was that she was part of the tribe by then. She had an old mama squaw that clung to her chattering faster than I could understand, but clearly intent on keeping her. And Nadauh, as they called her, was just as intent on staying, holding onto that squaw and looking away from me. And Peta Nacona was intent on marrying her, and thought that's why I wanted her, for a squaw, since she was coming of age then. He was there courting her, all decked out in bear claw necklace and eagle feathers and white buckskins, with a dozen horses."

"Hell, you's in a bad bargaining position," said LaPoint.

"Ah know dat's right. I ended up trading that knife for my life. Knife for a life, Captain, pretty good, huh?" said the big grinning man to Gabe as he tugged on his sleeve, prompting another laugh. "I could make up a ridin' song for ya."

"So what yer sayin' is ya lost that fine knife we pounded out and ground down during that fine spring of 39 in Taos, huh?"

"Captain, I was lucky to ride out of those twisting red sandstone canyons alive, with my big horse under me, thanks to that knife. Whoa-wee, thought I was a goner then."

"I can imagine. Peta could be a rough customer. So did you lead the rangers back to her?"

"Nah suh, ole Peta made me promise not to if I was to ride out atal. If I'd lost their faith in my word, wouldn't be nothin' else I could do again, far as bargaining for captives."

"Waugh, that's right. Yore word only has power with them if you are true to it. So you gave up on getting her back?"

"Yessir, I took ta scouting and guiding on the Sante Fe trail and hunting meat for Bents Fort then, like we used to. Naw, nobody found 'em for a long time. Until Mr. Charlie Goodnight and Captain Jack Cureton's rangers led Sullivan Ross's men to the camp, about ten years later, along with a bunch of soldiers intent on killing Indians. By that time she had children by Peta, and it was way too late...it was around 1860, as I recollect. They thought they killed Peta then, but that weren't so. He died later, maybe from the big cholera plagues. No fighter killed that man, nor many could. So I don't know what happened to that knife. Maybe his son Kiwih-nai got it. Nadua's boys were there and escaped together on two horses, you know. Escaped getting killed by the soldiers, I reckon. The soldiers got on a killing spree, is what I heard. "

"Yeah, so we heard from Charlie Goodnight, who was thar when ole Ross and tha soldiers raided that camp. He said the soldiers did some indiscriminate killing of women in that raid, which disgusted him, but that his rangers did not."

"About like that crazy Custer on the Washita, just murdering villagers for fame and glory. Abandoned his men too. Oughta be hung for it, or court marshaled and shot. I won't scout for the seventh cavalry anymore, on account of such. Nor for Miles, who fires the damned cannon off every morning and lets all the Indians for miles around know where he is. They hear General Miles for miles, captain. Another good one, huh?"

"That's what I heard also, from Ross's rangers, and you can bank on the word of Charley Goodnight. There's way too much crazy talk about wiping out all the Indians, from the likes of that Baylor fella and his type, then officers who can't tell and don't care which Indians they kill. It's gone plumb disgusting. Makes it impossible to talk peace to the tribes."

"Yes it has, and will get worse, I figure. But that Captain Jack Cureton's bunch was a good bunch, like you and Captain Hays, and Mr. Goodnight's a damned fine scout too. He gone to trail driving now. Have you seen him lately, since he made that cattle trail west in 66, out the Concho and up the Pecos?"

"Oh yeah, we's supplyin' him remudas, and he's badgerin' us to sell him some big grays we have, for his own mounts. Josh been trainin' them since they were born."

"Well, I'll be, tell him hello from ole Britt. And a howdy to ole one armed Bill as well, would ya Captain?"

"We will, next time we speak. And quit calling me captain, I'm a rancher now, Ole Pard."

"Ranger to rancher, you and scout Goodnight, ain't surprising atal. All the old scouts moving up. Rico hombres now, eh? Did you ever think you'd see me owning four freight wagons?"

"Nosir, I never. But I never thought Jack Hays would leave Texas neither. Speakin of old pards, ya ain't seen Mr. Alex lately, have ya?"

"El Aguilar? Why yeah, a while back. I visited with him at Lucien Maxwell's place on the Cimarron, maybe five years ago, in spring, around snow-melt time it was. He was consulting and helping re-build on what Lucien called the Aztec mill, so it would grind up about everything, with a set of different stones, ya see. He'd done spent the winter there, working with Lucien, with all his cleverness about machinery, like you."

"Wal, that's the nearest thing to a real location we heard on him for years."

"When I last seen him he was riding off with two mules packed with elk meat and gold nuggets de size o goose eggs, in rawhide parfleches. Lucien done struck it rich up there, you know, pays in blobs o melted gold he's got. Got a million acre grant on the Cimarron trail, and a gold mine. He ain't just no hunter guide any more. He showed me four hollow logs, each about three feet long, filled with them gold goose-eggs."

"Ya don't say. Good for him. Last I heard he married some Spanish gal with a sheep ranch or such. Whar was Mister Alex heading?"

"Said he's headed up to that Ute Country, with old Colonel Pfeiffer. Yonder up to that hot springs, the great Pagosa, tryin' ta heal his wounds. He had some lead in him, giving him hell. He got shot by Comanches when he was around Mora, heading down to help his old pal Ceran St. Vrain set up a grist mill down there. But he never made it, and like to died on the trail, with some lead close to his heart. So he had what I'd call a heavy load, lead and gold. He wasn't as spry as he used to be."

"Zat so," said Gabe, glancing at Josh. "By himself?"

"Naw suh, had three Apache guides with him to take him out along the ridges, so as to avoid robbers in the canyon to Taos. The bandits was laying in ambush along the Cimarron at that time, waylaying the Sante Fe trail traffic on the cutoff."

"Apaches for guides?"

"They lived on the big spread Lucien has up there, suh. Mr. Alex seemed to trust them. They was to guide and escort him up to the Pagosa country, to that big hot springs, up past Abiquiu and Chama, about sixty miles north of Chama. Up to ole Pfeiffer's place, on dat little creek runs into that Piedra River west of the hot springs, by the Chimney Rock. He was sorta stove up in the shoulder with lead, and was talking about it was the first time he ever had an Apache escort."

"Wal, thanks, that news floats our sticks."

LaPoint nodded. "Thanks for the news, Britt."

Britt was silent a moment, looking at them, then leaned in to Gabe and spoke again. "Say. Any chance of getting another McBride knife, you got any ta trade?"

"Why hell yes, after we eat and drink, got a bunch of new ones we made in winter, at my blacksmith shop, across the river. You'll come rest your mules there for a spell. What ya got ta trade?"

"The latest Spencer repeating firearms and the new Sharps fifties with long brass telescopes."

"Hot damn! Repeaters for the rustlers. Wal alright then, let's eat. What's fer supper tonight?"

"Steak, pork, or chicken, but no buffalo. Sho got some good mashed taters, for good measure, though. Smooth as silk, with butter too."

After a big meal of steak, onions, and potatoes, followed by apple pie, and a few more cool drinks at Muldoon's, the old yarns started spinning about great shots in the old days, and the three of them decided to try out the new Sharps 50's with telescopes which Britt carried, at 600 yards on some over ripe cantaloupes. Gabe took a new Sharps with telescope to do his shooting with, and took some practice shots, as did Josh. But when it came time to match shoot, LaPoint's choice was the gun he was used to, and pulled out the beautiful Whitworth with its four powered brass scope.

"Awww now, lookee heah!" said Britt, walking over to where Josh loaded the long Whitworth with the heavy barrel, smooth on the outside with a rifled twist inside, and the elongated octagonal slugs. "Whar' ya get that thing? I always wanted one of those. But heah now, yal didn't say nothing bout using a Whitworth."

"You didn't ask," said LaPoint, as he rammed the long slug down over a heavy power load. "Your scope on the Sharps is a lot stronger anyway."

"Yeah, but round galena balls don't fly true like those elongated slugs from the Whitworth. That rifle is engineered by the best English engineer to fly true."

"My thoughts exactly. I'm using the gun I'm familiar with, my good old reliable Whitworth."

"Alright, young LaPoint, load that thing and show me who you is!"

A small crowd gathered as the news spread, and they set up on the outskirts of town as the sun set in the west. Britt's big head covered with a wide felt hat could be seen above all as the group milled around the shooting meadow, with targets being set up across a long flat. He was several inches taller than LaPoint, at least six foot four, and thick-muscled like a black stallion, carrying two heavy Sharps in his arm like they weighed little. A lot of men were making cash offers for the new Sharps, but Britt said they were already promised to men in Comanche country up north.

Muldoon took charge of the whole affair, and had his men set up the targets while the shooters readied their guns. Some serious side betting began to occur when the word spread on who was shooting, and the size of the crowd increased steadily as they prepared and took more practice shots with the new Sharps.

The shiny new bass alloy telescopes made sighting in a lot easier, and they each shot from a rest. Britt and Gabe both preferred to rest on a wagon with chocked wheels, while LaPoint laid on the ground with a short forked metal rod that Gabe had made for him. He had been practicing from a low rest lately, and wanted to see if that had improved his shooting the big heavy Whitworth that tended to wear a man's arms out just in the handling, before he ever touched the trigger. Josh always handled the gun with his finger on the trigger guard until it was time to shoot. Gabe was enthralled with the new telescopes, since his eyesight had deteriorated over the years of smoky shops and pounding hot steel.

The long brass telescopes gleamed in the slanting rays of the afternoon sun as they began to shoot. Muldoon had to shush the crowd in his deepest bellow as the men began to aim at their cantaloupes. A hush set in, and then the crack of fire belching out of the long barreled gun.

The big Sharps and the Whitworth made startlingly loud booms that rolled for miles over the prairies, and the shooters were all keen on target. More folks hustled up from the town as the sound drew them to the growing crowd.

Another round of firing ensued. As the smoke wafted out of his line of sight with the binoculars, Muldoon could see no cantaloupes on the picnic table. They all hit three out of three, shattering the pale orange fruit to smithereens, so they moved it back to 900 and fired again, this time with heavier betting all around. The acrid smoke from the big guns was swept away by the light breeze.

"I thought you said your eyesight was failin' you, ole horse-trader," said Britt, impressed with Gabe's shooting. "Dat ain't too bad for an old half-scalped coon. And you done taught Mr. LaPoint pretty good with that old Whitworth, huh?"

"Maybe a bit old, but accurate, huh?" replied Josh.

"I see how you keep dat wood all nice and polished up. That thar gun is LaPoint's baby."

"I like it better than any."

Gabe nodded with a small satisfied smile. "He's got a better long sight, young eyes. But this here brass lookin' glass makes it easier for an ole coon. Lets go again while I'm on target."

"Alright then. This is like the old rendezvous days, huh, Gabe. I wish old Kit and Lucien was here too."

"It's good enough jus' ta see you, Ole Coon."

"Well suh, how bout betting one of these new scopes against a knife of yours?"

"Ya ain't seen tha knife."

"Well hell, it's a McBride, ain't it suh? I seen plenty of McBride's, lets see. Ole Kit's got one, Ceran's got one, Alex's Robinoix's got one, Dick Wooton's got one, Mr. LaPoint's got one, Colonel Pfeiffer's got one, everybody but me. Even several Comanche chiefs have them. Ain't none ta match a McBride, why Jim Bowie died longing for a McBride ta stab General Santa-Anna with, hiding in a storeroom at dat Alamo."

"Yeah, that's right, and don't forget it again."

"So how's about putting one up, if I promises never ta allow it to be referred to as a Bowie, or let a Comanche get it, lessen I have ta?"

"Bowie. Go ahead and out-shoot him, Josh," said Gabe as he spat a stream of tobacco juice.

"Captain, how 'bout dat knife, I know you want's one dese heah scopes, don't cha?"

"I put up my best for you, if yal shut up about that damned Jim Bowie, Britt, " said Gabe while loading.

"Well alright, then. Now that's just a side bet between me and you. It doan matter if Mr. LaPoint heah wins the match, which ah think he might with that Whitworth."

"Why hell yah he might, for he's been out-shooting me for years, since his pap gave him that Whitworth....but I'm fixin ta out-shoot your big ole black self, Buffalo man."

"Ah know dat's right. It's McBride and Britt Jonson agin, like's de ole rendezvous days. Now da pressure's on, go ahead and shoot, suh."

"You gentlemen going to leave me out of the betting? I'd like a chance at one of these scopes too, looks like I could fit it on to my Whitworth. Gotta keep up with technological advances."

"Alright suh," said Britt with another grin. His good-natured manner put everyone at ease. "What you want ta barter, dat nice gray Stallion? Might give ya two for him." A broad grin opened as he saw Josh smile and shake his head.

"No way."

"Just checkin'."

LaPoint offered a bet with Britt for silver coin against a new telescope. Britt glanced at Gabe, who gave a slight scowl and negative shake of the head.

"Trade for a whole new rig, rifle and all, plus a new telescope for your Whitworth. Then we'll have three long distance guns with scopes, Josh," said Gabe. "Offer him what you treasure, the mare."

"Whooa-wee, now we talkin' barter. What kinda prize sides silver yal got to offer for a whole new Sharps and telescope rig, an extra telescope, with saddle scabbard in the deal?"

"Josh has got a mare just big enough for ya that he's just finishing off. He trains the best saddle mounts in the country, ole coon, and he's got a big one that's a fit for you. I know you like a big mare with a proud head. She's well over 16 hands."

"I sho do. Well alright then, if Captain McBride says it's a fair trade, I takes his word for it. How's dat sit with you, Mr. LaPoint?"

"Sits just fine, Mr. Jonson. I'd love some new telescoped rifles, and the horse is ready and big enough to carry you. And you can call me Josh."

"Alright den, Josh LaPoint. Take your shot, suh."

"You older gentlemen go first, Britt," said Josh as he laid down with the beautiful long wooden stock cradled and laid on the rest.

"Well somebody shoot, boys," said Muldoon, who was perched in the chocked wheel of the wagon with LaPoint's field glasses on the cantaloupes. "Everybody shut yer yaps, now; they'll be aiming and firing soon, and plug your ears, boys."

Another round of cracking booms erupted from the big guns and echoed off the rolling prairie. Each shot in turn and loaded with the long ramrods while the other shot.

The crowd was quiet until Muldoon, standing in the wagon with LaPoint's binoculars, announced the results of each shot, then a short cheer commenced. Never had three such expert marksmen been gathered at Helena, demonstrating their skills on the latest weapons.

More people were riding out to the shooting match as word spread about the famous marksman Britt taking on some locals. A wagon full of supplies driven by Polish farmers stopped by, and a cart buggy with several ladies in it, one of them a beautiful petite blond lady that caught Josh's eye the moment she stepped from the wagon.

"Oh, my goodness. Who is that little lady there?" Josh asked Muldoon.

"That's Miss Hartman, the school teacher over at Panna Maria. They just come from town, heading back with supplies. They have a bunch of books for the school in the wagon, and other stuff. She's a fine little lass, smart as a whip, and perky too."

"Whew. She's got an angel face, and a lovely form, doesn't she?"

"That she does, but don't get distracted from shooting straight, I've got money riding on you, lad. Keep concentrating on that long shooting iron in your hand."

Miss Hartman and a few of the folks from Panna Maria edged up into the crowd to watch the shooting. She turned her head topped with golden curls, and he caught her eye and held it for a moment, then went to preparing for the shoot.

The crowd was murmuring louder and closing in on the shooters, with everyone wanting to get a close look at the big rifles. Josh noticed the lovely Miss Hartman up front by then, watching him, but he tried to fall into his groove of rifle concentration, his ritualized habit from years of practice. They went again for the long shot as Muldoon ended the betting and shushed the crowd. At a thousand yards Gabe hit once, Britt hit twice, while Josh hit three times from his prone position, and won the match and a reputation as the shooter who out-shot Britt Jonson. After congratulating him, Britt told LaPoint that he should match up against a new young shooter named Billy Dixon who was driving wagons for him, if he got the chance.

After the friendly shooting match, Josh invited Britt to the rancho to rest himself and his mules for a few days, which offer Britt was glad to accept. When they got there Josh offered him a very good deal on the big mare and a mule, trading for another scope for his old Sharps, one for Gabe, and the rest on credit for future considerations, which deal Britt accepted with great pleasure. Soon they were fastening the scopes and sighting them in on the little rise behind the barn where they had a long shooting range set up. There they sighted in and grew accustomed to the new scopes and guns.

Rosita performed beautifully as the gracious hostess and made special dishes that pleased everyone, and long nights were spent around the campfire out front of the house, listening to stories of the old days on the staked plains. Every night Josh recorded the gist of what he had heard in his journal, which held all the stories of the frontier that Gabe had told him since their journey began, as well as their experiences together.

They had a pleasant three day visit while Britt helped them track down a cougar that had been stealing calves from local drovers who were gathering herds for drives to the north. Britt had an uncanny ability to smell a cougar, and his instincts even exceeded Gabe's in hunting this elusive animal. LaPoint felt proud to hunt with the two great hunters of the frontier days around Bent's fort and the Sante Fe trail, and learned all he could about cougar tracking.

However, after hours of stalking in the dark, it was the stealthy LaPoint who sighted and killed the cat with a head shot on their return to the homestead, using the open-sights Spencer from about a hundred yards. Soon the neighboring ranches hired Josh to hunt and kill the cougars killing their stock. The cougars they saw out on the range, they left alone. But the ones who raided stock became rugs when Josh was called in.

When Britt left, pulling the gray mare behind his wagon, Gabe was filled with sadness and nostalgia for the old days, and assuaged those feelings by pulling out all their weapons and cleaning them, as well as adjusting the scopes solidly onto the old rifles. Josh was sad to see the fine horse leave, for he had spent lots of time with her and her brother, but he really liked Britt and felt the horse was a fine match for him. He knew Britt intended to breed her up at his place on the high plains, and produce big foals from her for his little ranch.

Once in '70 when heavy rains upcountry sent the San Antonio River up over its banks, Rosita asked Josh to take her and Rosa in the wagon to Panna Maria to church, for Pancho was out mustanging, and she was afraid to take the wagon over the brown swell of the river. Josh figured he could drop them at church, then drive to Helena for supplies, then pick them up after the service and lunch, a couple of hours later. He took Scorpio along, tied to the wagon, then used him with a lariat to help tow the wagon across, and they made it across the river and got the females in their Sunday best to church on time. Then he went to Helena and got supplies and lunch at Muldoon's, though the Irishman was off in Panna Maria for church as well. When Josh returned to Panna Maria with a wagon-load of supplies, he heard shooting from a shotgun and pistols. He stopped the wagon and listened, and upon hearing more shots he pulled off the road and tied the mules in the shade of a clump of live oaks, then rode Scorpio the remaining half mile to town.

As he spotted the church he saw the smoke of a shotgun blast emerge from the belfry, and saw three riders returning fire with pistols. They were cantering their horses around between buildings while yelling and firing potshots at what looked to be a priest in vestments in the belfry with a shotgun.

Stopping his horse, LaPoint tightened the girth strap and checked his weapons, then remounted and sprinted the stallion towards the altercation. The outlaws were too busy putting pockmarks in the whitewashed stucco of the bell tower to notice him coming, and he bore directly down on a Helena tough's horse. Scorpio lunged at the man's horse with his muscled chest and knocked it over sideways just as the fellow noticed Josh had arrived. The pistol was knocked from the man's hand as he fell and got rolled on by the horse. Without pausing Scorpio kept charging forward, and Josh pulled his big Remington pistol and began firing. He fired two shots and winged both of the men, one in his right shoulder, the other in his gun arm. They both hightailed it out of town as Josh pulled Scorpio up hard at the church, skidding into a turn to check on the other outlaw, who was just starting to crawl around looking for his gun. The church door opened and Josh saw the beautiful blond lady with her arms extended to keep the children from stepping outside. Muldoon rushed out past her and went for his carbine in the saddle of his horse tied in the shade.

Josh whirled away towards the outlaw on the ground and rammed Scorpio into him at full speed as he arose with the pistol. The man was shoved back into the air and then into the dirt, the pistol flying off. The man rolled over and Josh took his riata and bounced a loop onto his boot, snagging him and dragging him off with a trail of dust. He slowly drug the twisting and hollering man back down the road, stopping where the wagon was parked. Drawing his gun again, he pointed it at the man and told him to get out of his sight within one minute if he wanted to live. The dusty outlaw got up and ran off towards Helena, limping but still hurrying. Josh watched him go, then tied Scorpio to the wagon and went to pick up Rosita and Rosa.

When he got to the church-yard he saw the priest with shotgun in hand at the door of the church, his vestments covered with dust and chips of plaster from where the gun thugs from Helena had been peppering the belfry. Muldoon was standing with his rifle on a low masonry wall by the side of the church, scanning for further trouble. The priest made a sign of the cross over Josh and thanked him profusely, as did the others emerging from the church, most in a language he could not understand. The beautiful blond lady with the school children in tow was heading for the tables spread with food under the oak tree in front. He looked into her eyes and felt the same strange soothing sensation he used to get from his mother. She mouthed the words, 'thank you' at him with her full pink lips and continued on with the dozen or so children towards the schoolhouse.

Rosa and Rosita emerged from the church and introduced Josh to the priest, who invited him to stay for a visit, but Josh said he was in a hurry, with business waiting for him, and soon rode off with the girls in the wagon.

The sight of the beautiful blond lady with her bunch of trusting children stayed in his mind for a while. It was the same lady he had seen at the shooting match, the one whose face lingered in his memory. He asked Rosa about her and got a raft of information about her being a wonderful teacher, so kind and good with the children, and a good catch for any man. Rosita sensed some deep need in Josh that she felt the intelligent and kind teacher could fill. She told him he was a fool not to be courting her. Josh nodded and pushed the mules back home without comment. He thought of the killing he had done, and he thought a decent woman would reject him for it. Nor did he want to return home and find his woman dead because he had not stayed home to protect her.

Soon after the shooting match with Brit, the new model Spencer repeaters came in handy in driving off a crowd of rustlers from Oakville who tried to take a herd of about forty horses, in the summer of 1870. The LaPoint outfit was on its way back north from the Nueces valley with a herd of select mustang mares and colts, and had camped for the night in a small creek valley on the rolling prairies.

The rustlers came down from a small mesquite covered rise like wolves in the darkness, their howling and screaming soon turning to flapping saddle blankets, popping whips, and the firing of desultory carbine shots to promote a general stampede as they swept down from the surrounding rise on the herd in a watered valley. The horses panicked and bolted like bats out of hell back towards the range they were gathered from, as gunfire shattered the still night. The picket line was ripped out of the ground as the riding horses panicked as well.

The LaPoint outfit numbered eight men at the time, with LaPoint and Tom Jackson on the midnight night-rider shift, watching the stars wheel around as they circled the herd until the attack, then racing unsuccessfully to turn the herd. Both were shot at and narrowly missed by the rustlers, and had to pull off and seek the shelter of mesquite brush to avoid being hit. They pulled out the new Spencers and began to lay down heavy fire, which was returned in full. The men in camp ended up crawling on the ground avoiding bullets whizzing in from all directions, their bellies and faces covered with dust that was streaked by the sweat running from their heads. It wasn't until LaPoint and Jackson continued returning concentrated and deadly fire from the new repeaters at the flashes in the dark that the gang pulled off and followed the horses.

The riding remuda was also gone, heading off in a different direction, since the pins holding the rope were in ground soft enough to release when all twelve horses tugged on it in panic. After a brief conference with Gabe, LaPoint and Jackson took extra weapons and started for the remuda in the darkness, following the drag marks of the metal pins. It took them until dawn to spot the horses, still tied together on the picket rope, and until midday to get them back to the rest of the outfit. They never got the herd back, and two of the vaqueros were winged by rifle slugs and had to spend time recuperating at the bunk house. That was the only time the LaPoint outfit lost a herd of horses in South Texas. It galled LaPoint, and put a burr under his saddle regarding rustlers. Both he and Tom Jackson filled their spare time with target shooting, to better protect the stock.

When McBride, Jackson, and LaPoint got stale from overwork they could always make a trip to Muldoon's for some fine meals, good whiskey and brandy, and pretty gals playing the piano or the mattress springs. Jackson soon got a steady gal at the saloon, the lovely dark eyed Ruby, and even Gabe took a gal upstairs on occasion, especially after he had gotten a new order of ginseng root delivered. Meanwhile Josh had Delores, who was in love with him by that time, and arranged each Friday night for her extended lovemaking bouts with him. It seemed that after Josh had started to carry the image of the lovely Miss Hartman in his mind's eye, Delores went out of her way to please him in every way when they had their brief visits.

During the winters the partners got together in the blacksmith shop while the blue northers howled outside, and pounded glowing red steel, folding hard and soft layers over and over into the night, plunging them into a sheepskin soaked in a special brine brew, then grinding the edges the next days while the cold north wind decreased and the sun came back out. The knives were sold to locals whom Gabe took a shine too, or through Muldoon to various worthies.

Over the passing years, the blacksmith shop became a much used spot in the windy winter weather, with hot forge going and a pot of coffee simmering on the stove in front. With New Orleans Sazarak brandy and Gabe's special soothing kinnickinnick to smoke, good times were had by all in that warm and cozy workshop. The local vaqueros began to drop by to get their horses shod in a friendly environment, and soon they had Spanish guitars and guitarons thumping with German accordions to pass the long northers as the wind howled in the eaves. When the crowds got larger they moved to dance in the dogtrot area between the cottages. But Rosita saw Josh sitting alone during the fandangos, and thought of the schoolteacher, lonely also across the river in her little cottage.

It was the wet and grassy spring of 1871 when they got word from Muldoon that the big new anvil, pedal operated squirrel-cage bellows, additional water pumps, and other new blacksmithing tools had finally arrived. On a cool morning Josh and Gabe went to Helena to pick it up, with Josh armed and mounted on Scorpio and Gabe driving the wagon with the mules for the heavy blacksmith equipment.

They met Muldoon at his place for breakfast at 9AM Sunday morning on March 15th, as his note indicated. He informed them that the heavy load including the anvil was on a teamsters wagon at his livery, and that they wanted to load it into Gabe's wagon directly, instead of offloading it onto the ground and then back up into the wagon. The anvil was a big one, requiring four men to lift.

"Wal why didn't ya say so earlier?" said Gabe, "I'da left the wagon there."

"Because the teamster is just waking up anyway, and won't release it til he gets paid. He's upstairs."

"Wal listen, we gotta go over ta Butler's and get some sacks of corn and cement and such, then put the anvil on near the back, where it's easier to unload."

"Alright. I'll send him down to the livery after I stuff a breakfast taco and coffee in him."

"Okay, we're off for supplies," said Gabe. "Tom, you go with me and help lift."

"Alright, Gabe, that's what I'm here for," said Jackson.

"Oh wait, I forgot to mention. The priest at Panna Maria has been hearing about Josh here shooting all those rattlesnakes at your place and wants him to come over there and shoot the swarm they got."

"Well, that doesn't sound too smart, in a town like that, might fill the walls with holes, must be a better way," said Josh.

"I've been through enough snake killing at the ranch, way too many of them varmints," said Jackson. "I want no part of it. I'll stay home and guard the herd."

"Most I've killed have been with a revolver, outside," said Josh. "Shooting inside is no good."

"Waugh. Blow holes in all the walls. Naw. Ya do like these chapparal birds, the piasanos, distract 'em in front and pin 'em from the back with forked sticks, chop their heads off with sharpened hoes and machetes, or snag 'em with wire loops on sticks. Best time is right now when they're still sluggish from cold but coming out to sun on warm days. Could take shotguns and six shooters too, if we find them outside away from buildings."

"Like I said, I'll stay home and do what I'm good at, guarding the stock," repeated Jackson. "Those things give me the creeps, boss."

"That's fine," said Josh.

"We owe Muldoon some favors, let's clear 'em," said Gabe.

"Alright, we'll take Jesse too. And Pancho is deadly with a riata, vaquero style. I've got a bullwhip as well. We could clean out a bunch of them. Especially if we got some of the livelier farmers to help distract them with long forked sticks. I heard you could douse them with kerosine if they went back in a hole, and it will make them stupid for a while."

"Well, shall I tell 'em you will come over Sunday morning next?" asked Muldoon. "There's a grand Polish dinner in it for you, hopefully not like the first grand dinner the first priest threw for new arrivals, when a four foot diamondback fell from the thatched roof into the stew-pot. And that pretty little schoolteacher lass was asking me about you the other day, as well."

"Damn," said Josh. "Sounds like something we should attend to, being as we have a lot of practice at it. We'll do what we can, next Sunday."

Gabe glanced at Muldoon and nodded.

"Alright lads," said the saloon owner. "I'll set it up."

Chapter Nine: Vipers of Panna Maria

"Wal, I reckon we're goin' from roundin' up mustangs ta roundin' up rattlesnakes, boys," said Gabe as he put away his breakfast utensils.

"Not sure how I agreed to this, but let's get it done without getting bit," said Josh.

"I'm ready; let's kill some more rattlers," said Jesse.

"Don't get too eager," said Josh.

"That's right," said Pancho. "Keep your distance."

"If anybody gets bit we got to slash it and suck the poison out and spit it away pronto," said Gabe. That stilled Jesse's excitement somewhat, and the wagon rumbled along without much talking after that.

With the big freight wagon loaded with various items for snake eradication, at daylight they were at the river crossing near Helena the next morning after breakfast. The eagles followed them to the crossing and circled there as they forded and headed for Panna Maria, back upstream. In the wagon they carried an oak barrel, several sharpened hoes, several long sticks with wire loops to capture snakes, and some rakes and cans of kerosene, as well as lots of burlap tow sacks. Gabe had exercised his ingenuity in constructing wire loops on sticks that could be tightened around snakes, as well as specially made wire implements to flush them from holes, and long handled knife choppers and small hoes with razor sharp edges. He also had fixed two small tins of kerosene to squirt through a tiny hole in the lid, and a secure flip-top lid for a small gathering tub. As well, they carried a can for coals with a long snout to deliver smoke into holes. They had big buckets of sand and bags of lime and cement, with wire mesh to reinforce the plaster they intended.

LaPoint carried his sidearms, knife, and a bullwhip he was accurate with. Jesse was still keen for the hunt, messing around with one tool and then another as they made the river ford, then rumbled down to Panna Maria. Pancho rode alongside with a determined look, his riata already knotted on the end.

The priest was out in front of the small church when they arrived, together with about a dozen men who were ready to help with hoes and shovels. Pancho went up to the priest and knelt for a blessing, then joined the farmers in conversation. The stout men in cover-alls and tall boots were speaking in Polish, drinking coffee, and sucking on their pipes. The portly Polish priest had his robes on, white lace over a black cassock, and went into a long blessing in Latin. The men got on their knees in the grass for the group blessing. Josh impulsively made a quick sign of the cross and bowed his head, a leftover response from early childhood.

"Hope a snake don't crawl into any those tall boots while they're a-subjugating themselves," whispered Gabe as he shifted his tall riding boot in the dust.

LaPoint smiled and did not reply, hoping to get the prayer done without an argument with Gabe and the priest. The sonorous Latin phrases burbled on and on, lulling the mind into their soft rhythms. Josh gave sidelong glances at the lovely teacher, then at McBride, who shuffled his feet alongside him. Gabe had the traditional Appalachian hunter's disdain for Popish traditions, and he pulled out a chaw and cut a piece off to stick in his mouth. The farmers bowed their heads and murmured replies to the ending as the priest made the sign of the cross over them with his chubby hands.

"What'd he say, you know that Latin palaver, eh?" asked Gabe.

"The Lord is with you."

"Why heck, if his absentee land-lord is here why don't we go home and let him take care of it."

"Hush, don't start a row with him. Snake hunting is bad enough."

"Yore idea, as I recall."

"Please shut up."

The priest finally finished his blessing and motioned to everyone to get up. The farmers, speaking in Silesian Polish, grabbed their hoes and shovels and gathered around, collecting the other implements. Afterward Josh and Gabe outlined their plan and gave everyone a job with instructions on how to do it.

Then the portly priest came over to bless the implements and the snake hunters with their tow sacks.

"Oh glory," muttered Gabe, "not again, how long is this gonna take? Snakes will all be out hunting."

"Too long, I imagine," replied LaPoint, softly.

"I expect not much longer. The last priest got run out of town with a lynching party on his heels, is what Muldoon told me, the one that brought them to this rattlesnake den."

"Well, there's a good oak tree right there."

"Don't tempt me; Rosita might quit feedin' me if I strung him up. She thinks he hung tha moon, on account of schooling her kids."

"Well, she's got a point there. But he'd better not drone on too long, these guys look sleepy enough anyway." The priest cleared his throat and began to recite another prayer in Latin, causing everyone but LaPoint and Gabe to bow their heads.

Josh was unable to keep from glancing at the beautiful blond schoolteacher in a thin violet-colored cotton dress by the food tables. They had briefly met several times, and each time they had lingered in eye contact with each feeling the spontaneous attraction. Continually glancing at her out of the corner of his eye, Josh stood impatiently, sliding his boots in the sparse grass, as the priest murmured on in Latin. Finally he was done, and the men shifted to gather their tools. After the blessing, LaPoint made a quick and abbreviated sign of the cross and started to leave as he saw the priest headed for him. As he went quickly by the food table to start the rattlesnake roundup, he felt a soft small hand clutch his strong wrist, and turned to see the big blue eyes and sweet face of the lovely blond school teacher.

"I need you. At the schoolhouse, when you're done with the homes and outhouses. Our firewood and cloakroom is buzzing."

"Buzzing. Alright," said Josh, feeling her hand on his wrist, staring into her big beautiful blue eyes. He took her small soft hand in his big callused palm and held it gently. He was smitten when he locked eyes with her, unavoidably mesmerized. He had an urge to kiss her hand like he used to kiss the hands of lovely women in New Orleans back when he was a gentleman trader, but he stifled the urge.

"With rattlers, I mean. Really, the walls are buzzing."

"I'll be there," said Josh. He stood there wordless and did not want to let go of her hand as her fingers clasped into his, fitting so naturally. The pause caused the priest to catch up with him and take him by the other sleeve, pulling him aside.

"Mr. LaPoint, I wanted to thank you again for your help in

running those thugs out of town. We need a man like you around here, for we have lots of trouble with the gunmen from Helena. The ones you ran off before were not the first or the last, I fear."

"The sheriff at Helena should..."

"But he doesn't show, and you did. I saw you make the sign of the cross, so I know you are a Catholic. Could you not come on Sundays and protect us from those gun thugs with their lust for our girls? We are nothing but peaceful farmers here. We came to get away from the Prussian wars and live in peace, not fight pistol thugs. Sunday Mass is at eight, ten, and high mass at twelve o'clock."

"I'm not a Catholic, nor looking for gunfights. That's the county sheriff in Helena's job. I gave your religion up when I learned to think for myself, a long time ago."

"Fallen away from the flock doesn't mean you are lost from the love of Jesus."

"I've never seen any sign of the love of Jesus in the world I've been in. It's a nice, pretty myth, but I can't put any stock in it."

"Myth? Surely you're not an atheist, Mr. LaPoint, with a name like Joshua, the leader of the Israelites?"

"No. I'm just LaPoint to you. I leave survivors when I can, unlike the Israelite Joshua, who left none, according to the bible I read. I'm more of a deist than atheist anyway, like Thomas Jefferson. No use arguing religion."

"But God made all of us, deists and Catholics."

"Well. This world was obviously set in motion by some great creative intelligence, but I cannot see any sign of benevolent Divine active involvement since then, despite what priests would have us believe. He didn't stop the war."

"Maybe you haven't been looking in the right place."

"Did you notice a five year war with Christians slaughtering each other over high ideals and fine speeches? Each side using high-flown biblical phrases to hide the evil they were doing. Been going on all through Christian history, during the long reign of your 'Prince of Peace'. I suppose it was Joshua of the Israelites who started it off, rampaging through Canaan leaving no survivors, and justifying it with absurd theology. It's always been more Vene, Vedi, Vichi, than Dominus Vobiscum, the way I see it."

"But surely you see how you were sent to..."

"How anyone can cling to the dream that a merciful and all-powerful and all-knowing God is acting at the behests of priests or preachers after the war we just went through, with Christian soldiers slaughtering each other in sanctimonious rage, is beyond my understanding."

"That war was a punishment for slavery, I'm afraid. And Lincoln emancipated them."

"Emancipated to what, no job and no place to live? The war was caused by a plan of the Republican party to impose a bigger tariff, a national bank, and a transcontinental railroad, which they couldn't get through congress with southern senators opposing it. They used the fervor of Christian zealots in the abolitionist movement to mask their agenda, which was shove all the southerners out of congress to pass their bills. Lincoln had no sympathy for the poor suffering black slaves, only a desire to push the old Whig agenda and amass power."

"But the emancipation..,"

"The Emancipation Proclamation was a war measure meant to stir slave revolt, not a statement of black equality. The Republicans thought they could eject the South from congress, get their bills passed, then whip the South in three months and let them back in as a subjugated people. It just took longer than they thought, but it made a lot of money for certain folks, and gave control of the money supply to the big bankers. Lincoln planned to deport them all to Africa. The slaves are worse off now than they were. I was born and lived with slaves, and I know."

"Surely it's good that slavery has ended?"

"Not all of a sudden with a ruined economy! All the other countries with slavery had gradual emancipation without a war like this country just endured, for Mr. Lincoln never used his lawyer's gift of gab to move things in that direction, did he? A half million men killed and enough money spent and borrowed to buy every slave several times over."

"Well at least they carried through and ended slavery."

"Yeah, and left things in a shambles. With Lincoln's plan to deport all the blacks to Liberia, it damned sure wasn't a moral crusade to free the slaves and make them equal. Everything that has happened has changed the country forever, and from now on the government will get more and more centralized and corrupt. Big corporations like the railroads will unite with corrupt politicians to feed at the public till."

"But slavery has ended, the blacks are free."

"Free to starve in a shattered economy or vote republican for ten dollars each, meanwhile, the constitution and consent of the governed are dead letter notions. Anyway, slavery is justified in your Bible, along with a lot of other crimes, like what Sherman and your Joshua did, grind the cities unto dust, make war on innocents, and God never lifted a finger over it down through history. Hellfire, He promoted it. Slavery could have been ended without killing and maiming a million people to do it!"

"I understand you have thought deeply and hard on this horrible tragedy."

"That could have been averted."

"But we of Panna Maria did not support the republicans, the secession, slavery, or the war, and we suffered for it. We actually came here to get away from the Prussian militarists,and civil wars. Our men avoided the war as much as we could, at some cost...."

"Prussian militarists? What about the huge federal army right now? Bismark and Lincoln did the same thing, created a corrupt central government that overrules the rights of the states, and turns consent of the government into rule by bayonet. You ran from one frying pan to another. The German revolutionaries that came here pushed Lincoln into power."

"Well, we could argue politics for hours, but surely you still acknowledge the sanctity of mother church?"

"Sanctity? Well, I hear the bells ringing every morning, and I think you help with schooling the children and binding the community, but I don't acknowledge sanctity. I recognize your dedication. But I also recognize what your church did during the inquisition, the height of evil. And would do again, if it had the power it once had."

"The bells you hear ring every morning, they ring over good pious people. You hear bells every morning, as we hear your guns while you practice shooting, nearly every night, showing some dedication also. Surely you see the good that the church has done Pancho's family."

"Listen, I'm all for the schooling of children, but you will never convince me of your dogma, the virgin birth nor original sin nor a merciful God helping us out at the ritualized behests of priests...... but that doesn't mean I won't help these people."

"But you were sent to help us right now."

"Nobody sent me. I'm doing a friend a favor, which he deserves. I acknowledge that you have a school, which is a good thing. Right now the problem at hand is the rattlesnakes in the schoolhouse and homes of your believers, and I don't see Saint Michael or St. Patrick around to drive them off. So how about let's quit wasting time, and let us do the job. Nobody deserves to live with rattlers."

"Our God sent you to help us. You would not have appeared as you did when the shooting finally started to drive those gunmen away"

"Believe what you want, but it's time for the Panna Maria rattlesnake roundup."

With that the priest relented for the moment, made another quick sign of the cross blessing over LaPoint and his bunch of snake hunters, then went to praying on his knees under a huge live oak tree in front of the church while the booted farmers set out with smoking cans, kerosene squirters, and implements for capture and chopping. Pancho led the way with his riata, and kept telling Jesse to keep back from the snakes. Jesse was eager, pacing in place with his long pole with a wire loop on the end that he could tighten on the first snake head. Gabe walked alongside LaPoint, spit some tobacco juice, and spoke quietly.

"I thought ya didn't want no argument with ta priest."

"Hell, I couldn't get shed of him without one. He wanted me to sign up as church guard."

"Oh yeah, I figured that was comin', after ya run them Helena thugs out of town. Did ya tell 'im ya already shed that Roman Catholic snake skin, in yore youth?"

"Well, something like that. And I told him how you old Taos trappers like to bow down and subjugate yourselves to Popish ways."

"I bow to no man nor made up big spirit."

"Let's get these snakes done without anybody getting bit."

"Yeah, let's get 'er done, so ya can visit with the schoolmarm."

"Please shut up. Come on now. It's snake killing time."

They began at one end of town, sweeping through every

barn, outbuilding, lumber pile, rock pile, and hole in the ground, driving the snakes into the open where they could be shot, chopped, or captured. Many were beaten into disorientation by Pancho with his riata, then captured by Jesse with the wire loop on a long mesquite branch. A few times, when they got a single big one in a yard, Josh would use his bullwhip with deadly accuracy on the snake's head, impressing the farmers gathered to rush in with hoes.

Josh did some shooting when some snakes proved too dangerous and aggressively striking to handle, and easily blew their heads off with his .44 Remington New Model Army revolver, converted to metal cartridges. Usually they were able to fling or herd the snakes onto the porch or yard before he blasted them, but several time he left big holes in the floorboards. The farmers from Panna Maria used shotguns for the same affect, filling the air with the sounds of blasts and resulting blue smoke. Someone would yell snake, and one would come out a door or window, only to be dispatched by waiting hunters.

The rest of the community gathered at the churchyard, where the priest tried to lead them in prayer. From the upper floor of the barn with the tall pitched roof, Josh noticed the lovely blond schoolteacher walking towards the schoolhouse, with the sunlight silhouetting her trim figure through the thin but long and high-buttoned cotton dress. But soon excited yells and the buzz of rattlers took his mind back to the job at hand.

The barns and shed were finally cleared of rattlers big and small, then they made a sweep through and around every house, scouring rattlesnakes out of their holes, then leaving men to patch the holes in the exteriors where the rattlers were entering. The vipers which they could capture, they put into the burlap bags and emptied them into the barrel, which was soon a writhing tangle of buzzing rattlers.

"Hey," said one farmer, "we should get old Lilith here to read this coiling mass of snakes like entrails." He was quickly shushed by the other farmers.

"Well, they say she can read the future that way. I wonder if our future doesn't hold any more snakebites." The other farmers pulled him away and went to the next house, following LaPoint, who had circled it and spotted the holes by then, and couldn't help but notice the schoolteacher enter a small cabin past the schoolhouse. But there was another row of houses to clean up, and he kept pushing the hunters.

With one man squirting kerosene while several others used the implements to either catch or chop the snakes, steady progress was made in the eradication. Pancho stood by with this knotted riata and LaPoint stood by with his drawn Remington .44 with the long barrel, ready to shoot if necessary. They went from building to building and cleared out the vipers.

The Polish farmers were elated at the progress and amazed at the revolver shooting by LaPoint and McBride, and they spoke excitedly in their native language about his skill with the handgun. They sent runners back to the women gathered with the priest by the church, relaying the information to murmurings among the crowd in dresses, preparing meals and praying with the priest. LaPoint did not speak except to give directions and keep telling Jesse to get back some. He was concentrating on directing quite a few folks and endeavoring to keep anyone from getting bit.

At one point he had emptied his big long barreled Remington .44 when he saw a snake slip out of a hole in the wall behind a heavyset farmer. Quickly holstering the .44 into the left scabbard, LaPoint immediately drew his fast action stub nosed Remington Navy .36 from the right holster and blasted the big knotted head from the snake with two direct hits, so close together they seemed like one shot. All the farmers stared at him in awe, having never seen such fast and accurate shooting with a pistol. When he reloaded they were amazed at the metallic cartridges and ease of reloading, having never seen brass casings for pistols before.

"They be awantin' ya for a church guard, 'pears ta me," said Gabe. "Knight on a white charger. Wal, pearly gray, that is."

"No outside fights, we have enough of our own with rustlers," said LaPoint. "Just don't get so close when you're stirring them out, if a snake bites you, it might die in the hole and stink up the place."

"Naw, not this ole coon. I got a sharp blade. Let's eat; snake hunting makes me hungry. And thar's that pretty lil gal at the tables. She can help ya read all them books ya been agettin'."

"Yeah, there she is, boss," said Jesse. "Dang she's pretty, que bonita, que linda, no? She's very nice, too."

"Settle down. Stay focused. Let's get this last house before lunch." Josh glanced at the school teacher as they approached the square and stumbled on a log on the ground.

"Naw, he ain't interested in her, not by a long shot," said Gabe as Jesse laughed.

"Come on now, let's get this house cleared by lunch; somebody get a wheelbarrow of mortar mixing," said Josh.

By the time the noon bell rang at the church, they had at least four dozen captured rattlers, and nearly a dozen dead ones with heads blasted off by LaPoint's accurate shooting.

The lunch was served on long tables set up in the churchyard, and served by the ladies of Panna Maria. Potato salad, cold slaw, pork, bacon, roast beef in garlic onion gravy, green beans, corn, okra and tomatoes, and raw onions on the side, along with dark round loaves of bread, pies with criss-crossed crusts, and German chocolate cakes filled the tables.

While they were waiting for the priest to finish the blessing so they could eat the delicious smelling food, Josh could not help but notice the beautiful blond schoolteacher he was told came from Fredricksburg. Rosita had been talking about her for months, how she needed a good man around here to convince her to stay, because she was such a good teacher, and the children loved her. While noticing how lovely the teacher was on several occasions, Josh had decided to stay with his simple relationship with Delores at Muldoon's, lively sex when needed and no entanglements. He figured a schoolmarm from a religious town would probably marry a stolid Polish or German farmer and want nothing to do with a man like him, who had killed before, and would again to keep what belonged to him.

However, he had not figured on seeing such an enchantingly beautiful and refined female here. She was petite and shapely with an angelic face, full pink lips, and sweet manner, and was bustling around efficiently making sure everyone was served. Rosita had also mentioned that she was educated in a woman's college back east and could speak several languages fluently. It was hard for Josh to keep his eyes off her. He sought her eye and caught it continually glancing back at him. The meal was stupendous, and they were all famished and took to heavy eating.

The schoolteacher was very solicitous of Josh and Gabe,

the organizers and leaders of the rattlesnake hunt, and made sure they had the best of the meal at their fingertips. They could not set a half empty glass down without her refilling it with cool tea with mint leaves in it. At the end of the meal, she brought Josh the first slice of her homemade peach pie, apologizing for the canned fruit, and seemed delighted when he enjoyed and praised it. Then she took him a piece of her pecan pie, blushing as she did so, then busying herself with serving Gabe, obviously a bit embarrassed at her fluttering over Josh, which had caught the notice of the folks at the table. Gabe started grinning with a big gap-toothed gleam as he watched all this and kept eating the delicious Polish food.

The meal was washed down by excellent homemade German beer of the dark strong variety. LaPoint leaned back and relaxed for a moment, finding it very pleasant, the meal, the beer, the lovely woman in his vision, after scaring up snakes all morning with the threat of possible death ever constant. He relaxed and gazed around at the buildings and houses, each with tall pitched roofs, as if built for snow country in a place where they were lucky to see steady rainfall. He couldn't help but notice how shapely the schoolteacher was as she went around and poured beer for the snake hunters who sat around chatting in Polish. She had a perky athletic look, with muscular arms and legs, unlike the thicker Polish women tending the tables.

Soon she left while glancing and catching his eye, walking quickly to a tiny cabin by the schoolhouse. After the meal and relaxing sit down with a few beers, they went to the schoolhouse and met with the schoolteacher, who had changed into a wide-legged riding skirt and high laced boots. Josh stamped on the boards at the entrance of the building and could hear low buzzing of rattlers. "You hear what I mean?" asked the schoolteacher.

"Yes. I feel the buzzing."

"Let's get them out, boss," said Jesse.

"Now hold on, let's check it out first."

Examining the building in a circuit, Josh pointed out all the low openings that would need plastering after they got the snakes out. He had a Polish farmer mixing plaster in a metal-wheeled wheelbarrow with his weed-chopping hoe, getting ready to seal the holes with wire and stucco. Then they went inside and started jamming the wires and smoke spouts into holes and hiding places inside the firewood room. The lower boards on the walls had wet rot and holes in them. A few of the men began shifting through the split oak firewood while Kathy Hartman stood watching through the window in her riding costume, her eye on Josh.

"Why hell, the roof leaked and rotted the floor sills, gotta fix the roof too," said Gabe.

"Yes, I told them that at lunch," said LaPoint.

"That schoolmarm looks even better in that ridin' outfit, don't she?"

"Yeah boss, I think she likes you," said Jesse.

"Come on now, shut up about that. We got snakes to attend to."

"Waugh. Ah reckon. That firewood pile in her cloakroom is full of rattlers. Go on and clean it out, I'll see to tha plaster mixin', so as not ta cramp yer style."

"Well alright then, having Jesse to look out for is enough anyway."

"Well alright then, go save her from tha varmints."

"Shut up."

And there she was, standing at the doorway in her riding costume, looking all excited as Josh stepped into the cloakroom. Distracted with Miss Hartman and trying not to notice her so much, LaPoint and Jesse began removing firewood and pitching it out the door, hearing some steady buzzing start in the pile. Soon they were in a scramble with several big rattlers, coiled and striking out at Jesse, who brushed them back with the hoe while backing up. Several small rattlers were pouring out of a hole in the wall, beside the big ones, which were coiled and hissing with their rattles whirling a frightening buzz and their mouths open showing long fangs. They began to strike out, lunging from their coiled positions to considerable distances, making Jesse jump back in a hurry.

Then another big rattler came out of the firewood pile behind Jesse, and Josh yelled, "Don't back up" while rapidly drawing his Remington .36 and firing twice at the snake, hitting it in the head and neck, leaving it writhing in death throes and nearly headless. In a flash LaPoint stomped with his tall boots on the heavy flopping head of the snake, then leaned over the crouching Jesse and fired four more shots at the others, hitting them all in the head and filling the room with blue-gray smoke.

"Eeee-cuella! My ears!" said Jesse, looking all around with wide eyes. "Chin-gado! You done shootin' now you done ruined my hearing?"

"I hope. I saw that big one came out of the wall behind you, and was fixing to strike."

"Gracias, Josh, I never saw it, 'cause of those others. Too many to handle in here. Go ahead and shoot those little ones too, it's already smoky and full of holes in the floor now anyway."

So Jesse backed out of the room, and Josh pulled out his long-barreled Remington .44 and shot the rest of the snakes, blasting big holes in the boards while the splinters and blood went flying. Then they pulled the boards off the lower wall and found a hole underneath and several more big rattlers nested with lots of young ones inside. These they were able to capture into gunny sacks and load into the barrel. LaPoint stepped outside on the porch for fresh air as the room cleared of gun-smoke. He faced the excited schoolteacher with big blue eyes and paused for a gaze into them.

"Jesse, can you bring some of those bricks and mortar? We need to block this hole in the bottom," said Josh. She held his gaze into her dark pupils as he spoke to Jesse.

"Sure thing."

"So that's where they were getting in, behind the woodpile..." said Miss Hartman, who had pulled the window open to let the smoke out.

"Sorry about shooting holes and tearing out those boards, Ma'am, but they were getting too thick to handle with hoes. That firewood pile is full of them. The big hollow Spanish oak logs had the big ones in there. We've got to get all of it out of here to make sure we clean them out. We're going to just tear those wall boards out too. Sorry about using the gun in the building. I wanted to avoid that, but didn't want Jesse to get bit."

"My goodness. No need to be sorry. I can't believe what I just saw. You shot them all in the head. How did you learn to shoot like that?" replied the wide-eyed Kathy, standing in the doorway watching the snakes being removed. Josh could not help but notice how beautiful her pink full lips were, and those big blue eyes, and the feeling of soft soothing waves like from his mother when he was small.

"Practice. Like ole Gabe says, 'If ya wants ta be the best, ya got's ta do it the most.' Anyway, they were close."

"But their heads were swaying around too. Each shot killed a snake."

"Practice. Like anything else."

"Practice, eh? I wish you'd tell my schoolkids that. So that's when the shooting across the river started, when you started clearing out rattlesnakes," she said.

Jesse spoke up. "He practices his weapons every night. Pistols and rifles. Keeps the Helena crowd away, and he's teaching me too."

"Yes ma'am. I probably shot fifty big rattlers while building the horse-pens at our ranch across the river. Clearing them out seemed a good way to practice pistol work. The head is the biggest part to hit, and that way the skin can be used. It becomes a reflex after a lot of practice. But I was hoping to keep the shooting outside. I'll patch up the holes later for you."

"Don't worry about that. Getting rid of those snakes will end my nightmares. It's just horrible trying to teach children with them slithering around and rattling. Even the walls would buzz. Please, continue. Let me know if there's anything I can do for you, to help you, anything."

Josh looked into her eyes when she said that. She held his gaze, her pupils expanding in her bright blue eyes.

"We'll all be so grateful to be rid of these evil vipers. There's a million acres of brush land they can live in, not the schoolhouse."

"Yes ma'am," said Josh as he reined in his mind from her and back to the problem at hand. "I guess I'd better get back to the snake killing."

So they continued and removed every snake they could find from the area. With the crew working well under the firm guidance of LaPoint, they avoided injury or snakebite. The only casualties were two broken hoe handles from men chopping too hard in a fury. A second crew was working behind them, patching every hole with wire and mortar, or boards and sometimes bricks. Gabe oversaw that operation to make sure no snakes could enter the buildings through holes.

By the end of the day they had a tall wooden water barrel swarming half full of rattlers. It was a rare and fearsome sight, and many stepped up to view the writhing coiling twisting mass of snakes inside. Kathy stood there staring at them for a few stunned minutes, then got a shiver of fear, at which point she turned in the wagon, and LaPoint was there to catch her under the arms and lift her down. They stood close when her small feet touched the ground. He walked her towards her house until some farmers' wives took her the rest of the way, for she was feeling strange and shaky after seeing the writhing snakes, and wanted to lay down.

The late afternoon was getting cooler as they finished clearing all the vipers they could from the area. They started a crew patching all the outside holes they had found in dwellings, with a special tough mortar reinforced with wire, which Josh showed them how to install.

Josh mounted Scorpio when they were finished, and walked him to the small porch on Miss Hartman's cabin. He saw her angelic face in the window, gazing back at him.

"Miss Hartman, we've gotten all the snakes we could find out and patched the holes with mortar that will set up overnight. I'll come replace the blasted boards tomorrow."

She quickly appeared on the porch. "Oh thank you so much, I'm sorry I fell out on you, just the sight of all those snakes...sort of made me feel strange."

"I understand. I didn't want you to get up and look at it, but I was busy, then looked up and you were there."

"Thanks again for all you did, and I'll see you when you return."

"Alright."

Then the LaPoint outfit headed home with their buzzing cargo, where they methodically chopped the head from each one, stripped the skin off, and pegged it to dry on the west side of the barn. They harvested nearly seventy diamond-backed snake-skins and a big pile of rattles from the varmints. Rosita and Rosa would tan them to leather, making hatbands, sashes, and belts. They marketed the goods at Helena and sold all they could make. The meat would be given to a man who had hogs, in return for some salt pork. Rosita usually saved some and cooked it up for the vaqueros, who enjoyed it with peppers, onions, beans, and rice.

The next day Josh returned to Panna Maria and spent the morning fixing the torn-down wall and bullet-holes in the floor. He had mixed a strong batch of brick mortar and was laying some down to block the holes. Kathy was there, serving him hot coffee and yeast-cakes, watching him while she straightened up the room after the snake hunt had left it in disarray.

"I can't tell you how much I appreciate you cleaning out those snakes for us. I was actually considering giving up and going back to the hill country, or back to Virginia for school. In the church there's a statue of St. Michael trampling a big snake, while the whole place is infested with rattlers. I'm lucky I have two hens left for eggs to bake with. They've bitten several people in the two years I have been here."

"But you're staying now?"

"Yes, through the end of the school term. Thanks to you. At least the rattlesnake problem won't run me out before the end of the school year, when I go back East to finish my teaching degree. If they don't come back."

"Well, I imagine some will show up, that we missed. But we left those tools and showed the men how to catch them. And I'll come back to kill strays if I need to."

"Well, there's nobody around that can shoot them with a revolver like you. I remember watching my dad try to hit a stump with an old Walker colt and barely do it from a short distance, then switch to a shotgun for snakes. He never could shoot that pistol well."

"A shotgun works better anyway, just leaves a bigger hole in the wall. I'm intent on taking these floorboards up and replacing them, they're too shattered by those .44 slugs to be any good. Might take a while."

"So you can stay for lunch, then, Mr. LaPoint?"

"Why yes, I could. Miss Hartman."

"Is that what you like to be called, LaPoint, like everyone says."

"I'd like you to call me Josh."

"Alright Josh. And I am Kathy, not ma'am."

"Alright, Kathy Hartman...from?"

"Fredricksburg. My father and two older brothers live there now. I got offered a job teaching here because my father insisted we all learn to read and write, and sent me to school back East. I had just gotten back for a summer break after two years of college when the priest here came looking for a teacher who could speak English and German and Silesian Polish, which

I learned from my grandmother. So I came down here to this hot, humid, windy prairie, full of rattlesnakes and visiting gunmen from Helena."

"I see. I didn't know people volunteered to come here to this sticker-patch full of riffraff from Helena and Oakville, especially gracious and lovely ladies like you."

"Yes, some do, instead of marrying a simple-minded German farmer who will make a house slave out of you and leave you alone on a poor farm in Comanche country. At least there's no raiding Indian's here, lately. I don't want to be alone in a frontier cabin."

"Oh. I can understand that. And I really admire what you're doing here, so I hope you don't leave. It's the first step, really."

"How do you mean that?"

"Well, Kathy, in my view, the schoolteacher is the first real important element in civilizing this wild place. You are what we rougher fellas are trying to clean this place up for, so you can teach the children to read and write and do numbers, and treat each other fair. Guys like us just sweep through briefly to clear out the rattlesnakes and other killers. The school and the courthouse civilize a country, with the school teacher being most important of all, aside from being a good mother, I suppose."

"Why, thank you Josh, that's the nicest thing I've heard in a long time." Her eyes grew moist and she went and busied herself with cleaning up, leaving Josh to his rebuilding project, but with his usual concentration now interfered with by her lovely presence in the next room. He could physically feel the emotion pouring through her, and it intrigued him as much as her beauty. And she was so gracious and ladylike, the kind of women one dreamed of marrying. His eyes grew moist as he stared into hers. After sinking into her gaze for a while, he went back to work.

Josh labored for four hours and had the firewood-cloakroom vestibule completely remodeled and sealed up when Kathy came back again to look. She had watched him off and on during the day, bringing him coffee, admiring how he never broke his concentration and stuck to the job through step after careful step until it was done perfectly and looked better than before. Meanwhile, he found it hard to focus on the job while hoping she would just come and stand close again. Her presence was both soothing and exciting to him. She smelled like roses.

"Josh LaPoint has a French sound, and your speech has some accent, maybe Cajun French?"

"I'm a Creole from New Orleans, aiming to be a Texan," he replied, his eyes playing over the beautiful curves of her cheekbones, the startling big blue eyes with long lashes, the soft full pink lips.

"A Creole?"

"Mixed blood, French, Spanish, and some other, this and that." His gaze drifted to her lovely neck and high, firm looking breasts under the white blouse.

"And were you a carpenter there, Josh?"

He thought of how she would be making love, her strong emotions aroused to passion by his concentrated ministrations.

"Not exactly, though I did some. Mostly I was a student, then helped run a trading company. I was somewhat schooled in building trades, masonry, carpentry, and pottery, tile and brick making. I did some construction work." He couldn't help but take deep breathes, she smelled so good, as good as she looked. He imagined tasting the tender areas behind her little pink ear with his tongue and kissing her down the neck. He reined in his mind, remembering that she wasn't a bar girl. She smiled.

"And reading and writing and figures too, I'm told. I see you do excellent work. Last month I found some yellow clay along the river, and I'm trying to use if for art class with the children. Do you think you could come and show them some pottery making?" A tiny frown creased her brow as she asked, making her appear even more appealing to him. He wanted to kiss her very much, and knew he would not stop if he started.

"Well, I don't know, maybe. It's been years since the brothers taught me that, and I'm awfully busy building a ranch and training horses. Maybe I could later on, after I get some projects finished."

"A busy man, always working…So Rosita tells us. She says you won't come to church. Were you schooled by Catholic monks?"

"As a boy I was, but they were more refugee Cathars than Catholics, I think. They weren't tied in with the local church, just some monks imported from France to teach an orphan school. I'm not a believer anymore, or rather, I don't share the beliefs of the Catholic church."

"Oh? Are you like my brother? He says this world is a bad dog, and it'll bite you if you give it the chance."

Josh laughed. "That's not too far off, for these times, and this frontier. I just believe I've got to help myself, make my own life here, despite the vipers, without believing in somebody's fairy tale. I'm thankful for being alive, and intend to stay that way. I believe in having the best weapons, and being good with them to protect my outfit. I believe in working steady."

"You just believe in hard work, like my father? Rosita tells us you work, work, work, never stop. 'Spends more time with the horses than people', she says. And when you're not working, you practice with your guns. And you sleep with a little chihuahua that is totally devoted to you, like your horse is."

"Oh yeah? It's good work, you know. With horses. They are wonderful animals. Chihuahua is too. What else does she tell you?"

"That you read big books at night which you buy in San Antonio, and don't go to the bar and drink and gamble very much, which she sees as a good influence on Jesse, and that you love your horses and have a magic way with them. And that you won't talk about your past."

"I'm more interested in the present and future than the past. Nothing but ashes there. Rosita's been doing a lot of talking about me, it seems."

"Yes. The war, well, there's been some curiosity hereabouts. There's been a lot of questions, especially after hearing all the gunfire across the river. People talk about how you out-shot Britt Jonson with the long rifle and outdrew Ike Covington the gunfighter."

"Actually Tom Jackson killed Ike."

"You shot him twice before he drew his gun, though he started first. We heard the story. And the other gunfights with rustlers are still being talked about, and that gunman who was going to shoot Jesse until you walked up and shot him. And then when you came charging in like a knight on your magnificent dappled white stallion, running those outlaws off, you were the talk of the town for weeks. The priest has his hands full with gun thugs from Helena coming over. He started off threatening them with a shotgun from the belfry when they persisted in ignoring his warnings. Then they started shooting at him for sport. People were terrified that day you showed up."

"That was a lucky coincidence."

"Well, maybe, but it was a godsend as far as these people are concerned. At first everyone was afraid new gunmen had moved in across the river to raid us when we first heard you shooting over there. The priest had been praying to St. Michael to send help. And Mr. Muldoon has told us about Mr. McBride and you when he comes to church and lunch on Sundays."

"Oh, like what?" Josh kept tearing off the wall-boards on his knees as he spoke, trying to get it clean to put on a new board without holes.

"How you whipped the town bully Bratelske in his saloon when you first showed up, that nasty freighter and his pals. He's the one that bullwhips all the Tejanos when he gets drunk, or used to."

"Oh that...yeah, just sort of happened, caught us in a tired and cranky mood, after a long trip, I guess."

"Yes, I can imagine. And now he says that the gunmen in Helena and Live Oak are afraid of you, with your fast draw and sure shooting. We can hear you practicing with your guns almost every evening, and the firing goes on and on, sometimes with really loud booms that echo for a while."

"That would be the Sharps and Whitworth rifles, for long distance shooting," said Josh as he strained at the job. The wall boards were nailed with big square nails and hard to remove. Josh took off his weapons belt and got down on his side with a crowbar where he could apply full leverage, individually popping the broken pieces of board off while listening to Kathy, who stood in the doorway near his boots.

"Every night we hear it. I've never seen pistols like that either. One big for longer range accuracy and one little for fast action, right?"

"Yes. Exactly."

"Can I handle them? I know how, from my brother's guns."

"Sure."

"They load from this place in front?"

"Yes, they're the first revolvers with metallic cartridges we could get a hold of. Remingtons. We used to carry the big

Colts, cap and ball type, slow loading."

"My, pistols are advancing. Metallic cartridges. My brothers will want one of these. And you practice every night?"

"Well yeah, lately I've been teaching some marksmanship to the whole outfit, with the rustler problems. And we're clearing the swimming hole of cottonmouths with our new telescope mounted rifles."

"Oh, that would be so nice, to be able to swim in the river without those evil things coming after us. Is it a hole deep enough to swim?"

"Yes. We made a dam of oak and mesquite logs to raise the level, and now with the high water, it's great. Maybe you could join us for a swim there sometime."

"I'd like that, if you bring your gun for snakes."

"I always do. So what else have you heard?"

"Well, mainly everyone talks of your special way with horses, and your trained Spanish stallion with the high arched neck, and what good saddle-mounts you train and sell. And Rosita and her family are finally feeling secure now that you are there at the ranch."

"That's good, what we wanted. They are wonderful folks."

"That's what everyone wants out here, to feel secure, to sleep at night and not lie awake worried about being attacked. It's hard enough to make a living from this rough land without being attacked. I always dreamed of being a schoolteacher, but nearly gave up because of those snakes and the outlaws from Helena. Rosita says they quit raiding their rancho with you there."

"Yes. There's been no more raiding there since we've moved in. There's always a rifleman on guard, usually Tom Jackson, who doesn't often miss. And our horse business is doing well."

"Is Mr. McBride your father?" With a serious strain Josh got the last board off along the floor with a loud popping and cracking sound.

"No. My actual father wasn't around. Gabe is more like a cranky old uncle that raised me and schooled me about shooting and living in the wilds. Could you hand me that can of nails?" She bent down to get the can of nails and he was distracted by the view of the beautifully rounded tops of her breasts. She had chosen the day she was to be alone with him to wear a special blouse she kept packed in a cedar chest, with Spanish style design and not buttoned up to her throat like the day before. She smiled softly when she handed him the can, and as he took it and looked back at the wall, two rattlers came up from a hole in the plate.

Without thinking LaPoint smashed the hammer on the head of closest one and grabbed the other by the body near the buzzing tail just as it reared up to strike his face. Slinging the snake like a whip he popped it against the small cast iron cook-stove, repeatedly, whanging the head against the hollow steel shell with a fast knocking rhythm until the snake-head was too bashed to operate his fangs. Then he got to his knees and popped it like a whip, breaking his neck. Kathy had pulled back out of the doorway in terror as this was going on, reaching for his pistol to hand to him.

LaPoint flung the battered but writhing snake into a far corner of the room and looked again at the one he hammered, which was slowly coiling, the pale belly crossed with lines of scales, but basically dead of a smashed brain.

"Joshua. Are you alright, did you get bit?"

"No, I don't think so. Damn sure had to take the initiative, though. Hand me that big brick, I've got to stop up this hole in the plate for now and go mix some concrete to pour in there."

"Take the initiative, I'll say. I can't believe what I just saw. I've never seen a human being move that fast, with exactly the right moves, too. Weren't you terrified, with two of them after you?"

"Wasn't time for that. Hammering the first was easy, but the other was out of reach of the hammer and about to strike, so all I could do was grab it with my other hand. I've done it before, practiced quite a bit, actually, but usually with my right hand. When we find them inside the buildings at the ranch I often grab them by the tail and jerk them around until I get out the door, or step on them and cut their heads off. I watched the chaparral birds kill them for a while, saw the snake's weak points in combat, let's say."

"You have the quickest moves I've ever seen, and I grew up with brothers who wrestled every day. I'm amazed. What a snake killer, answer to our prayers around here."

"Glad to be of service. This is awful, having snakes in

the schoolroom. We'll block that out. I've got to go make some concrete for these holes going underneath."

Kathy took several deep breaths, still holding LaPoint's small Remington Navy .36. "So is that the ranger way, study the enemy?"

"Yes. And learn from his tactics."

"Is Gabe the old ranger, scout, and Comanche killer that everyone says he is?"

"Yes, except for the Comanche killer part. He's not on a vengeance warpath with them any more. Gabe is all I have left of family. We're just trying to build ourselves a spread to live on, and let other folks alone, including the Comanche. But it's proven hard to do that without some gun-play. We've had gunfights to hold onto what we've earned."

"So he was in New Orleans too, Gabe McBride?"

"Yes. He used to work for my former employer there, Alexandre Robinoix, in the fur trade, out in Taos and the Staked Plains, and when he was badly hurt by renegade Indians he was brought to the home plantation to recover under the care of my mother, who was a healer. She brought him back to life, and he was assigned to my training at the plantation on the Bayou Teche. Later he set up a blacksmith shop to be a part of the trading company business in New Orleans, when I went there to help run the business."

"Your mother was a healer! That explains the touch with horses. Pancho calls you el brujo del cabbalaros. Training in what?"

"Firearms, knife making, blacksmithing, horses, tracking, hunting, knife fighting, knife throwing, mule packing, skinning for pelts and curing, living in the wilds, stuff like that."

"And your mother, is she still there in Louisiana?"

"No. She was killed by federal marauders when the plantation was destroyed."

"Oh, I'm so sorry. It hurts for a long time when you lose family."

Josh stifled a lump in his throat, then went on. "My father is gone too, disappeared. There's none of my family left, except Gabe, my horse, and chihuahua." Josh spoke these words slowly, with a catch in his voice. It was the first time he had spoken of it with anyone but Gabe. Somehow she had reached inside his work-hardened raw-hided exterior with her calm blue eyes and kind heart.

"Oh lord... another murdered parent. I'm sorry to open old sorrows, Josh. That's what you meant by ashes." Kathy put the .36 revolver back in his weapons belt, and handed him the knife.

"Yeah. Loss and regret. I wasn't there to protect her." He looked down and grabbed the smashed snake and cut it's head off, then stepped over and did the same to the other, throwing all of it out the window.

"And did you shoot the men who did it, like Rosita thought?"

"Yes, some of them. But not the leader, though I'd kill him now if I had the chance."

"Oh. Still unfinished business of revenge?"

"I guess that shocks you, but I'd think no more of it than shooting those rattlesnakes. I've killed when I had too, Kathy, no use to hide it from you. I'm a killer, when I need to be, and that's maybe why I never came to meet you before, I guess. Despite what Rosita told me about you."

"And now?"

"Here and now, I'm very attracted to you, which I think you know. I can't help that. But probably a lady like you wouldn't want to get involved with a killer like me. I'm proud to know you, though, and help out where I can."

"Why Joshua, the whole country is full of men who spent five years killing other men, all claiming to be good Christians. Rangers and German farmers are killing Indians, Comanches are killing everyone. Those who can't fight around here seem to get killed."

"Yeah, I know. But I thought I had avoided all that. Then I killed in vengeance. And I've had to kill in self-defense just getting here, and trying to maintain a working horse ranch. I came to raise and train horses."

"But you still have a vow of vengeance, someone you must kill, a blood debt that must be cleared? You should try to let it go, or it will drag you down like my brothers, make your life a cup of bitterness."

"Well, not exactly a vow of vengeance, but I'd probably kill him if he crossed my path. I don't dwell on it or cling to the notion, but I can't say I don't keep my eye out for him."

"And what does that do to your peace of mind?"

"Not much. I hold my mind on building a ranch. This place is about a fresh start in life for me. The location is not my first choice, but it serves for now, and I hold my mind on building a horse ranch, what I've always wanted to do. Sometimes it seems like the best revenge is forgetting the injury and living a full life. If I let that scoundrel rob me of my concentration, then I'm allowing more plundering. I never wanted to get involved in killing, but folks can't live with miscreants that constantly attack them; it's like trying to live with rattlesnakes. If they would just stay in their natural zone, I'd let them be. I even avoided the war by supplying merchandise to Union troops occupying New Orleans, and supplies to the people. The killing just seemed to happen. The war seemed to bring out the worst in some folks, requiring gun-work to deal with them. So I got good at gun work."

"But I heard it's a problem for you now because the Helena gun thugs want to draw down on you and get famous."

"Yeah, well, I never wanted to hang out much in Helena anyway. Except for a friendly visit to Muldoon's and picking up supplies, I avoid it. How about you, Kathy?"

"I came for a fresh start too, Josh. But it seems that sometimes killing is necessary to stay alive out here. I don't hold it against you as you might imagine."

"Well, other than going after the men who killed my mother, the rest I killed were trying to kill me at the time."

"Then what else could you do? It's like those snakes. But my brothers want to kill every Comanche now. Revenge is on their minds day and night. If my dad could shoot like you, my mother would maybe still be alive."

"Oh, how do you mean?"

"She was killed by Comanche raiders in the Saline Valley, south of Fort Mason. They killed her and my aunt and stole my little brother, back in 1852. I was ten years old then, and I was out by the creek watching the goats grazing. I ran back to the house when I heard screaming, but all I could do was hide and tremble in a cedar bush as they finished raping and butchering my mother and aunt, who both had axes and fought them for a while, but ended up chopped to pieces, with their hair gone."

"Oh no, you don't have to go through this retelling..."

"No, I want to tell you. They had dad trapped in the corn crib. He was shooting at them with his old junky pistol while they laughed at him for being such a poor shot. They were having a grand old time, jumping out from behind cover and yelling ridicule at him when he missed them. He had a bigger gun, like your big one there, but old and in ill repair, and slow to load, you know, the power and caps and ramrod."

"Yes, Colt .44, we had that kind until recently, when we got these fast loading Remingtons. So tell me the rest of what happened, unless it pains you too much."

"The Comanches were wasting time in taunting my dad, and I was hoping the pistol shots would bring the neighbors and save us. I was too scared to move from my hiding place. One of the Comanches got a kerosine lantern from the house and lit it, intending to throw it on the corn crib and burn dad alive, or make him run out and get shot. Then the Indian got shot from behind when some local men came to the rescue with my older brothers, who were out haying with them a few miles away, and heard the shooting. After that I could not talk for a month or so, and dad found a buyer for the land. That's when we moved back to Fredricksburg, and then my father sent me to Virginia for schooling. I could talk again once I got away from the Comanche land."

"Oh what times we live in. You too, I'm sorry, Kathy. We both lost our mothers at a young age."

"Oh? I thought you said she was killed during the war?"

"Well, yes. But I was sent to an orphan boarding school when I was six, so I always missed her."

"Oh, I see. And then she was killed."

"Yes, right before I was going to meet with her and try to convince her to come here."

"I'm sorry. Life is cruel in these times. It seems so beautiful in Texas to be such a cruel place, even here in the brush-land, with all the snakes and sticker bushes. I loved the hill country until I saw the Comanches kill my folks and steal my brother. After that I was always afraid to be there. I wouldn't herd the goats anymore, or go out riding to Enchanted Rock. I never slept a wink on the nights of the full moon, even in Fredricksburg."

"I thought there was a good treaty between the Germans and the Comanche up there."

"It lasted for a few years, then fell apart when surveyors started moving north. Some renegades killed the surveyors, then the rangers raided the Comanches for it, and it turned back to war."

"And you never heard of your brother again?"

"No. He's been with them 15 years now, if he's still alive."

"How old was he when they stole him?"

"He was only eight, my baby brother, little Rudy," she replied, choking back a sob. "I try not to think on it, it makes my heart ache so. And the not knowing....make's me sad."

"I can feel that. What was his name?" Josh felt the wave of her sorrow wash through him, and it grieved him, and joined with the pool of sorrow he carried over the loss of his mother.

"Rudy Jim, Rudolph James Hartman. He'd be a young man now, if he is alive."

"If he's alive he's a Comanche warrior, Kathy....and there won't be any getting him back."

"That's what I'm told, but if only I could know if he's alive or not, that might ease my mind. I doubt that I ever will, though."

"Do you have a picture of him?"

"Why, yes, I have one of both of us together, a tintype. Several, in fact. Here they are, in the box of family pictures I pour over when I get lonely out here and the wind howls."

"Cute. Family resemblance. And this one, is this your older brothers with you?"

"Yes, in Fredricksburg two years ago."

"Can I have these two for a while?"

"Yes, but why, do you think you might..."

"I won't go looking for him, if that's what you're thinking. But I travel a lot, so it wouldn't hurt to have these pictures. With the close family resemblance, I would guess he looks somewhat like your grown brothers in this picture. And on the one in a thousand chance I meet up with him, he might recognize this picture. But please don't get your hopes up, it's just on an off chance."

"Alright. Some chance is better than none. I can't sit around worrying about it, so I try to get on with life."

"That's all we can do, try to make the best of things. Part of being a survivor is missing those who don't make it. But enough of this stirring bad memories of the past. How about the future? Would you like to go swimming with me next Saturday?"

"Yes. I'd like that very much, if there aren't any cottonmouths swimming after me."

"Well alright then, I'll come for you in the wagon."

"Wagon? Don't you have an extra horse for me to ride?"

"Sure, I've got some gentle mares and lots of geldings."

"Bring me a fast horse, I can ride better than you imagine, Mr. LaPoint," she said with a saucy smile. "I used to love to ride out to the Enchanted Rock with my brothers, before the raid. I could outrace them all. I'd like you to teach me to shoot that small pistol as well, if you would."

"Well, alright, that would be shining, as old Gabe says. I'll be here bright and early. And I've got a long legged mare for you that's shining too."

"That would be wonderful. I would feel safe with a man like you there, with your guns and fast moves. And I bet I could learn to hit something with that little gun, since it's not so heavy, so bring it."

"Oh, I always carry guns, but I don't have a sidesaddle."

"Josh LaPoint! I don't ride like some eastern schoolmarm, clutching a silly sidesaddle, sir. Those things are too off-balanced. I grew up riding bareback outracing my brothers, so a western saddle with stirrups is a treat for me."

"Well, alright then. You're an enchanting lady, schoolmarm and bareback rider, the last thing I expected to find in Panna Maria."

"Will you bring your little chihuahua? I think I should meet her."

"Suzette, sure, if I can pry her away from Rosita's kitchen. She likes the girls now."

So they met on Sunday for a horseback ride through the river valley and a picnic prepared by Kathy. Suzette immediately took a shine to Kathy and would not leave her lap as they picnicked. Josh was entranced again with Kathy's charm and beauty, as well as the excellent cooking. He felt he could relax with her, and they did so, together, under drifting white clouds on a big quilt.

Later she wanted to learn how to shoot a pistol, so they used a big oak stump for a target and she took hold of the small gun.

"Would you help me at first, on how to aim it?"

Josh stood behind her and steadied her arms. Her scent filled his head. "Here, hold your wrist with the other hand to steady it for the kick." His leg brushed up against her tight bottom as he enveloped her in his strong arms while steadying her hands. "Now remember, it's not like the big one, there's no trigger, so just draw back the hammer with your thumb and point and fire."

She did so, over and over again, until she got fairly competent with the small gun, which had much less kick than the large caliber pistols common on the frontier. The sound of the firing stirred a great blue heron from his fishing pond on the creek, and he circled above the water until he spotted a small bass, which he scooped up and carried to a large nest of sticks in the riverside forest treetops, and gave it to his mate to feed to their brood. Then he went back to fishing as they watched the resident eagle swoop along the water looking for fish.

The afternoon grew hot and they rode back towards the swimming hole after a short siesta on blankets following the big meal. It took twenty minutes of fast riding to get to the swimming hole. Kathy proved an excellent rider, and it was only because of his stallion's speed and endurance that Josh kept the lead. She did not ride like a dainty lady, but like an excellent horsewoman. What she had learned as a child had stuck with her, and she sat a horse beautifully, from Josh's point of view.

In fact, Josh could not help but noticing her tight little rump bouncing on the saddle when they slowed down to a trot and he pulled Scorpio around to the back so he could move up and ride on the left side. Delores had kept him satisfied sexually for years, but this lady was beautiful and full of gentility and culture, not to mention how well she sat a saddle.

They circled around the cool water, watering the horses, checking for snakes, before they dismounted. After graining the horses, Josh stripped to his underwear and waded into the water after propping a rifle against a tree on shore. Kathy stripped down to a slip over her underwear and followed, with Josh admiring her lovely trim figure. They cooled off and swam for hours in the moving current, with both of them soon skinny dipping, and enjoyed a wonderful afternoon at the idyllic river park that Josh and Jesse had worked so hard to create. Her pale and slender body was just as beautiful as he had imagined, but he did not try to make love with her. The time did not seem right, with her leaving so soon for a length of time to finish her teaching degree. He was thinking of her in the long term.

As they were starting to leave the water they saw a water

snake swimming away from them in a fluid serpentine motion.

"Oh no, is that a cottonmouth?"

"No, it's a banded water-snake. See the head is not a big knot like a viper?"

"Oh good, no shooting to spoil the peaceful mood."

"Right. No shooting. Let's get dressed and ride some more."

"Alright, let's. I love riding that horse you brought me."

"That's good, because I love watching you."

During the rest of the school year Josh paid occasional but regular visits to Kathy, usually picking her up after Sunday mass for a ride and a picnic and swim, and Delores was set on edge with her intuition that her regular lover had eyes for another. However, LaPoint kept visiting Delores for sex and affection at least three times a week, and carrying on a platonic relationship with Kathy, who left for more schooling back east at the end of the school term. He never even kissed her until he bade her good bye at the stage when she departed, and that kiss stayed on his mind for a long time. He had leaned down for a tentative peck on her sweet lips when she embraced him in a full hug and kissed him long and deep. The softness of her breasts under the red velvet jacket she wore was something LaPoint would remember for a while. Her receptiveness was enchanting to him. He held her close as they spoke. "I'll be back in two years, Josh LaPoint. Take care of yourself."

"I will. You too."

"Should I write you?"

"Yes."

"And will you write back and tell me how you're doing?"

"Sure I will."

"Don't let anybody shoot you, Josh LaPoint."

"I won't, if I see them first. Goodbye until we meet again, Kathy. I'm going to miss you."

Tears trickled down her rosy cheeks as she turned and boarded the stagecoach, and Josh walked away with a hollow feeling in the pit of his gut. He found it hard to stop thinking of her on the ride back, and finally took to racing Scorpio at top speed to engage his mind in the present, jumping sticker bushes in wild abandon as he ran the back pastures. He plunged back into corral building when he got back to the ranch, and worked steadily until after dark, as he did every day thereafter.

While the horse business continued to prosper when Kathy was gone, Josh found a bur of discontent under his saddle with his life there, the constant work and then a few overnight sessions with Delores at Muldoon's. He began to want more out of life, and imagined Kathy sharing a home and family with him. He checked the mailbox regularly for her letters, and spent considerable time reading and answering them.

With the idea of a ranch home to settle down in on the lovely Blanco river, where the countryside was rolling hills and every plant did not have a thorn on it, Josh began to feel nagging dissatisfaction with many aspects of life around Helena. He had never enjoyed a normal home life, and he began to long for that, away from the Helena and Oakville gun-thugs who were always looking for trouble, or trying to make a name for themselves by challenging him to a gunfight.

Helena was usually a troublesome place, which went through sheriffs one after another. The amount of riff-raff that had settled around the area during the cart wars and then the recent cattle rustling wars had not diminished. Racist killers, drunk braggadocios, surly teamsters, hired guns, rustlers, and wagon train robbers made it their headquarters, despite attempts by honest folk to rid the place of them. They were always shooting at each other and sometimes riding off to Panna Maria looking for girls and mischief, though fear of LaPoint had stifled that somewhat. None of the LaPoint outfit liked Helena, but Josh felt a growing disgust with the place, and imagined how life would be like in the hill country, near the German settlements, with a lovely German blond wife and several children, and a more educated and cultured class of people. It got to where he could not go to town without constant nervousness that somebody would want to try his luck on a fast draw to make a name for himself.

Once while getting supplies from Butler's general store in Helena on Saturday morning, they witnessed a brutal knife fight with a circle of men betting on it. Josh was inside gathering supplies while Gabe had the mules and wagon stopped at the loading door, near an alleyway with a fight breaking out. The fight was making the mules nervous and jumpy, as well as prompting an awful racket out of them as the yelling got louder. Gabe tried to talk them down while standing up to see the fight better. There was a ring of rowdy men around the fight, but

Gabe could see over them by standing in the wagon, although at some risk because of the jumpy mules.

The two combatants were tied together at the left wrist with leather bindings, and each had a short bladed knife to whack and slice at each other. The rowdy crowd was yelling at them and making bets as to who would go down first. A deafening racket bellowed out of the alley with men pounding on the building boards, egging the combatants on with chanting yells.

The small knives were too short to make a killing blow very easily, so there was lots of blood from slashing as they rolled around in a muddy mess. Having their arms encumbered by the left wrists being tied meant they were often jerked off balance, which situation soon favored the bigger man, who slung the smaller fellow around and jabbed him repeatedly in the trunk. Gabe's right hand instinctively went to the butt of his knife as he held the reins tight with the other, watching the melee.

The sound of the combatants yelling went from anger to pain as he watched the blood flow from both of them. The smaller man soon had a bloody flap of shirt over a long wound across his chest, squirting blood into the muddy street and onto the other man. He was screaming and slashing wildly at the other, bigger man, in desperation, which put the mules into a near bolting panic as the strong smell of blood assailed their long noses. Their big ears were back and their hooves were milling the mud as Gabe strained to see the fight while leaning on the wagon brake handle.

The bigger man jerked the arm of the smaller one each time he slashed, knocking him off balance, but when he fell it pulled the bigger man down into the mud, where they writhed around, rolling up against the building finally, exhausted and panting, but still slashing. The crowd moved into a tight loud circle and obscured Gabe's view.

The smaller man gave out a shrill scream as he got stuck in a vital spot, which caused the mules to start moving, nearly knocking Gabe over into the back of the wagon. Aggravated to beat all hell, Gabe moved the wagon around the corner to get away from the scene and calm the mules.

"Gol-dang, another Helena knife fight, as if there wasn't enough ways ta get kilt without makin' up that kind," he complained to Pancho, who had just come with Jesse from the

Post Office. "I guess bettin' on dog fights warn't enough for em."

"Hola, what's the commotion now?" asked Pancho.

"Hey Jesse, " said Gabe. "Go inta tha store and tell Josh I had ta move out front, on account of a knife fight back there was spooking the mules. He's in thar now, getting corn and coffee and such. Maybe ya can help carry some stuff. Oh yeah, they got some new brooms thar in the front window, I want one for the bunkhouse. Could ya grab one of them too?"

Jesse began to unload the stuff he had been carrying so as to go help Josh. Then he sprang off the wagon and went in the front door as Pancho peered down the alley to see what the commotion was about.

"What it es? A bull-whipping? Somebody drawing down on the boss?"

"Fuggin' insanity is what it is. Helena knife fight."

"Eeeecoilachingah," said Pancho as he climbed into the wagon seat beside Gabe. "It's always somethin' in thees town."

"Don't I know it. These sonsofbitches are the dregs of humanity, I tell ya. Makin' a sport outa slicing each other up while the crowd bets on it. Hell in a hand basket!"

"Eijos de diabos," said Pancho.

By then there were horses and mules all around growing fractious and spooky from the noise and smell of blood. Gabe made a renewed effort to still his mules while Pancho jumped back off the wagon to go hold them.

"Si, I feel sorry for Mr. Butler, they tried to make a nice town, but these crazy people always mess up everything."

"Crossroads of the crazy world, huh? No wonder LaPoint is sick of it."

"I'm sick of it too."

"That makes all of us."

Josh came out of Butler's store onto the small loading dock with two fifty pound bags of corn over his shoulders, and saw Gabe had moved the wagon around to the front, which started him to cussing.

"What the hell did you move the wagon for, damnit?" Gabe jerked his chin towards the altercation in the alley, which caused Josh to glance over to the commotion and grimace as he saw the bloody pair arise and start to slashing again. "Oh. Shit what a town. I'd like to come here just once without dodging a bloody disturbance."

Walking the heavy bags over and dumping them into the back of the wagon, Josh gave a disgusted look at Gabe, who was trying to steady the mules. "I told you we should have come on Sunday."

"I know. You was right, but I needed a good hammer."

"Did you see that, those guys were tied at the wrist and slicing each other up for sport and betting. Our own little version of the Roman coliseum, a muddy alley in Helena, huh? Nothing like a taste of Helena to make me appreciate the ranch. I despise this place."

"Well I guess we could go ta Live Oak and shoot our way into the general store thar, huh? Or maybe drive all day to Goliad?" Josh could hardly hear Gabe for all the mules snorting and braying and the men yelling in the alley.

"Yeah, or we could just move north to the Blanco and live around some civilized Germans. Or go make a ranch in the foothills of the Rockies, like Charlie Goodnight."

"Yeah, and fighting the raiding Comanches every full moon, we ain't had a lick o' Indian trouble down here."

"Comanches there, Helena-hand-basket here, racist gun thugs and rustlers, maybe the Comanches will leave us alone. This town is filling up with white trash, looking for trouble. They've gone through five sheriffs since we've been here, and it isn't getting any better."

"I know it. But they ain't raided us since we been at tha ranch."

"The only reason they're not raiding us is we're better at shooting. We ought to go up to Taos after this horse season is over, look for traces of Mr. Alex, do some elk hunting, go to that hot springs you told me about, the Great Pagosa. This mustanging is about played out, and we've picked the best all the way to the coast and the Nueces. I'd like to take our best brood mares and move up to the Blanco valley if the Comanche raiding isn't too bad up that way, or maybe even check out the mountains for a new ranch. I came out here to work horses, not dodge killers all the time."

"Wal, I'm fer getting' shed of this class of varmint, that's fer shore, but we're here now...you gonna stand thar deliberating on it while these skittish mules...."

"Alright. Just hang onto those mules, Old Coon, while we get the rest of the stuff. Josie looks about ready to bolt or start kicking, and drag Pancho down the street through the mud."

"Doan I fuggin' well know it? Get tha stuff and lets go eat at Muldoon's, if we're all done getting' yore supplies. All the riffraff is down here bettin' on the slashing contest, should have plenty of tables open thar. He said meals on the house for all the snake killin' at Panna Maria. And that goes fer tha whole crew, anybody that don't like Tejanos can clear out, he said."

"Alright, and Pancho, why don't you take our horses over there now," said LaPoint, who went back into the store to help Jesse carry the rest of the supplies to the wagon. Josh came out with an armload of books on the last trip. Then they had a nice meal and visit with Muldoon. Muldoon took that opportunity to tell Josh that Delores had taken the stage to San Antonio and a job at the Menger Hotel.

"She said to drop by and see her there when you pass through. I think she had a notion about you and Miss Hartman, and she got a good job offer. And maybe there's a spark between Mr. Winger and her, as well."

Josh felt saddened and then relieved to hear that, but moved on to the stack of mail on the table. There were several letters with the scent and handwriting of Kathy Hartman on them, and he pocketed them for later enjoyment. He noticed that his heart was beating very hard over the turn of events in romance, and he felt a fresh start was happening.

He opened the mail addressed to the LaPoint Outfit and found more requests to purchase horses from Mr. Winger and the Second Cavalry, and a printed letter from Charles Goodnight suggesting a mutual endeavor to go along with the remuda deal they had already arranged. The offer suggested a meeting in San Antonio later that month, at the delivery of the second remuda to a Goodnight herd, so LaPoint wrote a reply agreeing to this, and mailed it. Invigorated by the fresh business opportunities, they redoubled their efforts to meet the requests, working from before dawn to sunset, building remudas.

Chapter Ten: Goodnight Trail West

The early summer of 1872 was steaming hot in San Antonio, and the horse-ranchers Josh LaPoint and Gabe McBride were anxious to conclude their meetings with buyers, trail bosses, and General Augur's adjutant with army contracts, and to get up to the cool waters of the Blanco, where they had horses to gather and shoe and deliver back to San Antonio for Bud Winger's drive to Abilene, and others destined for the army forts. They had been in San Antonio for several days, and were tired of the city and the paperwork side of the horse business.

Texas had been readmitted to the Union in late March of that year, and their business with the army had increased greatly after that, as pressure built for the troops to stop the increasing Indian and border bandit depredations. The last meeting on their horse contract list was with Charlie Goodnight, whom they had supplied remudas to before, and he was already eating breakfast in the dining room of the Menger hotel when they joined him.

"Wal, good morning, Charlie, ain't ya puttin' on a little bit o weight?," said Gabe.

Goodnight just nodded and kept eating. "Trying to pack some on for ta burn off later, McBride, LaPoint, sit down and eat. Here, have a good cigar from my bag here, I know you like 'em. I couldn't wait til yal chose to arise from your long beauty rest, as ya can see. Got lots to do. I thought ole ranger McBride always got up before dawn to make his sourdough biscuits."

While Goodnight was talking, McBride was staring at his arm and hand holding the fork, then at the other one holding the coffee. He took the big rum-soaked crooked cigar Charlie offered and slipped it into his shirt pocket, all the while staring at Goodnight's arm.

"What the hell are you looking at, McBride?"

"I's just checking, seems like every time ya bend an elbow, yer mouth flies open."

"Seems like every time your mouth flies open, you put your elbow or foot in it, Ranger McBride. Waitress, get this guy some coffee, please."

LaPoint laughed, often amused at the interchange between the two ex-rangers, since Goodnight had been wrangling with them at the Menger over remudas for years, since he had began running herds west.

Gabe continued to check Charlie out, staring at the plate with three eggs and grits and potatoes with onions and biscuits and a scorched steak, with a plate of bacon on the side. Gabe scooted the chair back with a loud noise which attracted the notice of the whole room, and sat down with a grin.

"Wal Charlie, I already knowed you got extra helpin's of everything except patience, so don't wait ta eat on our account. I didn't get ta sleep til late last night, on accounta somebody next door playing rhythm on tha bed springs."

"Hell I been up for hours, rode in from Leon Springs this morning, already sent four telegraphs. That steak is so tough I ordered some pork after I tried to cut it. They burnt all the taste out too."

"How's the biscuits, or did ya just swallow 'em whole?"

"Bout half as tasty as yours. McBride. I guess you got it hand's down on sourness, huh? Mr. LaPoint, you got that remuda ready for me?"

"Almost. How's the potatoes and eggs?" replied LaPoint.

"Good. ...onions good too. Grits too thin. Coffee's weak, too. I'm used to a good chuck wagon cook who does it just how I like it. How many horses you got ready?"

"Forty finished out as saddle mounts"

"Wassa matter, coffee not thick enough, couldn't stand a horseshoe in the coffeepot?" said the older scout. Charlie was about four years older than LaPoint, who was thirty at that time, while Gabe was near sixty, though his movements didn't show it.

Ignoring Gabe, Charlie concentrated on LaPoint, talking while spearing a piece of steak. "Any more on line?"

"About a dozen nearly finished, already bridle trained and carrying bareback."

"How about that gray pacer, you must be done with training it now, eh, or maybe you're too in love with him to let go?"

"It's already under contract to the army, like I told you last time, Charlie."

"But no money has changed hands yet."

"We shook on it. And we're delivering horses to the forts next. We already supplied a riding mount for General Augur a few days ago. They're expecting the rest."

"One-armed Bill said you had a filly that was from the same stock, your stallion and the big mare."

"Sorry, Charlie. Traded it to Britt Jonson for telescopes and a new Sharps, and some cash."

"Mighta known. That ole squaw humper! Now that's a scout and shooter I could sure use. Britt still going strong with his business, freighting and trading?" Charlie never slowed down his eating, as he spoke between bites.

"Going strong, and he said to say hello. You told us you don't like mares as much anyway, too much nickering at passing Comanches."

"Alright, that's true, I prefer a gelding to ride and mares for breeding on my ranch, but I want the next colt from your stallion and that Kentucky mare."

"Deal." LaPoint offered his hand on it, and they shook.

"What if it's my buckskin that knocks her up, Charlie?" asked Gabe.

"That'd be alright too, though I hear his gray is faster."

"A touch, maybe, but that Buck is shore good for the long ride," said Gabe.

"Which forts do you deliver mounts to?"

"Martin Scott, McKavett, and Concho."

"And you already got Mr. Winger his horses?"

"We owe him a few more, gonna deliver them here in three days."

"You know he's going to Dodge this year, don't ya...the rail head is moving out by the fort."

"Trailing further west, through the staked plains then," said McBride. "Through the heart of Comancheria."

"Right. There will be a beaten trail there soon, a mile wide and bare of grass. No squatters to contend with, just Indians. When do you plan to arrive at Fort Concho?"

"We're heading out to get the horses after this meeting. Should be there in two weeks."

"Perfect. How are the saddle mounts?"

"Good, a sturdy mix."

"Good as last years?"

"Better, about half of them are the bigger crossbred mounts, but they can still live on grass like the mustangs. We've about stripped the area around the ranch of good mustangs a couple of years ago, so we're doing more breeding with larger eastern stock, producing a slightly bigger horse that can still live on grass if need be."

"Perfect. I need to watch you train horses someday, for you're sure getting the best results. They're horses that want to please the rider, and they learn working cattle real quick like. And they're tough, they all make it through the dry stretch to the Horsehead crossing."

"You'd be welcome to my round-pen, Charlie. I let them run, and I let them return to the fold, so to speak. It's a better way than beating them to submission. Makes a better, more willing, spirited mount. Horses want to be friends with us."

"Friends! Why I spend more time with Blackie than anyone else. I'd be nowhere without good horses. This whole frontier country would be empty except for a few starving digger Indians, chasing worms and grubs and grasshoppers."

"That's for shore," said Gabe.

"Yes, that's right," nodded Josh. "We owe it all to the horse."

Charlie quit eating and looked at them both in turn. "Men, I only need one more thing."

"What's that?"

"Hear me out now. I need ten horses now, today, and for you and McBride here to bring thirty to Fort Concho to meet the herd arriving there in about two weeks, and run the herd out west for me, scouting and ramrodding it. Mr. Loving my old partner who helped lay out the trail west, is gone now, rubbed out by Comanches, and I need some reliable men to get cattle to Fort Sumner. Last couple of years I had some fellas just wasn't up to the job, lost lots of the profit on missing stock. I'll make it well worth your while."

"Well," said LaPoint, and looked at McBride, then spoke.

"Our outfit is tied up with horse work, and we don't have any real cattle drovers, just horse wranglers. Haven't worked a cattle drive in many years either, and then it was in wet grassy country."

"I got experienced drovers who can handle the cattle, the cowhands are already there bringing the herd to Fort Concho. I need someone who can handle men, and can scout the trail, take charge and make sure it goes through. I know that you whipped up the best vaquero outfit and ranch operation to herd, breed, and train horses in a very short time. I figure you can do the same with cattle drovers."

"He can handle men like he handles horses," said Gabe.

"Sure you can. They're good waddies, half of them have been before, some have driven up north to the rail heads. Treat 'em right, they'll do the job. I need someone who treats everyone on their merits and performance, nothing else, not race, age, size, nor tall talk. I need a determined man who don't take no for an answer, and who whips slackers and fractious hands into shape fast or runs them off. One-armed Bill has already told me all about your outfit, and I think you're the man. And McBride's as good a scout as ever was, and knows how to stay hidden and watch for rustlers. Wilson says I should get Jackson too, for his shooting. What do ya say, men?"

"Waugh," said Gabe, looking at LaPoint. "You was wantin' ta go to Taos, this would be a way to get paid doin' it. Might find some family in tha bargain."

"I figured we'd go across the staked plains, see that Palo Duro canyon you've been telling me about."

"Hell, I wanted to see that since I first heard about it, ain't seen it yet. It'll still be there when this is done," said Goodnight.

Gabe finally said his piece. "Comanches really raising hell up that way now, Josh. Kiowa too, got that wild medicine man, Maman-ti, with a talking owl for a hand puppet, stirring the bands up ta kill all the whites. We can avoid them and ride up into the mountains just past Las Vegas, on the old trail to Taos, after this route up the Pecos. I know that country."

"You know that way, out the Concho and Pecos?" asked LaPoint.

"Why hell yes, guided mining parties out the Concho, and further to the west in '49 and '50, 'til I caught the cholera from them and liked ta went under, like lots of the Indians did. Later I guided miners inta the Cimarron canyon and Mt. Baldy, way on past the headwaters of the Pecos. The cattle trail's mostly the old trails we laid out to California, that the Butterfield stages take now. The worst stretch is from the headwaters of the Concho to the Horsehead crossing of the Pecos. No water thar."

"That's right," said Charlie as he sawed his tough steak and dipped it in gravy. "McBride knows his trails. Ranger scout. Probably watches swallows to find water too, eh?"

"Yeah, he does. Examines horse turds for insect tracks, licks the rocks to taste for horsepiss..."

The middle-aged blond German waitress had finally spotted the newcomers and had arrived to take their order.

"Hate to break up this interesting gab, but would guys like to order? We don't have any insects, nor horse...products, of any kind. "

"I'll have what Mr. Goodnight's having," said LaPoint. "but no meat..."

"I'll have the Spanish omelet, no meat, with potatoes on the side," said Gabe.

"No meat?" asked Charlie, "I thought that's all you ever ate, usually raw."

Gabe chuckled. "Only on the trail. I carry my own buffalo jerky in this little pouch, agrees with my old stomach better than that tough cow, or pig."

"You old tracker, gemme some of that jerky."

"I thought you might want a taste, made it myself, shot the buffalo on the Pedernales."

"Damn, that's good. This and sourdough biscuits too, huh? You know they was always holding you up for me to emulate when I was a ranger for Captain Jack Cureton, don't ya, McBride? You and Jack Hays."

"Naw, I didn't."

"Yeah, yal set the standard we tried to live up to, though we got blamed for some of the foul deeds that Baylor crowd was doing, by some folks. Hellfire. Tophat McBride. Then you and Britt getting them French gals back by yourselves after all the rangers gave up, a sure fire miracle."

"Luck and a giant black man with a good aim on that one. I got one or two of them at first, but when they moved back far away ole Britt arched some shots into them I still can't believe, at eight hundred yards at least. We was game for anything back then, like roosters on a dung-heap, I reckon."

"You game for this drive, you old rooster?" asked LaPoint, staring at McBride. Goodnight stopped eating, knowing this was the tipping point. He stared at Gabe, who stared back.

"Why hell yes, if you are, Charlie's already done packed the trail with several herds. Only tough part is that hundred miles between the Concho and the Pecos. We can deal with gyp-water when we have to."

"Alright then," said Josh. "I'm ready to get away from Helena for a while. It's been five years ranch building there, and the fighting for stock only gets worse."

"You two are pards in everything, huh?"

"I reckon so," said Gabe.

"Yes," said Josh. "He's like an old boot one grows used to, even with the heels run down and holes in the toes."

"LaPoint, you should treasure your old pard here, ornery as he is, for you never know when you will lose him.

"Yeah," said Gabe. "Who'll cook yore biscuits then, boys?"

"Yeah, or reads the tracks," said Josh.

"I had a good old pard, Mr. Oliver Loving, killed by Comanches, and I sure do miss him. He was a fine cattleman. He gave me this hat here. I call this my Loving crease, runs the rain off. Someday you'll be able to buy this type hat in any store in the west, I reckon. I'm gonna make it famous, gonna spread cattle ranching all up the plains in it, for my old partner's memory. This here's my Loving crease. Want me to put one in your hats?"

"No thanks," said Josh.

"It is a fine hat," said Gabe. "We's sorry ta hear about old Loving, and we heard about how you carried his body back in a tin box with charcoal dust. He dang sure didn't go down without a good fight, I expect."

"That's the kind of men I want to ride for me."

"Well, we'll ride for you, and we won't go down without a good fight, I venture," said LaPoint. "And we have a few good hands to bring with us. Jesse and Pancho are top vaqueros for any stock. Tom Jackson is as good with a rifle as with a rope, and don't back down under fire."

"Well, there's liable to be a fight. McBride here will be scouting more for rustlers than water, for the cattle trail just goes up the middle Concho to where there ain't no more water til the Pecos. Mostly he's gonna be using armed outriders like for a ranger party, watching for rustlers. He ain't too old for that, is he?"

"What am I, tits on a boar? I can still pull a trigger more than once, ya nippin' wolf pups, and nobody surprises me scoutin'."

"He can still scrap with the best of them. We're a good fighting team, when we need to be," said LaPoint. And like I said, we have Tom Jackson, a top hand and good shooter with a rifle. I'm pretty sure he'll come. And I imagine I can get two good vaqueros and a pretty good young wrangler from our outfit."

Goodnight stopped eating and stared into LaPoint's steady gaze. "I believe you can do the job, LaPoint. You and McBride and Jackson, and who else you chose."

"You got anything against bringing our vaqueros, Pancho and Jesse and maybe another, and a kid to help with the remuda. Tejano hands?"

"Why heck no, race nor age don't matter to getting the job done. Vaqueros is past masters at herding and roping."

"Alright then. So we're throwing in with ya, Charlie," said McBride. "If the reward is sufficient."

"That's what I hoped. The reward will suffice. Can you bring a wagon to gather calves and carry extra water and such?"

"Yep," said Gabe. You got one of your chuck wagons with the drive now, and a good cook?"

"Yeah, yal lucked out in that regard. We're using two wagons to cross that bad stretch now, with lots of extra water barrels, and space for calves born on the drive. I got a chuck wagon with the herd now, and a good cook, E. Earl, been on two drives already."

"Alright," nodded Gabe. "I'll fix ours up for it, build a rack for extra barrels. Maybe a travois setup too, for firewood and such, calves, and injured drovers?"

"Sound like you done this before, as I was told."

"Drove herds to New Orleans, before the war, both of us, LaPoint was the teenaged horse wrangler."

"So I can count on you advising him about pointing the herd, running the drive?"

"Why shore. He can handle men."

"You build what you think you need on the wagon, you clever ole rascal. Bill said yal got a hell of a nice smith shop down there, and really good mules. Really glad to have yal sign on. All I need now is another lead bull to hook a bell on."

"We happen to have one," said LaPoint. "I think he's sweet on Gabe, too."

"Yep," replied Gabe with a broken grin, "We still got old Plunger. We'll take a shot at it."

"Well, alright, then, it's signed and sealed.

"Well, alright then," replied LaPoint, and Charley

Goodnight dove back into his breakfast with relish, satisfied that he had achieved his first objectives of the day. The other breakfasts arrived, and they all filled their bellies while their heads filled with thoughts of the drives coming up. Charlie poured information into LaPoint as they ate, all the particulars of driving cattle west. Goodnight eventually nearly slid his plate off the table, trying to cut his thick steak with a dull knife.

"Here Charlie, try this," said McBride as he pulled out his razor sharp belt knife and handed it to Goodnight. Charlie laughed and took the huge knife to cut his steak into good sized pieces, the gleaming edge separating the meat pieces easily. He admired the knife and handed it back, shaking his head.

"So that's a McBride knife, huh? Heard about them for years. I'd like to have one, a little smaller, someday. That's a damned grizzly bear knife."

"Well treat us right and one might take a shine to ya, Charlie. I have stabbed a grizzly with that knife, come to think of it, but I cleaned it off since then, I think....not too sure, though, old and feeble as I am."

"You ain't gonna buffalo me, I've et bear and snake with equal relish, McBride, dog and horse too. And I drank horse blood on the staked plains. You know, there's more rustlers than before on this trail, and scouting's going to be dangerous for that reason. More watching for rustlers than looking for water holes, since there ain't any for a hundred miles anyway. But the rustlers are working on the headwaters of the Concho now, so you gotta see them before they see you...like the old ranger days, huh? See everything without being seen."

"We'll get the job done, Charlie, and get ya a nice knife too. I got some dandies that Josh and I pounded out this past winter, turned out beautiful and tough. With 64 layers."

"64 layers, sounds like my mom's hen house, McBride. Well you've already made my day, and it ain't past breakfast yet," replied Goodnight. "You want some more cigars, Gabe? I got several hundred. Trade you a dozen for more of that jerky."

"Alright, cigars are good for staying awake on a late night."

"Oh yeah," said Josh. "Like the time you dozed off and set your shirt on fire down on the Nueces."

"Waugh. It'll dang shore wake ya up, shirtfire. Here, I got some flint, lemme show ya."

"You sure you don't want to take Gabe with you, Charlie. I know he couldn't replace Mr. Loving, but the biscuits?"

"Naw, yal fit together like a pair of boots. You keep him."

They made their trade and concluded the breakfast with several cups of coffee, hashing out the particulars of the deal.

Josh signed the LaPoint outfit to work for top wages and a share, plus extra for the use of the wagon,mules, and lead bull. They stood up and made firm handshakes all around to seal the deal. LaPoint would oversee the remuda and ramrod the herd and crew, while McBride advised him while spending most of his time scouting for rustlers, leading the herd from water to water, and making sourdough biscuits when he was in camp, for his sourdoughs soothed many a grumbling stomach. They headed back out to the corrals near the old mission ranch outside of town, and filled in Tom Jackson and Jesse on the background and details.

The Goodnight-Loving trail had been established in 1866 by Charlie and his older partner, Oliver Loving, who had already driven a herd up the Arkansas River and front range of the Rockies to the mining camps at Denver. Since that time Charlie had delivered many herds to New Mexico and up the Rockies to the northern plains.

Starting with supplying the ill-planned and ill-fated mixed Indian reserve at Bosque Grande, Loving and Goodnight spread range cattle up the eastern face of the Rockies. Along with the cattle, the ranching culture was spreading up the high plains, though Colorado would not allow the direct importation of Texas cattle until they had wintered a year in New Mexico, which Charlie soon facilitated with his Apisha ranch just south of the line. He had made the transition from ranger scout to wide ranging cattleman with the same drive that characterized all his activities, and had pushed the frontiers of cattle ranching further than any man.

For the 1872 drives, Goodnight was prepared to receive the cattle at Fort Sumner, after they staggered up the bitter Pecos following the long hot trek across the scorching prairies between the headwaters of the south Concho and the Horsehead crossing. Goodnight himself took a mixed herd of 1400 soon after the meeting with the LaPoint outfit in late June, while LaPoint was to receive his cattle herd at Fort Concho on the first of July, the beginning of the scorching season, and head west with the Goodnight herd two weeks ahead of him.

Charles Goodnight had not been a bit shy about filling Josh LaPoint's head that morning with instructions and directions about moving the herd west in summer. He knew how to do it, from bitter experience, and wanted it done that way. Of particular importance was keeping the main body strung out and grazing as much as possible, until the grass ran out, with the remuda protected from Indians and rustlers by being kept between the herd and chuck wagon. The other main point Goodnight stressed was to avoid running weight off the cattle by avoiding overheating, over packing them too tight, and pushing them too fast while not letting them graze enough.

With Goodnight running several herds that year, and moving a big one himself up ahead of the LaPoint outfit, Josh and Gabe were sure that he would be dropping back by to check on the herd. He had worked out successful methods for driving cattle to the west, and he made sure those methods were applied when he could. He was already known for long hard horseback trips in remarkable times, for he left nothing to chance if he could see to it himself.

After absorbing all the cattle trailing knowledge they could from Charles Goodnight, they returned to the Blanco ranch and finished out the rest of the remuda, utilizing Jesse and Pancho for saddle training to speed the process.

It was a rush of work to get the horses finished on the Blanco, deliver Mr. Winger's remuda, and hustle with the rest of Charlie's remuda north to meet the herd. Since they were going to the army forts to deliver mounts and meet the herd at Fort Concho, LaPoint decided that he was finally finished with training the big gray pacer, Scorpio's first foal out of the Kentucky mare, and took the 3 year old stallion up to deliver to Lt. Peter Boehm at Fort Concho, fulfilling the last of their Army contracts for that year.

Lt. Peter Boehm had the gray pacer contracted for when it was a yearling. He said it was for Colonel Ranald Mackenzie, the new commander of the 4th Cavalry, who needed a smooth-gaited pacer because of all his war wounds. They got the best price they had ever received for a single horse, but Josh hated to part with the magnificent intelligent animal he had spent so much time training. He hoped the Colonel would appreciate what a fine stallion he received, with such a comfortable smooth gait, and war training besides, but he knew he would miss the clever and noble beast, the first colt of his own stallion, whom he had grown to love. Scorpio, on the other hand, seemed glad to see him go, since he had been taking so much of LaPoint's time.

When LaPoint got there with the gray pacer on the big open parade ground of Fort Concho, Lt. Boehm got the Colonel out of his quarters to watch the horse while LaPoint put him through his paces, displaying various gaits, his blazing speed on the open stretch, instant cutting and turning ability, rapid spins in either direction, skidding stops and turns, and the old time warhorse skills of kicking out with front and rear hoofs, or walking on his hind legs effortlessly while milling his legs in front of him, hoofs flashing in the sun.

Then LaPoint rode up to the Colonel and dismounted while laying the horse down flat on the parade ground, stepping away as the horse remained prone until given the command to rise. Then Josh got the horse circling riderless in an expanding circle as he stood in the middle, signaling with hand and whistle. At a signal the horse would reverse direction and circle in the opposite direction, another signal made him move faster, another brought to a standstill, and a sharp shrill whistle brought him hurrying back to Josh, whom he touched noses with and nickered. Scorpio, standing off to the side, gave a shrill scream and nicker, feeling left out, but he stood exactly where LaPoint had left him, his reins on the ground.

Colonel Mackenzie, a medium sized man with brown mustache, oft wounded, oft decorated, oft promoted veteran of the Civil war, was duly impressed, and selected the horse for his own mount. He thanked LaPoint for the excellent job of training the flawless gray Pacer.

"You're quite the horse breeder and trainer, LaPoint. General Grant himself would have been impressed with what I just witnessed, and he is a great man with horses also. Where did you learn all this? I've never seen a stallion so well-trained."

"I learned as a kid from an old Choctaw horseman, and then later from a Spanish gentleman who came over with some horses, from Andalusia. Also, I studied at the school in Vienna for a while, for the jumping moves. I learned on my own horse, Scorpio. And from laying on the ground watching a small herd for days at a time as a kid."

"Interesting. Your stallion there is the sire of this big

gray?"

"Yes Colonel. And a big Kentucky mare is the dam. Take a ride sir. He will walk at first click of the heels, then move into a long pacing gait at the second. I think that's what you want, sir, according to what Lieutenant Boehm told me. I have written down all the signals for each movement he knows."

The colonel looked at the paper, studied it for a moment, then mounted and quickly moved the big gray into his smooth fast pacing gait, making a smooth and rapid circuit of the parade grounds.

"Perfect, LaPoint," he said as he came back and dismounted. "My kingdom for a smooth-gaited horse."

"The better to suffer the 'slings and arrows of outrageous fortune' with, eh, Colonel?"

"And 'take up arms against a sea of troubles'! I didn't expect a reader of Shakespeare for a horse trainer. What a fine mount, LaPoint! He walks really fast and smooth. Such a fine disposition for a stallion, so collected. I'm told that you ride with scout Gabe McBride, who also rides a trained Andalusian stallion, and they never bicker."

"Right, sir. The cavalry in Spain would have a line of a hundred stallions with no bickering, in the old days. Only the most trainable Andalusian stallions are allowed to breed. This horse knows all the battle moves except jumping in the air and kicking out with front and hind legs."

"Oh come on man, no horse can do that."

LaPoint smiled, whistled Scorpio over and mounted him, circled out to attain speed, did a series of front lead changes, then skid to a halt, whirled the horse one way and then the other, had him rear and kick out, then kick out with his rear legs, then jump up and kick out with both. He did it again to make sure the Colonel got the full effect. Then he reared the stallion up and walked it forwards and backward while it flailed out with flashing hoofs, all while the reins were hooked on the saddle horn and his hands were held to his thighs.

"This one is the best to learn first, Colonel. Very effective in close fighting conditions, controlled with the heels while your hands are free to fire weapons. And all of our horses are trained to gunfire and do not bolt."

"Damned amazing, LaPoint. Look at that, Boehm! Damned amazing."

"I told you sir. Worth the wait, Colonel?" asked Lt. Boehm.

"Yes, that's a war horse worth keeping. My sincere thanks to both of you."

LaPoint rode another fast circle with hands resting on his thighs, reversed directions and rode back and dismounted, and the Colonel shook hands with him and held on to his hand while looking up into his eyes with his piercing gaze.

"That was the finest horse work I have ever seen, sir. You should be training horses for us here while your partner McBride scouts for us to find these Comanche raiders committing depredations and escaping back to reservations. You could scout for us too. We could have a special detachment with horses trained like that."

"No thanks, Colonel. We're tied up with big commitments now. Running a horse business, developing two ranches. Going to take a cattle herd out west, to boot."

"The Goodnight Loving route?"

"Yes. We're working for Goodnight."

"So Peter told me. You'll be slipping out of our patrol range on that route, and we've had complaints of whole herds being taken by marauders lately. I hope your men are well armed, with plenty of ammunition, and lots of water."

"Yes sir. We're taking two wagons for extra water, and we're armed with the latest weapons."

"Keep my offer in mind, LaPoint, and convey it to McBride. I need him to scout for me on the staked plains. My Tonks and Seminoles don't know it, and are baffled to find a trail in that wiry mesquite grass that springs right back up an hour later. All the old timers say scout McBride knows the Llano Estacado better than anyone, and he doesn't go anywhere without you along."

"I'll mention it, sir. We appreciate the offer, and hope the big gray helps bring in the raiders. Folks along the frontier are mighty upset about all the raiding and rustling."

"Don't I know it. Which is why I need you men to scout for me. The damned newspapers..."

"Oh yeah, that paper, Colonel," said LaPoint, pointing to the paper wadded in the officer's jacket. "Like I said, I wrote down all the signals on the paper. Work through them a few times with him, getting to know each other, he likes to be talked to, seems to understand everything."

"Alright, I'll learn it by heart with him."

"Then you might have your adjutant file it, for it will be standard for all officer horses. I always curry him a bit before riding, talk to him some, rub his head and withers. You will love him, sir. I hate to part with him."

"Yes, LaPoint. I think I will. Does he have a name?"

"Just been calling him big gray, sir, leaving it for you to name him. Boehm contracted for the horse when we met at a horse auction in Sherman, two years ago, after he saw Scorpio show his stuff. He tried to buy Scorpio, so I agreed to sale of the colt when it was ready. I knew I was training another colt for a general or something."

"Colonel. I was a brevet general in the war, not now. Maybe I will be someday, though stars are scarce now in this army. I hope to bring in Kicking Bird and Maman-ti and Lone Wolf and Kiwih-nai and Para-coom and Mow-way on this horse. Thank you very much, LaPoint. Keep my offer in mind. I have scout jobs for both of you, if you wish to help me rid the area of this scourge of depredations."

"I wish you good fortune in your job, Colonel, and hope this horse helps a lot."

"I wish you the same running that herd out west, LaPoint. It's gotten more dangerous every year with rustlers out there. We have patrols out on the Middle Concho right now, but only to the headwaters. After that you are unprotected until Fort Sumner, without good water or cavalry patrols. Watch out for those Comanchero rustling crews. Keep outriders, all the time."

"Well, I think we both have dangerous jobs, Colonel. We'll have to protect ourselves. Until we meet again, good luck," said LaPoint as they shook hands again.

Paperwork and silver changed hands, goodbyes were passed between LaPoint and the big gray, and LaPoint turned his attention to moving the herd, which was grazing upstream, just outside of town. He mounted Scorpio, who screamed a shrill goodbye to his offspring, and headed across the river over to the saloon in San Angela to find Gabe while the big gray called after them. His eyes ran tears of parting with the horse he had raised from a foal. When he looked back from a bluff by the river, he saw the colonel pacing the horse around the parade grounds and felt satisfied that the special stallion he raised went to a good man who appreciated him.

He rode fast to the saloon in the small village that had sprung up by the fort, offering booze, gals, laundry, and eats to the soldiers. Gabe was sitting at a table with a big soldier, tall and broad shouldered with a long brown handlebar mustache. The old blacksmith was a little tipsy and waved his hand to Josh to join them.

"Here's the man now. Josh LaPoint, meet Corporal, no, Sergeant John Charlton from the fourth cavalry. He's the fella I talked about, fooling the Indians at Mountain Pass, lining his men up with sticks to resemble rifles, and the one that shot that murdering Satank when he tried ta escape."

LaPoint shook hands with the big fellow with beer suds in his handlebar mustache, but remained standing. "That story about giving your men sticks to look like rifles was a damned good one, Sergeant Charlton. Gabe here says you're a good hand with mules too. A man who endures mules gotta be alright in my book. And I heard Satank left you no choice, and I've been in that spot myself."

"Call me Jack, LaPoint. Did the Colonel like the big horse?" asked the big muscular soldier with a strong grip, who seemed tall even sitting down.

"Yes, he did. Apparently a rough ride puts him in pain, so he really liked the smooth gait. That big gray can walk faster than others trot, smooth as silk."

"Well it's a good thing, anything to settle his nerves. You should see him grimace when we trot. Makes him grumpy, or grumpier."

"I saw him watching some black masons, and he asked me what I thought of the stonework, since the adjutant had told him I did masonry. So I mentioned that I saw quite a few stacked vertical joints, not a good thing. He proceeded to give some black masons the what for about it in no uncertain terms, and had me show them how to avoid it, level off, and cross over, by the book."

"He's by the book and then some. He's a bit irascible at times, sparse with praise for good work, but a heck of a good commander, determined. He's got a lot of war wounds, makes him grouchy. They made him a brevet General in the war, then bucked him back to Colonel here. Did you notice his hand?"

"Yeah, thought of Gabe's hand when I saw it. Actually, I

heard it before I saw it. When he was chewing out the black masons, he took to snapping the stumps of his fingers. Got them shot off, I guess. Pretty intelligent guy, I thought. Seemed to take in a whole page of signals for the horse in one quick study."

"First in his class at the Point, and Grant called him the most promising young officer in the Army. He'll take care of these Comanches, if the top brass and the Indian ring let him. We got this crazy new peace policy now, which I guess the religious folks talked Grant into, and Sherman and Sheridan are against, so things are at crosscurrents. Plus the goods for the Indian's are being stolen before they get there, so they go raiding the settlements, then skedaddle back to the reservation. It's a damned mess. Of course yal heard about those freighters on the Warren supply train getting butchered, which at least got Sherman's attention."

"Hell yes," said Gabe. "We knew some of them fellas."

"They finally gave us the go ahead to chase raiders after that. So we chased Kicking Bird back from a raid, but he just ran back to the reservation while our mounts played out for lack of grain. We need some better scouts than these Tonkawas and Seminoles, folks like McBride here that knows the area. Mounts that can live on grass too, and lots of them. They always have extra mounts, them we're chasing. While we're slowed down hauling wagon-loads of grain for ours. Why don't you guys..."

"No thanks," said Gabe.

"We're committed," said LaPoint.

"That's what Lt. Boehm said you'd say."

"Well, I'd like to sit and visit, but I'm sure Gabe's got the news from you, and told you more than you wanted to hear. We need to start moving that herd," said LaPoint.

"Hell, he's getting like Charles Goodnight now, can't sit down," said Gabe. "Next he'll be smoking thirty cigars a day and riding all night, burning out horses."

"You know better than that. Daylight's burning, pard."

"Well, good luck to you men," said Charlton as he stood up to shake hands, towering above them. "LaPoint, if you have any more of those larger mounts, I need a big horse like Mckenzie got, one that can thrive on grass too."

"Damn, you're big. Hate to have to wrestle you. I'll have some big horses in spring, Jack, out of other big mares I bought, and the Andalusians."

"Wrestle hell, McBride just beat everyone in the bar arm-wrestling for the price of beers. That's why he's tipsy, won about five matches. My arm's still sore. Sure strong for an old guy."

"Ain't old, just seasoned," said Gabe.

"Blacksmith arms. I'll keep you in mind for a big horse, Jack."

"May our path's cross again," said the big sergeant.

So LaPoint and McBride rode out to lead the herd west from where they were grazing on the Middle Concho River outside of town. As soon as they arrived and met with the point riders, Gabe rode off in front to scout while LaPoint conferred with Jackson. Pancho and Miguel, his best vaquero, were riding point, and Jackson was guard and outrider, with one rifle out and another in his saddle scabbard. Everyone signaled they were ready with waves of their big straw hats, then one by one the drovers slipped big bandana's up over their noses.

When all had signaled readiness, LaPoint gave a wave of his hat and a loud yell that rolled off the river banks to head them out. "Let's get it rolling! Move the herd!"

The wagons started moving, with E. Earl bellowing a loud hurrah and ringing the triangle from the chuck wagon. The clanger was un-padded from the lead longhorn's bell by Jesse, and the bull began to plod west, leading the mixed herd of 1500 as the drovers popped their lariats and did some yips and whistles. Dust began to rise from the already beaten trail as they pointed towards the Pecos.

They had a huge chuck wagon, well designed by Goodnight on an old Army freight wagon, and another smaller wagon that McBride had fashioned with a metal rack for extra water barrels. The horse remuda was always to be kept right between the wagon and the cattle, to protect them from rustlers, with the extra mules trailing them. LaPoint hustled around to get the drovers to stretch out the herd as Goodnight had lectured him, to retain weight.

Any other bull that tried to pass the old longhorn with the bell would get hooked with the horns, which spread about five feet, so the lead position was soon established, and the pace was steady behind the brindled old veteran with swaying horns. The drovers spread out the herd and they moved west along the middle Concho river with its grassy banks, sounds of cattle and drovers with their herding calls filling the dusty air.

    A cattle drive west into the alkali barrens was a slow, dusty, and monotonous process, with the cowboys surrounding the herd and pointing the lead, never pushing the animals, allowing them to graze as they moved, nudging the stragglers and rounding up strays, picking up calves to carry along, keeping them strung out just right so they didn't overheat and lose weight and endurance, keeping them calm, eliminating the stampede starters at the beginning, leaving the herd to satiate their thirst at the available freshwater creeks to sustain them on the long waterless stretches. Movement was constant except for bedding down at night.

    The drovers were rotated as well, except for the point riders, whose jobs required too much expertise to trade off. Pancho and Jesse quickly gained the point positions with their vaquero skills. Ben Burnett maintained the large remuda under the close directions of LaPoint, and Jackson was in charge of the out-riding guards, because of his sure aim with a Spencer repeater from horseback. LaPoint maintained outriders all around the herd, with mirrors and established ways of signaling by the positioning and movements of a scout's mount..

    The chuck wagon provided a home kitchen on the road, and LaPoint spared nothing on the food, but allowed no strong liquor, except when he provided brandy to the outfit on rare occasions. The second wagon carried extra water barrels, fresh calves that were dropped along the drive, shelves for storage, and a big meat smoker made by McBride. Since the familiar wagon with the mules were going, LaPoint allowed Suzette to go as well, for the chihuahua seemed to thrive on heat anyway. She rode with E. Earl in the wagon, sometimes hanging out on the shelf in back and watching Ben Burnett with the remuda right behind the wagon. She slept in the wagon boot and guarded the camp at night, ever vigilant with her big ears.

    With Gabe's help Josh learned to read cattle like he could read horses, knowing their condition at a glance. The long herd became like a single organism to him, and with a glance or cock of his ear he could tell how it was doing. He swung between the remuda and the point of the herd, where he watched for Gabe, up ahead scouting and signaling back with mirrors and horse positioning about the route.

    At Goodnight's directions they kept a bell on the lead bull

they had brought from the rancho, a trail veteran, who plodded a steady pace and pulled the herd along with the loud clanging. At night they stilled the clanger with a pad, only to release it when they were ready in the morning, and the old brindle bull would get up and start trudging and clanging, the whole herd rising to follow.

The drive went steady and calm at the beginning, without major incidents. Pancho and Jesse did a good job of riding point and keeping the nose of the herd tight and on line behind LaPoint, who followed the scout McBride.

Sourdough biscuits and deluxe coffee and breakfast got the men to working early in good spirits. E. Earl awoke very early and watched Gabe make his special recipe to learn to do it when Gabe was out scouting. Then he rang that triangle and blew his cow-horn to call the hands. They had a cask of honey and one of molasses to go with the biscuits, so several dutch ovens full were made every morning, and drovers nibbled all day on biscuits. The drovers soon found that LaPoint treated everyone fairly and well, so the trailing proceeded smoothly. There was enough grass from recent rains to sustain the grazing as they moved west.

As Gabe started to ride out from a conference with LaPoint on the second morning, a big black raven lit in a short live oak tree nearby and began to caw in a loud voice. They looked at the bird in amusement, his black feathers iridescent in the sun. He seemed to be eyeballing Gabe, who eyeballed it back.

Gabe began to caw back at it in a near perfect imitation. The bird responded with faster caws, as if in animated conversation. Josh laughed some more. "You old crow," he said.

"Buffalo nearby," said McBride as he turned Buck and readied to go scout the way. "Don't let the cattle bolt when we meet them. I'll flash my mirror continuous and circle Buck, then rear him up, when I come upon them."

"Ha! If you come upon them."

"When I spot 'em. According to my friend the raven, it's a big herd, too big to go around. We gonna mix herds, 'cording to him."

LaPoint gave back an incredulous look, shook his head, then burst out laughing. "So you say. That's a pretty good bird imitation, and I suppose the Comanches can do the same?"

"Yep, but ya can tell the difference from the echo, for the human imitation has more echo than a bird."

"So your friend says buffalo ahead, huh?"

"Lots."

"Okay, I'll lay in wait to see that."

"Could get both herds nervous. I'll signal back when I spot the herd, like I said."

"Okay, I never made any money betting against you."

"Alright, then," said Gabe as he whirled Buck towards the lead direction for the herd, which was bawling up behind them.

Josh shook his head, smiling and watching Gabe nudge Buck towards the west and charge off, as the raven sat and looked at him, then uttered three more raucous caws and flew off in the same direction.

Two hours later LaPoint saw Gabe's fluttering mirror signal, looked through his field glasses, and saw the buckskin stallion making a circle and rearing up, twice. Riding to a higher point on the rolling prairie, he stilled Scorpio and stood in his saddle stirrups with the field glasses, spotting a vast field of brown in the grassy flats behind McBride. He also saw McBride looking back at him with the brass telescope he favored, and grinning.

LaPoint alerted the drovers and had the word passed back, and forty minutes later they came upon a sprawling dark brown buffalo herd, too big to see the end of, and had to slowly make their way through it.

The tricky task was up to the drovers, Josh and the point riders Pancho and Jesse, to keep the animals from panicking as they met. You could see them all sniffing nervously as they met each others strange scents. Pancho started singing a Spanish lullaby as soon as he saw the buffalo herd, and was soon joined by Jesse as they tightened the front of the herd. LaPoint heard them and started humming along, not knowing the words. Soon every drover was singing softly, with lariats out and ready. They met the buffalo and the beasts all stared at them curious, slobbering and dripping drool as they watched the cattle plod along towards them.

Then LaPoint slow-paced Scorpio forward and the black tide of huge and powerful animals parted as the stubborn and steady bell bull plodded through behind Josh, his long horns swaying to clear a path. The cattle were nervous and spooky, but with the huge dark buffalo herd hemming them in, there was no place to stampede, and they plodded on through by the end of the day. The drovers had enough experience and savvy to know that a stampede by either group would be a disaster, and acted accordingly. Everyone picked up the melody sung by the point vaqueros as they eased through the black mass of buffalo. The cattle bawled and the buffalo grunted as the mass of mixed beef moved through the natives of the plains.

After they were through the brown shaggy sea of the buffalo herd and a few miles past, Jackson went back and harvested a fat cow to feast on, smoked in the metal oven Gabe had made for the second wagon, with the rest made into jerky for the trail. The tongue and hump were cooked for supper and enjoyed by the drovers, after a steady diet of beef. Gabe busied himself slicing the rest into thin strips to slow cure all night with a slow mesquite fire in the bottom of the smoker, which had firebricks on the bottom to hold steady heat, and valves to control air flow.

While they were hanging around the campfire, a scuffle started with one of the East Texas drovers yelling racist taunts at the two vaqueros who put their bedrolls near his. LaPoint fired him on the spot, told him to pack his rags and be gone from camp in ten minutes, looking at his big watch as he said it, then unstrapping the leather loop from his Remington .36 fast draw pistol. The drover was gone in five minutes, as LaPoint said anyone else would be, if they resorted to cheap racial or mocking taunts. With Cherokee and Seminole drovers riding with Tejano vaqueros and Anglo cowhands, LaPoint knew that fractious attitudes and actions had to be nipped in the bud. He was determined that all of his outfits would run smoothly on the merit system, and knew Goodnight would back him on that.

Heavy rains struck on the third day, from a rolling line of thunderstorms moving slowly from the west, indicating that grass might be freshened that way. The lightning of the storm got the cattle mighty nervous, but LaPoint had seen the storm coming and had all the wranglers out to forestall a stampede, which they did. The hard rain put more water in the upper Concho, and the stock fared well because of it, the fresh grass filling out their sides.

When they were about sixty miles from the fort after five

days out, LaPoint spotted a horseman with a streak of trailing dust, followed by another, riding fast towards the nose of the herd, where he rode about a half mile ahead of the point riders. Stopping beside the upper Concho bluff to take out his field glasses, he saw it was Charlie Goodnight followed by another rider, pushing hard in Charlie's dust trail, with his saddle trying to slip from under him on the bumps.

LaPoint rode over to a short sprawling mesquite tree and dismounted, took a leak against the trunk, then went to squatting in the small patch of shade until Charlie Goodnight rode up. When Goodnight reined in his lathered black horse, Josh was snacking on jerky and sipping his canteen. He then filled his hat to water Scorpio and Charlie's horse.

Goodnight, unlit cigar in his teeth, carried his repeating rifle balanced on his saddle horn, hooked on with a leather thong, and quickly undid the thong and slid it into the scabbard after scanning around the horizon. He dismounted in a hurry, his horse panting and blowing, his shirt soaked with sweat. LaPoint stood watering Scorpio with his hat, then gave some to Charlie's horse.

Goodnight exuded the powerful smell of a man who had been sweating into the same clothes for days. He looked sunburned, tired, and dusty, with streaks of mud on his shirt where the sweat had merged with dust in the wrinkles and dried to lines of flaking crust. His teeth were yellow from the juice of the cigar he chewed, and his goatee was caked in white dust.

LaPoint handed him a canteen and went back to squatting in the shade. "It's good water, but with a piece of cactus in the bottom to gather the dust. Don't shake it, nor take a bath in it, though you need one."

Charlie spit a pebble out of his mouth and took a sip, then another. Then he took off his glove and shook hands with LaPoint, saying, "Good to see you, LaPoint. I've been in the saddle twenty four hours. At first I thought it was you, but your horse seems lighter."

"Yeah, he's turning white while I get darker from the sun. Welcome to the only shade, Mr.Goodnight," said LaPoint as he gripped the cattleman's hand.

"Ouch, let off, gotta a tender hand. Damn, you got a grip like that old blacksmith. I got my hand jammed last night."

"Hell, I'm glad to see you, Charlie. I've never bossed a

herd before, and it's good to see the expert ride up, tell me how I'm doing."

Charlie spit his cigar out. "First McBride appears in front of me, nearly spooking my mount Blackie, then LaPoint appears, waiting in the only shade for miles. You two are quite a pair. Right where you oughta be, too, if there's a herd right back there. Scouting and pointing, you're making good time. How're the cattle looking?" Charlie tipped the canteen back, and his big Adam's apple chugged up and down for a while as he replenished his fluids, the excess stream dripping down his dark goatee.

"Good so far, Charlie, how are things with you?"

"Better now that I'm not drinking foul water from the bottom of a spent canteen. Where the hell's the herd?"

"About a mile back, or less."

"Any rustler trouble?"

"Not a bit, ran into a buffalo herd a ways out of Fort Concho, got the cattle a bit spooky, but no stampedes or rustlers, and enough grass and water to stay in shape. All the hands are doing well, though I fired one for some cheap race baiting."

"Did you do it loud, in front of the others?"

"Yeah."

"Glad to hear it. We got jumped by rustlers who cut out part of the herd, maybe a hundred head, but we laid into them and ran them off without a major stampede. I've been looking for sign of them or their compadres on the way back...reason for carrying my rifle out."

"Yeah, I saw how you rigged that with a leather thong, good idea, waste no time to start shooting, but won't drop if you're winged."

"Ranger days. Ready for ambushers."

"I've seen Gabe do it too."

"Yeah, he's doing it now. Hell,I started to ride over and tell McBride about the rustling band, but I'as too thirsty and hungry, so I figured I'd let you send word to him. Not that he wouldn't notice, but it's good to be forewarned."

"I thought the Indians were just after the remuda, that they hated cow meat, like Gabe."

"That's how it used ta be, but not now. This was renegades, whites, Mexicans, and Indians, over a dozen of them, very well mounted and armed, probably Comancheros trying to run the herd up to New Mexico for sale. About twenty miles ahead is where they jumped us, thought I'd come back and warn you while I could. When I rejoin my herd we'll cross the dry stretch to the Pecos. There will be no riding back then."

"So you saw Gabe, about two miles ahead, huh?"

"Yep, or he saw me, then I saw him, nearly spooked me..." said Charlie as raised his canteen to drink some more. After a long swig, he continued. "He gave me the all's well signal and kept scouting. Move over," Goodnight said as he squatted beside LaPoint, "You're taking every last bit of shade, I want to cool off a bit before Bill gets here.. hot damned sun today, no clouds...yeah....come on, Bill...he's a good pard, but his horse is jaded."

"Here he comes."

"He's gonna be pissed at me for not stopping earlier. The damned rustlers nearly shot him last night, put a hole in his hat, and he wasn't about to let me ride off alone, but his horse can't keep up with my big gelding there."

"Oh well, my ole pard gets pissed at me regular."

"Your old pard, Ranger McBride, damn sure don't show himself unless he sees who it is with that telescope he's carrying. He plumb scared the crap out of me, riding out of a gully in front of me before I ever knew he was around. Hell of a scout."

"He's got a nose for water and Indians, that's for sure. And a sense of direction that still amazes me. Want some buffalo jerky, Charlie?"

"Hell yes", replied the famished man as he went to gnawing on the reddish brown dried buffalo meat. "All I've had is some honey on a stale biscuit, and pecans with dirty water. Man, that's good, mesquite smoked, huh?"

The other rider pulled up and dismounted from a worn down mount, lowering the dusty bandana from his face, spitting a pebble from his mouth, snagging his horse reins onto his belt, then immediately grabbing his canteen and tilting it up with his good hand for long slow draws.

"Nice to see yer face, Charlie," he said, between swallows. "Thanks for the dust trail ta swallow."

"I said follow my dust trail, not swallow it, Bill. Have a drink, why don't ya," said Charlie as Bill's adam's apple glugged up and down.

"Wash it down so you'll have something to crap today. We both got the runs from gyp-water last night, drank some bad water in the Centralia draw."

After a long pull of fresh canteen water, Bill spoke. "Ooooh that's good." He leaned his chin towards Goodnight and half scowled, then addressed LaPoint.

"First he takes the best horse and don't hardly give me time to catch a spare, then he fusses at me for not keeping up, then he squats in the last of the shade. Charlie, you gonna tell me you didn't hear me hollering at you to stop for a minute for my saddle girth coming loose from my ganted horse? I about pulled the hair out of Shorty's mane trying to keep straight."

"Told ya he'd be pissed. Bill Wilson, shake with Josh LaPoint. Guess I don't have to mention his nickname is 'One-Arm', being he's got a hand missing."

Bill stopped his slow draining of the canteen and glared at Goodnight with a half grin. "That'd be like calling ole Britt 'Big-Black-Jonson' wouldn't it, boss? Anyway, I got the arm, just not the hand. Oughta be One-Hand Bill."

"Tuhubitu papii tasiwoo tenahpu! That's what the Comanche call old Britt. Black-headed Buffalo Man. What a good fella, hell of a scout and long-range shooter too. Set out to hire him too, you know."

"Yeah, but he's happy up on the plains."

Goodnight laughed, happy for a little bit of shade and fresh water, happy that he had reached his current goal, finding the herd.

"That was a long ride, even for me, glad to be out of the saddle," he said.

"How's that again, Charlie?"

"Tuhubitu papii tasiwoo tenahpu. Black-headed Buffalo Man."

"Shit, I never could figure how you could wrap your tongue around them Injun words. I think I'll just call him Britt, or Mr. Jonson. And I heard that LaPoint here out-shot him at a thousand yards down at Helena. Call me Bill, LaPoint, for Pete's sake."

"LaPoint," said Goodnight. "You got a reputation as a fine long-range shooter, but I notice you wear a small Remington in your right side tie-down quick draw holster and a big .44

Remington backwards on the left. You get better fast draw with the small gun and short barrel, I expect. I've heard you called lightning fast after you put two slugs in Ike Covington before he cleared leather. What caliber is it?"

"It's a .36 that Gabe modified, took the trigger out, adjusted the spring, fires with the thumb, real easy like."

"Can I take a look at it, or maybe you're superstitious about anybody touching it?"

"Sure, take a look, long as you don't thumb it and shoot your foot. I'm not superstitious. It fires as fast as the thumb will fan it, with a short action. The short barrel and small size make it faster to draw."

Goodnight took the weapon from LaPoint and studied it. "Trigger-less gun, never woulda thunk it, huh Bill? Light little bastard too. I think I see why you chose the Remington over the Colt, metal cartridges, loads from the front, fast and easy."

"Yeah. The trigger removal was McBride's idea, actually. The trigger was broken off anyway, so he experimented around with it. I had to practice with it a lot, on rattlesnakes, at first. Of course, the long barreled .44 has got a better whallop and accuracy for distance. I use one for speed when I need too, and one for knockdown, if I have the time."

"Well give me a Spencer or Henry rifle and good solid cover if I got the chance," said Goodnight.

"Me too," said Bill. "It'd save on hats, and heart quivers."

"Me too, if I get the chance."

"Nice balance to this thing," said Goodnight. "Is this what you outdrew Ike Covington with?"

"Yeah. Didn't know you'd heard about that."

"Hell, I've been in South Texas, LaPoint, heard the talk. But that ain't why I hired ya. Might be a bonus though."

Charlie tried to spin the gun on his big finger and nearly dropped it. "Opps, look-out now. Here, take it back before I shoot myself. Remind me to take you to the Trinchera Pass with me when they try to stop my herd at the Colorado line next time, and you can show me how you work them."

"Now that's a good idea," said Bill.

"Well I'd prefer to avoid any more pistol work, if possible, Charlie."

"I bet you have to work at that, with the word out about you being so fast and all, after the Covington shooting."

"Couldn't avoid that one."

"Yeah, well expect more of that kind coming up. Unavoidable. Though hopefully you'll keep them away with rifles. You got repeaters, huh? You're not hoping to keep rustler packs away with that single shot Whitworth I heard about."

"Oh yeah, I carry a Spencer seven shot on one side of my saddle, the Whitworth on the other."

Josh stood up with the canteen that Charlie handed back to him, and handed it to Bill after pouring some more into his hat for Scorpio and the other horses.

"Take a sit in the shade while you drink." LaPoint was glad to get into the breeze away from Charlie, who smelled like a man who had spent at least a day in the saddle. He went to each tired horse and watered it a bit from his hat.

Wilson slung the canteen on his shoulder and extended his one hand to rub his horse's neck. Both of their horses were worn out from the long hard ride. His other arm lacked the full hand, which had been shot off, according to campfire legend, but he used it pretty well anyway to clutch things to his body, or aim a rifle if he had to.

"Whew, that water is fine, glad to finally get ta see ya, LaPoint....been riding four hours straight at horse killing speed. Here's my hand ta shake, I don't have none ta spare when tippin' a canteen, if ya know what I mean."

"Yeah, howdy Bill. We've met before, when I delivered that remuda in San Antonio, and at the rancho on the San Antonio a couple of years ago. Didn't get to talk much then, with horse work and all."

"That's right, glad we meet again. If you weren't here I'd likely fallen off ole Shorty soon. I've needed to tighten my saddle girth for the last two hours, but damned it a man can get Charlie Goodnight to stop when he's on a beeline for something. I got ta tighten it now while he's stopped in the shade. How's tha herd? I done followed this man back twenty miles hellbent for leather after a pert near sleepless night ta find out."

"Herd's fine, Bill. Have some jerky, it's buffalo," LaPoint replied.

"Buffalo, damn!...thanks. Been eating tough ole pan-fried cow steaks for weeks. Hey, mesquite smoked, the best."

"Thank McBride, he made it. He's got a slow smoker set up on the second wagon."

"Oh yeah, that's good, sure 'nough. With his sourdough biscuits and this, I wish ole McBride was up with our herd," said Bill.

"Naw, you'll never shake those two apart," said Charlie. Bill Wilson set about tightening his girth strap, and then Charlie's. Both horses were snorting and blowing as he tightened the big belts around their shrinking bellies. Charlie's chunky muscular black gelding was shining with sweat, glistening like a crow's wing, and seemed in better shape than the bay gelding Williams was riding. LaPoint gave Scorpio some molasses corn feed after he finished the hat-full of water. Then he moved to the other horses to give them some, speaking softly to them.

"Charlie, I thought you would be further ahead of us," said LaPoint.

"I thought you'd be slower. Loving's son is up ahead of us with a lot of disorganization, and rustlers scattering his herd. Unless these miscreants got a big bunch of riders to steal the whole herd, they just scatter the herd and pick off the part they can handle, including the remuda if you don't keep it close. The Comanche always go for the remuda first. Comancheros go for a herd to sell."

"I've kept the remuda tucked away between the wagons and the drag, like you mentioned, about seven times."

Wilson let loose a gaffaw at that comment, and kept sipping water. Goodnight jerked his jaw around towards him but Bill spoke first.

"That sure is a fine lookin' stallion you ride, LaPoint. Does that long mane fly back in your face?" asked Bill with a smile.

"Well yeah, once in a while. I might trim it again soon."

"Well, it was good spottin' you and that pearly colored stallion. Charlie said you'd be on one, in front of the herd, and here you are."

"You're a man who does what he says he will, LaPoint. I like that. The boss up ahead of my herd ain't got your self discipline. They were leaving cattle scattered all over, so we slowed down to round them up. Then we slowed down when we found good grass and water to put the herd in shape to make that ninety miles of badlands. You'll come upon it when you hit the head-water creeks of the middle Concho, just a ways ahead.

Ain't much water in them but there's enough if you stop for a while and let the stock drink 'til they're full. Better fill your water barrels and water your horses first though, for it'll be a mud pit later on."

"So you spent a few days slowed way down, grazing and drinking, rebuilding their endurance?"

"Yep. And the rustling incident slowed us down a bit, re-gathering the steers."

"I'll vouch for that," said Bill. "Sonsobitches."

"Hellfire it's been one slowdown after another, then I got to worrying about this herd back here and slowed them down some more while I rode back to parley. The Comancheros and renegades are working this stretch now, since there are so many herds moving west. At first everybody told me it was impossible to come this way, and I was crazy. Then they all started following me soon as I made it." Charlie took another drink after his statement.

"Well, you got me following you."

"Yeah, someone with sense and reliability, finally. If you say you're gonna do it, you do it."

"I try my best to, Charlie, like you. Did the rustlers take a toll on your outfit?"

"Yep, the murdering varmints. Wounded four of our guys and killed one, but we only killed two of them, though we wounded several. Hell of a mess."

"Look at my good straw hat, put a hole in the crown, in and out, an inch lower and I'd been dead," said Bill, fingering the hole with his good hand.

"Got any idea who?"

"Mixed band of renegades, Comanches, Apache, and Comancheros. I think it was Polonio Ortiza and that damned Bison McCairn fella, got a big ginger colored mane like McBride used to, but thicker and more brown to it, dresses like an Apache, comes swooping in when you least expect it. These son's of bitches shoot to kill, mark my words. That renegade Bise McCairn used ta murder and rustle up around the Indian reserves in northeast Texas, part of the reason I left there, couldn't maintain a herd for the rustling."

Bill Wilson spoke up. "Some of the Fort Concho and Griffin officers say he's West Point trained and crazy from syphilis."

Charlie lit a cigar and continued. "Now the damned thieves come down here since there's lots of cattle coming this way. Only way to get shed of them is to kill them. Ride with your rifles out. Keep all your weapons cleaned and in good working order, and handy. Have all the outriders you can. Shoot them right out of the saddle if you get the chance."

"Alright, we'll double our guard. So maybe I should do the same with the herd, slow down and let the cattle fill up, huh?"

"Yep, about twenty five miles ahead, where the feeder creeks branch out north and south, two of them, that's the last of the good grass and water in the creeks, rest 'em there and let them fill up, and then move slowly south down those creeks until you run out of grass and water. Rest and feed them all day, then start in late afternoon and drive west all night and keep going til you get to Horsehead Crossing. Last time we made it in about sixty hours, with maybe ten hours of resting. And keep lots of armed guards up until then. After you get out past water you won't have to worry about rustlers anymore. Sounds simple,don't it?"

"Yeah, sure, Charlie. If you made it then we can."

"That's right, LaPoint. I made it several times already. Only ninety miles of alkali hell, part of it the damned gullies and gulches of the Centralia wash, with gyp water in it. We got caught in a cloudburst there and lost some cattle to drowning in flash floods last year. It's usually bone dry, though, and likely will be again when you get there."

"Alright."

"And then you got to do your best to hold them back when they smell the water, along around Castle Canyon. You'll see a sharp line of hills with a gap to head for, and that's the time to make ready for a stampede to water, get drovers out front to hold 'em back. We lost several hundred the first year, for they started a crazed run at the scent of water when they smelled it coming through that gap. We didn't have enough drovers up front to hold them, and they stampeded right into the river, then got bogged in quicksand."

"Oh no."

"Oh yeah. The front of the herd went over the cap rock bluff of about ten feet and the others ran over them and trampled them into that sandy bog....couldn't pull them out to save our lives, even with three or four ropes. We were roping them by the horns with several lines and breaking their necks trying to pull them out. Damned aggravating. It was hell, after getting them all that way, to have the river kill the crazed bastards."

Bill spoke up while Charlie puffed his cigar a bit. "They don't call it horse-head crossing for nothing. There's hundreds of skulls of horses that died there, after coming up the dry trail from Mexico and drinking too much salty water. It's the old Comanche crossing, from their raids on northern Mexico. There's salty pools alongside the river in spots, kill any stock that drinks it."

"Yeah, so I just heard from Gabe. Let's see, stampede for water, Comanchero raiders on the trail, and quicksand crossing, anything else, Charlie?

"Well, as Bill said, it's the Comanche raiding trail to Mexico, so a bunch of them could happen along at any time. Listen, if anyone knows quicksand river crossings, it's McBride, from all his scouting up on the Staked Plains. He's gotta scout the best approach early, before the belled bull leaves that gap, and you gotta figure the best approach before they get close and maneuver them in, not letting them run wild into the river. They ain't as smart as horses, you know. All their brains are good for is menudo. They just get plumb crazy when they smell water in that cool canyon after ninety miles without. You'll need most of your drovers up front to hold them back, especially if the wind is blowing your way from the river. Forget about the drag then, and get everyone up front holding them to a walk, and put them across right where you choose, not them."

"Alright, I've got it, and thanks for the warnings. We just have to stay a step ahead of their primitive minds, huh?"

"That's it. You'll do fine. You got lots of water barrels, limes, citric acid, a strainer, and all that I told you for gyp water, right?"

"Yeah, more barrels than you called for even. Gabe made a special rack on the calf wagon to carry more. That and a slow smoker with mesquite for smoked buffalo, or beef barbacoa."

"I mighta known that old rascal would find a way to improve my invention, or think he has. I'd like to watch him pound those knives sometime. So you got two wagons and all ya need, huh?"

"We're set to make it, Charlie, so far so good, and I want

you to look over the herd, tell me if I'm pushing them too hard."

"LaPoint, I'm damned glad I hired you two, even if ole McBride scared the crap out of me appearing out of a coulee like that...I had raiders on my mind. Tell him it's lucky he waved his hat and turned sideways or I'da knocked him off that nice buckskin and claimed it."

"Alright. I imagine he tickled himself over it. He seems to like you, the way he gigs at you all the time."

"Well, if he makes me nearly crap myself again he's gonna have to part with one of them knives to calm me down. I was gonna ask again, if he brought me one, but he rode off. So what about the drive so far, LaPoint, no stampedes or rustlers?

"Well, it's been pretty smooth so far, but here comes the hard part, huh?"

"Could be. Be primed and loaded, stay alert, have outriders watching for riders, lots of coffee for the men, don't let them fall out of their saddles asleep."

"Alright, we will. I was thinking of rigging the fuel travois from the wagon for a place to drop sleepers, if some couldn't stay awake."

"Good idea. We've lost some drovers to falling off and getting trampled in the later parts of that drive. Like I said, I'm glad I hired some thinking fellas."

"Glad to ride for you, Charlie."

"Yal ought to come on up the Rockies with me soon, help me run some herds in McBride's old stomping grounds. Them miners is hungry for beef up there, and ranching is starting where there's grass."

"Well, I'm intent on finishing what I have on my plate right now, we'll talk about that later."

"Charlie, what about horses?" asked Bill.

"LaPoint...We're gonna need some fresh horses after we see the herd and parlay with yal a while, some grub and good water too. I want to head back with four fresh horses before twilight. I got to wash in a creek too, can't stand the smell no longer, and I know it's gonna give Wilson something else to complain about."

"I'll say. It ain't sourdough starter I'm smellin'," said Bill. "Now I'm glad I was trailin' so fer back with my bandanna on."

"We've got all you men need in camp."

"You're a bit ripe yourself, Bill," said Goodnight, "See any bath-houses around?"

"We've got one," replied LaPoint, "...a big copper tub. A couple of hours ago I had the water barrels all cleaned and filled and prickly pear slices put in to gather the dust, should be settled clean by now. With the creek nearby you can have a hot bath each. Come on, lets ride back and get you some grub, and you can look at the herd and tell me if I've got them strung out right, not overheating to burn off weight, and all that stuff, Charlie."

Goodnight patted his black horse and said, "Let's go." So they all mounted and rode back to the east until they spotted the herd. Goodnight was pleased at the sleek-sided look of the cattle as they circled the front of the herd.

They rode back to the chuck wagon and Goodnight was well pleased with the defensive arrangement of the wagons, the camp fire with logs to shoot behind, and the remuda, well staked on a stout picket line, and guarded with riflemen. He liked the extra wagon setup, with a water settling barrel and siphon hose to the other extra barrels, for clear drinking water, and both men used the big copper tub to wash with hot water, a great relief to all nearby. The chuck wagon cook made a big fuss over feeding them and getting their baths hot and ready, trying to impress this man who was already becoming a campfire legend. The tired riders liked the grub and thought the bath was near heaven. Pancho and Jesse hung around the campfire instead of resting for their later night watch, for they liked Goodnight and wanted to be around him.

Tom Jackson sat off to the side cleaning his Spencer and big army Colt, watching the proceedings. He offered some extra clothes to Bill Wilson, who had taken off so fast after the rampaging Goodnight he had forgotten to pack any in his saddlebags. Then they sat around for a while and told stories of the trail drives and lonely graves that marked it, with the legend behind each one.

While in camp Goodnight had paced and talked the whole time, checking the horses, the camp, the chuck-wagon, the extra wagon innovations, the food supply, the extra mules, everything he could think of, never able to sit down by the campfire, even with a plate of food in his hand. Finally he sat down and listened to Gabe's ranger story and dozed off for an hour. When Bill heard Charlie snoring, he laid down by the fire and slept as well.

After a couple of hours of sleep, then replenishing food and water while constantly discussing things with LaPoint, the parley was over. Gabe downed his last cup of coffee and headed back west to scout, with Charlie and One-Armed Bill mounting fresh horses and taking two spare mounts to make fast time and catch their herd when it took off across the dry stretch to the Pecos. They hustled off together in a cloud of dust with Gabe racing Goodnight like a couple of kids, and Wilson bringing up the rear.

After Goodnight rode away Josh walked over by the campfire where Jackson had just finished writing in his journal and was showing Ben Burnett how to clean a Spencer repeating rifle.

"I never seen a man in such a hurry," said Tom Jackson, as they rode off leaving trails of dust. "Don't he ever set still, 'sides on a horse, I mean?"

"Maybe he knows he'll fall fast asleep if he stops, like he did by the fire," said Jesse.

LaPoint chuckled, watching the two riders race off. "Hell, he's usually whipping and spurring on his horse, even. Occasionally he sits down to eat, while in town, I suppose, and then he issues instructions as fast as the words will fly out. He's always got things to do. He's moved more cattle out this trail than anybody, and is moving the ranching life up the face of the Rockies. He'd been in the saddle pretty steady for twenty-four hours before he got here. Determined man."

"Ole Gabe's story put him out like a light," said Jesse, laughing.

"I'll say," said Tom. "I never would of thought of driving cattle out here through this barren hell in front of us. It shimmers like they say that the Sahara desert does. No grass, no shade, nothing but Spanish daggers, cactus, and coyotes scrounging for rattlesnakes in the worthless ground cover. Hawk country, looking for some landmark, and there's nothing but heat mirage. Who'd be out there to buy them if we get them there?"

"The fool federal government. They pinned up a bunch of Apaches and Navajos together, even though they hate each other, trying to teach them to farm land that won't grow crops and to live on salty Pecos water, according to Goodnight. They need beef, as well as the soldiers and forts up the line, and the miners in the mountains."

"Oh, I guess that figures. I read about Kit Carson and Col Pheiffer routing them Navajos out of their canyons and burning their fruit trees. But whatever gave Charlie the notion to drive herds out this way instead of up the staked plains, like folks is doin' now, to Abeline and Dodge."

"Oh, that's just Charlie Goodnight. He said he got tired of them stealing his cattle up around the Keechi valley. I guess things got too hot with Comanches up the Arkansas River trail way, which his old partner Loving used to get a herd to Denver a while back. And there's so many herds going north, the grass is sparse, with Comanche trouble to boot."

"His notion being that the Comanches live up there but only pass through here occasionally, on horse and slave raids to Mexico, I suppose?"

"Yeah, and with all the recent trouble with the Kiowas up there too, with that medicine man stirring them up, Maman-ti, with his hand puppet talking owl....that way ain't no picnic either."

"Yeah, I heard Gabe talking about that. It's a wonder that Catholic priest at Panna Maria don't copy that innovation, a hand puppet and throwin' your voice."

"Don't mention it to him."

"Hell, only time I seen him is when we picked up Rosa from school that time, and he tried to recruit you for alter boy or some such."

"More like church guard, I think," said LaPoint.

Jackson laughed out loud and continued cleaning with an oily rag on his gun.

"I seen Gabe ride into camp a while ago."

"Oh yeah, not much to scout anyway, glad he's back to get some grub and rest. I'm concerned about him making it on this long dry stretch coming up. No need for him to be out front anymore anyway."

"Why not?"

"Well hell, Goodnight's packed a trail like a cow tollway."

"Yeah, that Goodnight damn sure knows cattle trailing, I'll give him that," said Tom, as he cleaned the cartridge injection tube from the butt of his Spencer rifle. "Got a regular trail out here now. That durned chuck wagon is one of the best ideas I seen for moving herds in comfort. I'm for taking one on mustanging drives. But boss, it seems like all these cattle and horses will draw rustlers of whatever kind out here, where the pickings are slim, so it'll be a fight, just like the staked plains, except less grass."

"Appears that way. There wasn't any until all these drives started, no easy pickin's out here then. Thieves go everywhere there's something to steal. Lazy, is what they are, Tom, always wanting to steal the other fellas' work. Killers too, like that Helena and Oakville crowd, I don't want Gabe getting shot up front."

"I agree. Let me and the outriders take care of that. You just keep doing the thinking, I'll be ready to shoot killers."

"Everyone needs to clean their guns and get them working smooth like you're doing. Pass the word and pick some extra outriders with good night vision. They're most likely to hit us before we hit the dry stretch. Keep switching the outriders to different positions too, keep them alert. Feed them coffee and chaw. Watch the gullies of these draws coming up for hidden riders."

"Will do, boss. We'll keep a good lookout."

"Put only the most awake and alert on guard duty, Tom. A sleepy drover may fall off and wake up when he hits the ground, but a sleepy outrider may get us killed and the herd stolen."

"Right, boss. We'll get 'er done, like always."

LaPoint followed Goodnight's instructions to the letter and had the cattle spend a couple of days resting on the nourishment of the grassy creek valleys feeding the Middle Concho River. All day Sunday the men and horses rested while the cattle grazed and watered. LaPoint even gave the drovers each a dram of brandy and got the fiddler and guitarist to playing campfire tunes to relax the men before the big push. Jesse and Pancho revealed their beautiful singing voices after a few drinks, and soon others joined in. With shade tarps strung from the wagons, they kicked back and relaxed with cards and songs and stories. Gabe blew some ridiculous sounds on his bugle before the drovers begged him to stop.

The cook E. Earl Rhemnett made a huge peach cobbler in a big enamel pan, out of canned peaches and sourdough batter with eggs in it. His dirty glasses and dark beard combined with dirty apron, didn't help with the presentation of the feast. E. Earl's lower face was hung with a foot-long dense black beard into which he actually wove little braids along the sides. They tended to collect flour dust in the morning and other tidbits during the day's cooking. Ben Burnett was always ranting at him about keeping his pigtails out of the dough, and in recompense E. Earl would ring the triangle really loud when he was standing nearby.

The cobbler was so good the men ate until it was gone, lining up for more as soon as they gobbled down the first bowl. This was E. Earl's third drive in Goodnight's chuck wagon, and he had the routine down pat. Nobody went hungry when E. Earl ran the chuck wagon, and meals were even set out for the night riders when they came in late. He took good care of his mules too, and got consistent performance out of them. And the comforting constant smell of mesquite smoke told the drovers that meat was always smoking into tenderness and flavor in the metal smoker on the chuckwagon.

Chapter Eleven: Horse-head Crossing

As the blistering sun was starting to go down in the red sky of the west, and LaPoint was out checking the herd and the night-guards, he spotted a large covered freight wagon heading in from the west. Surprised, he left Jackson in charge and cantered out to meet it, and found the two big jenny mules just walking along while the driver slept on the bench of the covered wagon. Inside he heard the strangest noise, a deep buzzing that seemed to vibrate the whole floor of the heavy wagon. LaPoint could tell the wagon was heavily loaded from its motions and tracks.

Something about the mules looked strange from a distance, a disproportion in their long heads somehow. They were lathered and looked like they had been worked without rest for a long time. When LaPoint pulled up in front and stopped them, he saw their noses were all swollen with their nostrils nearly closed up and drool just pouring out of their misshapen snouts. He gently rubbed them between the eyes and on the withers, cooing softly to comfort them. They were feeling low and mistreated, and barely could breath through their nostrils, sniffling and snorting. He gave them some feed from his saddlebag, and gave some to Scorpio as he swung his big head back to receive it.

"Hello there, you in the wagon," said LaPoint as he watered the mules. The sweaty fellow woke up with a start and started grabbing for his shotgun. His hair was all tousled and stuck up in spikes with muddy dust on it.

"Don't shoot, I'm friendly, pointing a trail herd back there."

"Whoa! Naaaaw! Oh shit, ….lawd it's a white man. Thank God. You got any good drinking water? Are there Comanches around?" He set the shotgun down and reached for a canteen to take a few swigs.

"Hard to say, haven't seen any, where you headed, to a garden somewhere? You look like a scarecrow ready to light with that hair." LaPoint handed a canteen to the man.

"Fort Concho, I hope. I was having a bad dream in this heat, that I was headed back to hell, the other way. You're the second man that woke me up today. I just can't stay awake anymore, so dang tired. Am I close to the middle Concho river yet?"

"Yeah, within a mile or so to the creeks at the headwaters. Who was the other fella?"

"Charlie Goodnight, in a hurry as usual. Who is that riding up in such a hurry?"

LaPoint turned in the saddle to see Tom Jackson cantering his mount over a small rise towards them, with his rifle out. "He's my top hand, Tom Jackson." He rides guard at the front of the herd. Don't worry, we're friendly."

"Need any help here, boss?" asked Tom, as he slowed down within talking distance and stopped beside them.

"Yal want any honeycomb ta chew with mesquite honey in it?" asked the wagon driver.

"Why hell yes. Tom, rein in and listen. Have some honeycomb with me. Who's riding night herd?"

"Pancho and Jesse at this end, boss."

"Can I borrow your knife to cut some pieces of comb off?" asked the wagon driver. "I dropped mine somewhere"

LaPoint handed him his McBride knife, not as big as Gabe's, but still a foot long with an antler handle."

"I ran into a Comanche chieftain that had a knife just like this. He cut St. Paul's reins loose with it."

"Really. Cut loose Saint Paul, with a knife like that?" said Josh, deciding to humor the guy, who was likely sun stroked and addled. "Well, I imagine he was just a Roman agent anyway."

"Yes, same kind of antler handle and same kind of swirled pattern on the blade. St. Paul ain't no Roman. He's Comanche now."

"Alright. So what happened with Goodnight?" asked LaPoint as he remounted.

"He came and went, like always."

The driver delayed answering while dealing with the honeycomb, offering one to LaPoint, then a piece across the wagon seat to Tom.

"He was in a lather to get back to his herd, just bought some honey and pecans, chewed me out, then left."

Tom reined his horse to the other side of the wagon to get the comb. The traveler handed him a piece of honeycomb, then spoke again after putting a bit in his mouth and licking his fingers.

"That durned Charlie Goodnight yelled at me to wake me

up, then cussed me out and told me I was gonna get scalped riding around asleep, then rode off in a huff. Had a one-handed drover with him named Bill. We've crossed path's plenty of times before. He can be abrupt at times."

"No kidding," replied Tom.

"Thinks he's the manager on this trail or something. I was using it long before he ever dreamt of driving cattle out here."

Tom Jackson was turning his horse around on the side of the wagon opposite LaPoint, and had his attention caught by something near the back. He rode around towards LaPoint with a question to the honey man. "Holy cow, what happened there? I see broken off arrows in your wagon!"

"I broke them off with my hatchet 'cause I couldn't get them out, they were so deep, with those metal spikes. I had a scrape with a Comanche party this morning. About a dozen or more young bucks with a bunch of horses, probably coming back from a raid in Mexico. They tried to get my goods, but I scared them off. They called the leader Quiineah or something like that,,,,"

"Uuuuhooh," said Jackson, a look of apprehension clouding his brow. "We heard of him at the fort. Son of Peta Nacona."

"And his pal looked just like my ex-wife's German relatives, a white man gone Comanche, if you ask me. That fella wanted to kill me, and kept pointing one of those dreadful rusty tipped arrows at me and drawing his bow back all the way with big powerful arms, just holding it there, aiming it at me, asking this Quiineah to let him shoot me, but Quiineah wouldn't let them. Quiineah called him Asawaynah, Asawaynah, what ever that means. I guess it means don't shoot."

"I think it means gray blanket."

"I quit trading blankets. Some Kiowas accused me of having smallpox in my blankets."

"Probably his tribal name, Gray Blanket. Lucky for you this Kiwih-nai, which means eagle, I think, held him back."

"You scared them off, you say?" asked Tom, glancing at LaPoint, who looked incredulously back.

"I'd like to know how," said LaPoint.

"From the looks of it, they was firing arrows from close range, buried the heads in that hard wood," said Tom.

"Tell us everything that happened," said LaPoint. "From the beginning."

"Yes-sir, I was just riding along all peaceful like with my telescope in hand, looking for bee gums or pecan trees or walnut trees, and I saw them coming, so I stopped the mules by some cat-claw bushes and mesquite trees so they might not see my dust. I hid and prayed, actually, and sweated in there."

"You gather pecans out here?" said Tom.

"Will you let him go on, Tom?"

"Pecans and honey, mostly honey this time of year, but don't ask me where, 'cause I ain't saying. I plant pecans along the watercourses too. The pecans I have are last year's, so they're not fat and juicy, but have a lot of flavor, if yal'd like some."

"Why hell, sure would. Along the creeks we been grazing on, I've seen pecan trees, bees too, all back along the Concho," said Tom.

The man in the wagon handed them each some pecans while LaPoint ached for the rest of the story, wanting to know every detail about a raiding party so close.

"Dang, those are tasty, good flavor," said Tom.

"Aren't they, though."

"Heck, I'd like to purchase a bag of these here."

"So how did you escape the Comanches with a wagon of honey and pecans?" asked LaPoint. "Comanches would ride twenty miles for either one."

"When I saw through my telescope that they kept coming towards me, I hid in the back of the wagon, not knowing what to do. Then in desperation I put on my beekeeping gear, with my screened bonnet and white coat and pants with sealed sleeves and such, and opened some bee gums I had in the back there, had the whole area swarming with angry bees in a short time. They rode up as I was carrying a piece of hive with a queen towards them, with the worker bees all over my bonnet and gloves, just swarming all around me in fact, and lighting out to sting the first rapid movement."

"Sweet crimony and grits," said Tom, laughing.

"Good idea, I'd say," said LaPoint.

"Then Saint Paul got stung in his nose..."

"Saint Paul?" said LaPoint. "That who you were praying too?"

"Saint Paul is the horse I rode in on when I came down to Texas...and he went just wild and started kicking, which startled my jennies Eve and Lilith into a panic, and they started pulling and jerking, started moving the wagon against the wheel brake, screeching it, making an awful sound, stirring more bees out of the back from the open gum...."

"Damnation, what a tight fix," said Tom.

"Sounds like one of those Bible stories, made up by someone who's been in the damn sun too long and had a stroke," said LaPoint.

"I reckon so. I have. They came close as they could without getting swarmed and aimed their bows and arrows at the wagon and kept yelling, 'Puukuh, Puukuh, Puukuh'. I didn't understand, so they shot arrows into the side of the wagon by where I had my horse tethered. It was those dreadful rusty barrel hoop arrowheads, the kind that poison you, too. I'll never forget that awful sound they made thudding into the wood. That's the kind that killed that nice Mister Oliver Loving, poisoned him til his leg rotted off and killed him."

"Yeah," said Tom. "I seen they was rusty steel tips, buried deep, boss. He ain't lying. I'd like to get a bag of pecans before you get back to camp and everybody swarms up to buy you out."

"Forget that for a minute, would you, Tom. 'Puuku' is Comanche for horse. They wanted your horse," said LaPoint. "One of few Comanche words I know. Another is Kiwih-nai, means Eagle, he's a rising young chieftain of the Quohadis, we've heard, son of the late Peta Nacona and Cynthia Ann Parker. They were probably on their way back from raiding horse ranches below the border. I've heard his best friend is a white captive that grew up with the tribe, a German farm lad, name of Ficherman or something like that."

"Well how in the world can you know all this?"

"We sell horses to the cavalry, visit the forts, hear the news."

"Well, they durn sure got my horse. The arrows hitting so close caused St. Paul to throw a fit and start bucking and get all tangled up in the rope I was towing him with, so this Kiwih-nai rode over slowly into the bees, calm as you please without a sting one, and cut him loose, but St. Paul ran off, and two of them followed and catched it. I saw the knife, plain as day, just like yours, brass guard and all, with the wavy pattern in the blade."

"It probably was made by the same guy."

"You named your horse for a Bible character?" said Tom.

"I came from St. Paul, up north, Minnesota. The doctor told me to go to a dryer climate."

"Looks like you found one," laughed Tom. "Now about those pecans,and maybe some honey too."

"Okay, they got St. Paul, so what happened then?" asked LaPoint.

"I needed that horse, 'cause these mules won't carry a rider and go to pitching, so without thinking I walked out towards them pleading for it with a small queen-hive in my hands, swarming with worker bees. These Comanches got angry about that and started whirling their horses around, especially that Adolph Gray Blanket, and the quick movements attracted the bees. Adolph rode closer and drew back his bow to shoot, but Kiwih-nai had a pistol and pulled it out to make him stop, but he had attracted the bees by then, and got stung a bunch. His face was swelling up and red as hell."

"I can't believe you're still alive," said Tom.

"Go on with the story," said LaPoint. "I think we're at the miracle of St. Paul part."

"So the bees took after them both and started stinging their horses and them too. The horses started bucking, then the small herd they were moving started running. The last I saw of them was chasing their stolen horses, and pulling mine off with them, heading north."

"That's a good one. That's the best I've heard since Tom's story about his ma whipping some bucks with a frying pan of hot ham-grease and eggs, " said LaPoint, then laughing out loud for a bit.

"Aww-hell, this one tops mine, boss. Chasing Comanches off with stinging bees and a wagon-load of honey sitting right there."

"Well, it's all I had. Trouble is, it spooked my jennies, sweet Lilith and that bitchy Eve when they got stung too, and they pulled the wagon over a little gully and bumped the brake undone, so I had to walk after the wagon for miles after the Comanches rode off. It's Eve's fault, Lilith is wise enough to stay put, but Eve always gets in a dither and over-reacts."

"Oh man, all that garb on, in the hellish heat." said

LaPoint.

"Why yes. I was left standing there in my full gear, running sweat while watching my wagon disappear in one direction and my horse in another. I took out walking, carrying my beekeeping outfit, for hours in this infernal scorching heat, not a cloud in the sky for shade. I finally found it with the wheels hooked into a gully, swarming with bees all around, so I had to put my gear back on in the heat of the day and get it out of the gully and get the bees settled. That wore me out. It was so hot, I sweated out all my water, it seems. So I was so tired and woozy coming back this way, I fell asleep."

"Damn. Now I've heard it all. You're safe now. My name is LaPoint, I'm ramrodding that herd back by the creek. You're welcome in our camp, and well-guarded."

"I'm called Honey Allan. I got a wagon full of honey combs and a few pecans, heading to sell it to the soldiers at Fort Concho."

"You don't say," replied Jackson. "How's about we work a deal for some right now, before the line forms?"

Josh spoke to the man as he made up a bag of pecans for Tom. "We just come from there a few days ago. Why don't you make camp with us. I'll buy a lot of that honey and pecans, might be just what we need to help cross to the Pecos."

"I'd be glad to camp with some protection, after what I've been through. Always glad to sell honey and pecans too. I can always gather more."

"Well follow me and I'll clear you a spot fairly close to the chuckwagon. Tom, would you ride in and get some water and feed bags ready for these mules, and tell E. Earl to get out a plate of food?"

"Oh yeah, boss."

They settled the curious looking wagon with the steady buzz about twenty yards away from the chuckwagon, and E. Earl took care of his feeding. LaPoint bought lots of honey in the comb and had Earl divide it into small pieces with piles of pecans. The men feasted on the unusual treats, and Earl prepared packages of honeyed pecans to nourish them as they rode the trail. For the evening meal, he had made pies of canned peaches with honey sweetener and pecan crust with real eggs in it.

Figuring this was the time to enjoy life, before the hell of the desert overtook them, LaPoint had the cook prepare a big meal, and everyone feasted and partied around the campfire, sleeping late the next day. He sent a rider out to carry some to the well armed night riders and guards. Another big meal and all day preparations for the trip occurred in camp while the cattle and horses filled up on water and grass, the last full day of the rest.

Then, on Monday afternoon, with every water container brimming and all the men and animals full of fluid, they left the last water at sunset and prepared to head west for the Pecos, ninety miles away. The view to the west was foreboding, dry white land with scarce low ground cover and hundreds of Spanish daggers in the shimmering heat haze, back-lit with the setting sun, still a red glaring ball of fire.

On this strip there would be no water and no browse, just pushing forward through stinging alkali dust. The available hands gathered around the coffee pot and everyone drank all they could. The tension among the drovers rose as the sun set. LaPoint mounted Scorpio and spoke in a voice loud enough to be easily heard by all.

"Alright drovers, listen up and stay alive."

"Hey you guys, quiet, listen to what the boss has to say," yelled Jesse.

"There's no more water til the Horse-head crossing of the Pecos, which I figure is over ninety miles away. We're going to take it slow and steady, keep the herd strung out and moving all night until dawn, then take a food and coffee break. We push without haste and without ceasing, like a tree root in stone. Go easy on your water and keep drinking all this coffee we made so you don't fall out of the saddle asleep on this first night-ride. Just keep snacking on jerky, water, pecans, and honey as you ride, for big meals will make you sleepy. Jackson tells me you can rub tobacco juice on your eyelids to keep them open, if you so choose. There's a big tobacco chaw for anyone to cut a piece off, and a big bag of ready roll fixings. Whatever it takes to stay awake, do it. Slap your face, pull your hair, whatever, but don't fall from your saddle. I figure we have nearly sixty hours of solid riding ahead of us, with no waterholes, then a fight to keep the herd from bolting for the river."

"You guys pay heed or maybe go under 'cause ya didn't," said Gabe.

"That's right," said Jesse. "Boss LaPoint has saved my life more than once."

Josh continued in a loud voice.

"This is the tough part, what we've been getting ready for. Watch out for each other as sleep gets hard to fight off. If you can't ride any more then come in to the chuckwagon for a spell. We've got a travois rigged up behind it for unavoidable naps, if you just can't stay awake. Don't fall off your horse and get trampled by the herd."

"We aim to avoid losing drovers, so pay heed," said Gabe. LaPoint continued, since they all seemed to be listening.

"And you drag riders, don't think every cow and steer is going to make it. Some are going to fall out and die, but don't bother with them, just keep the main bunch moving steady, and don't let the herd get too strung out. But don't let them bunch in the heat of the day, either."

The drovers, quiet and attentive to a man, each took on a serious face, with the ones who had not made the trip before asking the others what it was like. They knew that many drovers like them had died on this route, and their graves would be passed by desperate men. Then they spread out around the herd and readied themselves for a tough go, everyone's belly full to the stretching point with water.

Steadily, E. Earl the cook and his helper cleaned up and packed the wagons, tying down everything tightly for the rough gullies of the Centralia wash, making sure the tops of all the barrels were secure. Earl was not fast, but he was thorough, and made sure nothing would come amiss or undone as the wagons traversed rough ground through the gulleys of the Centralia wash. LaPoint was impatient to be off, but sat waiting for E. Earl to finish in his meticulous manner.

McBride the scout rode out first with a helper to ride back messages, and LaPoint followed within an hour with the last half of the red sunset in his eyes, the sweat pouring from his face. He had wet his shirt in the last creek before leaving, and the breeze through it chilled him off, despite the blazing sun throwing its heat in his face. He was ready for darkness to cool the high desert trail as he spun in his saddle and signaled the point riders to begin moving the herd west.

"Let's get rolling, move the herd," he yelled. The wagons started forward, with a long bellow from E. Earl's cow-horn, while the wrangler Ben rang the triangle, and the old bull arose and began pacing west.

The cattle started out sleek and fat looking, full of grass and water, well rested. LaPoint spurred his horse to about a mile in front of the herd and spotted McBride signaling back about the route. He knew that signals would not be visible much longer, and tried to line up the route with the dimly appearing stars as the sun set. He found the dippers and north star, the Orion's belt, and reckoned west on other familiar stars. He knew that Gabe would get closer as darkness fell, and wished they were riding together already. He worried about the effects of this long drive on the older man, though Gabe had seemed to be getting younger and stronger over the last few years of ranching. He stared into the dim starlight ahead, looking for McBride's silhouette, then scanning for Jackson and his outriders. The beginning of the drive through the dry stretch started out well. LaPoint visualized the canyon gap ahead, that Charlie Goodnight had described as their goal.

An hour later he spotted McBride whipping and spurring back towards him, his arm flashing at his side as he flailed Buck with his quirt of a buffalo tail. He was being chased by several riders, who began shooting at him, the echoes rolling across the dry prairies. McBride had them out-horsed with Buck, and was slowly leaving them behind, eating his dust.

LaPoint pulled his Spencer and his trusty Whitworth from the rifle scabbards, near a leaning Mesquite tree. He pulled Scorpio down, prone in the dust, and got the ammo for the Whitworth from the saddlebag as the big stallion went flat with a nervous grunting. Scorpio whinnied in protest but stayed down.

Quickly loading the big gun and bracing on the mesquite trunk, he sighted into the darkness behind McBride, waited until he saw a flash of fire from the shooting pursuer, then squeezed the trigger and unloaded into that flash, knocking the rider from his horse, hearing him and the horse scream as they tangled and fell with the echoes of the big booming Whitworth rolling off the gullies. Through the telescope he could see a cloud of dust in the moonlight as the horse tried to rise but the rider did not.

Buck began to zig-zag on a piece of flat ground as the other riders pulled up and began to fire their rifles towards McBride with more accuracy. With his heart pounding hot blood through his temples, LaPoint switched to the Spencer and began to pepper fire towards those flashes as well, laying down seven accurate shots before he had to reload.

The firing stopped while LaPoint reloaded, and Gabe came hustling up out of the darkness, then stopped with a skid in the dust and pulled his rifle from the scabbard, scanning behind him. LaPoint reloaded both guns and peered into the starlit prairie. No more flashes came, but the empty horse of the first pursuer came rushing up, following Buck.

McBride spurred Buck over, reached down and grabbed the reins and cantered in the last thirty yards, pulling the frightened horse. There was blood on the fancy Mexican saddle with silver trim and huge silvered saddle horn. They peered into the darkness, waiting for further attack, but none came. Finally LaPoint aimed the big Whitworth up and fired into the darkness where he last saw them, so as to empty the charge and clean the gun.

"Hellfire, with yore luck, you probably hit one of 'em. You shore took that close one out fine, thanks."

"You're welcome, good scouts are hard to come by. Who the hell was that?" asked LaPoint as he began to clean the guns, with Gabe standing beside him with his own Spencer ready.

"A bunch of guys who wanted to kill me, I reckon."

"Yeah, like who?

"Comanchero rustlers, would be my first guess. I stopped for a smoke when I got sleepy, one of these cigars I got from Goodnight, been saving it.... they must have seen me light up. Started chasing and shooting at me. Had ta drop my cigar, tha sonsobitches."

"Well, hell, lets ride together, safer."

"Fine with me, I ain't peering down for no trail anyhow, since it's like a damn turnpike with all the herds been by here. Lucky for that rain a while back, or thar'd be no grass left." They both remounted and slowly headed off together into the dim starlight, carrying their repeating rifles balanced on their saddles, ready to fire.

Alerted by the firing, Tom Jackson and Jesse soon came charging up out of the darkness, rifles at the ready. Appraised of the situation, they spread out again, even more keen for trouble. Soon LaPoint and McBride heard firing and rode into the darkness to help. They met Tom and Jesse riding back, each trailing a riderless horse.

"What happened?"

"Tom shot them out of the saddle, both of them. We found the other one's body too."

"We got all but one, boss," said Tom Jackson. "He hightailed it in the dark."

"Well, that might deter them, three dead for coyotes and buzzards," said Gabe. "Let's get the herd settled now, all the shootin' mighta got 'em stirred up."

"Alright. Tom, stay out with Gabe and guard, Jesse, come back and settle the herd with me."

The drovers and their cattle rode that steady unhurried and unceasing way well into the night, Josh using the north star to orient his path and guide the herd, at times sending relay riders out to check with the well-armed outriders. McBride pulled out another cigar, and offered one to LaPoint. After a few minutes of it, LaPoint put the stub in his vest pocket, nauseous from the strong rum-soaked taste. They kept up the steady pace, the only sounds the lowing of cattle, the clanging bell, and coyotes singing in the distance.

Usually they followed the ruts of the Butterfield stage line and the trail of previous herds. The several years of usage since the original Goodnight drive had made a serious trace across the dry land, full of coyotes and rattlesnakes, and nothing much else. After the bolting cattle caused by the gunfire in the dark, LaPoint had given orders not to shoot at snakes or coyotes or anything else besides rustlers, for fear of stampeding the herd.

The cattle had started out fat, calm, and contented but were becoming somewhat restless in the wee hours of the morning, after the long steady night drive, when the smell of water had totally slipped away. LaPoint could tell by the sounds they were making how they were feeling, and it was a nervous feeling. The thick alkali dust raised by their hoofs was bitter and stung the eyes and throat. It even smelt sort of burnt and acrid in the nostrils, and caused a constant irritation. At least the high desert air cooled off a bit in the evening, making the temperature pleasant compared to the daytime.

Resisting the urge to push them in the cool darkness, LaPoint kept a slow and steady progress, listening to the monotonous clang of the belled bull behind him, and the confused bawling of the rest of the herd. Along around first light everyone got incurably sleepy. McBride rode ahead to check out the ground in the morning light, rubbing his eyes with a wet rag to try to brighten up his vision.

An hour later even LaPoint was starting to doze in the saddle as the sun rose up behind him, tinting the sky violet-pink and orange. Suddenly he felt bright light flashing on his eyelids and woke to see McBride's mirror several miles ahead, reflecting back the rising sun behind him. Blinded in his weary eyes, seeing blurred flashes, and feeling chagrined at falling asleep in the saddle, he then heard the old scout's bugle bellowing, a signal to stop and rest. He imagined Gabe seeing him sleeping with the telescope and chuckling about flashing his eyes to wake him up. He knew Gabe had been nursing the last bottle of Cypress Sally's stay-awake potion for this trip, and wished he had some at the time.

LaPoint rode back to the chuck wagon and called a halt for food and lots of coffee. E. Earl got to scurrying around, dishing out grub and boiling water for coffee, barking at anyone who got in his way. The old lead bull wouldn't stop, so they put a pad on his clanger and hobbled him, finally stilling the others into a restless stand. Then LaPoint sent a rider out to fetch coffee and grub to McBride, and made sure the men got all they could handle, as well as a few catnaps. After an hour of break time and attending to horses and gear, they started out again, moving at the same slow and steady pace into the day as it heated up. There was no more grazing the herd, only keeping them moving forward at a ceaseless crawl, following the belled longhorn bull across the badlands. A cloud of white dust was left in their wake, choking the drag riders. The sun arose and heated their backs, driving the cool air away and replacing it with air nearly too hot to breathe.

For dreary scorching hours they rode in misery, the drifting dust making mud over their sweat. The cattle, a mixed herd with somewhat different natural gaits, were growing restless and disturbed, with ribs showing and tongues lolling out, squawking and bawling while they looked for grass to eat. With not much point left to staying in camp with the cattle restless, the drovers quickly readied themselves and spread out to move the herd west again, thankful the glaring heat would soon be diminishing as they headed into the afternoon sun. To the west they saw nothing but white plains and the shimmering of heat mirages in the distance. A thousand skinny stalks of Spanish daggers loomed off into the distant shimmer, the only thing that rose above ground level. Hawks circled high above, waiting for mice or rabbits, hovering in rapid wing bursts at spotting the prey, then diving down at high speed to snatch them.

Most of the drovers were wearing wet bandanas on their necks by then, to try to lower the heat of the blood going to their heads, in this furnace of the alkali plains. The horses poured sweat and began to pant and blow in the increasing heat. On they trudged, mile after miserable mile, unable to do anything else in the dry heat like air out of a furnace. No more soothing songs floated up from the drovers, for their faces were now set in grim determination and their mouths were shut under bandanas full of dust. LaPoint rode from drover to drover, keeping his outfit intact.

The same steady plodding pace carried them through the day until late afternoon, when they stopped again for a rest, a change of horses, and grub with lots of strong coffee. The drovers' nerves were on edge by then, with some suffering the early stages of heat stroke, and everyone bone weary and moving slowly. Most had bleary red eyes and cracked lips with sun burnt faces highlighted by red noses.

LaPoint kept Tom Jackson in charge of maintaining a crew of alert outrider guards, riding with rifles out, ready to fire at rustlers. LaPoint went from man to man with a wet towel and several canteens, forcing fluids on them, offering the trick of a prickly pear held in the mouth to keep it from drying out, offering salve for their lips and red noses, making sure they tended to their mounts. They moved on after a short break, since it was just as hot sitting still and the cattle were restless. McBride stayed closer to the herd, since there was no water to find anyway, and they were following the obvious trail of Goodnight's herd by then.

The fear of rustlers even faded as they traveled into the bone dry Pecos flats, or at least it was too hot to imagine it. LaPoint signaled the outriders to come in closer so as to change their horses and get water. Everyone slowed down, trudging wearily through the baking heat and bitter dust in the rising dry wind, faces blistering from the sun above and reflections from the white ground, and lips swelling and cracking more. They searched the horizon restlessly and saw only the shimmering mirage of heat. The cattle and horses grew weaker, with gaunted ribs, and more fractious. The drag was filled with half-crazed wandering steers, bawling for water.

A wet bandana was the only protection against the bitter dust, and all the drovers were thus attired like outlaws, with another wet one on the neck. Fortunately the extra barrels of water meant they had plenty to keep their fluids up and their horses watered. They changed horses at shorter intervals than normal, trying to avoid burning them out. LaPoint had put Jesse to working with the young wrangler who was kept busy getting water to all the working and resting mounts, as well as handfuls of grain, for there was no grass worth browsing.

By the full heat of noontime McBride and LaPoint rode side by side, barely a mile in front of the herd, plodding through the baked air, at times dripping water onto a bandana to cool their necks. Tom Jackson and his armed outriders were up front by then, riding out a mile on each side, and LaPoint had pulled McBride back beside him for consultation, and to keep and eye on him in the terrific heat. He realized it was very tough on even young seasoned men, and that McBride was near sixty, though tough as a bull neck rawhide.

"Hot enough for ya, Old Coon?"

"It'll do, if hell's full up, ah reckon. I'm feelin' it. Buck too. How 'bout you."

"Just the sleep creeping into my head, and worrying about the men."

"Yeah, can't be helped, this stretch, done it several times before, but without a herd. I reckon Charlie's right, move 'em so slow they live through it."

"Yeah. A few hours ago I started wondering what the hell I was doing, driving cattle herds when I just wanted to raise and train horses. But we'll see it through."

"Nothin' else ta do, ah reckon. Sorta scorchin' though, ain't it."

"I'll say."

LaPoint had never experienced dry blistering heat for nearly a hundred miles without a water hole, and it required some serious effort keep pushing on towards the glaring heat of the setting sun. He put his drifting mind on remembering the cool swim in the San Antonio river with Kathy, and held it there for hours as he plodded through the air that scorched his eyes and nose like it was oven heated. The trace they followed of the herds in front of them was very clear, and the fear of rustlers was replaced by the fear of broiling alive and being eaten by rattlesnakes and coyotes, or the black buzzards that circled overhead. Josh began to worry more about Gabe as he saw him begin to sway a bit in the saddle. But the old scout kept plodding on steady and taciturn in his sweat-covered linen shirt.

In late afternoon, LaPoint circled back to check the drovers and found Ben Burnett asleep in the saddle. He ordered him to go take a nap on the big travois for twenty minutes, then alternate with another drover who was to do the same. That way everyone got a short break and a new position to stay alert and endure the monotony. They never stopped or slowed, just kept pushing on relentlessly.

Finally it was sunset, and they kept plodding, then twilight with no slackening the steady pace, then dark and the welcome stars came out to guide them ever west through the cooling air, the men, horses, and cattle suffering the effects of the constant movement. The coolness of the night air was the only relief they could enjoy.

It went on like that for over fifty hours, day and night, with one hour breaks at times, pushing through the bitter white alkali dust of the merciless badlands. It became nearly impossible to keep the eyelids open, and LaPoint himself dozed in the saddle, lulled to sleep by the baking heat and the steady creaking of the saddle, falling into hot dreams of his mother standing on a rise and warning him that the killer was near. He awoke from the disturbing dream and rode a few miles, only to doze off and fall back into the same chaotic mix of symbols and anxieties, until at late afternoon on Thursday when LaPoint spotted the Castle mountain range and the gap through them. He rubbed his bleary eyes and pulled out his binoculars to make sure he wasn't seeing a mirage or his dream.

The setting sun was lighting up the Castle hills ridge-line on the western horizon, and he was elated. He had been imagining it for hours, that ridge-line and gap through it which they must traverse, knowing the Pecos river was only twelve miles further. His last look into the water barrels on the chuckwagon had showed only about ten gallons left, so desperation was a factor in his thinking. Scorpio sensed his feelings and began to bristle with it, stepping livelier.

The excitement of the goal in sight woke him up into a

dull awareness that he had a lot to do then, and soon he saw the mirror reflection of Gabe catching the last rays of the sun and sending them back in a constant flutter. He put some canteen water on his bandana and rubbed his face and eyes, then put some into his hat to water Scorpio.

"Yeah, you found the pass, ya ole coon, come on Scorpio, we're almost done with this hell stretch," said LaPoint as he took a last swig from his coffee thermos, remounted, and wheeled around to go alert the drovers. First he alerted Tom and the point riders, Pancho and Jesse, then circled the herd on the left while Tom did the same on the right, talking with every man about the possible stampede towards water coming up. Then he rode to the dusty tail end of the herd and gathered the drag riders to come to the front in order to prevent a stampede to the river. Finding Ben Burnett with help at the remuda, he sent the youngster for water from the river, carrying all the canteens and casks he could on horseback. The herd continued on a steady gait, now hemmed in more tightly by the drovers.

Within an hour they were entering Castle Canyon, a gap about a mile long through the line of hills, and the faint smell of the Pecos river alerted the horses and cattle in the cooler air of the stony gap. The bell of the lead bull started clanging faster, and they began to speed up their long descent towards the river as they passed into the shadows of the canyon. The cattle were desperate for water, and becoming crazed and noisy. With their ribs standing out like bars in a jailhouse, their flanks drawn tight and ganted down, their tongues hanging far down and layered with white dust, some of them actually dragging on the chalky ground, the whole herd began a desperate push forward, while some just keeled over and died, the heat of the excitement too much for them. LaPoint was soon wide awake with nervous energy, making sure the front drovers were in place.

With a majority of the horns flopping back and forth, and a fearful bawling, they surged forward and pushed the front of the herd. But with extra drovers up front the LaPoint outfit was able to hold the cattle to a fast walk for the twelve miles towards the river, despite their wild craving to rush for the water. Goodnight's warnings had eased their situation, along with LaPoint's sure response and planning.

While riding up front searching for Gabe, LaPoint saw a rider moving fast towards the herd. An hour before the herd entered the gap, LaPoint had sent Ben Burnett carrying plenty of empty canteens to go on ahead to the river, fill them with the best water available, douse them with citric, then hurry back with them. Ben had developed into a good and reliable hand since they had given him a second chance after the Oakville incident, and LaPoint liked to use him for important work because he was so enthusiastic and thankful to be with a good outfit. Ben was approaching in front of a stream of dust, with the river glistening in the far background, or perhaps a mirage of the river, which seemed to wind all over the place.

The drover stopped and offered LaPoint a canteen. "I've still got some, but I'll try it, from the river, right?"

"Yeah, with citris acid in it already," replied Ben. "Not too bad, but scout McBride says to tell you that there's saline pools in the old false bends of the river."

"Saline pools, huh?"

"Yes boss, they are salty as hell from evaporation, and we got to keep the stock away from them. They're south of the crossing. He's found a spot to cross with no quicksand and a slope down. He'll signal with a mirror there. The water is about six feet deep, and maybe sixty feet across there. Also, he said to tell you that he saw tracks of unshod horses bearing riders, like Comanches bringing a herd of stolen horses up from Mexico."

"Alright. Good job. Let me taste this, then ride and alert Tom and Jesse to all that. "

As soon as he had a drink of the new water, slightly bitter with salts, but drinkable, he rode to a small rise, took out his glasses, stood in his stirrups, and scanned for Gabe. He saw a mirror flash with the shimmering river snaking along in a loop-de-loop behind it. He signaled back with his mirror and waited there for the herd, graining and watering his horse with the Pecos water poured into his hat.

"Here Scorpio, try this. It's a bit salty, but see if you can take it before the rest try. Ben, take some of this honey in the jar and put a dab into each canteen. Then take it all back and alert the point riders. I'll wait here." Burnett took off for the herd while LaPoint squatted to rest beside Scorpio, who kept nosing him, wanting to go to the river.

Feeling bone weary, LaPoint laid down to wait for the herd and fell asleep with the wet hat over his face. Awakened in less than an hour from a heat-strained land of jumbled dreams, he heard the bell of the lead bull and the bawling of the herd, and rode back to alert the point drovers to the route and dangers. He spotted Jesse and joined him, chagrined that he had fallen asleep on the job, but excited that the end was near.

The cattle were even more desperate to run to the water, just three miles further, but the extra drovers up front held them back, and they did a fast walk to the river, avoiding the quicksand and saline pools. McBride sat on Buck at the river bluff, flashing his mirror, and LaPoint spurred to meet him.

"Gabe! We made it."

"LaPoint. Push 'em over."

"You do it, Jesse. You've earned it."

"Thanks, boss." Jesse spurred his horse towards the lead bull and chased him towards the crossing. LaPoint sat with tears of relief in his eyes, rubbing his stallion's neck. Then he rode to the river to supervise the crossing and set up some men to try to get a rough count of the cattle.

The other herds had worn down the six foot cap rock bluff to a slope which the cattle poured over into the wide salty river. They drank as they walked into the stream, but soon had to swim, the push of the herd behind them too much to resist. They swam across and the drovers spread them along the other bank to drink as more crossed over and crowded them. The crush of the cattle herd was so thick that it dammed up the river flow for a while, raised the water level, and floated a bunch downstream, but even those were recovered. The wagons had a bit of difficulty crossing, but a bunch of drovers put ropes on them and helped drag them free from the deep ruts. Within three hours all the herd and outfit had crossed, and a headcount revealed no men missing.

Greatly relieved, LaPoint set the herd to grazing and the men to rest in shifts.

"That was a tough one," said LaPoint to Gabe, who rode up chewing a ginseng twig with a big smile on his sunburned face.

"Ya done good."

"You done good, just kept riding and riding, huh?... like the old days on the plains."

"Yep, put my mind elsewhar at times, like with my senorita at Taos."

"Yeah, I thought of Kathy a bit, when I could think, anything but thinking of the hell we were in."

"You done fine. You're a ramrod, a trail boss now."

"Everybody did well. Especially you, Old Coon. I'll never forget seeing you whipping and spurring to get away from those rustlers."

"Yeah, and ah reckon ah won't forget ya savin' my skin, neither."

"I'm mighty proud of our men, this outfit."

"Now's the time to tell 'em."

"Yeah, you're right about that. Toot that bugle to get their attention, huh?"

McBride pulled out the battered brass bugle and gave three toots and LaPoint spoke in his loud voice. "Alright, drovers, well done. Excellent work. Nobody missing, nobody hurt bad, and we kept most of the cattle, in pretty good shape too. There will be a good rest and some brandy and music tonight. Just hold them along the river grazing and drinking, is all I ask for a day or so. Break into shifts to rest and hold them steady here. Tom, will you take three men back as far as the gap, to see what you can salvage of the stragglers?"

"Shore thing, boss. Come on, Andy and Seth, bring some water bags."

"We did it, men!" yelled LaPoint, which McBride followed with a loud sour blast from his bugle. A loud cheer rose up from the drovers within hearing. The crowd of mules around the wagons did a bit of his familiar heehaw as well. Scorpio and Buck led the horses in spirited cries.

Tom and several drovers went with lots of water and rescued thirty odd stragglers and two calves from the drags, while the rest of the drovers made camp and watched the herd drinking, not allowing them to founder on too much salty water. They stayed in camp all day, washed clothes and swam in the shallow river while the herd was slowly moving up the west bank, grazing the sparse grass and directing the herd to rain-fed runoff creeks entering from the north, which were not so salty as the Pecos. Recent rains had brought up enough browse to keep the cattle happy. chewing and drinking.

At twilight they were not surprised to see Charlie Goodnight come hustling up, happy to see they had crossed without losing many cattle.

Their first drive across Texas was a success, and now they faced the trail north up the Pecos, which Charlie called the "graveyard of high hopes." They sat around the campfire and drank brandy, with Goodnight talking to LaPoint while the men sang and played music, happy to be past the worst stretch. For once Charlie seemed content to relax a bit in camp, now that his three herds had crossed the dry stretch, and the first two were already moving north. Of course, he was full of more big plans that included LaPoint and McBride, and took pains to keep them in his association, talking of his ranching plans until they fell asleep while he rambled on.

Charlie left early in the morning for the other herds, after grabbing a handful of Gabe's biscuits, while everyone else slept in for a change. After a couple of days of rest, the LaPoint outfit and herd headed north up the Pecos, happy that recent rains had put water into the side creeks, grass along the banks, and had diluted the saltiness of the dirty Pecos.

While in camp McBride designed a big water strainer of several layers of cheesecloth on a wire hoop, to clarify the red water of Pecos, to which they later added citric acid and honey to make palatable and reduce the alkalinity. Still the men began to suffer from the alkali runs, which struck a fellow in a big hurry. Fortunately there was a river nearby to wash underwear in the evening, for saddle chaffing in alkali country could drive a rider to distraction and madness if not remedied.

The drive up the Pecos to Fort Sumner was a long and dreary trip of nearly 300 miles, but without major incident nor severe strain upon the stock and men like the stretch to the Horse-head crossing. About the only incident of possible disaster started when a drover shot a big catfish in the river at twilight, prompting the herd, which had already settled down, to get up and try to run. Fortunately enough drovers were there to hold them down. Apart from the near stampede, the drinking of the Pecos water, even screened, decanted, and doctored with citrus and honey, was about the worst of it. But even that was endurable, especially with occasional better water in side creeks.

The advantage of the river, beside some grass in the valley all the way up, was a change in diet as Tom Jackson and E. Earl came in with catfish several nights, after fashioning a hook and a big gig and leaving out at twilight with pork fat. The herd averaged about twelve miles a day, and got there in another three weeks, delivering to Fort Sumner while Charlie sat counting a passing chain of cattle in his head.

When it came time to pay off the LaPoint outfit camping at Bosque Redondo under cottonwood trees, Goodnight recompensed them with a bonus over the agreed price. LaPoint was able to distribute it among the men, who would take the chuck wagon and chihuahua riding with E. Earl, then would gently drive the mules home. Goodnight tried to talk McBride and LaPoint into taking a herd north with him, up the trail that Loving had blazed, up into southern Colorado.

"You'd be taken 'em thru Dick Wooton's toll road at Raton Pass, I reckon," said McBride. "I know ole Dick. Rode with him in my mountain times. Give him my regards."

"Hell no, I ain't paying that toll again, ever. I scouted a pass to the east of there, after paying the man once. Trinchera pass. I winter them on a ranch south of there, the Apishi, so I can pass to Colorado legal. Got a herd there now that I'll replace with this one when I take it up to Wyoming. Texas herd's got to winter over in New Mexico to cross legal now."

"I remember that pass, near the Picket-wire river, long sloping approach from the southwest, goes right up to the high plains, with a clear trail to Trinidad."

"Knows his trails, don't he, LaPoint?"

"More than I can believe sometimes."

"Waugh, I know all the Sante Fe trail, that's fer shore. I hunted and guided from Bent's old fort on the Arkansas all along the Picketwire to tha Cimmaron canyons and inta Taos."

"You men gonna come with me?"

"We got some other intentions, Charlie, can't go this time," said LaPoint.

"Yep, we do. Goin ta Taos, first time in two decades. The rest of the outfit is headin' for home with the mules and wagon. But before we part, I got somethin' for ya," said McBride, who pulled out a knife in a scabbard made of a buffalo tail with braided leather over it, about two thirds the size of his own. "I even put some cow leather on the scabbard, in yore honor as a first rate cattle man."

"A McBride knife. Finally. I been waiting for this, Gabe. I'll treasure it." He clasped the fancy scabbard and unsheathed the beautiful knife with the wavy pattern in the blade.

"Ya better have it on ya next time we meet, doan be

losing it to no Comanche like Britt did his."

"Who'd Britt give it up to?"

"Peta Nacona."

"He's gone under now....I reckon his son Kiwih-nai has it."

"Probably."

"If a Comanche gets it, you won't be seeing me, 'cause I will have died fighting ta hang on to it."

"Well alright then."

"Britt said barter was better than fighting," said LaPoint.

"How about you two running a drive for me next year, same time, and bring it up the Rockies? Yal got thru this one in better shape than anybody, no loss of beef or men."

"Maybe. Next year we'll talk," said LaPoint after a glance at Gabe for approval.

"All right. Yal be sure and stop by my Apisha ranch below Raton Pass if you're in the vicinity. You could move herds for me from there as well."

"We can't commit on it now, for I know you'll hold me to anything I say, Charlie. We'll make that decision when the time comes."

"Well, what about that book you're always scribbling into, how about recording all the Texas brands you see while you pass through Comanchero country?"

"Alright, Charlie, I could do that for you."

After further agreeable discussion of future plans for delivering cattle up the Rockies, they turned Goodnight's repeated offers down with thanks, and headed for Las Vegas and the trail to Taos through the mountains behind it. LaPoint promised Charlie to look for and record Texas brands on cattle they might encounter up in the Comancheria country, where they were headed. They both wanted to look for Mr. Alex, and McBride wanted to show his old mountain haunts to LaPoint, who was eager to see them. Gabe had not been in Taos since he left on a trading trip to the plains, a couple of decades earlier, and had been captured and nearly killed by Comanches. He wanted to see his favorite town again, the haunts of his young days with Mr. Alex Robinoix, the father of Josh LaPoint. And he knew Joshua wanted to find his father and let him know how the dusty south Texas spread had been rebuilt into a prosperous working horse ranch, through the unceasing efforts of his only son.